Praise for *New York Times* bestselling author RaeAnne Thayne

"RaeAnne Thayne's *15 Summers Later* is fast-paced and deep-hearted, as compelling as mystery, as wise and tender as the best romance. I heartily—and heart is the significant word here—recommend this novel."

—Nancy Thayer, *New York Times* bestselling author

"I'm always eager to dive into a good story about sisters—and that's exactly what this book is! If you like heartfelt stories, you'll devour *15 Summers Later*!"

—Brenda Novak, *New York Times* bestselling author

"Seamless, graceful, gritty and big-hearted as only RaeAnne Thayne can do. I couldn't put it down."

—Kristan Higgins, *New York Times* bestselling author, on *15 Summers Later*

"RaeAnne Thayne will capture your heart with her beautiful, touching stories!"

—Robyn Carr, #1 *New York Times* bestselling author of the Virgin River series

"[Thayne's] books are wonderfully romantic, feel-good reads that end with me sighing over the last pages."

—Debbie Macomber, #1 *New York Times* bestselling author

Also by RaeAnne Thayne

The Lost Book of First Loves
15 Summers Later
The Café at Beach End
Summer at the Cape
Sleigh Bells Ring
The Path to Sunshine Cove
Christmas at Holiday House
The Sea Glass Cottage
Coming Home for Christmas
The Cliff House
Season of Wonder

Shelter Springs
Snow Kissed
The December Market
Christmas at the Shelter Inn

Haven Point
Snow Angel Cove
Redemption Bay
Evergreen Springs
Riverbend Road
Snowfall on Haven Point
Serenity Harbor
Sugar Pine Trail
The Cottages on Silver Beach
Summer at Lake Haven

Hope's Crossing
Blackberry Summer
Woodrose Mountain
Sweet Laurel Falls
Current Creek Valley
Willowleaf Lane
Christmas in Snowflake Canyon
Wild Iris Ridge
All is Bright

For additional books by RaeAnne Thayne, visit her website, raeannethayne.com.

The Rainy Day Bookshop

RaeAnne Thayne

MIRA

MIRA™

ISBN-13: 978-1-335-01320-0
ISBN-13: 978-0-7783-0743-3 (Hardcover Edition)

The Rainy Day Bookshop

For questions and comments about the quality of this book, please contact us at CustomerService@Harlequin.com.

TM is a trademark of Harlequin Enterprises ULC.

MIRA
22 Adelaide St. West, 41st Floor
Toronto, Ontario M5H 4E3, Canada
MIRABooks.com

HarperCollins Publishers
Macken House, 39/40 Mayor Street Upper,
Dublin 1, D01 C9W8, Ireland
www.HarperCollins.com

Printed in U.S.A.

26 27 28 29 30 LBC 5 4 3 2 1

For those who find comfort, courage, and joy between the pages of a book . . . and for the booksellers who make those discoveries possible.

CHAPTER ONE

—

Rosie

"WHO'S READY TO TAKE A TRIP TO THE MAGICAL LAND OF books?" Rosie Lucas asked as she set a plate of pancakes down in front of her granddaughter.

"I am!"

Olive's beaming face lit up every single inch of Rosie's heart.

The three-year-old girl and her mother, Rosie's daughter, Emma, had been back in Oregon for less than twelve hours but Rosie already knew she never wanted them to leave again.

"Can I get a new book there?" Olive asked. She sent a sideways hopeful look to her grandmother that Rosie found impossible to resist.

"I believe that can probably be arranged."

Rosie still owned The Rainy Day Bookshop after all, though she hadn't handled the day-to-day operations in years. What was the fun of owning a bookstore if a woman couldn't spoil her only granddaughter by letting her choose a picture book to bring home if she wanted?

The two of them chattered about some of Olive's favorite stories and television shows while the preschooler ate her breakfast. It was a thoroughly enjoyable time. Olive had nearly finished devouring her plate of pancakes when her mother rushed into the kitchen, her T-shirt still untucked and her purple-streaked auburn hair slightly messy.

"Sorry," Emma said, sounding frazzled. "I know we talked about trying to get there before the store opens in—" she looked at her watch "—five minutes. I must have overslept. I don't know what happened. I never sleep through my alarm."

"I turned your phone off," Olive informed her with a cheerful smile. "It was too loud. I didn't want it to wake you up."

Emma gave her daughter a frustrated look, even as she leaned down and kissed the top of her curls, the same auburn as Emma's own, minus the streaks of color. "That's kind of the point of an alarm clock, honey."

"Don't worry about it," Rosie assured her. "I know we said nine but nothing was written in stone. We don't have to leave at nine on the dot. We have all day. I only suggested nine when you said you wanted an early start."

"Right. I do. I need to know what I'm up against. From everything you've said, it sounds like I'm going to have my work cut out for me."

Had Rosie given her daughter a task beyond her abilities? She really hoped not. She wanted to challenge Emma, not scare her away.

Ever since she and her daughter had reconnected after years of estrangement when Olive was six months old, Rosie felt as if she constantly walked a tightrope suspended two hundred feet in the air. A thin wire covered in baby oil, where one misstep would ruin all their hard work toward healing the rift between them.

She didn't want to do anything to drive her daughter away again.

"You don't have to fix everything wrong with the bookstore in one day," she said carefully. "I hope I didn't give you that impression."

Emma poured herself some coffee. "I don't know. You were giving off some solid desperation vibes on the phone."

Rosie definitely needed Emma's help but if she had sounded

desperate, it was more from her burning desire to play more of a role in the lives of her daughter and granddaughter. Despite her and Emma's wary reconciliation after Olive's birth, Emma still lived in Las Vegas, hundreds of miles away from their small town on the central Oregon coast.

"You really are saving the day. I hated the idea of having to close the store for several weeks while your grandmother recovers from her accident, especially right as we're heading into the busy tourist season. The bookstore has barely covered its operating costs for years. I don't have time to run it myself and I don't really have time to train someone else to manage it. Not someone with your level of skill, anyway."

"You do know I have zero experience at this, right?"

"You managed a restaurant, though."

She made a face. "Not a restaurant. A Starbucks. That's not the same as handling the day-to-day operations of a busy bookstore."

"First of all, The Rainy Day Bookshop is not that busy, unfortunately. Mom hasn't exactly made drawing in crowds a priority."

"I'm fully aware of Grandma's philosophy. Books are meant to be enjoyed. Throwing in silly concepts like profit and loss somehow ruins the experience."

Rosie's mother, Sylvia, loved running the bookstore. She adored ordering new books, talking with customers, helping a reader find the perfect selection. All the things Rosie had loved when she ran the bookstore herself.

Sylvia did not, however, enjoy having to reconcile the budget or focus on the bottom line. As a result, the bookstore wasn't exactly a profitable enterprise.

Many people had asked Rosie over the years why she hadn't sold the bookstore after Gary's death. She never had a good answer for them, mostly because she didn't really know the reason. It made no business sense whatsoever. Her focus for years had been Lucas Construction, the company she and Gary had started together that she had muscled back from the brink of near bankruptcy after his tragic death.

She really didn't have time to focus on her dream of owning a bookstore, which had finally come true only a few months before he died and their life fell apart.

But every time she was tempted to sell Rainy Day, something held her back. Maybe her deep love of books, or sheer stubbornness, that determination to cling to her dream of keeping the bookstore doors open in a town that otherwise wouldn't have access to books except their small underfunded library.

"Your grandmother hasn't changed," Rosie admitted. "If anything, her time running the store has only reinforced her beliefs. I actually heard her say to a customer once that buying was optional and they were free to spend as much time as they wanted browsing, reading the books and admiring the dust."

Emma laughed. "Sounds like Grandma."

Rosie gave a rueful smile in response. She loved her mother dearly. For all her quirks, Sylvia was kind, compassionate, fierce. She couldn't help that a paltry thing like making money wasn't her first priority.

Emma, on the other hand, would be brilliant at running the bookstore. Rosie was sure of it.

"You have a business degree and plenty of experience managing people. As far as I'm concerned, you're perfect. I'm so grateful you agreed to help."

Rosie had no idea why Emma had finally acquiesced this time, when she had asked her to come home many times over the years since Olive's birth. She suspected her daughter had been ready for a change, especially as the lease on the apartment she shared with two other single moms had been ending soon.

"I won't be perfect for anything if I can't wake up in time for work." Emma turned to her daughter with a chiding look. "New rule, kid. You can't turn off my phone alarm, okay? Even if you think I need more sleep."

"Okay," Olive said cheerfully, taking another bite of pancakes.

"Looks like Grandma made you breakfast."

"Mickey pancakes. Except I already ate the ears."

"I hope that's okay." Rosie tried to keep the anxious note from her voice but was afraid it filtered through anyway. Perhaps after Emma and Olive had been here a few weeks and settled in, Rosie might relax, lose some of this fear of making a wrong move and sending her daughter running away again.

"Why wouldn't it be okay? I always eat the ears first. That way Mickey can't hear me chewing the rest of him."

"I meant the pancakes. I know you're vegetarian."

Emma lifted an eyebrow, the pierced metal post there reflecting sunlight. "Unless you have a special pancake recipe these days that uses beef tallow or pork drippings, they should be fine."

"No beef or pork. Plain old pancake mix."

"Then we're good. I appreciate you feeding her."

"It was my pleasure." Rosie hoped her daughter knew she was determined to do everything possible to make sure the two of them were comfortable in her home.

"I tried to pick up things at the grocery store I thought you might like. I even bought a vegetarian cookbook and I've been looking up recipes online for things I thought you might like."

"Thank you. I really appreciate that," Emma said. She looked slightly less frazzled now as she settled into a chair across from her daughter, sipping her coffee.

"Is your room comfortable? I did my best to update it. I've been slowly working on it since Christmas but after I talked to you last week, I had Bryce put a few other projects on the back burner to finish up here."

Emma's mouth tightened momentarily. What had Rosie said?

"It's nice," Emma assured her. "I really appreciate having two connected bedrooms and the Jack-and-Jill bathroom in between them. The rooms are perfect for now. If I end up staying in town longer than a few months while Grandma recovers, I'll probably look for my own place."

So many *ifs*. Rosie could only keep her fingers and toes crossed and do all she could to keep her daughter comfortable here.

"You know there's no need for that. You should save your rent money. I have plenty of room, especially with Mom insisting on staying in her own place."

Rosie was not sure who was more stubborn, her daughter or her mother. Sylvia had lived in the tiny self-contained guest cottage in Rosie's backyard for ten years, since she uprooted her life in Portland after Gary's death and moved here to help them through their grief.

Her mother did her own thing and always had. Why else would she currently be recovering from a broken ankle sustained while roller skating at seventy-two years old?

"I'll be ready in a minute," Emma said.

"Are you sure you wouldn't like a pancake?"

"No. Coffee usually does it for me in the mornings."

This was yet another thing Rosie did not know about her

daughter these days. This adult version of Emma was a virtual stranger.

The last time they had lived together, when Emma wasn't yet seventeen, her daughter had loved a big breakfast. Bacon, hashbrowns, pancakes. The whole thing. Now she was a vegetarian who apparently fueled up with coffee in the mornings.

She would figure all of those things out. They had time. Emma was here for at least a few months. If Rosie had anything to say about it, she could be here longer.

Her thoughts were interrupted by the back door opening. She looked over in surprise and found her mother peering at the three of them seated at the table.

Rosie jumped up and rushed to Sylvia. "Mom! What are you doing here? I can't believe you made your way all the way to the house on your own. Why didn't you call me?"

Her mother was on crutches and she wore sleep pants that had monkey face emojis on them. Her dyed magenta hair was crumpled on one side, as if she had forgotten to comb it out after she awoke.

"I'm hungry, if you want the truth. I was out refilling my bird feeders and thought I smelled pancakes coming from this direction."

"I wish you would let me refill your bird feeders," Rosie fussed. "The doctor says no weight-bearing for at least a month. You're supposed to be taking it easy."

"The doctor doesn't know what she's talking about," her mother grumbled. "I'm fine."

Sylvia was not fine. She had a compound ankle fracture that had already required one surgery and might possibly need another.

"I planned to drop some pancakes at your cottage before we head to the bookstore."

"Now you don't have to, since I'm here." She moved into the room, maneuvering carefully on her crutches.

"Hi, Granny Sylvie!" Olive beamed at her great-grandmother, her face sticky with syrup.

Sylvia grinned back at her. "Olive, darling. How wonderful to see you this beautiful morning. How did I get so lucky to see you two days in a row?"

"Guess what? You can see me every day now."

"Aren't I truly a lucky duck, then?"

"You're not a duck." Olive chortled. "You're a grandma."

"A grandma who needs to sit down," Emma said. Rosie's daughter pulled out a chair at the kitchen table for her grandmother. "Here you go."

The older woman settled heavily into the chair, her leg outstretched in front of her.

"That's better. Who would have guessed one silly moment out of your life could have such lasting consequences?"

Anyone with a shred of common sense could have guessed. A seventy-two-year-old woman with mild osteoporosis had no business even being *near* roller skates, forget about putting them on.

But Sylvia never asked advice before embarking on her escapades, she simply plowed forward. Or skated forward, in this case.

"Here you are, Mom," she said, putting a plate stacked with three fluffy blueberry pancakes in front of her. "And here's the syrup. What can I get you to drink?"

"Water is fine," Sylvia said, then sent her a hopeful look. "I don't suppose you have any bacon to go with this, do you?"

"I do, but I would rather not cook it right now."

"Why not? Bacon goes perfectly with pancakes on a beautiful Sunday morning."

Rosie sighed, sending a meaningful look at the other two people in the kitchen. "Emma and Olive are vegetarians, remember?"

Emma rolled her eyes, almost as if she were fifteen years old again. "You can eat meat in front of me, Mom. I won't have a fit of the vapors."

"I don't need bacon." Sylvia looked contrite. "I'll be fine. If I need more protein, I'll have a yogurt or something."

All of them were dancing around each other like boats navigating through a foggy harbor.

"What about eggs?" Rosie asked.

"Eggs are fine," Emma assured them. "I eat eggs. So does Olive. But bacon is fine for you, too. I'm not offended by other people eating meat, just because I've chosen a mostly plant-based diet."

Rosie would figure out this new reality of living with her daughter and granddaughter. At some point soon, she needed to sit down with Emma and have a good talk about her and Olive's dietary preferences—and anything else they needed to figure out so they could make this arrangement as comfortable as possible.

She had so much to learn about them. She and Emma hadn't lived together in eight years. Hadn't spoken for several of those.

Those years of silence had been a terrifying time for Rosie, as she had no idea even where her daughter was or what she might be going through. Her only comfort had come from knowing Emma had stayed in touch with her grandmother and always assured Sylvia she was fine. Sylvia, in turn, had passed that information to Rosie.

How *fine* was up for debate. Rosie suspected the full truth would devastate her if she ever learned all the details. Emma had been a seventeen-year-old girl, living with a man nearly a decade older who had dragged her into a life of drug and alcohol abuse. From the little Sylvia had told her about those years, Rosie knew her daughter had lived on the street for a time, had squatted in an abandoned house and had bounced from couch to couch.

She was here now. And doing incredibly well, all things considered. Clean and sober since before Olive was born, Emma had a college degree she had worked hard to earn on her own and she had left a decent job to come back to Wood Briar and help out at the bookshop.

The two of them had struggled to repair their fractured relationship but the occasional phone call, text message or rare short visit could only go so far.

"We always have eggs, thanks to our girls," she said, grateful for the five Rhode Island Reds who provided a steady supply.

When Sylvia first came to her during the Covid pandemic and said she wanted to pick up some chicks, Rosie had been reluctant. She adored them now. Together with her little dog, Dottie, and Sylvia's two cats, her house had plenty of creatures for Olive to love.

It was the perfect place for a precocious, inquisitive little girl to thrive. Rosie could only pray her daughter would come to see that as well during their stay here.

As she cracked several eggs and scrambled them together, she listened to the hum of conversation between the three women of multiple generations.

Emma and Sylvia chattered away with a familiarity that sent a twinge of jealousy through Rosie, though she knew she had no right to it.

She was happy her mother and her daughter got along so

well. It had been a deep comfort during their years of separation to know Emma had someone reliable in her life to count on.

She couldn't help it that she wanted Emma to confide in *her* instead of Sylvia.

After she finished the eggs, she plated them and took a seat at the table across from her mother.

"So what's on the docket for you ladies today?" Sylvia asked.

"We're going to the book place," Olive announced happily. "Grandma says I can have a new book."

"Are you?"

Emma nodded. "I want to take a look at things before I officially start tomorrow. Get the lay of the land."

Sylvia straightened. "What time are you leaving? I only need a few minutes to get dressed and do something with this hair."

"Are you sure, Mom?" Rosie said with a frown. "We might be there for a few hours."

"Positive. I won't do a single thing that takes more effort than lifting a pencil. We can't toss the girl into the deep end."

"You don't have to come with us if you're not up to it," Emma assured her. "You can stay wherever you're most comfortable. I can always FaceTime you with any questions."

Annoyance creased Sylvia's forehead. "I have a broken ankle. I'm not dying. I can handle a quick trip to the bookstore."

She ate another bite of pancake. "I still don't know why your mother felt the need to drag you down here," she grumbled. "I'm perfectly capable of running the bookstore. It all feels like a lot of fuss for nothing."

Rosie squelched her guilt. This was the right decision for her mother, even if Sylvia didn't want to admit it.

"Dr. Peterson is the one who said you should take several

weeks off. You have to stay off your ankle as much as possible. How can you do that when you're trying to take inventory or wait on customers?"

"Easy. I don't have to be on my feet at all. I can get around on a rolling office chair or something."

"We've talked about this, Mom." Rosie fought down her frustration. "Listen to the doctor. Take a vacation for a month. We need to let your ankle heal as long as possible, and then we'll see how you are after the doctor says you can put weight on it again."

She sincerely hoped her mother would decide that with the bookstore in Emma's very capable hands, she could relax and enjoy her retirement.

She could sleep in all morning, go thrift shopping with her girlfriends in the afternoon—once her ankle healed, anyway—and even catch the party bus to the nearest casino in Lincoln City to play the slots.

Sylvia made a face. "It sucks getting old, little girl," she said to Olive, who giggled as she continued eating her scrambled eggs.

To Rosie's relief, her mother let the matter slide.

They could do this, Rosie thought as she finished her own breakfast. Juggling four generations in one house—okay, one house and a guest cottage in the backyard—would be a challenge but Rosie would make any sacrifice necessary to protect her mother's health, heal the rift with her daughter and have an active role in her granddaughter's life.

It wouldn't be easy, but Rosie had been dealing with hard things for a decade. Compared to everything else they had endured as a family, this should be a piece of cake.

CHAPTER TWO

—

Emma

AN HOUR AFTER THAT PANICKY WAKE-UP SCRAMBLE, EMMA was still feeling frazzled as she and her mother loaded her grandmother into the passenger seat of her beat-up thirdhand Honda.

"It will be better to take your car than your mother's," Sylvia had said in her no-nonsense tone.

"Why?" Rosie had asked, looking almost hurt, as if Grandma Syl had said her Volvo SUV smelled like a dead raccoon.

"Because it makes the most sense. Emma already has a car seat for Olive. And you know how hard it's been for me to boost my fat tuchus into your SUV."

So there Emma was, embarrassed about her junk heap car. When she paid cash for it a year ago, depleting what was left of her savings after her final tuition payment, the car had represented all her hard-earned progress. She had a job. An apartment. And now a car of her own, so she wouldn't have to spend an extra hour a day catching public transportation to take Olive to day care before heading to work.

Maybe it wasn't the best-looking vehicle, but she had worked hard for every dent and rust patch.

They settled Sylvia into the front passenger seat, carefully adjusting her cast and her crutches, then her mother walked around to open the rear passenger door next to Olive.

"You can sit by me, Grandma," Olive chirped, looking delighted at the prospect of a bookstore outing with her grandmother and great-grandmother.

With everyone settled, Emma climbed in and backed

slowly out of her mom's driveway. She was fully aware she was a ridiculously cautious driver. She rarely exceeded the speed limit and always looked both ways twice before entering any intersection.

Killing her father while learning to drive could probably scar a person forever in that direction.

And, yes. She found it darkly funny that she was so careful behind the wheel when she had certainly specialized in every other kind of risky behavior over the past ten years.

Mindful that she was carrying three people she loved, she drove slowly through Wood Briar.

The town had changed since she last lived there. New businesses had popped up here and there and a few others had closed. The pizza place where she and her friends hung out now seemed to be a bakery and the former bike shop sold tourist supplies like beach chairs, kites and towels, at least judging by the window display.

The town had added hanging baskets from the old-style streetlights, and their colorful blossoms spilled over in wild abundance.

The bookstore looked the same, taking up a prime corner of real estate only a block from the seawall.

"You can park in the back now," her mother said. "A few years ago, the downtown alliance bought up the inner block area for parking."

That was new. Parking had always been a problem downtown, especially in the summertime when tourists flocked to every small Oregon beach town, even the more remote ones like Wood Briar.

The tourist madness apparently hadn't kicked in yet. On that early June Sunday morning, she could easily find a space close to the back entrance of The Rainy Day Bookshop.

Olive unhooked her own car seat, a relatively new skill Emma wasn't all that thrilled about. "Stay there," she ordered her daughter. "We need to help Grandma Sylvia first."

The girl gave a pout but picked up her favorite doll that she had named Penelope, for some reason, and began chattering to her as Emma opened her trunk and pulled out the collapsible wheelchair her mother had insisted they bring for Sylvia.

"I don't need this stupid thing. I've got crutches and a knee scooter. They're perfectly fine." Her grandmother's wrinkled features wore a disgruntled frown as she glared at the chair.

Rosie sighed, looking weary. This seemed to be a battle the two of them had fought before. Emma might have expected Sylvia wouldn't be a very easy patient. When had she ever taken the easy route? Her grandmother loved causing trouble, which was one of the many reasons Emma adored her.

"You know you'll heal better if you take it easy," Rosie said in an ultra-patient tone. "You're great at the crutches and the knee scooter, but why use them when you don't have to? We rented the wheelchair. We might as well use it."

"Fine," Sylvia grumbled. "But this thing makes me feel like an old lady."

"You *are* an old lady," Olive piped up from the back seat.

Emma winced. Olive basically had no filter whatsoever. Kind of like her great-grandmother. Maybe that was why the two of them seemed to get along so well.

"Thank you for the reminder, my dear," Sylvia said, sounding amused rather than annoyed. "I'm definitely not as young as I once was. I suppose it's fine this once."

Emma and her mother helped her grandmother from the car to the wheelchair. It didn't really take both of them, but Rosie seemed happy for Emma's assistance.

"Want me to push her in?" Emma asked.

Rosie shook her head. "I've got it. Go ahead and help Olive."

The two of them headed to the rear entrance of the bookshop while Emma opened the door for Olive and helped her out of the car.

"I love love *love* bookstores," her daughter announced, her voice bubbling over with joy as she skipped to the door.

Same, girl. Emma smiled at her, grabbing her hand as anticipation curled through her. This place would be her project for the next few months—assuming Rosie could convince Sylvia to step back, which seemed a formidable task right then.

And speaking of formidable tasks.

Emma walked inside the bookstore and was momentarily speechless. All she could think was *ew.*

She hadn't been in here in nearly a decade and it looked like not one single thing had changed. The bookstore seemed trapped in another era, with fluorescent lights, dingy paint the color of old bandages, and crowded, claustrophobia-inducing aisles stacked with dusty books.

Olive looked around. "This place is messy."

That was one word for it. Emma could think of several others, none of which were appropriate to say in the presence of her three-year-old child.

"We're in here," Rosie called out.

Still holding Olive's hand, Emma made her way to the office that ran along the rear wall. Dust motes floated like tiny shards of gold in the light coming through the front windows. She might think them pretty under other circumstances. Circumstances where she had not found herself suddenly responsible for turning a profit out of this cluttered, disorganized pit of despair.

Inside the office, she found her mother trying to move a chair so Sylvia's wheelchair could fit at the computer desk.

"Did you see the play area when you came in?" Sylvia asked. "I keep old books I find at Goodwill and yard sales for kids to read while they're in here. They can even take them home if they want. It's our own version of a Little Free Library."

"That's nice. A play area is a good idea," Emma said as she exchanged a look with her mother. Wasn't a bookstore supposed to *sell* books?

"It gives the children somewhere to hang out in the store so they don't pull everything off the shelves, plus keeps them occupied while their parents shop for books," Sylvia said. "The toys may be outdated. I only have some blocks, a couple of trucks and a play kitchen I bought at a yard sale. The kids seem to enjoy it anyway."

"Maybe Olive can play there sometimes while you're working," Rosie said, that anxious note in her voice again.

Her mother was trying so hard to make sure Emma was comfortable. Her eagerness made Emma's throat feel tight and achy.

"That will be great," she said, meaning the words.

Olive was the main reason she was here in Wood Briar. For her daughter's entire life, Olive had spent more time in day care than with her own mother. Emma had been busy working or going to school, though she tried her best to juggle her responsibilities around her daughter's schedule and take mostly online classes, where she could do the schoolwork while Olive was in bed.

Her daughter was smart, healthy, well-adjusted. But in her nearly four years, she had already been through eight day care situations.

In another year, she would be heading to kindergarten, then grade school. She was growing up far too fast. Emma wanted the chance to be with her more and to have her enjoy as much time as possible with her grandmother and great-grandmother.

Finding good quality childcare was the single hardest thing Emma had to do as a single mother. Harder than staying up all night with her when Olive was ill, even after a long shift at work. Harder than the constant grinding worry about finances. Harder than the equally grinding effort to stay sober so she could be the mother her daughter deserved.

Olive's father was not in the picture whatsoever. Depending on her mood, Emma found that state of affairs either far more simple or much more complicated.

Most of the time, she thanked her lucky stars that she didn't have to deal with Kevin Hollis on the daily.

Sometimes, though, she couldn't help thinking how much easier her path would be if she had someone else to help carry the relentless parenting load.

Kevin would have been a lousy father. She knew that. Emma hadn't wanted to let her child anywhere near him and she had been relieved when he had signed away his parental rights, though it certainly complicated things for her.

Day care shouldn't be as much of a problem in Wood Briar, especially if she could bring Olive along with her to the bookstore sometimes while she worked. Besides her mother and grandmother to help out on occasion, she still had friends in town, including one of her best friends, Josie. She was a stay-at-home mom with a daughter around Olive's age as well as a baby boy. When Emma told her she was coming home for the summer, Josie immediately offered her babysitting services. Yes, it would still be day care but in a homier environment.

Somehow, the office was even less appealing than the rest of the bookstore—windowless, cluttered, with dingy carpet and acres of dark paneling.

Emma pulled out her phone, opening a new note she labeled *Possible Changes.*

Beneath that, she typed in big letters, *Redecorate.*

The place needed new lighting, new flooring, new paint and a whole hell of a lot of elbow grease. She definitely had her work cut out for her.

You're going to screw this up, like you screw up everything else.

She tried to push away the negative voice in her head. She didn't screw up *everything.* She had already accomplished far more than she ever expected during those hard years when she only cared about her next fix.

"Ready for a tour?" Rosie asked.

Emma nodded, filled with renewed resolve. Her mother was counting on her to do a good job. More than that, *Olive* was. Her daughter deserved a better life than the one they left behind. If she could prove herself at the bookstore, perhaps she could figure out a way to convince her mother she was capable of more.

She simply had to use the same stubborn determination she inherited from both her mother and grandmother, the grit that had pushed her this far.

Sylvia opted to stay near Olive in the play area, so Emma followed her mother through the crowded aisles, jotting copious notes as they went.

The store was mostly empty except for a few customers and two employees, one at the checkout counter and one stocking books. She saw one customer looking at magazines and a couple of teenage girls giggling over what looked like a paltry collection of romantasy titles.

The comforting, familiar smell of ink and paper surrounded them, along with something musty and old.

"As you can see, your grandmother has let a few things go," her mom whispered.

Had it been hard for Rosie to turn over the operations of the bookstore to Sylvia?

Emma could remember how excited her mother had been when she purchased The Rainy Day Bookshop. When Rosie wasn't helping Emma's father at Lucas Construction, she had worked here part-time for the previous owner, a crusty old man who had been certain the future lay in renting out videotapes and CDs.

With big dreams and bigger ideas, Rosie had purchased it from him only a few months before the accident. Before everything had changed for all of them.

Now her mother ran the construction company alone and Grandma Sylvia dabbled in managing a floundering bookstore, between juggling her active social life and apparently roller skating.

Her mother was introducing Emma to the employee shelving books, a studious-looking boy named Ethan with shy dark eyes and a nervous smile, when Olive's voice drifted to them from one aisle over.

"My name is Olive. What's yours?"

A deep male voice answered something she couldn't hear. It was possible Emma listened to far too many true-crime podcasts, but her mind immediately went on stranger-danger alert.

In midconversation, she walked away from her mother and Ethan to hurry around the endcap to the next aisle.

There, she found her daughter chattering away to a gorgeous guy in a snug T-shirt and jeans.

Unlike Emma, her three-year-old seemed to excel at finding hot guys.

"Olive, honey, I thought you were sitting with your grandmother in the play area. She was reading to you."

"She fell asleep. I wanted another book. One about dogs."

"Hi, Emma. Great to see you!"

At the voice coming from the hot stranger, she looked up. He was tall, lanky, with work-rough hands and long eyelashes. She had the disconcerting thought that she should know him but couldn't quite place his face.

She narrowed her gaze. "I'm sorry. I've been gone from town for a few years. Do I know you?"

"Bryce!" Her mother's voice from behind her drew the guy's attention and he straightened, smiling broadly. Emma suddenly knew exactly who he was.

Bryce Kendall.

The man who currently had everything she wanted.

Rosie hurried forward, her features bright with pleasure. Ethan was nowhere in sight and Emma assumed he had resumed stocking shelves.

"I didn't know you were coming into the bookstore today," Rosie exclaimed. "I'm so happy to see you. This is my granddaughter."

"Of course she is. I immediately recognized her from the many, many, *many* pictures you have on your desk. Hi, Olive. I'm Bryce and I work with your grandmother."

"My grandma builds houses."

"I know. So do I. And offices and stores and restaurants sometimes."

Her mother wore a proud expression but Emma couldn't tell if it was directed at Olive or Bryce.

"I guess you know Emma," she said. "You were in the same grade at school, right?"

"Only because I graduated a year early and Bryce was held back a year."

As soon as Emma said the bitchy words, she regretted them. They made her sound like a spoiled, surly child in the playground, kicking sand all over someone else's bigger and better sandcastle.

"Sorry," she muttered.

He gave a cool smile that didn't quite hide the tiny glimmer of emotion in his hazel eyes.

She couldn't tell Bryce or her mother the reason for her pettiness, that she was fiercely jealous of his role as her mother's trusted second-in-command at Lucas Construction.

How had that happened, anyway? It still made no sense to her.

Bryce had been the class clown, always causing trouble. Though mostly annoying, he used to make her laugh the way no one else ever could.

Yet now, at twenty-seven, he was a respected builder whom her mother seemed to trust above all others.

Grandma Sylvia had mentioned to her a few months ago that Rosie expected Bryce to one day take over running the company.

Not if Emma could help it.

Lucas Construction was her family's legacy. Not Bryce's.

Her father had fought hard to build it from the ground up to the well-respected business it was today. Going on job sites with him had been her favorite thing in the world. She used to love handing him nails, helping him clean up the site or simply sitting beside him, chattering away about whatever came to mind.

She wanted in at Lucas Construction. While running the bookstore would do in the short term, eventually she wanted to prove to her mother she was capable of handling the responsibilities of a big operation like Lucas Construction.

"What brings you to the bookstore?" Rosie asked Bryce, her features bright with affection. At forty-five, she was still as lovely as ever, Emma realized with some degree of shock.

"You know me. I love to check out the new releases and sometimes Sundays are my only chance."

"I wouldn't have taken you for much of a reader," Emma said. "We had English together both our junior and senior year and if I'm remembering correctly, it wasn't your favorite subject."

"I love books, but not really reading them."

"Oh, just looking at the pictures?"

The words spilled out, despite Emma's best intentions to be civil. What was *wrong* with her?

"I'm an audiobook listener. I go through two or three a week while I'm working or driving from job site to job site."

"Listening to audiobooks still counts as reading," Rosie said, a sliver of censure toward Emma threading through her voice.

"I agree," Emma said. "But does The Rainy Day Bookshop sell audiobooks?"

"Not very many," she admitted. "We have a few old CDs, but that's it."

"I'm actually here to buy something for . . . a friend. But I like to come in regularly and see what's new and what looks good," Bryce said. "If I find something that appeals to me, I'll listen on audio. When I find a book I love, I like to buy a copy of the physical book here for my own collection or to donate to the town library. It needs all the help it can get."

"I love books!" Olive announced, her features wide with delight. "Grandma Rosie said I can have one. Will you help me pick it?"

Emma thought at first her daughter was speaking to her but then realized her daughter's grin was only aimed at Bryce.

He seemed disconcerted at her friendliness. "I don't know much about kids' books, I'm afraid. We didn't have many at my house when I was growing up."

Emma couldn't even imagine that. Books had been an integral part of her childhood. Both her parents had been avid readers and she picked up her love of stories from them. During the long, hard years in Las Vegas, public libraries had saved her more times than she could count. They had been shelter, sanctuary, a place of safety and peace.

"You don't need to bother Mr. Kendall," Emma said.

"Come with me, darling," her mother said, holding out her hand to Olive. "We'll go look at the books. I'll help you choose a good one."

"Okay." Olive stuck her hand in her grandmother's, and the two of them headed for the children's section. Emma was left with Bryce and her wholly unreasonable resentment toward him.

"Your mom tells me you're going to be running the bookstore until Sylvia is back on her feet," he said. Emma noticed again his long eyelashes fringing hazel eyes and his farmer's tan, visible when his T-shirt sleeve rode up, exposing a strip of paler skin that contrasted with his darker forearms.

She was a sucker for sexy muscled forearms.

Emma swallowed a sigh, trying to tell herself it was only a reaction to the sheer scope of the challenge ahead of her, not any quiver of awareness.

"That's right. The bookstore hasn't exactly been profitable for a few years." Or ever. "I'm hoping to use this summer as a chance to chart a different path. I would like to turn things around."

He looked around. "You have your work cut out for you."

"I'm fully aware."

"Any initial ideas?"

She looked at the note on her phone, up to multiple screens of to-do items now. "Too many," she admitted. "I don't know where to start."

He looked around. "What this place needs is something besides books to bring people in."

"This is a bookstore, Bryce. It's right there in the name."

"Ha. Yeah, I'm aware. But you want to entice people into the store who might not necessarily be in the market for books. They walk in for something else, something irresistible, then see a cover that speaks to them. And before they know it, they have a whole stack of new titles in their basket and you have instant sales."

Emma had been thinking along those exact same lines. For some reason, it irked her that she and Bryce were apparently on the same page. "I wrote down 'What about a small coffee bar?'" she admitted.

She wasn't sure if that was a valid idea or simply a knee-jerk reaction, coming from someone who until recently had managed a coffeehouse.

"That would be perfect. Maybe you could even work out a cooperative arrangement with one of the local coffee places to provide staff and product. We have some great ones in town. And you could sell pastries from Coastal Crumb, the bakery down the street. Their cinnamon rolls are as addictive as your books."

She could put the café setup near the display window facing Main Street, to bring in more foot traffic. They could start genre book clubs that could meet there over coffee and pastries.

The store could even host silent-reading book clubs, where people sat together, drank their coffee and enjoyed their latest read.

Her mind filled with possibilities, each more exciting than the one before. Then she took in her surroundings once more, and she fell back to earth with a hard thud.

"I think I need to focus on more basic renovations first before I think about expanding. Brighten things up. New paint, maybe, new lighting, and I could clear out about half the inventory, so it doesn't feel so cluttered in here."

"Not a bad idea. If you need help, let me know."

"I can't believe my mother hasn't put more energy into freshening up the place. It's not as if she doesn't have the resources. She owns a construction company, for heaven's sake."

His mouth tightened, as if he was annoyed at her for daring to voice anything resembling criticism of her mother. It was another unwanted reminder of their close working relationship.

"She's been a little busy trying to keep Lucas Construction afloat. That's why she brought in your grandmother to help with the bookstore in the first place."

Emma glanced over at him, surprised. "Lucas is doing great, isn't it? I mean, the town has grown so much. When we drove in yesterday, I saw construction projects everywhere."

"Wood Briar is definitely growing, but Lucas Construction isn't the only game in town. It takes a lot of effort to stay relevant in an evolving market, especially with plenty of healthy competition. It's not easy for a construction company to pay a living wage and also make a profit. Your mom has really turned things around the past few years, but it's been a rough road to get here."

Her parents had both worked hard to build the company. Emma remembered many hours spent hanging out in the office up on Kingfisher Road when she was a kid. That was when the company was a two-person operation and built maybe three or four homes a year.

Lucas Construction had soon branched out to commercial real estate as well as working more with property developers, and the business exploded. They had taken on more employees: project supervisors, designers, office staff. By the time she left town, Lucas Construction had a payroll of more than fifty people.

Including Pam Clarke, the office manager.

Her stomach clenched. From what Emma had heard, Pam still lived in town, still worked for the company. Emma would have to see her at some point. She couldn't avoid it. The thought left her feeling vaguely ill.

"I really would be happy to help you," Bryce said. "Let me know."

Emma probably would not be doing that. "Thanks," she said.

"It really is good to see you again, Emma. I know Rosie is thrilled to have you home."

"Right. Good to see you, too," she lied.

Okay, it wasn't completely a lie. What woman didn't appreciate a hot, ripped guy who loved books? But that wasn't why she had returned to Oregon.

She didn't want to mess this up. She had a job to do at The Rainy Day Bookshop. Her mother was counting on her . . . and her daughter needed the stability and connection to her grandmother and great-grandmother Olive was already finding here.

Emma couldn't afford to ruin everything by letting herself become distracted by a man who stood in the way of everything she wanted.

CHAPTER THREE

—

Bryce

OH MAN, HE HAD IT BAD.

Bryce walked through the cramped bookstore aisle, hardly aware of where he was. After all these years, Emma Lucas was actually here, within the same four dingy walls.

He had known she was coming back. Rosie had talked of little else for the past week, ever since Sylvia's accident when Emma had finally agreed to return to Wood Briar.

He had worked long hours to finish upgrading the two guest bedrooms and bathroom at Rosie's comfortable house overlooking Crescent Beach, aware with each nail he pounded and each board he measured that this would be for Emma.

Seeing her again felt like a punch to the gut. His heart raced, and his palms grew sweaty. He had wanted her for so long, dreamed of her countless nights, and now she was here, flesh and blood, more beautiful than he remembered.

The yearning he thought he had buried years ago came rushing back with a vengeance, threatening to overwhelm him.

She had certainly changed in eight years, since the last time he had seen her in person. That moment seemed seared into his memory, though.

Bryce had been standing in the hallway of Wood Briar High School, near his locker. He was late for his first-hour English class and knew Mr. Olsen would write him up. Again.

He had only been on time for first hour maybe a dozen times the entire second trimester of the school year, partly because he passionately hated English class. Dan Olsen was an ass, a petty tyrant who delighted in making someone like Bryce Kendall feel even more stupid than he usually did.

Unfortunately, even if the guy had been his favorite teacher, Bryce still would have been late. Every morning was a chore to make sure his mom was up and alert or she would never make it to her job at the cheese plant. If he didn't push her, he would come home from school before heading to his own part-time job at Lucas Construction to find Terri either drunk again or still in bed nursing a hangover, eight hours after he had left the house.

As he stood in the bookstore, the memory of that day eight years ago flooded back, vivid and painful. He could almost smell the musty scent of the school hallway, feel the cold metal of the lockers against his back.

Emma had come out of the principal's office looking triumphant and defiant, a dangerous glint in her eye that both thrilled and terrified him.

"What are you so happy about, Em?" Bryce had asked, startled by the unfamiliar expression on her face. It had been so long since he'd seen her genuinely happy that the sight was almost jarring.

"You can be the first one to congratulate me. I'm done here."

"What do you mean? Done with what?" he had asked, feeling slow and stupid, as he often did around her.

"School. This whole shit show."

He had stared at her, dumbfounded. "What do you mean? You can't drop out! We still have another trimester before graduation."

He could have told her exactly how many days they had left in school, down to the hour. He had been looking forward to that day for most of his life, when the endless torture session he called school could finally be over.

She had shrugged and hurried to her locker, which had been right next to his. As she yanked it open, she said, "I just took my last final. I have enough credits to graduate now. I could flunk every single class in the final tri and still graduate with a B-plus average. I've had enough."

"Of what?"

"All of it. School, Wood Briar. My mom. I'm done. Kevin has a job offer in Vegas so I'm going with him. We're going to find a little apartment off the Strip. Maybe I'll get a job as a cocktail waitress at a casino or something."

"You're only sixteen. You can't be a cocktail waitress unless you're twenty-one."

"I'll be seventeen this summer. But fine. I'll get a job at McDonald's, then. Anything is better than here."

Bryce had been stunned and upset, unable to reconcile this hard-edged Emma with the girl he thought he knew. There was a brittleness to her voice, a coldness in her eyes.

"What about prom? Graduation? College? I thought you were accepted to Oregon State?"

"You think I give a flying eff about any of that?"

Her words hit him like a slap. What happened to the brainiac who had once been on track to be their class valedictorian? He struggled to understand what had changed her so drastically over the past year.

"Does your mom know you're leaving town with a pot dealer who is eight years older than you are?"

Emma paused in her frantic locker-emptying. "No. And you can't tell her either. Not until I'm gone and she can't do a damn thing about it. Swear it, Bryce."

"No." He slammed his locker door closed. "It's not right. He's a grown man and you're still a kid."

Anger flashed in Emma's eyes, and she whirled on him.

"What I do is none of your business. Got that? It's my life. Keep out of it, Bryce, or I'll tell everyone in school you were the one who snuck into the faculty lounge and put laxatives in the coffee machine. "

That hadn't been enough of a threat. He wouldn't have cared if she told the whole school, even if it meant he was suspended. Again.

But even then, he had realized the futility of trying to stop her. Emma had been on a twisted path for more than a year, since her dad died, and she was determined not to let anybody drag her off of it.

Back in the present, Bryce was struck anew by the shock of seeing her again, so much the same but so different.

She still had the same high cheekbones, the same vivid green eyes that had haunted his dreams for years. She still had the same auburn hair as Rosie, like liquid fire, though now Emma's hair was tipped and streaked with purple highlights and she had plenty of piercings in her ears, her nose, as well as ink coloring the creamy skin of her arms.

He knew enough from the little Rosie had said about her daughter and granddaughter to know Emma's life hadn't been easy after she left town. The details were fuzzy, but he gathered it involved living on the street for a time, drugs and even a brief stint in jail. Then she had become pregnant with Olive when she was barely twenty.

Despite it all, or maybe because of it, Emma looked beautiful and wild. There was a strength to her now, a hard-won resilience that drew him in even more than before. Bryce felt the old attraction flaring up, stronger than ever.

That didn't matter.

Bryce sighed, paid for the stack of magazines and the coloring book he always picked up for his mom to help her pass the time at her memory care center, and left the bookshop.

As he walked to his truck, he couldn't help but think that while he might be drawn to her, Emma had never looked at him as anything other than the local screwup class clown. That was where he was stuck with her, forever the dumb, goofy kid who couldn't get his act together.

Maybe it was for the best.

He didn't have room in his life right now for anything else, not when his mom's early-onset dementia required so much of his time and emotional energy.

Still, a small part of him couldn't help but wonder what might have been, what might still be, if only things were different.

CHAPTER FOUR

—

Andrew

"I HOPE THERE'S A BATHROOM AT THE BOOKSTORE."

At the slightly strangled voice of his seven-year-old son, Finn, coming from the back seat, Andrew Morgan flashed a quick look in the rearview mirror.

"I'm sure there is. Hang on, bud. We'll get you taken care of."

"Why didn't you go before we left?" Zara demanded. At ten, she considered herself superior to her younger brother in all things.

"Because I didn't need to go then. Now I do. Anyway, I don't like that bathroom much."

You and me both, kid, Andrew wanted to say.

"It is nasty," Zara agreed. "I can't believe we only have one bathroom with a toilet that actually flushes. I feel like we're camping or something."

When they finally moved out of the carriage house apartment and into Stormhaven, they would have five bathrooms but as of now they were all unfinished.

His entire house was unfinished. Like his current manuscript. And, hell, the rest of his life.

"I liked our old bathroom," Finn muttered.

"Me, too," Zara said. "Wood Briar blows and our house is creepy."

"I'm sorry you feel like that. I hope once we've been here awhile, you'll like it better."

"I liked our old house," his daughter muttered. "And our old school and our old neighborhood."

"So did I," Finn said. "But then our house burned down and so did our school."

The lingering sadness in his voice made Andrew's heart ache. Those damn Santa Ana winds. Hadn't his kids lost enough already in their short lives? Their mother had only been gone three years. They were finally beginning to find their way after Tracy's death when the wind-fueled firestorm had decimated their house, their neighborhood and the life they had been trying to rebuild.

"We all needed a change," he said, trying to inject a cheery note in his voice. "And your grandma is here. Won't it be fun to be near her?"

"I guess," Zara said.

"And we're close to the ocean."

"We were close to the ocean in LA," she retorted. "And it was warmer there. Grandma said you can't swim here in Oregon unless you have a death wish."

Zara's negative energy was beginning to grate on his last nerve, though he tried to give her a little grace. He knew this move had been hard on her.

She had wanted them to rebuild their house in Los Angeles. She loved her friends, her school, their small house on a hillside above the ocean in a thriving neighborhood. While he understood where she was coming from, Andrew had plenty of reasons for wanting to start over somewhere new.

"You need to give Oregon a chance. Once the renovations to the house are done, you're going to love it," he assured her. "You'll have your own room and bathroom. You won't have to share with Finn like you did at our old place. Everything will be closer. You can ride your bike to the library, to the park, to the beach. We won't have to spend half our lives in the car like we did in Los Angeles."

"But Mom is in LA. We're so far away, we can't even go visit her."

"Mom is in heaven," Finn reminded her.

"You think I don't know that?" Zara glared at her brother. "I meant, her grave is in LA."

Andrew sighed, wishing he was better at this whole single dad thing.

For the past three years, they had all been in survival mode. He had felt pulled in a dozen different directions while he tried to juggle the kids' school and sports schedules, his book deadlines, publicity tours for his two books that had come out since Tracy's death, as well as the movie that had been made of his first book, released at Christmastime.

It had left little room for him to think, breathe, grieve for his wife, who had died two years after being diagnosed with an aggressive form of leukemia.

A year ago, he finally felt as if things were coming together. And then everything had gone to hell.

"We will still make trips to LA to put flowers on her grave," he promised.

"It won't be the same," she muttered.

He wanted to tell her that was an inescapable part of being human. Everything changed. Life was a constantly evolving river, ever reshaping its banks.

He didn't bother waxing philosophical. It only annoyed his kids and they were pulling up to a convenient parking space near the bookstore anyway.

The Rainy Day Bookshop had a charming facade, but unfortunately that was about the only charming part about the store. The interior was cramped, dark, dingy. Utterly unappealing.

Still, it was the only game in town and did carry a nice selection of kids books and esoteric research books.

Finn was first out of his seat belt. He opened his door, jumped out of the Range Rover and raced for the entrance to the bookshop.

"Slow down," Zara snapped. She unfastened her own seat belt and rushed after her brother, slamming the door behind her.

Andrew followed more slowly, feeling as if he were a decade older than his forty-three years.

Some days his kids exhausted him. As much as he adored them, they had boundless energy and they seemed to expend most of it bickering with each other.

Andrew didn't really consider himself an older father—he had been thirty-three when Zara was born, thirty-seven for Finn—but there were definitely times when he wished he and Tracy hadn't waited five years after they married to start having kids.

He pushed open the bookstore door to be met by the musty, delicious, addictive smell of dusty paper, old wood and possibilities.

If he closed his eyes, he would probably enjoy the vibe of The Rainy Day Bookshop more.

Books were cluttered everywhere, stacked sometimes two or three deep on shelves. Finding the exact book you wanted in this bookstore would be like trying to find a single star in a sky full of countless flickering lights. It would require patience, dedication and more than a bit of luck.

Still, it was a bookstore.

As long as he could remember, Andrew had always felt most at home in the world when he was surrounded by books.

Finn must have found his way to the bathroom. Zara, he saw, was already looking through the books about horses, her favorite subject right now. If he had purchased a ranch in Montana instead of a crumbling mansion in Oregon, she probably would have been much happier.

She looked up as he approached. "You said I could get two books, right?"

"That's right."

She sent him a sidelong look, obviously calculating how far she could push. "What if I find three?"

"We can talk about it."

Both of them knew Andrew was a sucker, especially when it came to books. He had a hard time saying no to his kids, which he knew wasn't helpful for any of them.

He could certainly afford three books for his daughter, if that would make her happy. His success and the subsequent movie and licensing deals had been lucrative beyond anything he might have imagined in his wildest dreams when he first decided he wanted to become a writer.

"I think I want to get two books about horses, one fiction and one nonfiction, and then maybe that new book in the Castle Door series."

"Okay. Maybe you can help Finn find a book, too."

She nodded and went back to perusing the shelves while Andrew headed over to the cluttered nonfiction section.

The bookstore did not seem to be crowded for a Sunday in early June. The town's tourist season hadn't really picked up yet. He expected in a week or two, the place would be hopping. Though Wood Briar was not as popular as some of the towns farther up the coast, like Cannon Beach, Lincoln City or Newport, it still drew plenty of people wanting to enjoy the rugged Oregon coast.

He had a pleasant time combing the shelves, looking for more research books to add to his collection. He was looking specifically for a book on alchemy. He could always order it online but he preferred to buy local when he could. Anything he could do to help out the town's only bookshop.

As usual, being in a bookstore seemed to settle something restless deep inside. He expected those soothing properties had started after his brother's death, when their already stiff and formal home had become a place of darkness and grief.

His father had been too busy burying his emotions in work while his mother had retreated into herself. More often than not at loose ends, especially during the summer months, Andrew would escape to the library and if he couldn't find what he wanted there, he would find his way to his favorite bookstore.

Books had been his refuge, his sanctuary. He lived in books more than real life when he had been young.

He couldn't regret it. How could he, when his obsession with books had led to his career as a bestselling author?

He was browsing the shelves when he overheard a snatch of conversation from the next aisle over.

"Yes, that's Andrew Morgan's latest," he heard a female voice say.

Naturally, his attention perked up at that. He liked surprising his readers in bookstores. It invariably gave them a jolt of happy serendipity and helped connect him to readers, random moments he could take out to help push him forward during the long hours he spent alone at his laptop.

"I haven't read that one yet," a second, younger-sounding woman said.

"You could skip it," the first voice said in a dismissive tone. "It's not nearly as good as his last one. And that one didn't have the same promise as his early works. He's massively overhyped, in my opinion."

Okay. This was awkward. Andrew stiffened, keeping his features turned to the bookshelf in front of him.

"You think so? I feel like his books have gotten better and better."

"I had no idea you liked his books so much, Em," the first voice said, sounding surprised. "You know he's moving to town, right?"

"Grandma told me that. How exciting! I hope I get the chance to meet him. I started reading him years ago. I saw the movie last Christmas with some friends and it was amazing."

"It was good. The books aren't as good as the movie, if you want my opinion."

Andrew didn't know about Em, but *he* certainly didn't want the other woman's opinion.

He couldn't approach the other customers now, when it was clear one of them was definitely not a fan of his work—and that she likely would know he had overheard her.

Andrew looked around, wondering how he could escape the bookstore with his son still in the bathroom and his daughter engrossed in finding bookish treasures.

"I can't believe you don't like them," the one named Em said. "I think the whole Starbound Chronicles series is amazing. The world-building is unbelievable, the plots are gripping and his dialogue cracks me up. You've never been a big fan of fantasy novels. Is that why you don't like his books?"

"It's not my favorite genre but there are some fantasy novels I enjoy. I just don't like overexposed male authors who tell the same trite story again and again, with wooden female characters who are basically one-dimensional nerd fantasies. Andrew Morgan writes love scenes like he's never even met a real woman."

The other woman laughed. "You must not be paying attention to the tabloids lately. Andrew Morgan has definitely met a woman. Didn't you see he was hot and heavy with Willow Voss? They were seen everywhere a few months ago."

The other woman snorted. "Publicity hype. That's all. I

find it more than a little coincidental that the leading actress of a new movie franchise had an apparently tumultuous relationship with the person who wrote the book the movies are based on. They were just trying to get attention."

"Mom, I don't think they really needed attention. The first movie broke box office records, and it's still breaking them. The second one is going to be even bigger when it comes out at Christmastime."

Andrew was still trying to figure out how to extricate himself from the unbelievably awkward situation when the two women moved closer, still concealed from him by the tall bookshelf.

"I would love to have him do a signing here at the store," the younger woman said. "Wouldn't that be epic? I wonder if he might consider it during the busy summer months, when all the tourists are here."

"I doubt that will happen. We're a small fish in a big publishing pond."

"We are the only bookstore in town. As he's our new celebrity author, I would think he might want to have a good relationship with us. Plus Grandma is friends with his mom. That has to count for something."

He should leave, grab his kids and sneak out the door before these women saw him. He didn't want to embarrass either of them. The only trouble with that was Zara was scouring the shelves for a book, and her brother was still in the bathroom.

Andrew slunk down, trying to look as inconspicuous as possible. He turned his face toward the shelves until he realized he was fiercely concentrating on a selection of books about coping with menopause.

To his vast relief, the women's conversation shifted to other subjects. Andrew headed over toward the bathrooms as Finn came out.

"Did you wash your hands?" he asked automatically.

His son nodded, shaking off his still wet palms. "Where's Zara?"

"She's looking at the horse books. What are you looking for?"

With luck, his son would say he didn't need a book and they could wrap up this excruciating bookstore visit.

"I want another *Star Wars Origami* book. Can you help me find it?"

"Sure thing."

Since the two women seemed to have moved to another section of the store, he directed his son to the children's area. Finn quickly found several books he wanted to peruse, including the clever book that taught readers how to make origami versions of popular *Star Wars* characters.

Andrew had returned to the research section right as the two women walked around the endcap into his aisle.

Even if he hadn't heard the younger one refer to the other one as Mom, he would have known they were related. Both women were remarkably pretty. They shared the same green eyes, the same delicate features, the same auburn hair, though the younger one—the very insightful reader who loved his books, apparently—had purple-tipped highlights, several piercings in her nose and her lip, and a tattoo of a crescent moon on one arm and an iridescent dragon on the other.

"Oh!" The older woman drew up short. He saw a dawning look of horror cross her striking features. "You're Andrew Morgan."

With all his heart, he wished he could deny his identity in that moment but that would be stupid. "I am. Hello."

He offered a smile, his polished meet-the-readers kind of expression—the one that concealed all the struggles and strains of life.

Maybe she would assume he hadn't overheard their conversation. He had no problem going along with that. With luck, they could avoid any awkwardness.

"Welcome to Wood Briar," she said. "I had heard you were moving to town. My mother is friends with your mother. She's been so excited to have you return."

He arched an eyebrow. "Why would your mother possibly care about me moving to Wood Briar?"

She grimaced. "Not my mother. *Your* mother is the excited one. Nancy has been talking about it nonstop. She's so thrilled to have your children close to her again."

Being near his mother had been one of the main reasons he had decided to settle here. Nancy had been extolling the virtues of the area since she moved here herself on a whim several years after his father died.

During the final days of Tracy's illness, Nancy had moved down to California temporarily to help him out with the children. He would be eternally grateful to her for that. Her calm presence had been a lifesaver.

His mother had talked about moving down to California permanently to be closer to them, but he could sense the reluctance in her voice every time she brought it up, so he had managed to dissuade her. She had made a life here, with a tight group of friends who looked out for each other. He didn't want to take her away from that. She deserved to find whatever peace she could after being married to William Morgan all those years.

After the fire destroyed his house, moving here to be closer to her had made sense.

He still didn't know if he'd made the right decision. The endless chaos of the house renovation along with Zara's negative attitude made him question everything, but he supposed only time would tell.

"My kids are looking forward to being close to their grandmother."

"How are you liking Stormhaven?"

"Stormhaven? Seriously? That's where you've moved?" Her daughter looked astonished at that information as she gave the older woman a look Andrew couldn't interpret.

He frowned. "I'm afraid it's not so much a haven right now as a disaster. We're in the middle of a construction zone. It will be nice when it's done, but right now we're squeezed into a couple of rooms above the old carriage house. The renovation is taking much longer than I expected."

"I know. I'm sorry about that."

"Why are you sorry?"

"Oh." She looked flustered. "I should have introduced myself. I'm Rosie Lucas."

He narrowed his gaze at her. "Rosie Lucas, as in Lucas Construction?"

"Yes, that's right. And this is my daughter, Emma."

"You need to do a hell of a lot better job meeting deadlines," he said. "I was led to believe most of the work would be done before we moved here."

He sounded like an ass, but he didn't really care. Rosie Lucas hated his books *and* apparently she was also responsible for the current chaos in his living situation.

The woman looked chagrined. "I'm really sorry we're behind schedule but everything turned out to be more complicated than we expected. It's a big job. The place has been abandoned for years. It takes a great deal of effort to bring it back to its full glory."

"And money," he grumbled. "Every time I turn around, the costs for things have gone up."

"Things are tough right now in this economy. Construction material is harder to get and costs twice as much. Believe me, my subcontractors are frustrated, too, which is another big reason for the delays. But I think we're back on track now. I'm hoping another few months and we should be done."

Great. Another few months of trying to focus on meeting his deadline with subs coming in and out.

"And you're living there in the midst of the work?" Emma said. "Is there anywhere for you to write?"

"Not really. Eventually I'll have a very nice office in the turret of the house but it doesn't have paint or carpet right now, so I'm mostly working at the kitchen table after the kids are in bed."

"Oh dear." Rosie looked distressed. "Maybe we can prioritize that and at least get you a decent workspace sooner rather than later. I'll talk to Bryce, your project manager."

He did like Bryce Kendall. In every interaction he'd had with the guy, he found him knowledgeable and hardworking, dedicated to restoring the old house to its former glory.

"I would appreciate that," he said, holding back his sarcastic rejoinder that he was paying them to finish on time and thus far Lucas Construction had failed miserably.

To his great relief, Finn wandered over from the children's area at that moment.

"I found the book I want, Dad."

"That's great."

His son, invariably friendly, turned to the two women. "Hi. My name is Finn. What's yours?"

Rosie smiled at him with far more warmth than she had shown him. "My name is Rosie and this is my daughter, Emma. We're your neighbors, actually. We live down the street from Stormhaven. We're in the house with the red door."

"And all the flowers! My sister said it looks like a fairy garden."

"That's right."

"Mr. Morgan, I have to say, I love your books!" Emma said after a moment. "My mom and I were just talking about them."

Yes. He was aware. He glanced at Rosie and saw her cheeks suddenly matched her name. "Were you?"

"You have a huge readership here in Oregon. Since you're our new celebrity author, we would love to have you do a signing here at The Rainy Day Bookshop once you settle in."

His confusion must have shown on his features because Rosie cleared her throat.

"Did we forget to mention that I own the bookstore?"

"Do you?" He should have known. She obviously had poor taste in books, and the general air of neglect of the bookstore reinforced that.

"I'm what you might call a silent owner. I've been busy running Lucas Construction for the last few years, so my mother has taken over the bookstore."

"Grandma had an accident a few weeks ago, so I've moved back from Las Vegas to help out," Emma informed him. "We are going to be making some changes and one of those is hosting more book events. I would love to have you be the guest author for our grand reopening."

"What changes?" Rosie did not look thrilled at the prospect. "What grand reopening?"

"Cosmetic, for the most part," Em said. She looked nervous suddenly. "I was talking with Bryce about some things we could do to brighten things up."

She turned back to Andrew. "What do you think? Would you be willing to be our first featured author?"

He tried to do his part to support indie bookstores but right now he had enough on his plate. "I don't want to commit to anything at this point, while my life is so chaotic."

"Fair enough. I'll talk to you again when Stormhaven is renovated, shall I?"

"Sure."

Andrew forced a polite smile, but inwardly he was already looking for an escape route. The last thing he wanted was to be further entangled with this bookstore or its owners. He had come to Oregon seeking solitude and a fresh start, not to be roped into local events or forced interactions. Yet as he glanced between Rosie and Emma, he realized with a sinking feeling that avoiding them entirely might prove impossible.

Rosie owned both the bookstore and the construction company working on Stormhaven. Her daughter seemed eager to involve him in their plans. Andrew found himself trapped in a web of small-town connections he hadn't anticipated.

As he returned to help his kids make their final selections, he couldn't shake the uneasy feeling that the peaceful life he had hoped to find here was already more complicated than he had bargained for.

He would need to find a way to maintain his distance without burning bridges—a delicate balance he wasn't sure he was prepared to strike.

CHAPTER FIVE

—

Rosie

EVEN AFTER NEARLY THIRTY YEARS IN OREGON, ROSIE STILL sometimes found it hard to believe she actually lived here in this beautiful place by the ocean.

It seemed even more unbelievable that she was currently walking in this serene setting with her own beloved granddaughter.

Rosie sighed with contentment while a giggling Olive skipped ahead of her, sunlight glinting on her auburn curls and Dottie's leash gripped tightly in her fingers.

Olive and Emma had been in Wood Briar for over a week and Rosie felt as if she had been holding her breath that entire time, bracing for disaster. She finally was beginning to relax and almost believe they might be able to make this work.

She still weighed every word she said to her daughter, afraid she might say the wrong thing and dredge up all the previous conflicts between them again. She sensed Emma was being as careful around her. So far, they seemed to be managing together in the same house better than Rosie had dreamed possible.

This was the payoff. Walking along her favorite beach with Olive on a sunny afternoon in early June while the ocean murmured beside them.

"Look, Grandma. A crab!" Olive exclaimed, her features lighting up with glee.

Rosie suspected there were thousands of them on the beach, but she wasn't about to tell this precious child her discovery wasn't particularly unique.

"Look at that. You found one. That is a mole crab."

"It looks like a potato with little squiggly legs."

"You're right. That's exactly what it looks like."

She didn't want this moment to end. When her daughter had asked her if she might be available to watch Olive that afternoon while Emma had a staff meeting, Rosie had been quick to rearrange her schedule, even when her own plate had been full.

As usual, her week had been a hectic one, filled with meetings and jobsite visits. She had barely spent a moment with either of them and Rosie relished this chance to be still and simply listen to the sound of the gulls, the music of the surf and her granddaughter's giggles.

Rosie would be spending all evening with Olive and tucking her into bed later, the most time she had spent with her granddaughter at a stretch since Emma and Olive moved in.

She hoped the fact that her daughter had asked for her help indicated Emma was beginning to settle in and feel more comfortable.

She suspected her daughter had big plans for making changes at the bookstore, though Emma hadn't talked much about them to her. Rosie could only hope she would share her ideas when she was ready.

During the years Sylvia had run the bookstore, Rosie worked hard to step away and not micromanage all the day-to-day operations of the bookstore she loved. The whole situation felt different now, with Emma at the helm.

"Can we find more crabs?" Olive asked eagerly.

Rosie considered, shifting her gaze to the edge of the beach, where the rocks presented the perfect place for tide pooling, especially now, at low tide.

How much time had she, Gary and Emma spent at this

very same beach, perusing the tide pools for anemones, starfish, crabs?

Their family had passed so many joyful hours on Crescent Beach building sandcastles, hunting for sea creatures, flying kites in the coastal wind. Rosie regretted that it had been years since she had taken the time to indulge in what had once been favorite activities.

That she had the chance now to share these moments with her daughter's child seemed a rare and priceless gift.

She could see two problems right now, though. For one, they didn't have the right footgear for tide pooling. She and Emma and Gary always used to wear muck boots to protect their feet and help them walk carefully on the slippery rocks without damaging the fragile ecosystems.

The second problem was Dottie. Her little dog, placid and easygoing though she was, would frighten the sea creatures.

She solved the second problem by finding a shady spot for Dottie nearby and securing her in place with her leash.

For the footwear issue, they would simply have to make do and stick to the tide pools closest to shore.

She and Olive were kneeling down admiring one of the larger crabs they found when Rosie heard the sound of approaching children. Apparently someone else had decided this was the perfect time for tide pooling.

Rosie pushed away the twinge of momentary annoyance. Crescent Beach was surely big enough for everyone who wanted to enjoy it, as long as they did so respectfully.

"Hi! You're the bookshop lady!"

She turned at the greeting to find Finn Morgan along with a girl who had to be his sister racing toward the rocks wearing rain boots and floppy hats.

Olive beamed at them. "Hi! My name is Olive."

"I'm Zara. And this is my brother, Finn," the girl said.

"We found a crab!" Olive said. "I named him Bob. I think he likes me."

"I'm sure he does," Zara answered, giving the preschooler an indulgent smile.

"How do you know if a crab is a boy or a girl?" Finn asked.

"Easy," Rosie answered with a smile. "You ask it."

She heard a muffled snort and looked up to see the children's father approaching them. For some silly reason, Rosie could feel her heartbeat accelerate. The man was far too gorgeous for his own good, with his lean features, stunning eyes and hint of afternoon stubble.

"If the crab doesn't answer," he said, "there are other ways to figure out whether a crab is male or female."

"How?" his son asked.

"A crab has what's called an apron that you can see when you turn it over. A male has a long, narrow apron like the Washington Monument and a female crab has a wider, shorter apron, more like the Lincoln Memorial."

"Is that true?" Rosie asked. She had lived in Oregon most of her life and had never heard that. Not that she had spent much time studying the gender characteristics of crabs, but still.

"I swear."

"Are you some kind of marine expert?" she asked.

"Nope. Just a guy with too much curiosity and a passionate love of trivia. I bought a book about the local flora and fauna of this part of Oregon when we were at your bookstore the other day. I read that particular fact in there."

Olive frowned. "But we can't pick up the crabs. My grandma said. We're not supposed to touch the creatures unless a grown-up is there to help us."

"Your grandma is absolutely right. About crabs, anyway."

He said the last part in an undertone and Rosie sent him a sharp look. What did he mean by that?

Her mind immediately went to their previous encounter in the bookstore. She had been worrying ever since that day that he might have overheard what she said to Emma about his books. She truly hoped not.

"How are things going at Stormhaven?" she asked, hoping to change the subject. "I asked Bryce to light a fire under our subs and I made a few calls myself."

"Whatever you did must have worked. We've seen a lot of progress this week."

"Oh good. I'm glad they're moving forward. I'm only sorry I can't expedite the entire project. Bryce tells me there's a problem with some of the materials that your designer ordered. They've been delayed because of a shipping problem and are somewhere stuck on a boat in the Pacific right now."

"I had hoped all these details would be worked out before we arrived."

"I'm sorry for all the delays. How is the carriage house apartment working out?"

"It's tight quarters, only two bedrooms, one bathroom and a kitchen/living area, but we're making it work. It helps that your crew has mostly finished my office in the main house. The kids are heading to the first of several summer day camps next week so I should have more time to focus."

Before she could answer, his daughter called for his attention. "Is this an urchin, Dad?"

He turned away from Rosie, leaving her feeling an odd mix of relief and disappointment. When he bent to take a look at the creature in the tide pool, she couldn't help but notice the gold streaks weaving through his brown hair.

As she watched him interact with his children, a shiver of awareness thrummed through her, taking Rosie completely by surprise.

Where did *that* come from? Okay, she couldn't deny Andrew Morgan was an attractive man, with those serious features and blue eyes. But she wasn't in the market for any man, attractive or not.

Rosie studiously turned her attention to her granddaughter. Her *granddaughter*, for heaven's sake. The fact that she was here with her daughter's child ought to help her keep her head, no matter how sexy she found her new neighbor.

Rosie knew she wasn't exactly ancient. She was only forty-five years old and barely heading into perimenopause, after all. She hadn't lived like a nun in the ten years since Gary died. She had dated on and off, usually when friends insisted on setting her up with a friend of a friend or when she needed a plus-one to some event.

A few years ago, she actually had dated a divorced Lincoln City restaurant owner for nearly six months. On paper, they worked well together and she had tried hard to fall in love with Jim Rylan. She enjoyed his company and they invariably had fun together, but that elusive spark never quite materialized, no matter how hard they tried.

Eventually they both decided they were better off as friends. Only a few months after they broke things off, Jim had started dating one of his neighbors and the two of them had married the previous Christmas.

Rosie was happy for them but had accepted that if she couldn't fall for a decent, kind, good-looking guy like Jim, maybe she was destined to spend the rest of her life alone.

She found it grossly unfair that she had only exchanged a few words with Andrew Morgan and wasn't even sure she liked the man, yet her traitorous body suddenly decided to wake up and instinctively respond to him.

"I don't know what kind of creature that is," he said to his daughter. "I'll take a picture of it, though, and we can look it up after we get home."

Rosie peered around him to the tide pool all three children were gazing into. "That is a frosted nudibranch, or 'sea slug.' They are incredibly rare. You're so lucky to have found one!"

"It's too pretty to be a slug," Zara declared. "Slugs are gray and slimy. This one is almost see-through and is all frilly and cute."

"It is cute. You're right," Rosie said. "She probably prefers to be called a frosted nudibranch rather than a slug."

The children admired the creature before moving to a larger tide pool where several sea stars clung to the rocks.

"Why are they all different colors?" Finn asked.

"Lots of different reasons. Their diet, their age and their particular species all play a part," she answered. "Sea stars are actually more rare than they used to be. Unfortunately, many of them have died of a disease. It's one of the most widespread marine wildlife diseases ever."

"That's so sad," Zara said.

"It is. But there are a few signs that they're making a comeback. You can see more of them now than even a few years ago."

"How do *you* know so much about tidal creatures?" Andrew asked when the children moved on to admire a tide pool brimming with colorful anemone that undulated in the water. "Have you read the book about local flora and fauna, too?"

"No. I'll have to look for it. I've lived in this area for years and have spent a lot of time on the beach. You learn a thing or two along the way."

"Where did you live before you came here?"

His question took her by surprise and she paused a moment before answering. "All over the place, actually. My dad was in the military, so we never spent long anywhere. He died when I was twelve. My mom was restless for a few more years. I went to six different schools in four years. Finally, she took a job here as the director of the high school library right before my junior year. I've been here ever since."

Where did the time go? It felt like only yesterday she was that scared, defiant, angry kid moving to yet another school.

From the very beginning, Wood Briar had felt different. More like home. Unlike some of the other places where they had lived, the other students had been kind and welcoming. She had loved the scenery even back then and would take long walks on the beach or drive down the coast in her beat-up Toyota to find a long stretch of sand where she could be alone.

"Was it tough, moving around so much?"

Rosie considered his question as she watched the children tire of the sea creatures and go over to Dottie's shady spot to pet the little terrier-Chihuahua mix.

"It was all I really ever knew. I can't say I loved never staying put in one place for long, but it did teach me a lot about the world and about people. That was also where I developed my deep love of books. There was inevitably a lonely time in every new place when I didn't know anyone, but I always had friends inside the pages of the books I loved."

"I'm worried my kids will struggle to make friends, with the move. They've been through so much over the past few years. Losing their mom, then losing everything we owned in a wildfire. I want everything to be perfect for them here. Finn is doing okay but Zara is still struggling with the move. I hope I haven't messed them up for life by dragging them here."

It was an admission she suspected he did not make easily. That he would be so frank and open with her, a woman he had only met once, touched something deep inside her.

"They'll be fine," she assured him softly. "They seem like lovely children and this is a very warm community. Once your house is finished, I'm sure they will feel more settled."

She would have to see what she could do about moving things forward even faster on that front.

"Is that what compelled you to stay in Wood Briar all these years? That warm community?"

"And the lovely surroundings." She inclined her head to take in the long stretch of beach and the soaring rock formations offshore that added drama and beauty to the area.

"This has felt like home since Mom and I moved here. I met my late husband on the first day of school only a few weeks later. We started dating and never stopped."

"High school sweethearts, then."

She nodded. "We were married a year after I graduated and had Emma a month before my twentieth birthday."

"That's young."

She shrugged. "We were in love and both knew what we wanted."

"The whole hearts and flowers, white-picket-fence thing?"

"Is something wrong with that?" she demanded.

"Not as far as I'm concerned," he replied.

Okay, perhaps she was a smidge too defensive about the choices she had made twenty-five years ago. She knew she and Gary both had been far too young, but they had known their own minds.

"We had planned to marry after I graduated from college but then I got pregnant with Emma and we didn't see any point in waiting."

Those early years had been tough. She would be lying if she said otherwise. They had both been forced to grow up together. Because she had always been a good student, Rosie had earned enough credits while still in high school to attain her associates degree by the time she graduated and she had been attending college in Eugene, working toward her bachelor's in business administration, when she found out she was expecting.

Gary had been working in his dad's drywall business here and working toward his own contractor's license. Everyone from his parents to Sylvia to their friends had encouraged them to wait a while before settling down.

Rosie could only be glad they hadn't listened or she would have had even less time with Gary.

"Can we take Dottie for a walk down the beach?" Zara asked her.

Rosie smiled at the sweet girl. "Sure. She would love that. Make sure you walk above the high tide line, though. We don't want to scare any sea creatures."

The small dog pranced around them with excitement as they bickered over who would hold the leash first. Zara won by force of will. Rosie suspected that was not an unusual occurrence. The girl struck her as possessing a very determined personality.

As if by tacit agreement, she and Andrew fell into step behind the children and Rosie was again aware of the sheer physicality of the man. He seemed surprisingly fit for a man who probably spent a lot of time at his laptop.

"How long has your husband been gone?" he asked.

She blinked at the unexpected question, hoping he couldn't read the direction of her thoughts. "Ten years," she said after a moment. "It feels like a lifetime in some ways and like yesterday in others."

Though she didn't really want to talk about Gary, she knew his next question before he even asked it. She might as well spare both of them.

"He was killed in a car accident."

"I'm sorry."

The compassion in his voice had an undeniable ring of sincerity to it.

"Thank you. And I'm sorry for your loss as well. Your wife died of cancer a few years ago, isn't that right?"

"Yes. Leukemia." He sounded surprised and not particularly pleased that she knew that much about him.

"Your mother and my mother are good friends," she reminded him. "I know we're all strangers to you but some of us already feel like we know you through your mother."

"Perhaps my mother ought to stop gossiping about me with the neighbors."

"You'll have to take that up with her."

"I will. Trust me."

She smiled at the annoyance in his voice. "As far as I'm aware, your mom doesn't blab your business all over town, if that's what you're worrying about. I probably know more than most people, simply because I worked with your mom on her own renovations and then she hired us again after you bought Stormhaven. In the course of our working relationship, she has told me a few things about your situation. I know, for instance, that you bought the house basically unseen and wanted to completely renovate it."

"What was I thinking?"

Oh, she liked him, far more than she might have expected. "You were thinking you and your children needed a fresh start somewhere and it made sense to move closer to your mom. For what it's worth, I think you made a great choice."

He smiled down at her and Rosie suddenly felt warm despite the breeze blowing off the water.

"Thank you. It's good to hear at least one person in town

doesn't think I'm reckless and irrational to pick up and move my kids hundreds of miles from the only home they've ever had."

"I'm not the only one. Trust me. Everyone is thrilled that someone is finally doing something with Stormhaven. It's a gorgeous property and most people in town would much rather see a family live there then have it be turned into vacation condos, like the previous owners planned to do."

"I suppose that's something."

"I'm sure people will tell you the same thing themselves when they have the chance to meet you."

"I'm not exactly a hermit. I've met a few people."

"If you're ready to meet more, we have our summer neighborhood party coming up soon."

"What summer neighborhood party?"

"When you live in a small town with a big tourist presence, you have to work hard to socialize with your neighbors or you end up disconnected and outnumbered."

"I can see where that might be a problem."

"A few years ago, a core of about ten of us decided to start up occasional gatherings. It's grown exponentially since then. We take turns. Every few months we have a potluck and everyone is invited. There are usually brats, burgers, chicken breasts and a few vegetarian options. I can't promise you grand entertainment or gourmet food, but it might be a good way for you and Finn and Zara to meet some of your new neighbors."

She could tell at once that he did not look thrilled at the idea. Did he have something against meeting his neighbors or was he simply naturally introverted?

"We could do that."

"I'm sure your children would enjoy it. This time it's a barbecue at my house, as long as the weather cooperates."

"What if it doesn't? It's Oregon, after all. You get your fair share of rain."

"True. Then we'll move the party to the community center, over on Thimbleberry Drive. We have a standing reservation. But keep your fingers crossed for good weather."

"I'll be sure to do that," he said, his voice dry.

"I should give you fair warning that you will probably be the center of attention. Don't be surprised if you end up fielding a bunch of questions about The Starbound Chronicles. You have a lot of fans here."

A funny expression crossed his features. He opened his mouth as if to answer then appeared to think better of whatever he intended to say, leaving her to wonder again if he had overheard her talking about his books with Emma.

More than ever, she hoped he hadn't.

"And of course," she went on, "everyone is going to want to talk to you about Willow Voss."

"Hate to break it to you, but you're not exactly making your little neighborhood shindig sound appealing."

She again had to smile at his dry tone. She really did like the man, she decided.

"If anybody becomes too intrusive, you can give them that exact death stare. It's quite intimidating."

He made a face. "For your information, I know how to occasionally make small talk with people. It's not my favorite thing but I have to go on book tours and speak with strangers all the time."

"Good to know." She could do dry, too.

"But if I get into trouble with some talkative neighbor or other, it will be your job to rescue me."

She snorted. "My job? Why me?"

"You're the one trying to drag me out of my writing cave for a neighborhood party."

"Fine. Be a hermit crab if you want to. Your mom can always take your kids to the party without you."

Before he could answer, Olive raced over to them, her hand outstretched.

"Grandma, look what I found. Zara says it's a sand dollar. My friend Finn found one, too."

She dutifully exclaimed over the shell in her granddaughter's hand, trying to decide if she was grateful for the interruption or not.

Either way, Olive was a great reminder that she and her sexy new neighbor were at completely different places in life. She was a grandmother, for heaven's sake, while he was a single father of two young children who were still grieving for their mother.

As attracted as she might be to him, she had to keep all that in mind before she did something stupid like develop a serious crush on the man.

CHAPTER SIX

—

Andrew

FOR SOME REASON, ANDREW STILL FELT LIGHT AS EIDERDOWN as they returned to his place, though walking into the depressing apartment above the Stormhaven carriage house definitely put a damper on his mood.

The place wasn't terrible. It would probably be a decent place for a single guy on his own. Not for a dad with two active children. A guy who also needed his own writing space.

"I'm hungry," Finn said. "What's for dinner?"

He thought of the nearly empty refrigerator and the equally bare pantry shelves. He needed to get to the grocery store again, since the few staples he had bought a week ago were running out.

They couldn't continue to eat takeout or peanut butter and jelly sandwiches for every meal.

He had hoped to hire a housekeeper by this point, someone who could cook and clean and help out with the kids when he needed it, but Andrew didn't feel as if he could hire someone until things were more settled in their lives.

Would that day ever come? Right now it seemed a world away. Andrew felt as if his whole life was on hold.

"How about if I order pizza?" he finally said. Could he be more of a single dad cliché right now?

"Yay!" Finn exclaimed, pumping a fist in the air as if he had won his second grade spelling bee.

"Yum," Zara said. "Can you order half cheese for me?"

Unlike her brother, Zara could be a picky eater sometimes,

yet another reason he wasn't particularly enthusiastic about cooking.

"You bet," he said.

He made the call to the better of the two pizza places in town—yes, they had tried both—and was unloading the dishwasher when he heard a knock on the door.

Andrew frowned. That couldn't possibly be the pizza. He had only ordered it ten minutes earlier. The place was fast but not *that* fast.

"I'll get it." Finn raced to the door and flung it open before Andrew could caution him.

He seriously needed to have another talk with both of his kids about exercising a little common sense. He didn't want to scare them but he had already experienced a few security concerns because of overenthusiastic fans. One of the improvements he was planning to Stormhaven was a state-of-the-art security system and eventually a high fence to encircle the property.

He didn't consider himself a celebrity whatsoever, but he had two children to think about. It would only take one rabid fan to upset their entire world.

To his relief, this time they had nothing to worry about. His mother walked through the door with a bright smile.

"Oh good. You're home. I thought I saw you walking back here from the beach."

Nancy only lived three houses away, in the opposite direction from Rosie Lucas's house. He suspected that proximity was the main reason she had worked so hard to persuade him to purchase Stormhaven.

In her cozy Craftsman cottage, his mother had a lovely view of Crescent Beach and the ocean beyond. He couldn't begrudge her that. She deserved any peace she could find after years of pandering to his father's controlling demands.

"We're here. I just ordered pizza. Have you eaten?"

"No. Pizza sounds delicious, if that was an invitation."

"Consider yourself invited."

She gave a sunny smile. "Thank you. How was your walk on the beach? Did I see you talking with someone?"

He again questioned the wisdom of moving into the same town as his mother, especially if she was going to be so watchful over his every move.

"We bumped into Rosie Lucas. Our contractor. You know. The one who was supposed to have this house done before we got here."

His mother looked guilty.

"I've told you over and over how sorry I am about that. I really thought things would be further along, or I would never have told you the house would be ready at the end of the school year. I underestimated how much work would be involved."

An understatement of epic proportion. And he had been too busy trying to dig himself out of the hole he had created for himself to pay any attention.

"Rosie is a lovely woman, though. Don't you agree?"

He gave his mother a suspicious look, hoping she wasn't looking to do any matchmaking in that direction. "She seems very nice. But I've only met the woman twice. Once at the bookstore in town and today on the beach."

"I expect you'll see more of her. Rosie is very involved in the community. She's on the board of directors of the library and volunteers every year to help with our holiday festival."

"She invited us to a party. Some neighborhood thing."

"Oh good! I was going to mention that to you. I'm so glad she did. I know how you are about big gatherings of people. You would much rather be home with a book, wouldn't you?"

He could not argue, so he only shrugged.

"That might be your own preference but you should think about Zara and Finn. They need to get to know the other children in the neighborhood. What better chance than a party like this?"

"That's what Rosie suggested," he answered.

"Grandma, guess what we saw down at the beach?" Zara said. "A sea slug that looked like it had on a frilly dress. Rosie said it's a frosted nudibranch."

"Is that right?"

"And I found this shell. Isn't it cool?" Finn held out the sand dollar.

His mother dutifully admired the shell as well as the agate that Zara had picked up on the beach.

The doorbell rang soon with the pizza and he grabbed it, paying the driver and adding a generous tip.

He had delivered pizza himself when he was in college, after he had refused to let his father pay his way when William Morgan had declared no son of his would waste his money earning a worthless English degree.

The next few minutes were busy setting out plates, finding drinks, grabbing some precut veggies and fruit out of the refrigerator for the kids so that he didn't feel like a complete failure of a parent.

No, he corrected. He would never be a complete failure. He loved both of his children and tried hard to make sure they knew it. He certainly made plenty of mistakes but he would never let his children spend one moment feeling as if they would never be enough.

When they finished devouring nearly all of the pizza, the kids asked if they could stream a new episode of their current favorite cartoon.

"After you load your dishes into the dishwasher."

They both sighed as if he had asked them to reshingle the entire roof of Stormhaven in the middle of a heavy rain but hurried to comply so they could enjoy their limited screen time to the fullest.

"How's the book coming?" his mother asked when the children left the small kitchen.

Andrew couldn't quite manage to get across to his mother how much he disliked talking about his work in progress.

"It hasn't been easy," he admitted. "I feel like I'm climbing a mountain that keeps growing taller as I go. Hopefully I will feel more in control once the kids start their day camps next week."

"I'm so glad they have that to look forward to this summer," Nancy said. "Remember how much you and Will enjoyed summer camp?"

His older brother had been in his element at the sleepaway camp in upstate New York the Morgans had always been sent to. Popular and vivacious, William Jr. had never struggled to make friends. He had invariably been right in the middle of the action, planning mischief, devising fun games, having swim races.

Andrew, on the other hand, had hated every moment of it. He had silently cried himself to sleep every night, missing his bed, his room, his books.

But he had only been eight the one and only year he had endured sleepaway camp. Later that year when they had returned to their lake house for the final few weeks of summer, his brother had gone out in the early morning for a swim and never made it back.

He pushed away the difficult memories and realized his mother had continued speaking.

"The children have art camp first, don't they?" she asked.

"That's right. Art camp for a week then nature camp, drama camp and sports camp."

"How delightful for them. They should make plenty of new friends, plus it will give you some time during the day to write."

He sincerely hoped so since he was trying hard not to panic about his deadline.

"Have you thought more about hiring someone to help you with them?"

"I'm planning to start looking, but I probably won't hire anyone until the house is done."

"That makes sense. I hope you know I'm here to help you as much as I can, though. I can pick them up after camp and even take them back to my place for a few hours to give you more time, if you would find that useful."

Impulsively, he hugged his mother. While his father had disdained his writing aspirations, Nancy had been invariably supportive.

She stayed long enough to help him put away the rest of the pizza and wipe down the kitchen, then left amid a flurry of kisses and hugs.

Nancy truly did seem to be thriving here in Wood Briar. He wasn't sure how much of that was from her surroundings and how much stemmed from her finding her own way out of his father's shadow after his death.

He sincerely hoped he and his children would find a similar peace here eventually.

He was gearing up for a long night of work at the kitchen table when he went into Finn's room to tuck him in. He found his son sitting up in his bed, gazing at the fragile sand dollar he had found.

"Are you planning to sleep with that thing?" Andrew asked gently. "Maybe you ought to set it on your bedside table so you don't crush it in the night."

"Did Mom like going to the ocean?"

He caught his breath at the quiet question. Finn had been so very young when his mother had first been diagnosed, a sweet, chubby preschooler with energy that could power an entire city block.

He had been four when she died. Finn hardly remembered the bright, laughing, joyous woman Tracy had been before her diagnosis. Andrew hated that Finn's memories were mostly hospital rooms, oxygen masks, and a mother too frail and fragile to play much with him.

"Do you think Mom would like it here in Oregon?"

"I am sure of it. What about you? Are you liking it?"

"I liked looking in the tide pools today. That was fun. And I like Rosie and Olive. They're nice."

After he finished tucking in Finn, he checked on Zara, who was rereading one of her favorite horse books.

"Did you have a good day, kiddo?"

"I guess. The pizza was good. I really love Rosie's dog, Dottie. She's so cute. Can we get a dog?"

At least she wasn't asking to get a horse. Yet. "Maybe once we're moved into the main house," he said.

After kissing her good-night, he headed into the kitchen to set up his laptop. Rosie had apparently made a big impression on his children. He wasn't sure how he felt about that.

She had also made an impression on him. He definitely knew he wasn't thrilled about his instinctive reaction to her. What was it about the woman that intrigued him so much? She didn't like his books. That alone should be enough to keep her at arm's length.

Despite that, he liked her, far more than he should.

He shook his head, trying to clear his thoughts of Rosie. He had too many other things to worry about. He was woefully behind schedule, and the pressure was mounting. Every day that passed without significant progress only ratcheted up the stress.

His fingers hovered over the keyboard as he pushed thoughts of warm green eyes and a quick wit from his mind. He had a story to tell, characters to bring to life. That was his priority. It had to be.

Taking a deep breath, he began to type, the gentle tapping of keys filling the quiet kitchen. As the words began to flow, he felt a sense of relief wash over him. This was what he needed to concentrate on. His work, his family, his new life here.

Everything else, including any budding interest in a certain auburn-haired neighbor, would have to wait. He had responsibilities, deadlines and two young lives depending on him. Those were the things that truly mattered, and he couldn't afford to lose sight of that.

CHAPTER SEVEN

—

Emma

THE JOB AHEAD OF HER WAS OVERWHELMING.

Emma looked at the stacks and stacks of boxes and tried not to panic. This was her first real chance to make progress in cleaning out the bookstore and she had so much to do, she didn't quite know where to start.

All week long, she and her staff had been boxing up books in preparation for the town's street fair sidewalk sale that would start the next morning and run throughout the next week.

She was really hoping to get rid of a lot of the extra inventory, especially dusty tomes that were twenty or thirty years old and should have been cleared out years ago.

She was all for having a large inventory. Reading tastes varied and not everyone enjoyed the same book. A good bookstore tried to cater to everyone.

But readers also needed to be able to find what they were looking for without having to wade through overcrowded shelves stacked two or three deep with outdated titles.

They also needed an environment for shopping that was pleasant and organized, not a wild jumble where nothing made any sense. She planned to clear out the extra inventory then move out the shelves so she could paint behind them.

It might take her all night, but her mom had agreed to feed Olive and put her to bed so Emma could make some progress.

She didn't mind hard work. She had a goal and needed to demonstrate to her mother she was capable.

She was immersed in her work, a fascinating audiobook playing through her earbuds, when she heard a knock.

She glanced at the large clock above the checkout counter. She had ordered a pizza for her dinner but hadn't expected it for another ten or fifteen minutes.

Maybe they were having a slow night.

She had left instructions for the pizza to be delivered at the rear door but maybe that message didn't make it across to the driver.

She hurried around a bookshelf to the front of the store as she heard a second knock.

The tall, muscular figure on the other side of the glass door made her catch her breath.

Not a delivery driver, then, unless Bryce Kendall was moonlighting.

He wore a snug T-shirt and jeans. With his hair slightly shaggy and that sexy beard, he looked delicious enough to eat with a spoon.

Maybe she didn't need pizza, after all.

She sighed, half tempted to turn around and retreat into the bookstore interior, pretending she didn't see him. She had thought about him entirely too much since she came to town nearly two weeks ago.

That would be the coward's way out, though. She was better than that, right?

She disarmed the security system, which really wasn't anything to write home about, and opened the door. "I'm sorry. We're closed. Maybe you didn't see the sign."

"I did. And I'm fully aware of the bookstore's hours. But I saw you in here when I was walking past and thought you might need a hand."

He had a dog with him, a sleekly elegant silver lab. Emma

couldn't resist kneeling down to the dog's level, always a sucker for a gorgeous canine.

"Hi there. What's your name?" She scratched the dog behind the ears and was rewarded with a happy sigh.

"This is Pearl. She's my best girl. She comes along with me to jobsites."

"Hi, Pearl. Nice to meet you."

The dog gazed up at her with a probing look that left her feeling disconcerted.

Something in that wise expression reminded Emma of her childhood dog, though the two animals didn't resemble each other in the slightest. Heidi had been a miniature dachshund and had been bad-tempered to everyone except Emma, whom she had adored.

"It's kind of you to stop," she said, straightening back to Bryce's level. "But I'm sure you've already had a long day. You're busy working on the Stormhaven project, aren't you?"

"I am."

"How's that going."

"Slower than I would like but we're trying to restore what we can, not simply rip everything out and start over."

"You mean like I want to do here? If I had my way, I would burn the whole place down and start over from scratch."

He smiled. "How about I help you stay out of the slammer on arson charges? I'm happy to help. I love The Rainy Day Bookshop and will do whatever necessary to keep the doors open."

Did he truly love the bookstore or was he simply being loyal to Rosie?

She pushed down her instinctive annoyance. Emma knew she had no right to resent their close relationship or her mother's trust in him. He had been here for Rosie when Emma had been off screwing up her life.

While she wanted to tell him she could handle this by herself, that would simply be stupid. He was here, offering to help her. She would have to be either foolish or pigheaded to refuse.

"Thanks." She forced a smile. "I actually could use some muscle. Originally the husband of one of our staff members planned to be here tonight to move boxes for me but their granddaughter has been playing in a soccer tournament down in Coos Bay and made it to the finals."

"Oh, that must be Jenny and Paul Cortez. Their granddaughter Annabel is a real star."

Did he know everything about everyone? Of course he did. This was Wood Briar, where people thrived on gossip.

"I can pay you in pizza. I have one that should be here any minute. In fact, I thought you were the pizza delivery when you knocked. I'm afraid it will be vegetarian."

"I like vegetables, only not mushrooms."

"Too bad for you, I ordered extra mushroom. You'll have to take them off."

"I can do that. Now where can I start?" He looked around the chaos. "I'm sure you have a plan here, but do you want to explain it to me?"

She sighed. What had looked so good on paper now seemed impossible.

"The overriding plan is to brighten up the place."

"That's a good place to start."

"The town sidewalk sale starts tomorrow. We're going to try to unload as much inventory as we can during the sale. Obviously, I can't leave the books outside tonight, especially where it's Oregon and there's always a chance of rain, but I thought we could move them closer to the door perhaps so the staff can take them out first thing in the morning."

And by staff, she probably meant herself.

"I can help with that. What else?"

"I want to repaint the place. I picked a warm white that will look much nicer than this disgusting color."

He looked around the space. "Repainting. That's a big job. You'll have to move all the shelves."

She sighed. "I know. I wish I could close the store for a few days and do it all at once. Since that's impossible during the tourist season without taking a big hit, I figured I could work in stages. One wall at a time. I wanted to start behind the checkout counter, since that is what most customers hopefully see as they're paying for all their books."

"I can help you move the shelves out of the way. Where are you planning to put them?"

"We have a storage room next door filled with odds and ends. I'll have to make room."

"Got it."

"If I had my way, I would start over with all new shelving."

"What don't you like about them?"

"The shelves against the wall are fine even though they go all the way up to the ceiling, but I feel like the interior shelves are too high. You can't see over them, they don't allow light to filter into the aisles and it makes the whole place feel so cramped and small, though it's actually a decent space. But I'm afraid I would need brand-new shelves and I'm not sure Mom wants to budget for that."

He went to one of the shelves in question, which stood well over eight-foot high. He studied it from several angles.

"These are decent and appear well-built. Instead of starting over, what about cutting them down and painting them a lighter color? That would brighten up the place, plus it would make the book covers pop."

She moved beside him and couldn't help noticing that

he smelled good. Really good. Like sandalwood and ocean breezes. She wanted to lean in and sniff his neck.

She ignored the impulse and focused on his suggestion. "Is that even possible?"

His half smile made her insides jump. "Anything is possible. You just have to work out how to do it. We could take the upper two rows of shelves, reusing the same top surface. It will reduce your shelf space, but I think you have good instincts. Some open space above the shelves will take away some of that claustrophobic feeling in the aisles and will make the entire store feel bigger."

"We could really do that?"

"Absolutely. It wouldn't be hard. I can take care of that for you, if you want."

Emma blinked, not sure why he had offered, especially when she had been so rude to him that first day she had bumped into him in the bookstore. "That's very nice of you but why would you offer?"

"Why not? I love to work on projects like this in my spare time. I have a good workshop in my garage."

She suddenly was intensely curious about him. Where did he live?

Was he *married*? Her mother had never said anything like that, but Emma couldn't imagine the women of Wood Briar leaving a guy like Bryce alone for long.

"Are you sure your wife wouldn't mind?" she asked, taking a chance.

He raised an eyebrow. "I was not aware I had a wife."

Well, that was something, at least.

She could feel her face heat. "I guess I made an assumption."

"Why would you make that particular one?"

"I don't know. It seems like in small towns like Wood Briar, people settle down early. My mom was twenty when she and my dad got married."

"Nope. Not me. No wife, no fiancée, no girlfriend. I am cheerfully single."

"I guess that's why you're spending your evening with your best girl. Who happens to be a dog."

"I thought I was spending my evening with you."

Something in the way he looked at her made her insides tingle. Before she could formulate a response, she heard a sharp knock coming from the back entrance.

"That must be the pizza," she said, grateful for the interruption.

"I can grab it if you want."

She shook her head. "It's fine. I paid online but I need to get to know the pizza delivery people in town, since I suspect I'll have a lot of late-night deliveries here over the next few months."

She hurried to the back door and opened it. On the other side was a young teenager with shoulder-length hair and braces.

"Hey, Jack." Bryce gave the young man a smile. "I wasn't aware you were delivering pizza these days."

The boy made a face. "Trying to earn some cheddar since my truck needs new tires."

"That's right. I thought I saw you driving a sweet Chevy."

The teenager looked delighted to talk about his ride. "I bought it from a friend of my grandpa's in Corvallis. It's in great shape. Has a lot of miles but the engine and the transmission were replaced a few years ago."

"Tires can be spendy. If you want, I can see if we might be hiring anybody on our cleanup crew this summer. We usually take on a couple of high school kids to clean up jobsites at night. Pick up nails, throw away scrap lumber. That kind of thing. Pays pretty good and the hours can be flexible, to work around your pizza gig."

"That would be great!"

"I'll be in touch."

Bryce was obviously well-liked around town, Emma thought as she listened to the two of them talk about the kid's new truck.

What a strange set of circumstances. For most of her life, Emma had been the good girl. Teacher's pet, winner of the spelling bee, singled out for the accelerated learning classes.

Bryce, on the other hand, had struggled in school. He had been bullied by some teachers, she could see now in retrospect. In elementary school, she remembered him being pulled out for extra attention—resource classes, they called them—as he had struggled to read.

He had been the class troublemaker, always the first one to talk back to teachers or be sent to the principal's office, something that would have mortified her.

Their paths couldn't have been more different back then.

And then the accident happened, and her life changed forever.

Now she was the recovering addict, a single mom who had barely enough in the bank to cover the pizza, while Bryce was universally well respected, by every indication.

When the two seemed to be wrapping up their conversation, she slipped the teen another tip, though she had already added one to the online order. She could remember too well her own days of waiting tables and delivering food as she struggled to make ends meet after Olive had been born.

"Thanks for the pizza," she said.

"You're welcome, ma'am. Enjoy." He closed his padded, insulated bag and after bidding a farewell to Bryce, he hurried out the door. Before it closed behind him, she could see a pickup truck even older than her own beat-up Honda.

"Where would you like to enjoy this feast?" Bryce asked after they were alone once more in the bookstore.

Emma considered their limited options. They could sit at the counter, lean against the checkout counter in the front or try to crowd into the tiny chairs at the children's table. She really did need to come up with some sort of café to draw people—or at least add a few seating areas for people to curl up with a book or have a conversation with a friend.

"How about the office? There's a desk chair and a guest chair. Neither is comfortable, but I suppose it's better than sitting on the floor. I'm afraid we both might get stuck if we tried to sit in the kids' chairs.

"I would pull you out," he assured her.

"Not if you were stuck, too. We would be trapped here all night, until my staff came in tomorrow morning."

"We would think of something. I could write a note and attach it to Pearl's collar and send her out to flag down a passerby. She's a genius. I'm sure she would find someone quickly."

She had to smile at the whimsical picture he painted.

"Why don't we save Pearl all that trouble and sit in the office, where we're almost guaranteed not to get stuck?"

She led the way. It did look less cluttered in here than when she first arrived, as she had already started packing away some of the extraneous items. Mugs, half-empty candy containers, scratch pads.

She didn't want to throw anything away that might be a cherished belonging of her grandmother's so she had boxed it all up and put it in the storage area of the bookshop. As soon as she could manage it, Emma planned to bring down her grandmother for an afternoon to sort through things.

Yet, one more thing on her list. Emma sighed, feeling overwhelmed all over again.

She could do this. She was a strong, smart woman who was willing to work as hard as necessary to prove herself.

CHAPTER EIGHT

—

Bryce

BRYCE STILL WASN'T SURE WHAT HE WAS DOING HERE AS HE followed Emma to the back of the store, where she let him through a small doorway into a cramped office.

He couldn't seem to stay away from her. He had tried. For two weeks, he had purposely not stopped in at the bookstore. Cowardly on his part, he knew, but he didn't seem to have much willpower when it came to Emma Lucas.

Despite his best efforts, thoughts of her intruded during the oddest moments. First thing in the morning while he was shaving, while he was driving to a jobsite that passed by the high school, when he heard a certain song on the radio that reminded him of her.

It wasn't anything new, really. He had certainly thought often of Emma over the years. Working for her mother made it impossible for him to completely work the fierce crush he used to have on her out of his system.

For the first few years he worked at Lucas Construction, Rosie seemed to go out of her way not to talk about her daughter. The subject was obviously painful for her.

She had told him Emma was pregnant, though. And that she had broken off with the baby's father.

After Rosie and Emma started to work on healing their relationship when Olive was born, his boss had talked about her daughter and granddaughter often, usually with a mix of admiration and worry in her voice.

What had once been a childhood crush, a desperate effort

to get her to notice him by whatever means possible, had begun to feel . . . deeper.

It was ridiculous, he knew. Emma didn't even know him. Not really. She knew the troublemaking, wisecracking kid he had once been but Bryce had tried to leave that persona behind a long time ago.

Now, as he followed her to the office, he reminded himself of all the reasons he had to keep his feelings to himself. If he ever told her how often he thought about a woman he hadn't seen in a decade, she would probably want to get a restraining order against him.

His dog trotted along behind them, sniffing eagerly at the pizza box Emma set on the desk after she cleared away a stack of papers.

"Settle down, Pearl. You've already had dinner," he said.

The dog sighed and plopped down in the doorway. Emma opened the pizza box and handed him one of the paper plates she dug out of a cabinet in the small corner of the office that appeared to also serve as the employee break area.

"Would you like something to drink? We keep some soda in the employee fridge, or I have tea."

"I'll grab some water. Would you like one?"

At her nod, he went to the watercooler and poured two cups for them then returned to set one beside her.

"I haven't had pizza from this place yet. Is it decent?" she asked.

"I think you will be pleasantly surprised, as long as you like wood fired."

"Who doesn't?"

"Maria Delmonico makes a fantastic dough and she tops it with fresh local ingredients. She even has a local farmer provide homemade mozzarella."

"Yum."

"The next time you order, you've got to try her hand-mixed ice cream. She has a salted caramel that is divine."

"I'll keep that in mind. I love anything with salted caramel."

"Same."

He picked off the mushrooms and took a bite of the delicious pizza. As she took a bite as well, she made a small sound of appreciation that felt oddly arousing.

He cleared his throat. "What are you doing back in town, Emma? I never thought you would return to Wood Briar. You always seemed pretty determined to stay away."

She took a sip of water. "While Grandma is on the injured list, my mom needs me. Or at least she says she does."

"She does," he assured her.

"I am hoping this summer will be good for Olive. I would like her to have a closer relationship with my mother and grandmother. I'm also hoping my schedule will be more flexible here than it was in Las Vegas so I can spend more time with her."

"Where is she tonight?"

"With my mom, who sent me a couple of pictures from the beach earlier. They went tide pooling apparently and ran into our new celebrity author and his kids."

She took another slice of pizza. "What about you?" she asked. "Why have you stuck around Wood Briar all these years? I always had the impression you couldn't wait to leave either."

He hated thinking about the kid he had been in school, embarrassed about his chaotic homelife and filled with shame because learning had been so tough on him.

"I couldn't wait to leave *school.* I like the town fine. I had . . . reasons for staying."

"Let me guess. A woman?"

"In the literal sense of the word, yes, but probably not what you think."

He weighed how much to tell her then decided he had no reason to keep it a secret. She would find out soon enough, if she didn't already know.

"My mom is not well," he finally said, doing his best to keep his voice emotionless. "Early onset dementia. She's in a nursing home up in Lincoln City. I'm all she has, so I haven't felt like I could go far, even if I wanted to."

Her face tightened with shock and sympathy. She hadn't known, apparently.

"Oh man. That's rough. I remember your mom from elementary school. Wasn't she a lunch lady for a while? She was always very kind."

He took a swig of water, aching for the woman Terri Kendall hadn't been for a long time. And would never be again.

"My mom hasn't had an easy life, I'm afraid. From childhood on, things were rough for her. Some of the things she's had to deal with were out of her control, but she also made some pretty poor lifestyle choices. After my dad left when I was ten, she did whatever she could to ease the pain. Drugs. Alcohol. Men."

He paused, then admitted what he had told no one else. "Intellectually, I know this isn't possible but sometimes I wonder if her dementia is simply another way for her subconscious to help her escape her demons."

Her eyes flashed bright and glittery, as if she were blinking back tears. "Oh, Bryce. I'm so sorry. I never realized you were dealing with all of that. I can't imagine how tough that's been for you to handle by yourself."

"Don't make me out to be some kind of a hero," he said, his voice low. He could give her an earful about the frustration of those early years after his mother's initial cognitive decline and about all the times he had railed against God or fate or biology or whatever was slowly stealing away his mother.

"You stayed in town to take care of your mom. I call that pretty heroic."

"It's not as if I'm doing the hands-on care. She's in a good facility. I visit her every Sunday for a few hours and that's about the extent of it."

She gave him a long look, her expression still drenched with compassion. "Is your mom the reason you bought a coloring book and all those magazines that first day I saw you here in the store?"

He shrugged. "She likes all the colorful pictures in magazines, especially the celebrity ones. Sometimes she cuts out pictures she likes and tapes them up on her wall. I never know exactly what is going to grab her interest. She had a John Deere tractor ad up for about three months, for reasons I still don't understand."

"And she likes to color? I found a bunch of adult coloring books I had planned to sell at the sidewalk sale. I would love to give them to your mom and the other patients at her facility instead."

That was what he remembered about Emma. She was always kind to everyone, even long-haired skateboarder punks like he had been.

"That would be great. She and her friends all love to color. But I'm happy to buy them. You don't have to donate them. Your mom pays me a very good salary and I don't have that many things to spend it on."

"I want to," she said. "Remind me to grab them before you go."

"Thank you."

"How did you come to be working for Lucas Construction?" she asked after a moment.

"I started when we were back in high school. The summer before our senior year."

He wasn't surprised she didn't remember. That was around the time she had basically become a different person, more interested in hanging out with the stoners and partiers than anything else.

"You remember that job I suggested to Jack? Cleaning up jobsites at the end of the day? That's where I started. After graduation, your mom offered me regular employment, though I didn't know much about construction except what I learned in high school shop class. Rosie has been great to me. I owe her more than I can say."

"She thinks very highly of you," Emma said stiffly.

"And vice versa."

They talked about people they both knew until Emma pushed her plate away. "Well, you're right. That pizza was deliciously addicting."

"See? Wood Briar has a few other things to recommend it besides the nice people and the beautiful scenery."

Her mouth twisted into a smile and he wondered what she would do if he leaned over and kissed her right here in this cramped office.

"Thanks for sharing with me," he said instead. "Now put me to work so I can pay for my supper."

"I won't turn down your help, if you're sure you don't mind."

"Not at all. I'm at your service," he said. *For whatever you might need.*

"You're probably going to be sorry you offered. I need *a lot* of help."

"Point me in the right direction."

She put him to work moving boxes of books for the sidewalk sale the next day. He hauled a dozen heavy boxes and stacked them near the front door while Emma continued going through shelves to pull out inventory.

"How are you planning to display all these books for the sale?"

"Apparently Grandma uses a couple of folding tables and puts the boxes on that. The bookstore also has a shelter she puts up in case of a sudden rainstorm. I guess I need to bring those out, too. They're back in the storage area."

"I'll grab them. Point me in the right direction."

"I'll have to show you."

She led him through a small hallway near the single restroom to a doorway with a sign that said Staff Only on it. The space was perhaps fifteen or twenty feet across, running nearly the entire length of the store.

He looked around, taking in their surroundings. The area was windowless and narrow but the high ceiling gave an impression of space. His mind raced with possibilities. "Why is this used for storage instead of retail space?"

"Believe me, I've wondered the same thing. If I had unlimited resources, I would love to create a doorway through the wall of the main retail store and expand into here."

"That coffee and pastry shop we talked about would be perfect in here. You could take the whole front half for that. You could even punch a window out onto Main Street."

"Is that possible?" She looked intrigued and excited at the idea, her features bright and animated.

"Why not? Rosie owns the whole building. She can do what she wants, as long as she doesn't break any zoning restrictions. As this is already zoned commercial, she should be fine to expand into here."

Emma looked around and he could almost see the wheels spinning in her head. "We could move several sections of books here, which would free up room over on the other side for a few reading nooks."

"You could even set up a small area in the back for book events and author readings."

"Oh, that would be fantastic!"

He loved seeing her face light up with excitement. She looked younger, happier. Her eyes sparkled and her smile seemed to brighten the whole room

For a moment, he allowed himself to imagine what it would be like if she could always be this happy and carefree. Too soon, her excitement seemed to ebb away. Her shoulders slumped slightly, and a small furrow appeared between her brows.

"It would be so much work, though. And I'm not sure Mom wants to put that much money into the bookstore right now."

"She asked you to come home to revitalize the place. She has to expect some degree of capital outlay as part of that."

"I don't know. I'll have to talk to her."

He wanted her to have this. He wanted her to succeed in Wood Briar and make a new life for herself and her daughter here.

"My evening schedule is pretty open right now, except for Sundays when I go to see my mom and Wednesday nights. That's when I play on the Lucas Construction softball team. On the other days, I usually work till about seven but I could come here after that."

She sent him a long look and he didn't miss the shadow of wariness there, as if she didn't know how to deal with someone offering to help her. His chest ached at the thought of her trying to handle everything by herself for so many years.

"Why are you being so nice to me? Is it because you feel like you owe my mom?"

Her mother had nothing to do with it. While he did owe Rosie for channeling his youthful restlessness into work he loved that provided a comfortable living, he wanted to help Emma for her own sake.

"I love the bookstore and agree it definitely needs a refresh. I want this place to be here for a long time," he said.

And I want you and Olive to be here for a long time, too.

"I can come tomorrow and help you paint the wall. If you give me the paint color you're using, I can pick up a can or two of the same color for the bookshelves."

"That would be great," she exclaimed, her eyes shining with excitement. "I don't know how I could ever repay you for all your help."

He could think of several ways but decided it probably wouldn't be wise to mention any of them.

He wanted to do more to ease her burden somehow. But he knew Emma well enough to understand that she wouldn't accept charity or pity.

For now, he would focus on one bookshelf, one wall, one day at a time. And maybe, just maybe, he could help bring some of that light back into Emma's eyes and help her feel like she truly belonged back home.

CHAPTER NINE

—

Rosie

AT THE END OF A LONG WEEK, ROSIE WALKED INTO THE LUCAS Construction office, grateful for the comfortable familiarity of the place.

How much of her life had she spent inside the walls of this sturdy brick building at the edge of town? Over the past several years—after she had been forced to step in to save the company—she had been here nearly every day.

It wasn't the life she might have chosen for herself, but she was still proud of all they had achieved.

Inside the door, the first person she greeted was Pam Clarke, who had been with the company nearly from the beginning. Pam handled the accounts receivable, payroll and office admin. Rosie considered her both her right and left hand.

"Morning," Pam said without looking up from her computer. "Happy Friday."

Rosie paused beside her desk. "How's Phoebe today?"

Phoebe was one of Pam's two cats, both as beloved to her as children. Worry creased the other woman's brow as she finally saved whatever she had been working on and looked up.

"Not great. I was up all night with her. She threw up twice."

"What does the vet say?"

"I talked to the emergency line first thing this morning. Dr. Mahmood says I can take her in later today."

"Do you need a personal day to be with her? I totally understand. I can handle things here."

"No. It's fine. I've been watching on the cat cam and she seems to be resting comfortably. One of my neighbors is going to pop in to check on her this morning and I'll go home on my lunch break."

"Okay. But if you need to run out before that, let me know. The only thing on my calendar today is the weekly meeting with the project managers. I should be able to handle that on my own."

"Thanks, Rosie. You're the best."

They both knew that was not true. Pam was the glue holding everything together here. She had been instrumental to the success of Lucas Construction. During the early years after Gary died, Pam and Victor Blackwood, Gary's second in command at the time, had done their best to run the company. It hadn't been their fault that everything seemed to go south at the same time, with supply shortages, economic hardships in the area and a long string of bad luck.

Only after Vic left to start his own construction company when she refused to sell to him did Rosie realize what bad shape Lucas Construction was in. With no other choice, she had stepped up. Along with Pam's considerable help as well as other loyal employees who had stayed with them, they had managed to yank it back from the brink.

Pam and her other coworkers were the most valuable asset Lucas Construction had. For a time, Rosie had left them all to flounder alone. She wouldn't do it again.

"I've left the agenda for today's meeting on your desk in case I have to rush out," the other woman said.

"Thanks for that. I meant to be here earlier to organize my thoughts, but I had Olive again this morning."

"How is that cute little girl?"

Rosie could feel her heart sigh when she thought of her

granddaughter, who already had brought immeasurable light and joy to her world. "Adorable. She never stops talking."

Pam chuckled. "A lot like her mom was, if I remember correctly."

"You most certainly do."

"You're so lucky to have both of them staying with you this summer."

The other woman's voice held only a trace of envy, but it was enough to make Rosie feel sad for her.

This was not the first time Rosie had caught a few glimpses of envy in the other woman's tone or expression. Pam had no children. She had been married and divorced three times and had a few stepchildren she didn't stay in touch with.

Rosie certainly didn't think every woman needed a husband and children to be happy. Definitely not. There were plenty of women who were happily single and/or childless and had created exactly the life they wanted.

Unfortunately, she suspected Pam was not among their number. As much as Rosie enjoyed her friendship with the other woman and valued her highly in a professional manner, at times Pam exuded an indefinable air of discontent. Whether that was from her personal life or something else, Rosie didn't know.

"Thank you," she said now, then picked up a stack of papers out of her cubby and headed into her office.

She had redecorated the space a few years ago, though she had kept Gary's desk. If she closed her eyes, she could still see him sitting behind it, completely in his element as he made plans for another project.

He had loved Lucas Construction and had been so very proud of the work they had done.

On her desk were pictures of her and Gary together and

another one of Olive and Emma. Her family. The walls were covered in framed photographs of some of the larger projects they had finished, touchstones that filled her with pride.

She was double-checking the agenda for the meeting when someone knocked on the frame of her open door. She looked up and smiled when Bryce came into her office.

"Morning," he said. "I was hoping to catch you before the meeting, but you look like you're in the middle of something."

"Not really. Just going over what we need to talk about." She set the agenda aside. "Come in. What's going on?"

He sat in the visitor chair across from her desk. He looked nervous, as if he were about to confess a dark secret.

"I thought you should know I've offered to help Emma out at the bookstore in my free time. I was there last night and I'm heading over again tonight."

"Emma? My Emma," she asked in surprise.

"How many other Emmas do you know who work at a bookstore?"

"None," she admitted. "I'm sure there are plenty but not here in Wood Briar. What are you helping her with?"

"Last night I helped her move a bunch of boxes full of books for the sidewalk sale that starts today."

"I forgot about that."

"She is trying to rearrange things to make the store more open and welcoming."

"It needs it badly. That place is oppressive inside, even for the most dedicated book lovers. I've been trying to convince Mom to clean things out and declutter for a long time, but you know how stubborn she is."

Rosie might ostensibly own the bookstore but that didn't make her mother amenable to any of her suggestions, unfortunately.

Bryce hesitated, appearing to weigh each word before he spoke. "Emma is trying really hard to turn things around there."

"I know. I'm so proud of her. I knew she would be great at it."

"Has she talked to you about doing a few more extensive renovations?"

She and Emma seemed to mostly talk around each other, always careful not to offend the other. "She's said a few things, but has been vague on details."

"It's not my place to discuss it with you. It's hers. But I get the impression she's trying to do whatever she can to refresh things on a shoestring. She doesn't want to ask you for help."

Rosie frowned. "That's silly. It's my bookstore. Anything she does to improve it will only help me in the long run."

"Well, you may want to bring that up with her. Don't tell her I said anything. I don't think she would appreciate my interference. I wouldn't have said anything, but I feel like you need to know I've offered to help her out in my off-hours. I'm going over tonight to help her paint behind the checkout counter and move some bookshelves."

"You don't have to explain yourself to me, Bryce. And you don't have to work for free either. You are a valued employee of Lucas Construction. I'll pay you for the time you spend helping her."

"What if I don't want you to pay me? I want to do this to help Emma."

She frowned. "What is she thinking about doing?"

"Again, probably better you hear it from her."

"I'll ask her. But you can tell me your thoughts, can't you?"

He looked torn for a moment, then nodded. "Last night I was grabbing some tables and a rain shelter out of the storage room for the sidewalk sale. Seems to me you're wasting valuable retail space by using that area to hold stuff you could store in a shed somewhere and not in the store."

She sighed, feeling guilty. "That was always in my master plan when I bought the building, but then I got busy here at Lucas Construction and put everything at Rainy Day on the back burner."

"You might want to think about moving it to the front. I'm happy to help out with the work if you want to budget for some of the construction materials."

He told her a little about what Emma wanted to do at the bookstore, all of which made perfect sense. She should have done most of it years ago.

"That sounds like more than you can do in your spare time."

"It might take longer after hours, but we could still make it work."

"With you working sixteen-hour days already? I don't think so. Not to mention it would only stretch out the chaos for months at the bookstore. It seems to make better business sense for you to hit it hard for a few weeks and be done, rather than extend it out all summer."

"I suppose that's something you can talk about with Emma."

If Emma was determined to renovate the bookstore, perhaps that was another indicator that she meant to stick around. Oh, Rosie hoped so.

"We need to come up with a plan."

He nodded his agreement as ideas spun through Rosie's mind. She quickly pumped the brakes when she realized what she was doing.

"I can't take over," she said. "This is Emma's baby. I want her to own it."

"Good call."

"I'll talk to her tonight." She gave him a steady look. "You know I wouldn't trust anybody but you to handle something as important as renovating the bookstore, right?"

She liked and admired all four of her project managers and considered each a valuable part of the company but there was something about Bryce that was different from the others. He went the extra mile on every single project, offering smart suggestions to improve the plans and coming up with creative solutions whenever problems arose. He was the hardest working employee she had and she respected him for not only his work ethic but the strong relationships he fostered with subs and crew alike.

When the time was right for her to walk away from Lucas Construction, she knew Bryce would be an excellent successor.

"I'm pretty busy right now with the work we're doing at Stormhaven, the Pine Beach house and the new East Ridge subdivision development."

She made a face at the reminder. "Right. You're maxed out. I can't ask you to take on more than you're already doing."

"You know," he said slowly, "I could probably find room in my schedule if you reassigned the Stormhaven project. Or you could take it over yourself."

She stiffened. Stormhaven. The house had once been her and Gary's dream house. Imagining what they would do with it had once brought her so much joy . . . and also so much pain, after he died.

After the accident, she couldn't summon any enthusiasm for fixing up that big place for only her and Emma to live.

But what was more important to her? Keeping her daughter here in Wood Briar, or confronting her own ghosts? Easy. Emma would win every single time. She owed her daughter every chance at success.

Rosie had been a mess after Gary died. No doubt about it. She had loved him since she was seventeen years old, and losing him at thirty-five had seemed the cruelest trick of fate. In the midst of her deep pain, she had withdrawn into her grief, shutting out family, friends and especially her daughter.

Emma had pulled away as well, relying more on her friends than her mother, and then eventually turning to anything she could find to block out the pain. And Rosie had been completely oblivious to how badly her child had been hurting, all the self-destructive ways Emma had found to escape.

Rosie hated that she hadn't stepped up to be the mother her daughter had needed during that time of grief and sorrow. She was ashamed of herself for giving in to her self-pity until it was far too late to do anything to help Emma.

She could help her now. Fixing up the bookstore, making it as productive and as profitable as possible, would not only increase the profit margin, but it could be exactly what Emma needed to stay in Wood Briar and to give Rosie this chance to make things right.

Freeing up Bryce by taking over the Stormhaven renovation was a small sacrifice on Rosie's part.

Rosie hadn't managed a construction project since handing more and more responsibilities over to Bryce and the other project managers a few years earlier. The challenge of fixing up the old house would be exciting, even if it meant working with Andrew Morgan, who affected her far more than she wanted to admit.

"I can do that, I suppose," she said.

Before he could answer, his phone rang. He ignored it for two rings, then looked at the caller ID and grimaced.

"It's Vista del Mar."

The nursing home where his mother lived, she knew.

"Answer it," she said. "That's your priority."

"I'll take it out in the hall."

"Hello. This is Bryce," she heard him say as he walked out.

After he left, Rosie turned to her credenza, pulled out a drawer and withdrew the folder she hadn't looked at in years. She should have thrown it away a long time ago, especially after she sold Stormhaven, but she hadn't been able to bring herself to do it.

This file held all her and Gary's hopes and dreams for the crumbling old mansion.

Before she could do more than page through the top few papers, Bryce came back into her office, his features pale beneath his tan.

"What's wrong?" she asked. "Is your mom okay?"

He ran a hand through his hair. "No. She fell in the bathroom, apparently. They're not quite sure how it happened since she was alone in there, but she somehow broke her hip. She's in the hospital and is going to need surgery."

She rose instantly and went to him, giving him a quick hug. "Oh, Bryce. I'm so sorry."

As if he needed one more stress concerning his mother. For a man so young, he had a great deal on his shoulders.

"Thanks."

"You need to go be with her. Don't worry about anything here."

"What about the planning meeting?"

"You and I can catch up on your projects later. Your mom comes first. Always."

He released a heavy breath, his expression dark with worry. "Thanks, Rosie. I really appreciate this."

"Take as much time as you need. And please keep me posted about your mother's condition."

"I will."

If she had a son, she would want him to be exactly like Bryce. Dependable, hardworking, incredibly loyal.

She only wished she could take away more of the burden from his shoulders.

"Oh man. I forgot I have an appointment this afternoon at Stormhaven with Andrew Morgan to go over the final phase of the work we're doing on the house. I'm not sure I'll be back in time. I'll reschedule on my way up to the hospital."

Rosie shook her head. "I'll handle your meeting. If I'm going to take over as project manager, I might as well start now."

"I'm sorry about this."

"Stop it. You don't need to apologize for one moment. Family comes first. You know that has always been the philosophy of Lucas Construction."

It was the main reason she had stepped in when it became clear the company would not survive without drastic measures. She had fifty employees who counted on her. Fifty people who needed good jobs from an employer who paid decently and rewarded them for their effort.

She knew there were some in the construction industry who held a very different philosophy. They cycled through employees like they went through finish nails. She and Gary had always felt strongly that part of the reason they wanted to start a small business was to not only improve their own situation, but hopefully improve the lives of their employees as well as providing benefits to the local economy.

Her employees had an average tenure of fifteen years. Some, like Pam and a few others, had been there almost since the beginning.

During those tough years after Gary died, when the company had been faltering, she had received a few decent offers to buy her out. The size of those offers would have left her quite comfortable, especially with Gary's life insurance policy. She could have devoted herself wholly to running the bookstore, which she had loved.

She hadn't been able to do it, especially when she could not get any guarantee from those making the offers that any of them would keep her employees. How could she reward her workers' years of hard work by abandoning them?

"Don't worry about anything here," she said now to Bryce. "Focus on your mom. We'll see where things stand next week. We can even assign out some of your other projects to one of the other managers."

"I hope it doesn't come to that, but I will keep you posted."

He hesitated at the doorway. "I mentioned to Em that I would come help her again after work if I get the chance. Will you let her know I might not make it back?"

"Of course."

"Thanks, Rosie. You're seriously the best."

He rushed away before Rosie had the chance to tell him she knew better. She was simply a woman with a mountain of regrets and a desperate need to make things right.

CHAPTER TEN

—

Andrew

AS HE STARED AT THE BLANK SCREEN ON HIS LAPTOP, ANdrew's head throbbed in concert with the pounding coming from somewhere in the house.

The crew was working on the drywall in one of the upstairs bedrooms, if he wasn't mistaken. Either that or they had decided to play a John Philip Sousa march using nail guns and hammers.

He was finding it increasingly difficult to create in the middle of a construction zone but he didn't have the liberty of time now. This book should have been finished before they left California. That had been his goal, but between packing up their apartment, end of school year requirements for the kids and tying up all the loose ends, time had gotten away from him.

He couldn't imagine how much worse it might have been trying to pack up their lives if they hadn't already lost most of what they owned in the wildfire.

He hated writing under the gun. He usually tried to be done with his books well ahead of his deadlines so that he had time to caress the prose to his satisfaction. He did not have that luxury this time, though how he was supposed to feel creative in the middle of a construction zone, Andrew had no idea.

He sighed and rose from his desk to put in a few steps walking around his half-finished office.

Today was supposed to be a great writing day. His mom

was collecting the kids from their day camp and taking them to a movie they had all wanted to see and then she was picking up takeout from their new favorite Chinese place.

He had been looking forward to finally having a long stretch of time to hopefully reach his creative flow state without the distraction of the kids in the next room.

He had made progress on the book, writing at night after the kids were in bed and in the morning before they awoke, though he was not a huge fan of working at the cramped kitchen table of the apartment.

Besides the ergonomic pain from sitting in a bad position, his creativity needed more room than that to thrive. That probably would sound stupid to anybody who wasn't a creator, but Andrew knew his imagination craved space to unfurl, to stretch its wings and soar. The confines of the tiny apartment, with its constant reminders of daily life and responsibilities, felt like invisible bars caging his thoughts. He longed for a dedicated space where his ideas could run wild, unencumbered by the mundane realities that surrounded him at the kitchen table.

Today, he had decided to set up the room that would eventually be his office, in the highest turret of the house.

When it was finished, the space would be magnificent, with views in all directions from the windows that circled the room. As he walked around the room, Andrew could see the mountains on one side, the ocean on the other, the town below.

Gulls flew past his windows and from here he could see a man and child on the beach below flying a kite shaped like a dolphin. It dipped and soared in the wind like a sea creature riding the waves.

He saw yet another vehicle approaching the house, this one

with the logo of Lucas Construction on the side, an oval with a stylized silhouette of a couple of pine trees surrounding the name of the company as well as their brand identity: *Built on Family, Rooted in Oregon.*

As he watched, the driver's side door opened and a woman emerged, carrying what looked like a bundle of blueprints.

Sunlight glinted off auburn strands and he immediately recognized Rosie Lucas.

If he were smart, he would stay right here in what he was already starting to call his writing tower. His neighbor affected him in ways he did not want to think about.

He had dreamed about her twice since the day he and the kids had encountered her and little Olive on the beach. Spicy dreams filled with tangled mouths and twisted sheets.

He hadn't had an erotic dream in a while. To have two of them about the same woman, a virtual stranger, annoyed and embarrassed him.

He was busy trying to tell himself to stay planted with his butt in the writing chair when an alarm on his phone rang.

He glanced at it and winced. Apparently, he was supposed to be meeting with the project manager today, something he had completely forgotten.

When he was on a deadline, he had trouble keeping track of anything but absolute necessities. In California, he'd had a personal assistant to keep him on track and handle all the details of his life. Saima Rashid still worked as his extremely efficient assistant but she handled things virtually for him now, mostly focused on handling his marketing and social media instead of his daily schedule.

Since moving to Oregon, Andrew had fallen back on setting copious reminders on his phone to keep track of his to-do list.

This particular phone reminder was his fifteen-minute

warning, which meant that if Rosie was here for the meeting, she was fifteen minutes early.

And why was she here instead of Bryce Kendall?

He really hoped her presence didn't indicate another problem with the project, which had already been beset by delay after delay.

With resignation, he saved his manuscript and closed out of the word processing app he used, picked up his laptop and headed for the winding stairs that led down to the entry hall.

He was nearly down to the first level when she opened the door and walked in. At first, he felt peevish that she walked into his house without knocking, until he reminded himself that she worked for the construction company and none of the other workers ever knocked.

Maybe if he and the kids were living inside the main structure, things might be different but this was a construction zone.

As he moved closer, he saw her looking around with an expression on her face he could only describe as wistful. She was taking in all the original woodwork that had been restored already in the project.

"Looking for me?" he asked.

She jumped, dropping some of her papers, and whirled around, eyes wide.

"Sorry. I thought you heard me coming down the stairs." He hurried the rest of the way and helped her pick up the papers.

"No. I was thinking about something else."

What might have put that expression on her face, a sort of sorrow mixed with a curious yearning.

"I was deep in my book and forgot I was supposed to be meeting with Bryce Kendall this afternoon. Did he come with you?"

He did not tell her he saw her arrive alone in the company truck. That sounded too much like he was spying on her, which he absolutely wasn't. It was his house, after all.

"No. Bryce had a family emergency and had to run up to Lincoln City. I told him I would take care of the meeting and show you the updated blueprints."

"Thanks."

"Is there somewhere we can spread them out to take a look?"

"There's a sawhorse in the kitchen with a couple of planks over it. That's what Bryce has been using when we need to go over something on the plans."

She studied the house with interest as he led her through to the kitchen. "Oh, you're adding a bay window here in the kitchen. That's a great idea."

"I thought a dining nook would work well for our needs. The kids can do homework there while I fix dinner."

"Good idea. I wanted to do the same thing."

He frowned in confusion. "You did?"

"A bay window and dining nook was actually part of the plan my husband and I made when we purchased the house."

He stared at her, completely nonplussed by the information. "You once owned Stormhaven?"

"I'm surprised you didn't know. I would have thought Bryce or one of the subs might have mentioned it to you."

He shook his head. "Not a word."

"This was once my dream house," she admitted with a rueful smile. "From the time I moved to Wood Briar with my mom in high school, I wanted to buy Stormhaven and fix it up. It's been abandoned for years, waiting for the right owner. Gary and I worked for years to finally afford it."

He shifted, uncomfortable at the idea of snatching her

dream home out from under her. "I had no idea. Your plans obviously fell through."

She looked away then turned back with a wooden smile. "My husband died the week after we signed the papers for Stormhaven."

"That must have been tough."

"I was too battered after Gary's sudden death to move forward on the renovation. At first I didn't have the mental or emotional strength for it. I was too busy with the bookstore and trying to keep the construction company alive. Plus, I was dealing with . . . family problems. I held on to the house for a few years but ultimately decided to sell it when the company was struggling and needed an infusion of capital."

"Ah."

Did she resent that he owned the house now? Was that one of the reasons for her negativity toward his books?

He did an internal eye roll at his own creative arrogance. His books simply weren't her style. It likely had nothing to do with his ownership of her dream home.

"Unfortunately," she went on briskly, unaware of his internal monologue, "I didn't do my due diligence when I sold the place. The next owner spent the next three or four years trying to push through condominiums. They wanted to tear down the whole house and build something else in its place."

He was beginning to think that might not be such a bad idea, given the headache of renovating it. "It does have a lovely view."

"Yes. And I'm sure it would have made a great spot for some condos. But this house is a beloved part of our community history as the first truly grand home on this entire part of the coast, built by someone who made his fortune in mining."

He had read some of the history of the house before his

own purchase went through. He knew it had a tragic past, with the original owner dying in a hunting accident before he ever had the chance to live here and his widow dying of consumption a short time later.

"When the consortium that owned it decided to finally list it again," Rosie went on, "I was trying to spearhead a fund-raising effort to purchase it and turn it into a museum or art gallery."

"Until I bought it out from under you. I'm sorry."

"Don't be. Please. I'm thrilled someone purchased the place who seems to be committed to preserving and protecting it. I was honored when you chose Lucas Construction to do the renovation."

Was she really? He wasn't sure he would be magnanimous enough to willingly help someone else renovate his own dream house. She was obviously a better person than he was.

His mother had been the one to persuade him to use Lucas Construction, delighted by the work they had done on her own cottage. He remembered being impressed by the bid he had looked over. It had not been the lowest, but he remembered their plan showed integrity to design and attention to detail, with the clear goal of restoring the home with authenticity instead of simply renovating it.

"I've been happy with your work," he said. "I only wish you could move faster."

"I know. We're working on it. On that note. I need to let you know that I will be taking over as the project manager here at Stormhaven."

He frowned, not at all thrilled by the announcement. He didn't need the excuse of propinquity to give him more inappropriate dreams about Rosie Lucas.

"Where's Bryce? Don't tell me he quit."

She looked aghast at the idea. "No. Heaven forbid. I would be lost without him. We had to make a few changes as Bryce is a bit overextended right now. I assure you, you won't see any disruption in the project. In fact, I might be able to accelerate things for you. It made sense for me to be the one to take on this project, since I am intimately acquainted with the house and the challenges it presents."

Some of his misgivings must have been clear on his features. She gripped her bundle of papers more tightly and took on a haughty expression at odds with her soft, lovely features.

"I'm a fully capable project manager. Since taking over the company, I've overseen more than two dozen builds or renovations. Beyond that, Gary and I managed just about everything on our own in the early days of the company. We were a good team."

Something in her voice, some shadow of old pain, struck an answering note in him. Perhaps their shared experience losing a spouse explained why he felt this unwilling bond with Rosie. They were part of the same unfortunate club.

She turned brisk once more. "I haven't been on-site in several weeks. Would you mind walking through with me so I can familiarize myself with the progress over the past few months and what still needs to be done?"

He thought of his manuscript, always waiting with the impatience of a hungry toddler for him to return to it. He felt the pull of the scene he had been working on as well as his inescapable deadline. On the other hand, Rosie was here, and needed his help.

He had scheduled out time to meet with Bryce Kendall. He couldn't avoid the obligation simply because his attraction to his new project manager seemed a complication he could definitely do without.

"Sure. Let's go.

He walked her through the house, starting on the main floor. He showed her through each room, pointing out areas still to be completed.

When they encountered the dry wall team in the space that would eventually serve as a luxurious media room, she greeted them all by name. She spoke Spanish to a couple of the guys and asked another one how his granddaughter was doing after her appendectomy.

It was clear she was well-known and well-liked among the contractor's crew.

They moved from the main living area up to the bedrooms. His own bedroom was huge, far larger than he needed, with a spectacular view over the ocean.

He had to admit, the en suite bathroom was his favorite part on this level. The clawfoot tub was original to the house, though it had been resurfaced. The rest of the bathroom had a massive shower with three different heads, as well as a huge window if he wanted to scrub up with a view.

She paused in the doorway, taking in the fittings and the view both.

"Wow. Great bathroom."

"It will be when it's done."

"I'm hoping you're putting in blinds. Otherwise you'll give anyone down on the beach quite a show."

He made a face. "I've checked it out from down there and you can't even see the bathroom from that angle. But yes. Automatic blinds are on the way."

Seeing the renovation through her admiring eyes as they walked through the rest of the house gave him a new appreciation for all the work that had been done so far.

The construction crew really had worked miracles to take

the house as far as they had in only a few short months. He had an unfortunate habit—in life and when it came to his work—of focusing too much on all that had to be done instead of how far he had come.

"Have you been to the secret room?" she asked when they returned once more to the main living area.

He stared. "What secret room?"

She grinned as a shaft of sunlight came in, lighting up her features. She looked breathtakingly lovely.

"I wondered if you knew about that."

"Obviously not, since I have no idea what you're talking about."

"Apparently during Prohibition, the owners of Stormhaven installed a hidden door behind the fireplace in the dining room that leads to a small room. Inside, they set up a bar where they could entertain guests with booze they smuggled down the coast."

He gaped at her. "You're joking."

"I'm not. I swear. Why would I joke about something you can prove yourself in five seconds?"

"Are you seriously telling me this house has a secret room that no one has bothered to tell me about? My real estate agents never mentioned it and neither has Bryce."

Her smile widened. "I'm not sure anybody else knows about it, to tell you the truth. I only stumbled upon it by accident after we bought the house, when I was walking through making initial plans for our renovation. For all I know, some of the old Prohibition bottles might still be there."

"You have to show it to me. Right now."

She laughed at his burgeoning excitement, the sound ringing through the empty house like a melody, soft and musical, brightening the room.

"Come with me."

She led him into a room they had already walked through, the formal dining room with its marble fireplace and Tiffany-style chandelier. The room was lovely and elegant, though he expected it would have little use while he was here. He wasn't exactly the kind of guy who threw elaborate dinner parties.

A secret Prohibition bar, though, might change his mind about entertaining.

She went to the fireplace, feeling around the carved embellishments. "If I'm not mistaken, the button is right . . . about . . . here."

She pushed something on the fireplace mantel and a gap suddenly appeared as a door swung open.

His younger self would have adored discovering a door like this, a secret portal to untold adventures.

Hell, his current self thought it was pretty spectacular.

"We have to go check it out."

"After you," she said, turning on the flashlight of her phone. He did the same and, with anticipation bubbling through him, he led the way past cobwebs through a small hallway and into what was little more than a walk-in closet, possibly six feet by six feet.

He aimed his phone light around the room, taking in the huge dust-covered mirror against one wall and an old polished wood bar that must have been assembled in this room, since it certainly wouldn't have fit through the doorway.

No more than three or four people could squeeze in here. Even he and Rosie were a tight fit. Andrew was suddenly intensely aware of her. She smelled of sunshine and lemons and he suddenly wanted to press his face to her hair and inhale.

That wouldn't be weird, would it?

"I can't believe I never knew this was here."

"I am not surprised. The previous owners you purchased it from were only interested in demolishing the home. I doubt they visited more than once or twice and they probably completely forgot about it, if they even knew."

"The kids are going to love this. I can't wait to show them."

"Emma was really excited about it. We were going to make this our secret reading room. My plan had been to take out the bar and add bookshelves around the whole space as well as a couple of big, plump chairs."

He loved that idea and was always down for anything he could do to foster a love of reading in his children.

On the other hand, a secret Prohibition-era bar was next-level sick.

"I'll have to give it some thought before I figure out what I want to do in the space. In the meantime, show me how you open the door again."

They went back out, with him resolving to clear out the cobwebs and dust as soon as humanly possible.

"The button is right there, in the middle of that flower. It releases the handle for the door. When you pull the door closed again the button slides back into place."

He leaned around her to try his hand at it, doing his best to ignore the urges clamoring through him to lean forward a few more inches and press his mouth to hers.

What was *wrong* with him? He had never reacted to any other woman like this. He tried to tell himself it was because she had revealed something amazing to him but he suspected the hidden room had nothing to do with his reaction to her.

"What other secrets does this place have?"

"That's part of the fun of restoring an old house, all the mysteries you can discover along the way."

"Did you renovate your own house?"

"Oh yes, but not all at once. It was Gary's parents' house and his grandparents' before that, so it needed a lot of work. After his father died, his mother decided to move to Portland to be closer to Gary's sister, so we bought the house from her. We worked on it here and there, whenever we had a bit of extra money. Which wasn't often in those early days."

"I'm sure it's lovely."

"It is, though not on the scale of Stormhaven. It's about a third the size of this house. We have a very nice sea view as well and it has a lovely garden, along with a small guest cottage on the property where my mother lives now."

As if on cue, his own mother and the kids came in through the front door.

"Hi, Rosie," Zara said cheerfully.

"Is Dottie here?" Finn asked, looking around.

"I'm afraid not. Sometimes she comes to work with me but today she's hanging out with my mom."

He hugged both of his children, then sent his mother a look of inquiry. "I thought you guys were going to a movie after day camp."

"I should have bought tickets online. Turns out, they were completely sold out. I bought tickets for tomorrow afternoon instead."

So much for his long stretch of writing time. He sighed. Apparently he would have to plan for another late night to get all the words.

"Hello, Rosie." His mother smiled brightly at her. "You're looking lovely today."

"Thank you."

Rosie stepped forward and gave his mother a kiss on the

cheek. "I've been catching up on the progress here at Stormhaven."

"Doesn't it look good? It's turning out even better than I had hoped. It's going to be such a wonderful home once it's done."

"Did you know Rosie once owned the house?" he asked.

His mother nodded as she unwrapped her scarf. "Sylvia told me that. It must be tough for you to work so hard restoring a home you once dreamed of owning yourself."

He watched a tiny flare of color rise up Rosie's cheekbones, though she gave his mother a cheerful smile. "I was telling Andrew how happy I am that Stormhaven ended up with someone who will love it as much as I did."

Rosie was far more generous than he could ever be.

"You'll never believe what Rosie just showed me. It's the coolest thing, something I had no idea the house had."

"What?" Finn demanded. "Does it have a secret dungeon?"

"Close," Andrew said with a grin. "Rosie, do you want to do the honors of showing them, too?"

She led the way over to the mantel, gave the children a mischievous look, then pushed the button.

Zara and Finn both gasped as the secret door opened, both children wearing matching incredulous looks.

"What's in there?" Zara asked.

"Is it a monster's lair?" Finn asked.

"Nothing so exciting," Rosie assured them. "Your dad should show you."

As he led the children inside the narrow passage to the hidden room, he couldn't help thinking about Rosie's generosity and grace. Her ability to show such enthusiasm for a home she once loved, now in another's possession, spoke volumes about her character.

Andrew found himself increasingly drawn to her. Her strength, her kindness and the way her eyes lit up when she spoke about the house.

But even as he felt the pull of attraction, Andrew knew he had to keep his feelings in check. He was here to give his children stability, to rebuild their lives after loss. Starting anything with Rosie, no matter how tempting, would only complicate his life in ways he couldn't begin to contemplate.

CHAPTER ELEVEN

—

Emma

"CAN I GET ANOTHER BOOK, MOMMY? I ALREADY READ THE one I got last time."

Though Olive knew the alphabet and could pick out her name, she couldn't read yet. For her, *reading* meant paging through a book again and again until she had the whole thing virtually memorized. Emma found it adorable and did all she could to foster the same love of reading in her child that had sustained her most of her life.

"You absolutely can get another book. Why don't you pick one from Great-grandma Sylvia's special shelf?"

She still could not quite believe her grandmother had been giving away children's books in the middle of a bookstore whose full purpose was to *sell* books. On the other hand, she couldn't argue with her grandmother's philosophy, similar to Dolly Parton's, that all children deserved to have books of their own to read and cherish.

"Okay. I'll find one. Maybe I'll play with the dollhouse while I'm there."

"You do that. I'm going to be here moving books."

Her mom was coming to pick up Olive after she finished a meeting. Her daughter was tired. Emma could tell. One part of her wanted to take Olive home and put her to bed, have a lovely evening reading stories and holding her sweet-smelling child as she drifted to sleep. The other part had so much to do that she did not know how she was going to accomplish all of it.

Keeping an eye on the play area, where her daughter seemed happily occupied for now, Emma continued bringing the books from the sidewalk sale back inside the store for the night.

They ought to have rolling shelves, she thought. If this were her store, she would definitely invest in them so they could simply roll them in and out each night. At least they had sold a couple of boxes' worth of books. That was something, even if the prices were steeply discounted.

She had pulled the final box inside when she saw two familiar figures approaching, a man and a sleek silvery dog.

Bryce wore jeans, a snug T-shirt and an exhausted expression. She held open the door.

"Bryce! I never expected to see you today. Mom told me you had to run to Lincoln City. Some emergency with your mother, she said. Is everything okay?"

His sigh was long and heartfelt and made her wish she felt comfortable enough in their growing friendship to hug him.

"Not really. It's been a rough day. She fell and broke her hip. She's in the hospital and probably will be there for a few more days."

"What are you doing here, then? You should be with her."

"The hospital has my contact info. I can't do anything more for my mom tonight. She's settled for the night and the nurses basically pushed me out the door. I told you I would be here again tonight to help you paint and to grab the bookshelves. I didn't want to leave you hanging."

Emma was not used to men who kept their promises and did exactly what they said they would. She was not quite sure how to respond.

"After what Mom told me, I totally didn't expect you."

"I've had a long, hard day of sitting around in the hospital and I could use something physical to do."

Her unruly mind instantly flashed with several physical things they could do that would be far more fun than hauling out some old bookshelves, but she quickly shoved the inappropriate thoughts away.

"I brought my trailer and furniture movers to take the shelves home with me. I can start working on them over the weekend. I thought I could load them up after I'm done helping you paint, if they're ready to go."

"They're ready. But let me handle the painting. The bookshelves would be more than enough."

"I want to help," he said again.

How could she argue with that? "If you're sure," she said, as Olive wandered over from the children's area.

"Hi. There's my friend Bryce," she exclaimed, beaming at him.

"And there's my friend Olive."

"Is this your dog?"

"Yes. This is Pearl."

"Hi, Pearl!" She hugged the dog and both of them looked instantly smitten with each other.

"Is Grandma here yet?" Olive asked.

"Not yet. I'm sure she will be soon."

The words had barely escaped her mouth when the rear door opened and, as if on cue, Rosie came through, looking smart and stylish as always.

"Grandma!" Olive raced toward Rosie, arms out. The naked love on her mother's expression made Emma's throat close up. Every time she saw her mother and daughter, Emma knew she had made the right choice to come home, even with all the baggage between them.

Olive needed Rosie in her life.

Okay. And perhaps Emma did, too.

Those years of their estrangement had been lonely and hard. She had yearned for the close relationship they once had. She didn't quite feel comfortable yet around her mother but she hoped with time that would continue to improve.

Rosie and Olive hugged for a long time, as if they had last seen each other months ago instead of early that morning.

When her mother set the girl back to her feet and straightened, her gaze instantly fell on the two of them. Her eyes widened.

"Bryce! What are you doing here? You're supposed to be with your mother!"

"Exactly what I told him," Emma said, not wanting Rosie to think she was selfish enough to insist the man rush back to town in the midst of his family crisis simply to help her.

"I was telling Emma that I've been in a hospital room all day and needed something physical to do."

"That is so kind of you," Rosie said. The affection in her expression gave Emma a little burst of jealousy that shamed her.

She had to get over this. Bryce had earned his spot in Rosie's affection, while Emma still had a long way to go. It wasn't fair to resent him for the close relationship he obviously had with her mother.

"Did Bryce tell you the news?"

Emma looked between the two of them in confusion. "About his mother's accident? Yes."

That surely couldn't be the reason for her mother's suddenly bright expression.

"I, um, haven't had a chance to tell her yet."

"A chance to tell me what?" she asked, feeling a sudden sense of foreboding.

"Bryce will be helping you with more than rearranging shelving and clearing out clutter. I've asked him to handle the whole bookstore refresh. Top to bottom."

Emma stiffened as all her plans seemed to crash through the front windows.

"The refresh."

Rosie beamed. "Yes! I'm so excited. He was telling me some of the things you wanted to do and they sound exactly what the bookstore needs to rejuvenate sales. I love the idea of expanding into the space next door and adding a coffee stand as well as more retail space. Genius!"

"Genius," she repeated, feeling numb.

"We all need to sit down and go through the blueprints for the building and decide the best use of the space. I've told Bryce to make this his number one priority for the next few weeks. When he's not with his mother, anyway."

Emma felt as if a whole bookshelf had fallen on her, knocking the breath from her lungs.

She had wanted to prove herself to her mother. Show Rosie she was more than capable of stepping up at the construction company. How was she supposed to do that if Bryce stepped in to take over all the details of the bookstore renovation? How had he wiggled his way into *her* project?

He must have read some of the turmoil in her expression. He gave her a careful look, hazel eyes murky with concern, before he turned back to Rosie.

"Emma and I will work as a team. I would never consider doing anything not in line with her vision. This is her project. I will simply be the hands helping her get it done."

"The tool, in other words," Emma muttered too low for her mother to hear. Bryce heard, though, and sent her a sudden flash of a grin, there and gone again, before he turned back to Rosie.

"That sounds like an excellent plan," her mother said.

"Since Bryce and I talked yesterday about expanding into the storage space, I've made a few sketches," Emma said. "I can show them to you to make sure I'm not doing anything you don't find acceptable."

"You have excellent instincts, sweetheart. I'm sure I'll love anything you do."

Emma was almost sure her mother did not mean that in the condescending way it sounded. Almost.

"Right. Well, I can show you what we were thinking, if you want to come take a look."

Olive yawned, one of her huge, jaw-stretching yawns that took over her whole face. Rosie looked down with concern at her granddaughter. "I do want to see what your plans are," she assured her. "But I also think this sweetheart needs to get home to bed."

Her mother was right. As usual.

Rosie reached for Olive's hand. "Should we head back to the house and grab some dinner? How do you feel about grilled cheese sandwiches and tomato soup on a rainy day like today?"

"I like grilled cheese sandwiches," Olive said.

"Same," Rosie said. "We'll leave the two of you to your work, then. Bryce, take as much time as you need next week to be with your mother. I insist on it."

"Thanks, Rosie."

He smiled at her mother with such warmth, Emma felt that twinge of jealousy again, though this time it stemmed from a very different cause. She suddenly wondered what she would have to do in order for him to look at *her* with warmth and affection.

"You've removed everything from the bookshelves?" he said after her mother and Olive left.

"Yes. They're pretty heavy. Can you move them by yourself? Do you need me to call somebody to give you a hand?"

"I'll take a look but I should be fine with the dolly I brought along. I might need help steering them through the door. I already called one of my buddies and said I might need him to run over. He's on standby and can be here in five minutes."

"I can help you as soon as I'm done checking out the final customers and shutting things down for the evening."

"Sounds good."

She returned to the checkout counter as a young mother with two children approached, a stack of books in hand.

She slid them across the counter and Emma rang up two storybooks for her children along with a book on writing fiction and an elegant journal with flowers on the cover.

"Are you a writer?" Emma asked as she bagged the books.

The woman looked embarrassed. "Trying to be. I have no idea what I'm doing."

"I'm thinking about starting a writing group a few times a month, where writers can brainstorm or work together. No real organized program, just sharing the same creative space for a few hours and cheering each other on. Do you think you might be interested?"

"Definitely! When do you think you might start? I would have to find a babysitter or work around my husband's schedule, but I would love something like that."

"Wonderful! I don't expect the renovation to be done for some time. We're only in the planning stages now but I would love to move forward as soon as possible." She paused. "If you're interested, I also would like to implement a few genre-focused book groups as well as a regular children's story time."

"That's fantastic. I would definitely be interested in all of those things."

"Check back in a few weeks. Oh, and follow us on social media," Emma said, slipping in the quarter-sheet flyer she had created with a QR code leading to the various social media pages she had created. "We'll post updates about the project as we go."

"That's great. Thank you!"

The woman seemed almost giddy as she left, leaving Emma with a deep glow of satisfaction.

Would she feel that same sense of accomplishment working for Lucas Construction?

Maybe she wouldn't have the same kind of personal interactions that she had always enjoyed while working in the service sector, but building something from nothing would offer a different kind of fulfillment.

Even as she considered the possibilities, negative thoughts intruded. What made Emma think she had any right to step in at Lucas Construction, simply because the company had been started by her mother and father? Yes, she had a business degree, but she hadn't really worked in construction at all, except when she was young and living here with her parents.

She had not earned anything nor did she really deserve that kind of chance after all she had done to hurt her mom over the past decade.

And what about Bryce? He loved working for her mother and was obviously great at it or Rosie would not place such trust and reliance on him.

With a sigh, she moved to the aisle where Bryce was hefting one of the big bookcases onto a wheeled furniture mover.

"You aren't supposed to be doing this by yourself," she exclaimed. "I thought you were going to call someone to help you."

"They're not as heavy as I figured they would be. I can handle it," he assured her.

"I'll help," she said.

The two of them worked together to maneuver the heavy bookcases outside to his waiting trailer. It took muscle to push them up the small ramp into the back but they managed, then returned to the store for the other three.

By the time they were done, she was sweaty and her muscles ached. She really needed to get back to the gym, once she felt more settled here in Wood Briar.

"Thank you," she said as they returned to the bookshop. "It looks so much brighter in here already!"

"It might take me a week or so to have these ready, by the time I strip the finish off so I can paint them."

"Can I get you a drink?" she asked.

"Water is great," he said.

When she came out from the office holding two cups of water from the watercooler, she found him wiping his brow with his sleeve. Emma couldn't help but notice how his T-shirt raised up as he lifted his arms, revealing a thin strip of hard muscle above the waistband of his jeans.

Awareness bloomed inside her like a long-dormant seed finally pushing through soil.

Cut that out, she told herself. She was not supposed to be interested in Bryce in that way. He was helping her, and she was grateful. And apparently, they would have to work together if she wanted to whip the bookstore into the shape she desired.

But she was not about to fall for the man.

CHAPTER TWELVE

—

Bryce

HE WASN'T QUITE SURE WHAT HE WAS DOING HERE.

Yes, he had promised he would help her out, but he was certain Emma would have understood his reasons for not fulfilling that promise. Now that he was here in the bookshop with Pearl stretched out at his feet and Emma across from him, Bryce realized he didn't want to be anywhere else.

"Tell me how your mom is really doing," she said, sipping at her own water. "We didn't have a chance to talk about it earlier."

"It was a tough day," he admitted. "She doesn't understand what's happened or why she has to be in the hospital, out of her comfort zone at the care center. She was so agitated, they finally had to sedate her."

"How scary that must have been for her. I'm so sorry. That couldn't have been easy for either of you."

The compassion in her voice touched him. Emma had always been caring and kind to everyone they went to school with. She was the first one to stand up to the bullies, the first to fight injustice. It was one of the things he had always liked most about her.

He lifted a shoulder. "It is what it is. I've always hated that expression, but it fits in this case. I can't change her condition."

"Right."

"I also can't go back in time and pick a different dad, one who wasn't a selfish ass and didn't leave us penniless by walking out."

As soon as he said the words, Bryce wished he could yank them back. He never talked about his dad or the scars that still ached from Mark Kendall's abandonment of them.

He took a long sip of his water. "The only thing I can do is move forward. Try my best to get through it."

"Sounds like that's exactly what you're doing," she said. "Trying your best."

"Most of the time it doesn't feel like my best is very good," he admitted.

"Don't be so hard on yourself. Most of us feel like our best isn't quite good enough. Will your mom be able to go back to the nursing home after she's released from the hospital?"

"Yes. But she obviously won't be as mobile as she was before, at least until the new hip heals. She will have to be watched more carefully. It puts a big burden on the staff, but they're really caring there. I'm sure they'll do a good job of keeping her safe."

"How long has she been in the memory care center?"

"Two years. It probably should have happened at least a year before that, but I did my best to get by with home health and a caregiver I hired during the day while I was working."

"And then you took care of her in the evening, after spending all day at jobsites?"

He didn't like to remember the bleakness of that time. His mother had been slipping away for a long time, but those early years after her dementia diagnosis had been nothing short of hellish.

"It wasn't that bad," he lied. "She slept a lot, so I was able to have a bit of downtime after she was in bed."

"Still, 24/7, with no vacation or sick leave allowed."

"The world is filled with a silent army of caregivers, quietly doing whatever is necessary. I was only one of millions."

"I think it's wonderful," she said. The admiration in her voice left him deeply uncomfortable and eager to change the subject.

"What about you?" he asked. "How are things going at home with your mom?"

"You probably know more about my rocky relationship with Rosie than I wish you did," she muttered.

"I don't know much at all," he assured her. "Only that she is really glad to have you back in Wood Briar. She worried all the time about you when you were in Vegas. It was tough on her."

Emma looked uncomfortable. "I was fine. Okay, maybe not the first few years after I left but eventually I was able to put my life back together. For the most part."

"That couldn't have been easy."

"No. It wasn't."

Her simple words concealed what he knew must have been a Herculean effort.

"How did you get clean?" he asked, genuinely interested.

He thought at first she wasn't going to answer him. After a long pause, she spoke in a low voice.

"When I found out I was pregnant with Emma, I quit everything cold turkey. I had no choice."

"That must have been rough."

She gave a tight laugh that told him far more than her words ever could. "You could say that. Would not recommend. One star out of ten."

"Good to know." He wanted to smile but her bleak expression stopped him.

"It helped that I had stopped using regularly before I got pregnant. A combination of reasons, really. I had a job I didn't want to lose. I was thinking about going back to school. I was trying to get out of a bad relationship. And then I found out I was pregnant. The timing couldn't have been worse."

"Why did you keep Olive? Most people wouldn't have."

She again was quiet, looking down at her hands. "I'm not sure it was a conscious decision at first. I sort of did what I knew my mom and dad would have expected me to do, and then, I don't know. Somehow everything changed. I came to love her. She was mine, and I wanted her."

He nodded, touched at the fierceness in her voice. "And you were hers."

"Exactly. I'm not sure I can adequately convey the miracle of feeling her move inside me for the first time. It felt like the first distant star in the middle of a dark, dark night."

He hated knowing she had endured such a difficult time after she left Oregon. He wanted to make it right for her, to give her back those years she had lost to despair and hopelessness.

She gave a little laugh. "As you might expect, Olive's father wasn't exactly thrilled at the possibility of being a dad. Kevin wanted me to give her up. Not terminate, necessarily, but consider adoption. I did. Believe me, I did. It would have made the most sense for her. I even had a couple of appointments with a social worker but in the end I couldn't do it. The most selfish thing I've ever done, in a lifetime of selfish things."

"What happened with you and Kevin?"

Bryce wanted to drive to Vegas right then and find the son of a bitch, give him a few lessons about how real men took care of people they loved. He had never liked the guy. Now he loathed him.

"He signed away his parental rights before she was born, which I thank God for every day."

"So you went through with the pregnancy all alone."

He had a sudden wild wish that she had come home at that time. Hadn't she believed Rosie and Sylvia would be there for her?

He would have liked to have been there for her, too, even though he knew he had absolutely no right.

"I wasn't really on my own," she assured him. "By that point, I had a job. Friends who rallied around me."

"That's great."

"And I was luckier than most people my age. I had a small inheritance from my dad to help fill in the gaps. Nothing huge, but enough to help me get by. My mom blocked access when I was using, which infuriated me at the time, as you could probably guess."

"I'm sure Rosie was only trying to protect it for you."

"I know. I can see that now, at twenty-five. If I could have accessed my trust fund after I first took off, I would have drained it within a month. When I was seventeen, I thought she was only trying to punish me because I left and she could no longer control me."

Bryce found it desperately sad that she and Rosie had turned away from each other after Gary's tragic death. How much pain could they have avoided if they had leaned on each other instead?

"I'm sure she wasn't. She was only concerned about you."

"I know. For a long time I didn't want to touch a penny that came from her, even indirectly. Finally I had to swallow my pride. I knew my dad would have wanted me to take care of his grandchild."

Her voice broke on the last word and she looked instantly horrified.

"Sounds to me like you did exactly the right thing," he said quietly and he couldn't resist reaching out and covering her hand on the table with his own.

They both gazed at their entwined hands for a long time. Bryce was aware of each slow inhalation of breath she took, each pulse beneath her skin.

He wanted to kiss her.

The urge was almost overwhelming, his body leaning forward slightly, his breath catching.

But before he could even consider asking, she shoved her chair away.

"Thanks again for all your help. I think that's all I'm going to do tonight. I'm not ready to start painting. I'm sure Olive's in bed by now, but I don't want my mom to have to worry about keeping an eye on her all night."

He nodded, and the moment was gone. The air between them seemed to cool instantly, the connection they had shared seconds ago evaporating like morning ocean mist in sunlight.

Bryce felt a pang of disappointment, but he understood. They both had responsibilities, lives that extended far beyond this quiet moment.

As Emma busied herself gathering her things, Bryce stood, shoving his hands in his pockets to resist the lingering urge to reach for her. He watched her move about the room, graceful yet hurried, and wondered if she felt the same mix of attraction and hesitation that churned within him. But now wasn't the time to explore those feelings.

Instead, he focused on helping her tidy up, their movements careful and distant, a stark contrast to the intimacy they'd nearly shared.

When they finally said their goodbyes and he gathered up Pearl and headed for his pickup, Bryce couldn't shake the feeling that something significant had shifted between them, though whether it was a beginning or an ending, he couldn't quite tell.

CHAPTER THIRTEEN

—

Rosie

ROSIE SPREAD A TABLECLOTH ON ONE OF THE EIGHT TABLES set up around her backyard, keeping a close eye on the few dark clouds overhead that punctuated the sky like shadowy specters haunting an otherwise perfect day.

She hosted these events once every few years, but that was more than sufficient. Every time, she forgot how much work they involved, though she wasn't responsible for anything but providing the venue and contributing a potluck item.

Rosie didn't consider herself an overly social person. While she enjoyed her book club and the occasional dinner out with friends, she was mostly happy here in her garden or with her books.

Still, these neighborhood parties were always enjoyable. They were a great opportunity for her to keep up with things happening in their small town, to connect with neighbors and friends she only saw in passing.

Even hosting it wasn't particularly onerous, when she really thought about it. How hard was it to straighten up her yard and set up these tables and chairs other neighbors had been dropping off throughout the week?

"Are these for the tables?" Emma asked as she carried out a tray of vases holding simple flower arrangements Rosie had put together from her garden.

"Yes. That's the plan. There should be a few extras. They can go on the food table."

This would be Emma's first neighborhood party, her first

social gathering of any sort, since she had returned to town. How would Rosie's neighbors accept this prodigal daughter who had finally returned to the fold?

She had no idea. She could only keep her fingers crossed that people would be welcoming to Olive and Emma.

She didn't really have misgivings about that. Most of the people who lived in and around Wood Briar were kind and generous. There were always a few outliers, unfortunately, strongly opinionated folks who seemed to think they knew what was right and proper for everyone else in their sphere of influence.

"What time will everyone be here?" Emma asked.

"In about an hour. Thanks so much for coming home early from the bookstore to help me set up. I know you're in the middle of a hundred different things."

"They will all be there tomorrow, too. If I had stayed late again, I'm not sure how much I would have gotten done anyway."

Her daughter looked tired, with circles under her eyes that hadn't been there earlier in the week. Rosie gave her a look of concern. "Is everything okay? I thought I heard you moving around pretty late. Did you have trouble sleeping?"

Emma gave a tight smile. "I'm fine. I have a lot on my mind right now."

"The bookstore refresh?"

"That's a big part of it."

"Was Bryce there late last night?"

Emma looked away. "Not too late. We didn't end up painting but he took about half of the shelving units to work on at home in his spare time. And, yes. I tried to talk him out of it without much success."

"Bryce can be stubborn when he wants to be."

"I am beginning to figure that out. Thanks again for taking care of Olive last night."

"Oh, you're so welcome. I love having her here."

Rosie slanted a look toward the sandbox she had created by pouring bags of sand inside an old tent. Olive seemed to adore it.

Gary probably would have called it silly to put a sandbox in the yard when they lived right next to a beach full of miles and miles of sand, but Rosie adored the idea of a tent sandbox so that Olive could have a covered place to play, even if the weather was bad.

Sylvia had seen the idea on social media and immediately suggested it for Olive. Now Rosie's mother sat outside the tent opening in her favorite lawn chair, chattering away to her great-granddaughter.

"How many people are you expecting tonight?" Emma asked as she set out biodegradable plates, napkins and utensils on one of three tables set out for food.

Rosie held up her hands. "Maybe two hundred. It's hard to know for sure, especially in the summer. People come and go."

Emma blinked. "Two hundred people. And you all do this several times a year?"

"Yes. Everyone enjoys them."

"Where do you have them in bad weather?"

"We always schedule out a year in advance and reserve the community center in town as a backup."

"Smart."

"It's not as formal as it may seem. We try not to make a big deal about it. Everyone brings potluck salads and desserts and we all donate a few dollars for the main dish, which is usually pretty basic in the summer. Grilled brats, burgers, chicken breasts. Don't worry, we always have a few meatless options too. We have plenty of vegetarians in the neighborhood."

"Good to know."

"Looks like somebody's here early," Sylvia called.

Rosie turned in time to see a small late-model luxury convertible heading up her driveway.

"The party's not supposed to start for an hour. Are you expecting a friend to help you set up?" Emma asked.

Rosie shook her head. "No. That's just Pam. She's dropping off a few papers for me to sign for one of our projects that needs an extension on the building loan."

For some reason, Emma's mouth drew into a tight line. Her eyes suddenly seemed as hard as agates as she watched Pam walk toward them.

Pam, as usual, was stylishly dressed, with perfect makeup and not a hair out of place. Rosie always felt a bit frumpy next to her. Still, she was beyond grateful for Pam's dedication to the company.

"I need to go in and work on my salad," Emma said, her voice suddenly flat. "Is Olive okay out here?"

Rosie gave an airy wave. "Totally fine. Your grandma and I will keep an eye on her."

Emma hurried into the house without even taking time to say hello to Pam, whom she had known most of her life.

Rosie frowned after her but didn't have time to do more than wonder at her strange behavior before Pam reached her.

"Your yard looks fantastic, as always," Pam said, looking around with admiration at the flower beds and the winding gravel paths that led to Sylvia's charming little cottage, the chicken coop, the gardening shed. "I honestly have no idea how you do it. You make me sorry I only have a boring old condo instead of all this gorgeous space."

"I enjoy it."

Rosie didn't bother telling Pam that working in the yard

was therapy of sorts for her, a way to unwind after long hours at work.

"And I always forget what a fabulous view you have from here."

Rosie looked out at the ocean she could see beyond her yard. She never tired of watching the clouds roll in or the sun setting on the waves.

"Are you staying for the barbecue?" Rosie asked.

"Not tonight, sorry. Tony and I are heading into Lincoln City for a concert at one of the casinos."

She named a group that Rosie remembered as being popular when she was younger. "Oh, are they still together?"

"Reunion tour, apparently. It should be fun. I went to see them when I was in high school. I think I got high just from the secondhand pot smoke. Now I'm sure the audience will smell like arthritis medicine and heart disease."

Rosie laughed. "No doubt."

Pam held out a manila envelope. "I only need two signatures and three initials. I've put stickies on the spots for you."

Efficient, as always. Rosie scanned the papers to be sure all was in order then quickly signed the indicated spots.

"Thanks for dropping them by."

"No problem," Pam said. "I should have had you sign them in the office yesterday but I was so worried about Phoebe it slipped my mind."

"Any improvement?"

"Yes, actually, or I would have called off the whole concert. She is doing much better today."

"Oh good."

She and Pam chatted a bit longer before her friend excused herself to get ready for her date and with a breezy wave, headed out again.

Rosie found Emma in the kitchen, slicing cucumbers for a salad with unsettling vigor.

Every line of her daughter's body seemed tense. Rosie frowned, wondering what she might have said or done to upset her now.

Not everything was about her, she reminded herself. Emma had the right to be upset about things that had nothing to do with Rosie.

"Is something wrong?" she finally asked as she took out the fruit plate she had prepared earlier.

Emma opened her mouth as if to answer then gave a slight shake of her head.

"No," she said, clearly lying. "Everything's fine. It's been a long day."

"If you're too tired for the party, don't worry about it. People will understand."

"I'm looking forward to it. This will be fun."

Emma still seemed distracted over the next hour but she seemed to throw herself into the party preparations, even after people started to trickle into Rosie's yard.

Most neighbors walked, since everyone invited lived within a few blocks of her place, but a few of the older residents with mobility needs parked in her driveway.

Rosie directed them and had finished helping Polly Anthony, one of her favorite people, from her vehicle when she spotted Andrew Morgan and his children approaching on foot from the direction of Stormhaven.

To her surprise, Finn pulled away from the other two and rushed to her, throwing his arms around her waist. "Hi, Rosie!" he exclaimed.

"Hi there, Mr. Finn," she said as she hugged him back. "I'm so glad you could come."

"Me, too. Dad says we'll only stay a few minutes, though. Only long enough to eat and meet a few people."

She met Andrew's gaze and saw with amusement that he looked chagrinned at his son's candid revelation.

"Sounds like a good plan," she answered. "There should be plenty of good food. Thank you for coming."

Zara smiled back, already looking around with an eagerness that told Rosie she was probably looking around for someone she might know.

"Where's Dottie?" Finn asked.

"She's over with my mom in the shade there by the tent. I believe your grandmother is over there, too. That's a sandbox, by the way, if you're interested."

He looked skeptical and confused. "A tent in a sandbox? That's weird," he said.

"Finn," his father said, again looking mortified at his blunt child.

"I thought it was weird, too, when I first heard the idea. But it's pretty fun, actually. The sand stays inside and you never have to worry about cats using your sandbox for a litter box."

"Ew," the boy said but he headed in that direction with his sister close behind.

Rosie couldn't help noticing how gorgeous Andrew looked in a navy-blue polo shirt and khaki pants. "You came. I wasn't sure you would."

He made a face. "I almost changed my mind. Meeting everyone in town at once is an intimidating prospect for an introvert like me."

She rolled her eyes. "You attended the Academy Awards this year, if I'm not mistaken. If you could handle all the fancy people there, surely you'll be fine at a little neighborhood barbecue."

"I attended the awards show, but I didn't enjoy it," he assured her. "It lasted for hours and I couldn't wait to get home and out of my tux."

"I can't promise this evening will be more entertaining than the Academy Awards. But let me introduce you to a few people. I know they'll be happy to meet you."

"Will the kids be okay? Maybe I should stay close to them."

Oh no. She wasn't going to let him escape meeting their neighbors that easily. "My mom and yours are keeping an eye on things and there are a few other moms who have volunteered to be on kid patrol. I've locked the gate that leads down to the beach trail and put away my chickens. That's the only hazard I can think of in my yard."

With a sigh, he followed her to a group of the friendliest, most bighearted people she could think of, several people she considered most unlikely among all of those in the crowd to make a fuss about his books or his notoriety.

She had already figured out that Andrew wasn't completely comfortable talking about his successful book series or the movie that had been made of them, something she couldn't quite understand.

She introduced him, explaining the others' connections and where they lived. She was relieved, as she hoped, when everyone was friendly and welcoming. Polly Anthony immediately started asking him about the renovations to Stormhaven and telling him about parties she remembered when she was young, when the place had been the most luxurious house on this part of the coast.

Satisfied that he was comfortable for now, she moved away and headed to check on the paper product supply at the food table.

She was stopped before she could reach it by Nina Patel,

her dear friend and owner of Rosie's favorite clothing boutique in town, who gave her a wide-eyed look.

"I can't believe you were able to drag Andrew Morgan out to one of our neighborhood bashes. Most of us have hardly caught a glimpse of him since he arrived. He's like our own version of the Loch Ness Monster."

He was far too gorgeous to be compared to any kind of monster, Rosie thought.

"I believe he's still trying to settle in, but it hasn't been easy since the house is still a construction zone. I'm glad he made it. It must be so overwhelming to come here and meet half the town at once."

"Wait. We're overwhelming?" Nina asked with a wide-eyed, innocent look that made Rosie laugh, even as she felt a pang of sympathy for Andrew.

She knew only too well what it was like to be the new kid in town, the center of all the attention.

If he was truly as introverted as he said, this must definitely be a challenge. She had a wild urge to run to his rescue and pull him away from everyone.

"I have to say," Nina went on, "the guy is even hotter in person than all the pictures I've seen of him in the tabloids with Willow Voss."

She looked over to find him smiling down at something Polly said, his expression somehow gentle as he looked at the frail octogenarian. Her skin suddenly felt hypersensitive and she was oddly aware of the soft evening breeze blowing off the water.

She swallowed hard, doing her best to rein in this silly response to the man. His previous girlfriend was a movie star. They went to the freaking Academy Awards together. Why would he possibly be interested in a frazzled grandmother who ran a construction company in a small coastal town?

"You should ask him to come talk to the Sea Witches!" Nina exclaimed.

Rosie blinked back to her friend, trying to imagine any scenario where she could find the nerve to invite him to join their rambunctious monthly book club.

"He's busy trying to meet a deadline right now. I'm sure he doesn't have time for something like that."

"You should ask him anyway."

"Who are we asking? And what do we want him to do?" Their other good friend Mei Lin Chen joined them. The nurse practitioner at the women's clinic Rosie went to looked as gorgeous as a movie star herself tonight, as usual.

"I was telling Rosie she should ask our sexy new neighbor to speak at our book club." Nina grinned, inclining her head in the direction of Andrew.

Rosie could feel her cheeks heat. She could only hope he was too busy talking with Polly to notice all the middle-aged women ogling him.

"He's great looking," Mei Lin agreed. "But Rosie doesn't like fantasy."

"She should make an exception in Andrew Morgan's case. And I'm not talking about the books he writes, if you know what I mean," Nina said with a grin.

Almost against her will, she looked over at Andrew. Their gazes met and he gave her a tentative smile. Rosie could feel her face heat even more, feeling as if she had swallowed a hummingbird. She smiled back but quickly looked away again.

"I saw that!" Mei Lin murmured.

"What?" Rosie tried for an innocent tone.

"The two of you exchanging longing glances in the middle of a party."

"You didn't see anything. We're friends, that's all. I'm taking over as the project manager of the Stormhaven renovation."

"Even better," Nina joined in. "You'll have to see each other all the time, at least until his house is done."

Yes. She was fully aware of that. In fact, she hadn't been able to stop thinking about it.

"You should go for it," Mei Lin pressed. "He's really hot, Rosie."

Sheer force of will was the only thing stopping her from stealing another look. "No thanks. I have enough on my plate right now. I've got Emma and Olive and my mom and two businesses. Who has time for romance?"

"You should," Nina said firmly.

"Gary's been gone for ten years," Mei Lin said. "Don't you think it's time to move on?"

"I have moved on. I've dated."

"Nobody seriously, except for that restaurant owner," Mei said, her features frustrated. "How many times have we all tried to set you up with somebody great? You date them one or two times and then say there was no spark."

"I can't help that."

"Have you ever thought that maybe the reason you haven't generated any sparks with anybody is because you do everything you can to blow out any fires before they can get started?"

Rosie instinctively wanted to argue, but she knew they were right. She had dated several perfectly nice guys but always made excuses for why they weren't right for each other.

And yes. She was tired of being alone. That didn't mean she was self-destructive enough to want to jump headfirst into a relationship destined for failure.

"Seriously. When am I going to find time to date? Even if Andrew Morgan and I were not completely wrong for each other, this isn't the time for me to start something with *anyone*."

"When is the right time?" Nina asked. "You can make excuses for the rest of your life."

"And what's wrong with that? I don't need a man to be happy. My life is full and rich and beautiful, just as it is."

If she had nights when she ached to have someone's arms around her, early mornings when she would love to have someone to walk on the beach with, evenings when she yearned for conversation and laughter and *fun*, that was her business.

"It is," Nina agreed. "That doesn't mean you should automatically shut the door on anything without seeing where it might lead."

"You could merely have a wild affair with him," Mei Lin said.

"Okay, first of all, I don't plan to have a wild affair with anyone. You both know that's not in my nature. Second of all, what would Andrew Morgan see in someone like me? He dates tight, hot, young actresses. I haven't been tight, hot or young in a long time."

"You're forty-five years young, honey," Mei Lin said. "Perimenopausal doesn't mean dead. Take it from me. I'm a professional."

She was grateful when another friend came over to talk to them, interrupting the conversation she did not want to have, about a man she could not stop thinking about.

CHAPTER FOURTEEN

—

Andrew

ROSIE LUCAS'S GARDEN WAS TRULY SPECTACULAR.

As Andrew followed another of the winding paths, this one leading along the fence that separated her yard from a trail down to the beach, he was surrounded by a sensory overload.

Soft twilight cast long shadows across colorful beds. Some of the flowers had closed for the night while others were only beginning to bloom, sending their intoxicating fragrances through the air.

One of his favorite coping mechanisms when he felt overstimulated was to try describing every real-life scene in his head as he might try to write it. How the dark silhouettes of partygoers moved around the yard like graceful shadows, how the rhythmic crash of waves below mingled with muffled laughter and conversation on the light breeze that rustled through the leaves, how the rich, earthy scent of damp soil and bark mulch mingled with sweet jasmine, spicy carnation, delicate roses.

A sense of tranquility washed over him like those waves against the sand, and he eased down onto a wooden bench overlooking the water.

He was enjoying the taste of salt on the air when he became aware of someone else walking along the path toward him. He felt an instant magnetic pull, as clear as the inexorable rhythm of the tides, when he recognized Rosie in the fading light.

"No fair hiding out," she said as she approached. "You're supposed to be out there meeting the neighbors."

"My threshold for meeting new people was exceeded some time ago. I'm taking a breather, then I'll probably grab the kids and head home."

"You're not enjoying yourself?"

"I am. I like meeting people. Maybe not a few hundred at once. That's one of the reasons I became an author, so I can spend the day with my imaginary friends."

"How do you handle book tours? Press appearances? I saw some of the publicity you did when your book was made into a movie. You seemed to have no trouble with that."

It seemed odd, wrong somehow, to think of Rosie watching him in interviews before he ever knew she existed.

"I can handle anything in small doses. More than that, and I end up exhausted. I have another book tour coming up later this year when the new book comes out. I'm not really looking forward to it."

They both turned their heads at the sound of children's loud shrieks and laughter. He spotted Zara, her face bright with happiness as she raced across the lawn, followed quickly by her younger brother.

As usual, his heart ached with love for these two extraordinary little humans.

"Your kids seem to be having fun. I believe they're playing freeze tag with some of the other kids, organized by my friend Nina's teenage daughter and her friends."

"It's nice that they've made a few friends."

"And you haven't?"

He made a face. "A few. There's you."

Even as he said the words, he had to ask himself if they were true. Were they friends? He wasn't entirely sure. He only knew that he definitely liked Rosie Lucas. Of all the people he had met in Wood Briar, she was the one who most intrigued him.

He certainly hadn't dreamed spicy dreams about any other women in town.

Thank heavens.

"I was admiring your garden. It will probably be years before I can enjoy the same kind of lush escape at Stormhaven."

"The gardens there are in pretty rough shape," she agreed. "But you can always hire people to help you with them."

"Do you have any recommendations?"

"Sure. We work with some great landscaping companies on the properties we develop. I'll come up with the list."

"I want the one you use," he said on impulse. "Your yard is gorgeous."

The sound of her soft laughter rippled through him as if she had caressed his cheek.

"I don't use anyone. Only myself, I'm afraid."

He blinked, taking in the neat flower beds, the trimmed hedges, the exquisite trees. If anything, seeing her garden and knowing how much passion she must have poured into it only added to his fascination.

"It's lovely," he said truthfully. "I feel more at peace here than I think I have since I came to Wood Briar."

"Oh," she exclaimed, a sound of sheer pleasure. "That's lovely to hear. I'm so glad. I'm sorry I interrupted your moment of zen."

She rose to go and he immediately regretted his words.

"That's not what I meant. Stay. You've probably been on your feet all day, getting ready for the party."

She shook her head. "It hasn't been that bad. I do have to go, though, as much as I would love to stay here with you and enjoy the sunset."

"Why?"

"Because it's lovely, especially with the storm clouds building off shore. We'll probably have rain later tonight."

"I meant, why do you have to go."

She sighed. "I have guests. I need to grab a few more things out of the kitchen."

He rose as well. "I'll help you," he said.

Though she looked surprised at his offer, she led the way to her comfortable kitchen. Along the way, she pointed out her herb garden and the heirloom roses she had rescued from a jobsite when they were going to be torn out.

In the kitchen, she handed him a few platters of cookies. "We're running low on desserts. Would you mind taking these out? And, yes. They're storebought but the bakery in town does such a good job that nobody ever seems to care."

"No problem."

He grabbed the platters and carried them outside, dropping them at the long rows of food tables. On the way back, he bumped into a couple of women he had been introduced to earlier. For the life of him, he couldn't remember their names.

"There you are," the shorter of the women said. She was a lovely brunette with sharp dark eyes and graceful features. He could easily see her as a courageous warrior in his books, with a fragile loveliness that he suspected concealed steely strength.

"Remind me of your names," he said.

"I'm Mei Lin and this is Nina," the woman who had spoken to him answered.

"We're Rosie's good friends," Nina said. "In fact, we're in a book club with her. Has she mentioned it to you yet?"

Andrew could feel his shoulders tighten. He really hated book clubs. He loved the idea of them, and he was flattered whenever one of them wanted to feature his books, yet he always felt uncomfortable with the idea of trying to interact with people who read his book to dissect it and parse every word.

Talking about his books was awkward enough. It was even harder to answer question about a process that still seemed mysterious and magical to him most of the time.

He was not a writer who analyzed everything he did. He simply wrote. While he admired those who planned out every word and constantly focused on subtext and imagery, that wasn't his process and book clubs tended to make him feel inadequate because of it.

"We call ourselves the Wood Briar Sea Witches."

"Ah. Great name."

"We're not really witches," Mei Lin assured him.

Nina rolled her eyes at her friend. "Obviously. We are strong, fierce women who like to take care of our own problems. We also like to read books about strong, fierce women. We would love to have you come and talk to us about your various series. Rosie was supposed to ask you."

"She did not."

"I think she felt nervous about it," Mei Lin said. "Rosie doesn't really like fantasy."

Yeah, he figured that out already, when he heard her in the bookstore dissing his books.

"Most of our other members love you and your books. And, of course, the movie. I know they would be thrilled to have you."

"Would you consider it?" Nina asked. "It would be a very casual affair. Stress-free is our motto. I promise, we're mostly harmless."

"Mostly?"

Nina grinned. "Yes. We can be savage toward the patriarchy. Fortunately, your books are very women-empowered and we love that."

He instinctively wanted to say no. But this was his new community, along with his children's. They needed to live with these people and *their* children. He didn't want to potentially risk alienating a group called the Wood Briar Sea Witches. Something told him that would not be a very wise move on his part.

"I can definitely check my calendar," he said, hoping an evasive *maybe* would suffice for now.

"We try to meet the third Tuesday of the month," Mei Lin said eagerly. "We're free anytime. You could come this month, if you want. I know most of us have read your books."

So much for that idea. They were determined to pin him down, apparently.

"I'll have to see. I'm on a book deadline and don't have a lot of free time."

She seemed undeterred by his evasiveness. "Great. I'll reach out. What kind of contact do you prefer? Email, text, carrier pigeon?"

"Email is fine. You can find my email through my website."

Nina looked suspiciously at him. "We need the personal one, so we can be sure it will reach you. You must have a different one than the contact info on your website."

"That one will reach me, I promise."

Mei Lin rolled her eyes. "You seriously can't read every single letter from readers that shows up in your inbox."

"I do."

He didn't tell her he loved connecting with his readers. He did have the occasional angry reader, annoyed by something he had written or quick to point out a mistake, but he mostly enjoyed them.

Hearing how his words touched someone or made them laugh or motivated them to make a change helped the long hours spent over his keyboard feel not quite so solitary.

"We'll email you, then. I really hope you can make your schedule fit."

"I'll do my best."

After checking on his kids, who seemed to be having a great time now playing cornhole with several other children their age, he returned to the kitchen. He wasn't sure what drew him there. He could have easily struck up a conversation with one of the groups of people who gave him friendly greetings.

Still, something about Rosie called to him.

In the kitchen, he found her preparing another tray, this one full of small pinwheel appetizers.

When he walked in, she lifted her head and gave him a bright smile.

"I totally forgot I made these a few weeks ago for the party and stowed them in the freezer. People are probably done eating but there's no sense leaving them in my freezer. They'll thaw in only a few minutes."

"Ah."

She narrowed her gaze suddenly. "Why are you back here? You should be out meeting people."

He certainly could not tell Rosie Lucas that he was drawn to her like iron filings to a powerful magnet. "I came to see if you needed help with anything else."

"Oh. Thank you."

"And I have met plenty of people. I actually just bumped into a few of your friends out there."

She looked up from arranging the pinwheels on the plate. "You'll have to be more specific. For the most part, every person out there is my friend in some capacity."

"A few of the Wood Briar Sea Witches. Mei Lin and Nina."

Somehow, she managed to laugh and grimace at the same time. "Don't tell me. They asked you to come speak to our book group."

"They did."

"You don't have to do that if you don't want to. Everyone will understand."

Perversely, her words only made him want to agree. "I told them to reach out with some dates and I'll try to make my schedule fit."

"That's very generous of you. I know your life is chaotic right now, living in a construction zone while you're trying to meet a deadline."

"I'm always happy to talk to readers," he said. "Even readers who find my work trite and overhyped and my female characters wooden nerd fantasies."

She froze, her gaze flying to his. He watched, fascinated, as color seeped across her lovely features. "Oh. You heard that. I was afraid you had."

"I shouldn't have eavesdropped. It was rude of me."

"You weren't rude. I was. I should never have said that about your books."

"Why not? If that's how you feel, you shouldn't lie about it. I had to accept a long time ago that not everybody will love my books."

"I do like them. You're a great writer and wonderful storyteller. I can't help it that fantasy has never been my jam."

He wished now he hadn't said anything. He had only made her uncomfortable, when they were truly beginning to establish a friendship.

On the other hand, better to get it out into the open than have it simmering between them, at least on his part.

"Rosie. It's totally fine. I'm sorry I mentioned it."

"I'm so embarrassed. What must you have thought about me and about The Rainy Day Bookshop?"

"I thought you were a reader expressing your opinion of my books."

"Rudely."

"Okay, I was a little put out at first. It's like somebody telling you your kids are ugly. But if everybody in the world all loved the exact same books, publishers would only put out iterations of that very same book again and again."

"I suppose that's true."

"The other day you showed me a secret passageway to my house I had no idea even existed. Books are like portals to a magical land. The thing is, everybody's magical land looks different. Every reader steps through and creates a world there that is uniquely his or her own."

"I've heard it said that every reader takes something different away from a book, depending on their own life experience."

"I can tell you that's true. I'm always amazed at what readers tell me they glean from my books, things I never thought about or intended. It's one reason I struggle to know what to say at book clubs, because they sometimes want to add deep, layered meaning to each paragraph and sentence and story choice, when I'm really trying to tell the best story I can."

"You do, Andrew. Your books are beloved for good reason."

He shrugged, embarrassed that he had revealed so much about himself to her. He gestured to the platter. "Do you think these are ready to go out?"

She blinked and looked down. "Yes. They should be."

He wanted to kiss her.

The urge swept over him out of nowhere like a sneaker wave, fierce, sudden and inescapable.

"I'll take these out," he said, his tone curt.

As he hurried out to the party, the rush of noise hit him hard. He would stay only a little longer, he decided.

His social budget was about spent and right now he wanted nothing but to grab his kids and return to his manuscript, their cramped carriage house apartment and his crumbling house overlooking the sea.

CHAPTER FIFTEEN

—

Emma

HER MOM ALWAYS DID KNOW HOW TO THROW A GOOD PARTY. Emma looked around at the crowd of happy neighbors and friends hanging out in her mother's backyard and felt a mingled sense of pride and envy.

Rosie was so good at this. She instinctively knew how to make everyone feel comfortable, no matter their circumstances. Right now, she was talking with a group of teenagers, and they all seemed to be engaged in what she was saying. She could chat as easily with older people, children, those Emma's age. Everyone.

Emma hadn't inherited the same skills. She liked to think she was pretty good with people, after years working in the service sector, but she could never interact with the same ease as Rosie.

She kept her eye on Olive, who was playing with a small group of children on the swing set. Her daughter was also having the time of her life, making new friends in that unselfconscious way of young children.

Even Sylvia seemed completely comfortable with this crowd. Emma was the only one who felt out of place, wondering if people were talking about Rosie's wild daughter who had returned to the fold.

She was relieved when she spotted her friend Josie arriving with her husband and kids in tow. When she spied Emma, she beamed brightly, handing her baby to her husband. He shepherded both kids to the food table and Josie headed straight for her.

"Hey you." Josie hugged her and Emma felt her nerves relax. Josie had been so kind to her since she returned to Wood Briar, going miles out of her way to make Emma feel welcome here.

"I'm so glad you're here," Emma said.

"We went to dinner with Brandon's parents tonight. I can't believe after everything we ate at dinner that my family is still heading to check out the potluck offerings."

"There's some good stuff over there. Somebody brought macadamia chocolate bar cookies that are sinful."

"Probably Nina Patel. That's her specialty. And you're right. They're delicious. I'll have to grab one before we leave, if there are any left."

"Here," Emma said, picking an untouched square from her plate and handing it over.

"You are a true friend." Josie grinned, took a nibble and closed her eyes in ecstasy. "The absolute best. So have you seen any of the old crowd here?"

"A few people. I saw Jake Holder and Lucy Carmichael together. I had no idea they were dating."

Josie grinned. "Engaged, actually. As of a few months ago."

Emma shook her head in surprise. The two struck her as complete opposites. Jake had been part of the wild, hard-drinking crowd Emma had started running with after her dad died, while Lucy had been straitlaced and stuffy, even as a teenager.

Still, they seemed to work together.

"How are things at the bookstore?" Josie asked. "I've been meaning to ask how you are liking it but we never have a chance to chat when you come to pick up or drop off Olive. She's always so happy to see her mom when you pick her up, and I'm usually in the middle of chaos with my own kids."

Emma was deeply grateful again that Josie had offered to

babysit her daughter. She found it heartwarming to see Olive interacting with Josie's children.

"It's going, I guess. Sales still aren't super great but I'm planning a big renovation project. I hope it will brighten up and refresh the place to bring in more shoppers."

"That's awesome! Do you need any help? I'm sure we could get the old gang together to help you paint or whatever. We love projects."

Emma could feel her cheeks flush. "Actually, this is an official renovation of Lucas Construction now. Bryce is helping me."

Helping her be filled with turmoil and angst and want things she couldn't have, anyway.

"Oh, that's terrific. You won't find anyone better in town."

She nodded. "He's already been a big help."

"What all do you plan to do?"

She told the details to her friend, who seemed genuinely interested.

"I love all of this. I can't wait to see it! You can bet I'll be bringing the kids in for story time once you get those started and I'd love to participate in a couple of book clubs."

"Follow us on social media," she said, which was becoming her mantra these days.

Emma really wanted to make The Rainy Day Bookshop a town gathering space while she was working there. Yes, Wood Briar had a small library but it kept sporadic hours and the offerings were pretty sparse. She would love to see the bookstore fill in the gaps.

"Emma!"

She turned at the excited greeting to find another good friend, Brooke Velasquez, heading toward her, arms outstretched. Brooke didn't appear to have changed at all from high school. She was still short, cute, bubbling over with energy.

"I am so darn happy to see you," Brooke said as she first hugged Emma then did the same to Josie.

"I'd heard through the grapevine that you were back in town, but I've been so busy at work this month, I haven't had five minutes to drive down to see for myself. I came down for a few days for my dad's birthday and when my folks said they wanted to come to a party here tonight, I tagged along, hoping I would see you."

"Here I am."

Emma forced a smile, though she again felt uncomfortable. What did her friends see when they looked at her? With her purple-tipped hair, her tattoos, her piercings, she was a far cry from the popular, outgoing girl she had been before that horrible day when her dad died.

"Where are you these days?" she asked Brooke.

"I bought a condo in Newport a few months ago. It's closer to my work at the hospital there."

She knew from their social media friendship that Brooke worked as an X-ray technician and loved every minute of it.

"Well, you look fantastic," Emma said. "Like you still should be cheering at the fifty-yard line down at the high school."

Brooke grimaced. "Not in a million years. I'm so glad to be done with high school and college."

"Same," Josie said fervently.

Emma had left before graduation and had gone to college mostly online, studying at night while her baby slept. She told herself again to take pride in how far she had come, not feel an ounce of embarrassment at the nontraditional path she had taken.

"And you're running your mom's bookstore. What a dream job!" Brooke exclaimed.

"It's getting there," Emma answered. "I still have a long way to go, though."

"She's doing a big reno. And guess who's helping her?" Josie asked, then answered before Brooke could try. "Bryce Kendall."

The other woman made a low sound of appreciation in her throat. "Lucky you!" she said. "The man is fire, as my younger sister would say."

"Definitely," Josie said. "He's a lot different from the annoying pest he was in fifth grade. Remember how he always teased you at recess and loved to pull your hair?"

"I always thought he had a thing for you," Brooke said to Emma. "He watched you a lot when we were in school."

Emma could feel her face heat and hoped the twilight disguised her reaction from her friends.

"I doubt that. If he watched me at all, he was probably only trying to figure out the next way he could make my life harder."

"Speak of the devil," Josie said, gesturing with her head.

All three of them turned to see Bryce walk into the backyard carrying a box from a bakery up in Lincoln City. As they watched, Rosie hurried to him and hugged him, taking the box from him with a scolding kind of look.

"Fire. That man sizzles," Brooke said.

"You are an engaged woman," Josie reminded her.

"I am, and I adore my fiancé. That doesn't mean I can't appreciate a good-looking guy like Bryce."

"Engaged," Emma exclaimed. "I hadn't heard that. Congrats! Who is he?"

"His name is Ben Warner, and he's a hospitalist where I work."

"Why didn't you bring him tonight? I would have loved to meet him," she said.

"He was working. Had a late shift this week, unfortunately. When he's not working, we tend to be out having adventures."

"Oh? What kind of adventures?"

"Anything outdoors. We love to hike, kayak, camp. He's from Iowa and loves any opportunity to be close to the ocean."

As she listened to her friends chat about some of their favorite recreational opportunities around the Oregon coast, Emma felt again the sense of *otherness* that had been simmering under her skin.

This whole situation was completely out of her comfort zone. The whole suburban block party was worlds away from the life she had been living since she left, trying mostly to survive in a world that too often felt dark and hard.

They chatted for a few more minutes, until Josie's daughter started crying over by the swing set. Her husband wasn't in sight, so she left them with an apology before heading over to deal with whatever was wrong.

"How are you really, girl?" Brooke asked after Josie left.

Emma sent her friend a swift look. "Fine. Why wouldn't I be?"

"I imagine this is a big culture shock to you, coming back to small-town Oregon after all the glamour and glitz of Las Vegas."

Her life in Vegas had not been glitzy or glamorous in the slightest. She could tell her friends about the best place to grab a free meal and all the things she had learned about how to survive on the street without being forced to sell your body, but she had a feeling they didn't want to hear about that.

"I've missed everyone," she said. "It's great for my daughter, too."

"Oh, where is your daughter? I have to meet her!"

She pointed out Olive, busy playing on the swing set with Finn and Zara Morgan and some other children.

"She is adorable!" Brooke exclaimed.

"Thanks. She is a joy. She has definitely changed my life."

She and Brooke chatted about her friend's wedding plans and about other friends and where they were now.

"Are you dating anyone?" Brooke asked.

Emma quickly shook her head, though for some silly reason, Bryce's image popped into her head. "No. That's way down on the priority list right now. I have enough to do with the store and with Olive."

"I get it. But when you're ready to date, make sure you let me know. Ben knows everyone. He's one of those guys who makes friends wherever he goes. You know the type."

"I do."

Her dad had been like that, gregarious and friendly to neighbors and strangers alike. One of the hundreds of things she missed about him.

"Most of the time, I love that he's so social and so interested in other people," Brooke went on. "But it's not always easy. We went on a trip to Hawaii last year, and I wanted to spend the whole time at the beach with my book but when I looked up, Ben was in the middle of a crowd of a half-dozen people. He had all their names and addresses and was making plans to hang out with them later that night."

She laughed. "Did you have fun with his new friends?"

Brooke made a face. "We had a great time and are even inviting a few of them to the wedding. My point is that we can totally find somebody for you, when you're ready."

"I'll keep that in mind," she lied. She was relieved when Josie returned and the conversation could turn to other things.

Throughout the remainder of the evening as she chatted with neighbors and friends, she was aware of Bryce, who seemed to know everyone here.

She didn't have a chance to talk to him until nearly the end of the evening, when she had retreated to one of the arbor swings her mother had set up around the yard. From here, she had a good view of Olive, who was trying to wring every last bit of fun from the party. The solitude gave Emma a chance to catch her breath and regather her composure.

"What are you doing over here by yourself?" a deep voice asked and she could feel her pulse jump when she recognized Bryce through the fading light.

"Hiding," she admitted. The words spilled out, though she wasn't sure why she was compelled to honesty with him, of all people.

"Hiding from what?" Chains rattled as he sat down beside her.

"It's not easy meeting up with everyone in town after so many years away, especially considering . . . everything."

"Everything?"

She sighed. "Most people have been very nice but there are a few Judgy McJudgersons who have been looking at me like they're waiting for me to break out a crack pipe any minute now."

He raised an eyebrow. "I hope you're exaggerating."

"Maybe a little. But I'm sure there are plenty of people who are wondering why my mom has welcomed me back with open arms, after all the pain I've put her through."

"I think it's amazing what you've done, Em. You are so down on yourself, but I think you need to focus on how far you've come. You've completely turned things around. That's nothing but admirable."

She wished she could see it that way. Instead, she only saw her own mistakes, laid out in front of her like runway lights on an airstrip.

She saw the poor choices she had made and all the opportunities she had missed out on. When she had been an angry, hurting girl, she never would have guessed how running away, seeking her freedom, had closed so many other doors.

"What about you?" she asked. "Shouldn't you still be out there flirting with all the women?"

"I don't believe I was flirting with anyone. It's called being friendly."

"It's called putting out the vibe, and you're doing a very good job of it."

He raised an eyebrow. "Am I?"

There was something sincerely baffled in his question, as if he wasn't at all sure of his own appeal. How could that possibly be?

"Surely you know that every woman with a pulse has her eye on you."

She was amused to see a hint of color creep up on the tips of his ears.

"That's ridiculous."

"Is it?"

She considered teasing him more but the summer night was too lovely, one of those rare, beautiful Oregon evenings when the world seemed fresh and sweet and filled with possibilities and it seemed too perfect to be swinging beside this man who fascinated her entirely too much.

CHAPTER SIXTEEN

—

Bryce

IF ONE OF HIS BUDDIES HAD TOLD HIM A FEW WEEKS EARLIER that he would find himself sitting on a swing with the lovely Emma Lucas—and feeling more peace than he had all day—Bryce would have laughed out loud at the absurdity.

What was it about her that soothed him so much?

He wasn't entirely sure. She didn't exactly have a restful personality. Emma could be caustic, sharp edged. He knew that was a defense mechanism, though. He couldn't imagine all that had happened in the past ten years to give her those pointy prickles.

He was content to let the soft breeze eddy around them while the noise and hubbub of the party played in the background.

She was the first to break the silence. "I didn't expect to see you here tonight," she said after a moment. "I thought you would be busy with your mom."

He sighed, feeling that heavy weight descend on his shoulders again. "I was there most of the day. She's supposed to move back to her facility tomorrow, where they're going to work on rehabbing her hip, so we had some details to work through. They have to keep a closer eye on her and plan to install some bed rails and a bed alarm so they know if she tries to get up in the night. She will hate it and won't understand why she can't get up when she wants."

"That must be so tough. I can't even imagine."

"I hope you never have to go through it," he said quietly.

He didn't want to talk about his mother tonight or care centers or broken hips. Eager to change the subject, he gestured around to the festive background. The crowd had begun to break up but there were still plenty of people gathered under the café lights on the patio or clustered in cozy conversation areas.

"Your mom always throws a good party."

"Are you surprised? My mom always does everything well."

At her glum tone of voice, he sent her a searching look.

"I don't think Rosie would agree with you there. I suspect she spends plenty of time feeling inadequate and overwhelmed."

"She hides it well. Mom seems like the epitome of a woman who has fought hard for her success and won't let anything or anyone take it from her."

"I would agree with that," he said. "She's also a woman who loves her family fiercely and worries for them just as fiercely."

She sighed. "I know. And I get it. You and my mom are close."

He gave her another careful look. "Your mom has given me some amazing opportunities and I will never be anything but grateful that she took a chance on a dumb punk like I was."

"You're not dumb, Bryce."

"Even though I was held back a year and you skipped a grade ahead?"

"I shouldn't have said that. I'm sorry."

"It was the truth."

"Not completely. I was a fall baby and always a little bit ahead of the rest of the kids in my grade. And you . . ."

Her voice trailed off.

"And I had to take remedial English and math classes because I struggled in school. For what it's worth, I was diagnosed with dyslexia in middle school."

Which probably would have happened much earlier if his mom had ever been sober enough at parent-teacher conferences to push the matter.

"Do you struggle at jobsites? There's plenty of math and English required."

"No. You never grow out of dyslexia but I did figure out some coping mechanisms that help a lot."

"Oh good."

He was about to add more when her daughter rushed over, her brow furrowed and her mouth pursed. She had tears on her cheeks but she seemed more mad than angry.

"I fell on the swing and hurt my knee and a boy named Charlie laughed at me."

Emma gathered her daughter in her arms and he watched all of her prickliness disappear in an instant, replaced by soft concern.

"Well, how rude of him. Maybe he didn't understand that you were really hurt."

"Maybe." Olive looked between the two of them. "Can I sit by you on this swing?"

Emma glanced over at Bryce with a questioning look. He willingly slid over and Olive hopped up between the two of them, warm and sweet and clearly tired.

"Hi. You're my friend Bryce."

He smiled, already adoring this open, friendly child. "And you're my friend Olive. It's good to see you again."

"Guess what? My friend has a new puppy. I'm going to see it when I go play there on Monday."

"A new puppy," he said. "How exciting!"

She grinned happily. "And she has a new Barbie doll, too, and she's going to have a new baby sister, but that's not as fun as a new puppy."

"Absolutely not," Bryce agreed solemnly.

"Guess what?" she asked again.

"Um, another friend has a new kitty?"

She giggled. "No, silly. I'm going to have a birthday. I'm going to be four." She held up her fingers.

"Four! You are growing up."

"I know. I go to kindergarten in one more year."

She leaned against his shoulder and Bryce felt as if a warm sunbeam had suddenly broken through clouds he didn't even know were there.

The warmth of her tiny body, the trust in her gesture and the innocence in her voice all combined to create a surge of protective affection he'd never experienced before. Somehow Olive had effortlessly slipped past all his defenses, nestling not only against his side but deep within his heart.

"Guess what?" she asked for a third time. It was apparently her favorite phrase. "I have a new bedroom, and I have a pink bed, and my grandma says she's going to find a dollhouse that my mommy had in the attic and have somebody fix it up."

"Is that right?"

She nodded, her head moving against his arm, then the little rascal sent him a sidelong look. "Can you fix it for me?"

"Olive," Emma admonished, sounding mortified. "You don't just ask people to do things for you."

"Grandma said she wanted to ask him. So I did it myself."

"Bryce works for Grandma, honey. He doesn't work for you."

"Does he work for you, Mommy?"

Emma shifted on the swing and Bryce could see the question made her uncomfortable. "He doesn't really work for me, but he is helping me fix up the bookshop to make it a little bit nicer and not so crowded."

"We're going to put in a place that sells cookies and muffins and cinnamon rolls. Things like that."

"Yum. Can I have a cookie?"

He laughed. "We can probably arrange that."

"Okay."

Rosie's little dog, Dottie, wandered past and Olive jumped up to follow the dog, leaving the two of them alone again on the swing.

"She is pretty adorable," Bryce said as they both watched Olive race back to her friends.

"She is. She's also extremely busy. Some days trying to keep up with her is more exhausting than running a marathon while juggling flaming torches."

He was quiet, not sure how to ask the question he had wondered about since she told him about going through the pregnancy alone.

"Why didn't you come home when you were pregnant with Olive? You had to know Rosie would welcome you back with open arms."

She looked toward the terrace, where Rosie was chatting with a couple he didn't know.

"I wanted to," she said, her voice low. "I started to text her so many times, begging to come home. I always deleted it and didn't send."

"Why?"

"I don't think I was ready. I was still dealing with so many emotions around my dad's death." She looked out at the ocean, barely visible in the twilight. "Besides, I knew my mom didn't want me here either."

He stared at her. "That's the most ridiculous thing I've ever heard. Of course, your mom wanted you."

Her laugh sounded ragged. "You don't know how things were that last year before I left town. We fought constantly. It was ugly. If not for Sylvia trying to keep the peace, it might have been even worse."

"What did you fight about?"

"What *didn't* we fight about? My hair, my clothes, my friends, the tattoo I went to Lincoln City to get. She hated everything I did. I was pretty sure before I left that she hated *me.* And, yes. I know I sound like a whiny teenager. Mom didn't really hate me. I was running wild and she hated that she couldn't control me. And, of course, every time she looked at me, she was reminded that I caused the death of my father."

Bryce stared at her in shock. Despite the low light, he could tell she looked as if she regretted saying the words.

"That's not true, Emma. You don't really believe that, do you?"

She fidgeted with a loose thread on her jeans but didn't directly answer his question.

"Things were so tough that last year. I'm sure she was relieved after I left."

"And I'm just as certain she wasn't. I don't know all that transpired between you and your mom back then. I can tell you I know for absolute fact that Rosie missed you every single day you were gone."

She made a small sound of disbelief and he couldn't resist reaching out and covering her hand with his. "Your mother loves you, Em, whatever happened in the past. That's the most important thing. She loves you and she wants to make things right between the two of you, whatever it takes."

Her fingers were small and cool in his. She curled them into a fist under his hand but she made no effort to pull away. Instead, she smiled unexpectedly, a sudden ray of sunshine breaking through storm clouds. It started small, a slight upturn of her lips, but quickly blossomed into something radiant and transformative, as if touched by starlight.

"You are full of advice tonight, aren't you?"

"Full of something," he muttered.

He wanted to kiss her with a fierce need that made his chest ache.

What would she do if he tried it?

Probably smack him, if he knew his Emma.

Not his, Bryce reminded himself. She was her own strong, courageous, fascinating self. If he'd had a thing for her since elementary school, that was *his* problem.

CHAPTER SEVENTEEN

—

Rosie

AS MUCH AS SHE ENJOYED THESE NEIGHBORHOOD PARTIES, hosting one was such a pain in the butt. Rosie looked around her yard at the devastation two hundred people had created. She had to be grateful her turn to host only came around every few years.

Her neighbors weren't really a wild crowd. Everyone was respectful and kind and did their best to clean up after themselves. But anytime a group of people gathered together to eat and talk and enjoy a summer evening together, some level of mess was inevitable.

She was working on cleaning the area around the grill when she heard her granddaughter complain to her mother about something, in a whine Rosie couldn't make out.

Olive wasn't a big whiner. She was likely exhausted from a busy day of helping them set up for the party and an evening spent with new friends. Poor thing.

Rosie approached the two of them, who were collecting trash. "You don't need to stay and help, Emma. I've got this. Why don't you take her to bed."

Emma frowned. "That's not fair. You did all the work throwing together the party. The least I can do is help you clean it up. It's too much for one person to do alone."

Over the past decade, Rosie had become an expert at handling the world on her own. What other choice had she been given?

"I'll be fine. Take her up to bed. If I'm still at it after she's asleep—and if you have any remaining energy—you can come back down and help me. It's not necessary, though. I don't plan to do much more than straighten up the yard for now so we don't draw every raccoon in Oregon. I'll take care of the rest in the morning."

Though Emma looked as if she wanted to say more, Olive yawned. Emma sighed.

"Fine. Say good-night to your grandmother, then."

"Night, Grandma."

When Rosie bent down for a hug, Olive threw her arms around her neck. She hugged the little girl tightly, her heart full.

"What can I do to help?" As she made her way toward Rosie on her crutches, Sylvia looked almost as exhausted as Olive had.

"You can go to bed, too. Please, before you fall over. The last thing we need is another broken bone."

Sylvia sighed. "I'm sorry. I feel mighty worthless these days."

"Are you kidding? You kept the whole party going tonight. Every time I looked over, you had a crowd around you and everyone was always laughing about something."

She envied that about her mother. Sylvia could make conversation with anyone. She was always the life of the party.

"Leave the dishes for me to do in the morning," her mother said. "I can't do much but I can stand at the sink with my leg on a chair and do the washing up."

"Sure," she said, though both of them knew most of the dishes would go through the dishwasher just fine.

"Let me help you to your place," she said, setting down the bag of trash. "It's dark and I don't want you to stumble."

Her mother must be tired, Rosie thought. For once, Sylvia

did not argue, she simply started making her slow way to her cottage.

Rosie moved ahead of her, clearing from her path a few toys the children had left out.

At her mother's door, she hugged her.

"It was a lovely party," Sylvia said. "It's always fun to get together with our neighbors."

"I'm glad you had fun, Mom."

Her mother might be frustrating sometimes, stubbornly insisting on doing her own thing, whether it was wise or not. But Rosie was deeply grateful for Sylvia's constant love and support.

Her mother had upended her own life after Gary died, moving in to help however she could. Rosie would never be able to repay her, though she knew Sylvia would insist that was simply what mothers did.

That was what she wanted to do for Emma. Help her daughter in any way Emma would let her.

"Well, Dottie," she said after she was alone in the yard again. "I guess it's just you and me and the chickens."

The dog snuffled, then jumped up on one of the padded lawn chairs, where she circled a few times before settling down to watch Rosie work.

On one of her trips inside, Rosie grabbed her earbuds and set her phone to play the audiobook she had been listening to earlier in the day. She was clearing away the rest of the food containers, keeping an eye on the storm clouds that had begun to gather, when a deep male voice came out of the darkness, rising above the sound of her book.

"Do you need a hand?"

She yelped in surprise and whirled, spatula outstretched reflexively.

"Oh no. Please don't scoop me with that thing," Andrew Morgan said in an amused tone as he moved under the café lights.

He looked gorgeous, all lean and sculpted and . . . Andrew.

She set the spatula back in one of the bowls, feeling foolish, and pulled her earbuds out, returning them to the charging case in the pocket of her sweater. "You scared the life out of me."

"I'm sorry. I thought you heard me come back into the yard."

She shook her head, holding up her earbud case. "I didn't hear anything. Earbuds."

"Good music?"

"An audiobook. It's the latest from one of my favorite authors. A mystery."

"So mystery novels *are* your jam?"

She winced, reminded again of their conversation earlier in the kitchen. She was still mortified that he had overheard her talking smack about his books.

"Yes. I love just about everything. Mysteries, romance, historical fiction. Sometimes even nonfiction if it's a subject that interests me."

"Just not fantasy."

She sighed. "I still can't believe you heard that. I'm so embarrassed."

"Don't be. I'm not fragile, I promise."

"For what it's worth, I'm giving your books another try. I've downloaded a couple of them on audio."

"You don't have to do that."

"I want to, especially since my friends invited you to talk to our book club."

He shifted, looking uncomfortable in the low light. "I'm still not sure about that. It's awkward enough for me to be the new guy in town. Having to talk about my books at the same time might be excruciating."

"Don't feel obligated. The Sea Witches will understand if you can't make it." She paused. "Is that why you came back? To tell me you had changed your mind about the book club?"

"No, actually. Finn lost a LEGO minifig somewhere in your yard."

"Oh no!"

"I told him not to bring it here for the party. I warned him he would lose it if he did, but apparently he didn't listen and slipped it into his pocket anyway. And, surprise, surprise. He lost it."

"Poor kid. He must be so upset."

"He's devastated. The kids are staying at my mom's tonight, so I told him I would stop back here and see if I could find it. If not, maybe we can come back and look tomorrow. I don't have very high expectations of finding a little minifig in a big yard, but we have to try."

"Of course you do." It touched her to know he would make the effort against seemingly impossible odds.

He was a good father, she thought. For some reason, she found that even more attractive than his obvious physical appeal.

"I'll help you," she said. Yes, she had a million things to do, but wouldn't rest easy unless she did all she could to reunite a boy with a favorite toy. "I've got a couple of good flashlights inside. I'll grab them."

"You really don't have to do this."

"I know I don't. But I want to."

After grabbing the lights from the utility drawer in her mudroom, she returned outside to find him looking around the tent sandbox area.

"Where do you think he was playing most?"

"Every time I saw him, he was somewhere else in the yard. They played tag, cornhole, everything. It could be anywhere."

Her yard had never seemed so big, but they set off, both shining their flashlights on the ground. A cool breeze whispered through the trees, carrying the salty tang of the ocean and the promise of rain. Leaves rustled overhead, punctuated by the distant crash of waves against the shore. The beam of their flashlights cut through the growing darkness, dancing over the grass in erratic patterns as they searched.

The temperature had dropped noticeably, and Rosie hugged her arms around herself, chilled despite her sweater.

In the distance, clouds gathered on the horizon, their dark silhouettes barely visible against the night sky. The air felt charged with anticipation, as if the very atmosphere was holding its breath, waiting for the storm to break.

"This is a big waste of time," Andrew said, his tone apologetic. "If we don't find it, Finn will survive. He can save up to buy another set that has the same minifig. Maybe it will be a good object lesson. Listen to your dad."

She laughed. "I hope it works. I spent a long time trying to get my daughter to listen to me, to no avail."

"Finn is only seven. I'd like to think I still have a little cred with him at this age."

"What about the swing set?" she asked, after they had been looking for a while. "I believe I saw him playing there a few times. Maybe it fell out of his pocket while he was swinging."

Andrew gave her an appreciative look that made her glow. "You might be onto something there."

The two of them walked over to the swings and she aimed her flashlight beam at the area around the poles of the swing set that Gary had built for Emma when she was about eight.

At that age, she had probably been too old for a swing set and would outgrow it soon anyway but Gary hadn't cared.

Someday we can share this with our grandkids, he had said.

It made her sad to think that her late husband never had the chance to meet Olive, with her funny personality and her bossy little brain.

"I'm not seeing anything. What about you?"

Andrew scanned the area. "No, nothing." He sighed. "He has a zillion minifigs. I don't know what stands out about this one so much. I guess he loves that particular Darth Vader."

"When are they going to make LEGO sets of your characters?"

"They're talking about it," he admitted. "They made action figures and other merch after the movie came out but a LEGO set would be mind-blowing."

She could not imagine creating something that was so universally loved that it had been made into a movie—soon to be a second and a third, from what she understood—and now had the potential to be a building set.

"That is amazing. Did you ever imagine when you started writing that you might one day be in this place?"

He gave a rough laugh. "When I started writing, I couldn't even imagine ever finishing a book. I'm not sure any writers think that their words are going to resonate so strongly with readers that one day their books are going to become a franchise with a huge fandom. I wouldn't have expected that, with my weird, esoteric fantasy novels."

"I think it's wonderful. You should be so proud."

"Even though I write love scenes like I've never even met a woman?"

She groaned. "I have a feeling you're never going to let me forget that."

He chuckled, a low, rich sound in the night. She turned away with her flashlight, and as she did, she caught a glimpse of something out of place in the grass. Immediately, Rosie dropped to her knees. "I saw something. Not sure what," she said.

Andrew dropped as well. They scoured the grass as the first few raindrops began to fall.

"Is that it?" Rosie asked, caught up in the thrill of the quest.

He dug around in the grass, then pulled his hand back. A small figure rested in his palm, dwarfed by the size of his hands.

"Yes!" she exclaimed. "I'm so happy we found it. I would have hated for Finn to lose something he loved in my yard, and then forever associate us with disappointment and loss."

He rose as well, graceful and masculine. "Oh, he'll be thrilled that we found it. I don't believe he expected to see it again."

He gave her a close look. "Thank you for helping me look. I'm sure you have a million things to do. I know it's no fun cleaning up after a party."

"Not a million. Maybe half a million."

"I can help you. You helped me. It's the least I can do."

She thought of that mountain of dishes inside awaiting her. She wasn't about to let her mother balance on her crutches at the sink to take care of them.

"That would be great, actually. Would you mind helping me put the folding tables and chairs back in the garage?"

"Not at all."

After pocketing the minifig—and zipping his jacket pocket for safekeeping—he grabbed some of the folding chairs and began collapsing them, carrying two on each arm. "Where do they go?"

"Against the back wall."

"Are these all yours, or do you need to leave some out to return to neighbors?"

"All the neighbors who brought some have taken them home. The rest are mine."

He looked at the collection of chairs. "Why do you have a dozen folding chairs? Just curious."

"You never know when you need a folding chair, right? We have various meetings here sometimes for the construction company. And parties, book clubs, Thanksgiving dinner when I need a few more chairs. Every homeowner should have at least a few extra chairs."

"I don't. I don't believe I've ever owned a single folding chair."

"Because you are an established introvert. You already told me that."

He smiled, apparently unoffended by her teasing. "What else can I do?"

"I will probably save the rest inside for tomorrow."

"What else?" he pressed.

"I have a sink full of dirty dishes but I'm not sure I'm up to washing them."

"Fine. Sit down and I'll do it. I don't know you as well as I would like, Rosie, but I suspect you're not someone who usually leaves a task undone. I think you'll feel much better if we finish tonight so you don't have to face it in the morning."

What did he mean, he didn't know her as well as he would like? Did he *want* to know her better?

Either way, she could not deny he was right. She probably would have ended up washing the dishes herself and then spending all night drying and putting them away. Two hands definitely were better than one, and she was foolish to reject his help.

"Thank you. I appreciate that. We could at least start a load of dishes in the dishwasher, and then I can take care of the rest."

He nodded, and together they walked into the kitchen, with Dottie following close behind. Inside, the dog immediately went to her bed, curled up and fell asleep.

Rosie loved her kitchen, which she considered the heart of her home. During the day, soft, natural light streamed through the large window above the sink, offering a glimpse of the ocean beyond. The walls, painted a soothing seafoam green, complemented the weathered white cabinets that lined the room.

The well-loved wooden table that occupied the center of the space bore the marks of countless family meals and friendly gatherings. Mismatched chairs surrounded it, each with its own character and story. Open shelves displayed an eclectic collection of beach-themed mugs and plates, interspersed with jars of sea glass and shells collected over the years.

Of course, the kitchen she had dreamed about for Stormhaven would have been spectacular. She had envisioned soaring ceilings, natural light, perhaps a skylight, and two huge islands with storage underneath.

That dream was gone. His own plans for the kitchen were still lovely but not quite as extravagant as her own had been.

By the time they organized the dishes, loading what they could in the dishwasher and clearing out the sink, she had decided they might as well do all of them.

"Do you want to wash or dry?" she asked.

"I don't know where anything goes in your house. I'll wash, you dry."

She handed him a dishcloth, and Andrew went to work.

She was fiercely aware of him. He smelled delicious, male and clean and outdoorsy, and she wanted to lean her head against his shoulder, close her eyes and simply inhale.

"Thank you for pitching in," she said instead as she dried one of her favorite serving bowls. "You're absolutely right. I'm not very good at leaving things undone. How did you know?"

"Lucky guess," he said, his shoulder brushing against hers.

Oh, this was incredibly seductive, standing here beside him in her quiet house, even doing a mundane task like washing dishes.

"I had a minute to talk to Emma tonight about the bookstore. She's excited about making some changes," he said.

"She's really taken charge. I'm thrilled. I hope that means she and Olive will stick around longer."

"She's only here temporarily?"

She looked toward the stairs but heard nothing. No footsteps, no water running. She suspected Emma might have fallen asleep in Olive's room while reading to her. It wouldn't be the first time that had happened.

"I asked her to come back to Wood Briar to help me run the bookstore while my mom is laid up with her broken ankle. But I'm hoping Emma loves it so much, she decides to stay. It's so lovely having my daughter and granddaughter here."

"Where were they living before?"

"Las Vegas," she said.

"Oh, wow. That must have been tough on you."

She debated how to answer and finally decided there was no reason not to simply tell him the truth.

"Emma ran away right before she turned seventeen and cut off all ties with me." She looked down the hall to make sure her daughter didn't suddenly wander into the kitchen, but again heard nothing.

"We've only reestablished our relationship since Olive was born. I'm working hard to make things right with her now that she's back in town."

"*Make things right with her?* What went wrong?"

She pondered her words before she finally spoke. "Her father's death was tough on both of us. I didn't handle it well, I'm afraid. I wasn't the mother she needed me to be during that time."

She glanced at him. "You probably understand better than most people how hard it is to lose someone you loved with all your heart."

A muscle flexed in his jaw and he seemed to focus on the cookie sheet he was washing. "Yeah. It's a rough road."

"Your kids seem to be doing well, though."

"Finn had nightmares for months after Tracy died, afraid I was next. Zara kind of shut down and didn't want to talk about it at all. I had to push her into therapy so she could figure out how to process her grief and her sadness and her anger."

"I didn't insist on counseling for Emma. Nor did I go myself. I should have. Instead, I fell into a deep hole for a long time and didn't want to climb back out."

"You must have loved your husband very much."

"Our marriage wasn't perfect, but he was my best friend."

"Were he and Emma close?"

"Very. They adored each other."

"You said he died in a car accident?"

"Yes. He was taking Emma to practice her driving when the accident happened. They were driving on the cliff road. She skidded on a wet patch of road and overcorrected. The car rolled down the cliff and into the water. It's a miracle Emma survived."

"Poor girl. How traumatic for her. Was she badly hurt?"

"Broken arm, scrapes and bruises. And, of course, she blamed herself for the accident, even though it could have happened to anyone."

"Rough."

"She needed me to assure her I didn't blame her for what happened. Instead, the two of us seemed to drift farther and farther apart. I wasn't there for her. I'm not sure she will ever be able to forgive me for that."

"Sounds to me like you need to forgive yourself first."

His words seemed to punch her right in the throat. "That's a big ask," she said, her voice gruff.

"You were doing your best at the time. Everyone processes grief differently. That's one lesson I've learned since my wife died. Also, grief is not a straight line. It's more like . . . the ocean out there. Some days, it's calm and you feel you can breathe again. Other days, it swells and crashes, threatening to pull you under. But even in its stormiest of times, you have to remember that the tide always recedes and in time learn to navigate its ebbs and flows."

He cleared his throat, looking embarrassed at his own eloquence. "Or so I've heard. I'm still waiting for those calm seas."

She pondered his words as they finished with the dishes, even as they talked about other inconsequential things. She almost didn't want to be done but finally they washed and put away the final dish and he drained the soapy water from the sink.

"I should go," he said.

Was that a similar reluctance she heard in his voice?

She didn't allow herself to wonder long. Surely she was mistaken. Instead, she walked outside with him.

"I can't thank you enough for helping me."

"My pleasure. It's the least I can do after you rescued Darth Vader from a potentially horrible fate."

Why was she so darned attracted to him? This was definitely going to be awkward, especially since she would have to work with him over the next few months as they tried to finish work on his house.

The night air was cool and fragrant with the scent of ocean and flowers and rain. Andrew stood close, his presence both comforting and electrifying. Rosie looked up, meeting his gaze, and felt the world around them fade away. The intensity in his eyes made her breath catch, and she found herself drawn to him like a magnet.

Andrew's eyes dropped to her lips, and Rosie felt a thrill of anticipation course through her. Without conscious thought, she swayed toward him, closing the small distance between them. Time seemed to slow as Andrew leaned down, his intention clear.

When his lips finally met hers, it was as if a spark had ignited. The kiss started soft, almost tentative, but quickly deepened. Rosie's hands found their way to his chest, feeling the solid warmth beneath his shirt. Andrew's arms encircled her waist, pulling her closer.

The kiss was everything Rosie had forgotten she needed. It was passionate and tender, awakening sensations she'd thought long dormant. She lost herself in the feeling of his mouth on hers, the gentle pressure of his hands on her back, the solid strength of his body against hers.

As the kiss intensified, Rosie felt a warmth bloom in her core, spreading outward until she felt flushed from head to toe. It had been so long since she'd felt this alive, this desired. She melted into Andrew's embrace, savoring every sensation, every gentle caress of his tongue against hers.

When they finally parted, both breathing heavily, Rosie felt dizzy with desire. She looked up at Andrew, seeing her own hunger reflected in his eyes. For a moment, they simply stood there, wrapped in each other's arms, the weight of what had just happened settling over them like a warm blanket.

CHAPTER EIGHTEEN

—

Andrew

WHEN HE DECIDED TO MAKE A MISTAKE, HE NEVER DID ANYthing by half measures.

Even as he kissed her, Andrew knew he would regret this. Rosie was the contractor he was going to have to work with on the house renovation for the next few months. Now he had made everything extremely awkward by throwing in a spontaneous, unprovoked kiss that would definitely tangle their relationship.

Even as he thought the words with one part of his brain, the rest of him was consumed with the taste of her. She was small and soft in his arms, her mouth tasting of mint and sugar cookies. The kiss was intoxicating, awakening a hunger in him he'd long forgotten. Her lips were pliant against his, moving with a passion that matched his own.

Andrew found himself lost in the sensation, his body responding with an intensity that both thrilled and terrified him.

He pulled her closer, one hand sliding up to tangle in her hair, the other pressing against the small of her back. Every curve of her body fit perfectly against his.

The world around them faded away, leaving only the sound of their ragged breathing and the pounding of his heart. He deepened the kiss, savoring the small gasp that escaped her. A primal part of him wanted to sweep her off her feet, to carry her inside and explore every inch of her. The desire coursed through his veins like liquid fire, consuming all rational thought.

Time seemed to stand still, and yet it wasn't enough. Andrew knew he should stop, that he should pull away before things went too far. But he couldn't bring himself to end it. Not yet. He wanted to memorize every detail. The softness of her lips, the warmth of her skin, the way she melted against him.

The rumble of distant thunder made her body jerk and sent reality crashing into him like a rogue wave.

She eased away to gaze at him through the darkness, eyes wide and her breathing ragged.

He drew in a breath, fumbling for a way to explain his actions.

"I'm sorry, Rosie," he finally said. "I'm not exactly sure where that came from."

Had he ever felt quite so awkward and socially inept? Even at the Academy Awards ceremony, he had been more at ease—and that entire experience had been far outside his comfort zone.

He was fairly certain none of the characters he wrote would actually apologize for kissing a woman they were attracted to. They would simply go for it and damn the consequences.

In his experience, real life was a great deal more complicated than fiction.

Unfortunately.

She released a shaky breath. "I think we *both* were not expecting that."

"I hope you don't think I'm the kind of guy who goes around randomly kissing the people who work for him."

Oh Lord. He was making this worse.

She blinked, her gaze fixed on his. He couldn't read her expression. Was she annoyed? Offended? Disgusted?

"I don't."

He wanted to slip out of her yard and rush home as fast as he could but he couldn't just kiss and run, as it were.

He sighed. "I'm attracted to you, Rosie. I don't see any point in trying to pretend I'm not. You're a lovely woman and you've been everything kind to me and my children."

Except for that unfortunate moment in the bookstore when she didn't know he was eavesdropping, but this wasn't the time to mention that.

"I'm attracted to you. More importantly, I like you. Very much."

Her cheeks turned pink and she looked both surprised and flattered by his words. "I like you, too," she said. "And I'm obviously attracted to you as well. I don't go around kissing every guy who helps me clean up after a party."

"Good to know." Some of his discomfort seemed to ease, replaced by amusement. She seemed as unnerved by their kiss as he was.

"But we have to work together for the next few months, especially since you've taken over as project manager for Stormhaven. I shouldn't have kissed you. It was . . . inappropriate."

"Inappropriate," she repeated slowly.

"I would hate for things to be awkward between us now. Could we backtrack a bit and pretend that kiss never happened?"

She said nothing for several beats, as if trying to gather her thoughts. Finally she nodded. "Yes. You're right. A hard rewind would be better all around."

Perversely, hearing her agree with him made him rethink the suggestion. He didn't want her to forget the kiss. He knew he certainly wouldn't.

"I should probably take off."

"Right," she said again. "Thank you again for helping me clean up. It was very . . . neighborly of you."

He didn't want to be neighborly with her. Nor did he want a business relationship. He wanted to go on kissing her here on her porch steps while the ocean murmured below them.

"Will this make things weird between us?"

"Not if we don't let it," she answered in that matter-of-fact voice he was beginning to recognize as sheer determination.

"Right."

"I plan to spend the rest of the weekend going over the Stormhaven project and reaching out to all your subcontractors to check their status. I will try to do everything I can to fast-track the project for you."

Not only did he want to be done with the renovation for his and his children's sake, now he wanted it to be done so that he might have the chance of kissing her again.

"Sounds good," he said. "Have a good evening."

"Same to you."

As he trotted down her steps, the rain misted in his hair and pearled on his exposed skin. Andrew didn't mind. He welcomed the cooling effect as he walked the short distance between her house and Stormhaven.

When was the last time he had reacted so instantly to a woman?

He certainly hadn't to Willow Voss, despite the media firestorm that had erupted after they went out a few times.

He'd liked Willow but she had mostly been interested in picking his brain about her character and the direction he intended to take it in the remainder of the series.

He suspected she had also loved the publicity they invariably generated when they were seen in public together.

Sighing, Andrew ran a hand through his hair, trying to clear his thoughts. As much as he wanted to pursue this connection with Rosie, he knew the timing wasn't right. His life was in flux, with the house renovations still ongoing and his career at a critical juncture. Maybe when his house was finished and his life more settled, he would be ready to explore a relationship with her.

For now, though, he had to put any romantic notions about Rosie out of his, which might be a more Herculean task than anything he threw at his characters.

CHAPTER NINETEEN

—

Emma

EMMA LOOKED OUT AT THE GRAY DAY THROUGH THE WINdow of the bookstore where rain pattered relentlessly down the glass.

She had seen the same view for the past ten days. Rain, rain, and more rain. So far, The Rainy Day Bookshop was definitely living up to its name, but unfortunately the rain still wasn't bringing in the customers.

She looked around at the mostly empty bookstore, actually missing the hectic days at her Las Vegas coffee shop when she would hit the ground running at 6:00 a.m. and not stop to catch her breath until her shift was over, sometimes twelve hours later.

The slow pace at the bookstore was frustrating, especially when she had so many great ideas, none of which had yet come to fruition.

She needed to be patient with herself. She knew by experience that change did not happen overnight. It took long, hard, concentrated effort to make a lasting difference. She couldn't expect the bookstore would suddenly become a thriving hub of community activity with only a bit of effort and time.

"I've put away the books that we ordered and shelved all the returns," Maya Thompson said. "Is there anything else I can do?"

"No, thank you. You've been great." She really did like the employees her grandmother had hired. They were all hardworking, earnest and loved books. She couldn't ask for more from her staff.

"If you want to go home for the day, I can handle the last hour before we close. I don't expect we'll have a sudden mad rush of people."

"We can always hope."

Emma felt as if she'd been doing nothing but hoping since she came to town. Hoping she had made the right choice, hoping she could figure out what she was doing, hoping she did not let her mother down.

"I'll see you tomorrow, then," Maya said. She grabbed her book bag, slung it over her shoulder and headed out to where her bike was secured in the rack out back.

The poor thing was in for a very wet ride home. At least she didn't have to go far. Emma knew Maya lived only a few blocks away from the bookstore, in the apartment she rented with three friends.

Though she was only four years older than her employee, Emma felt ancient in comparison. A single mom with years of bad choices behind her.

Had she ever been that young and carefree?

After Maya left, the store seemed abnormally quiet, especially without what had seemed like the ever-present sounds of construction from the expansion and renovation project.

Bryce hadn't been working at the bookstore for several days but Emma refused to acknowledge her bad mood might have anything to do with his absence—or that she might be coming to rely on seeing him to lift her day.

Emma would have thought a rainy day would bring more browsers in to peruse the shelves, something to distract them.

What was cozier than a bookstore during the frequent rainstorms that hit this part of the Pacific Northwest?

Unfortunately, their customers didn't agree. At least not tonight.

She was dusting off the new and improved bookshelves that Bryce had installed only two days earlier when she heard the chimes ring out front.

She gave her polite smile of greeting but when she raised her head, Emma could almost feel her facial muscles freeze.

Pam Clarke walked in, looking trim, pert and energetic.

Emma wanted to punch her right in the face.

She was extremely tempted to tell the woman she was not welcome in the bookshop. The words seemed to swell up in her throat but Emma forced herself to swallow them down again.

As much as she wanted to take the higher ground, business was business. She forced her features into what she hoped looked moderately polite.

"Hello, Pam," she said.

"Oh, it's so good to see you, Emma. You look fantastic. I wanted to have a chance to talk to you the other night when I stopped by before your neighborhood party but you disappeared."

"I was busy helping my mom get ready for the party."

And avoiding you at all costs.

"Well, it's great to see you! You look fantastic. Love the ink!"

"Thanks."

She fought the urge to hide the tattoo she had designed to remember her dad, a heart entwined with a crescent moon and the words *To the moon and back.*

"How are you, dear?"

"I'm good. Busy."

If she hoped Pam would take the hint, she was doomed to

disappointment. "It can't be easy to try to make something of a small-town bookstore in this day and age. It's so much more convenient to buy things online, don't you agree?"

"Maybe. But convenience doesn't keep a bookstore going in a small community."

She didn't bother telling Pam all the reasons The Rainy Day Bookshop was important to the community. About how it served as a community hub and offered locally curated books people couldn't find easily elsewhere. About how a good bookstore could provide a gateway to reading to community members. About how she wanted to foster creativity and connection here.

"Is there something I can help you find?" she asked instead.

"Just browsing, really. I'm looking for a gift to take to a friend who just had surgery."

"Books are the perfect present. I'll leave you to it," she said.

"Thanks," Pam answered. When Emma returned to her work, she saw the other woman perusing the shelves as if trying to memorize each title.

For the next twenty minutes, Emma was painfully aware of the presence of the other woman. A few other customers came in: a couple of tourists looking for a guidebook about the town, a young girl seeking the latest in a series of fantasy novels she was reading, a teenager looking for manga.

More customers came in during that final twenty minutes before the store closed than she'd seen in the past hour.

Through it all, Pam seemed to be browsing the shelves, book by book.

Just go, already, Emma thought as she checked out the manga titles for the teenager. She'd never been so eager for a customer to get out of the store as she was for Pam to leave.

She had hoped she could avoid further conversation with

the woman but by the time Pam finally approached the check-out counter, all the other customers had left and they were the only two people in the store.

"Found something?"

"Yes. I think she'll love it," Pam said, setting a Mediterranean diet book on the counter.

Emma had thoughts about the wisdom of giving a cookbook to someone who was feeling under the weather, but she chose to keep them to herself. She didn't know the recipient nor the circumstances. Maybe a diet cookbook was the exact right gift to lift the spirits of this person who was having a rough time.

After ringing up the sale, she held out the small machine for Pam to swipe her own credit card. When the transaction was done, Emma handed the book and the receipt to the woman. "Would you like a bag?"

"Do you offer gift wrap?" Pam asked.

Emma wanted to say, *Hell to the no. Not for you.* But there was a stylized sign behind her that clearly indicated The Rainy Day Bookshop offered free gift wrapping.

Suppressing her frustration, she pulled out the long box containing their three styles of gift wrap available, two book-focused prints and one silvery generic style.

"Which one would you like?" she asked.

Pam pursed her lips and studied the gift wraps before she pointed to the generic silver one.

Emma had never wrapped a gift so quickly, nor had she ever been as relieved to tie the final ribbon.

"Here you go," she said, giving a tight smile that felt like it was going to freeze off of her face as she handed the gift-wrapped cookbook to the other woman.

Pam took the book, eyeing Emma carefully.

"Have I done something to make you mad?" she asked.

Oh yes. Plenty of things that she did not want to get into right now.

"Why would you ask that?" she asked instead.

"You seem so short with me. We used to be buds. I miss those days."

"We weren't ever buds. Not really. I was a child and you were an employee of my parents."

She sounded ridiculously rude, but she couldn't seem to shove the words back in.

Pam looked hurt but she nodded. "I remember those days with fondness, when you used to come into the office and tell me about your friends and the boy you liked and your latest book obsession."

"That was a long time ago." Before, when Emma had been young and innocent and stupid.

"I suppose it was. Well, I'm glad you're back. Your mom has been terribly worried about you over the years. She missed you so much. It's great to have you back in town."

"Thanks," she said, through lips that felt numb. Emma didn't bother telling Pam that *she* was one of the reasons Emma had stayed away so long.

"I'm about to close the store," she said when Pam made no move to leave. "You're my last customer of the evening."

Before Pam could answer, the bells on the door chimed.

She felt a rush of relief and something deeper when she saw Bryce come in, pulling the hood back on his raincoat and shaking drops off on the mat.

His expression brightened when he saw Pam.

"Hey there, Pam, how are you?"

"Fantastic," the other woman said, beaming back at him.

Emma ground her teeth, fighting the urge to pull Pam away

and shove her out the door. She didn't want her anywhere near Bryce, which Emma knew was a completely irrational reaction.

The two of them worked together at Lucas Construction. Of course they would be friendly. Her parents had always fostered community and connection, treating their coworkers more like family than employees.

"How's your mom?" Pam asked, her features the very picture of concern.

"About the same," he answered. "She's back at her care center, where she's already started physical therapy for her hip."

"And how did things go with the Pine Beach project today? You're nearly done, aren't you?"

"On the home stretch. They're supposed to close on Monday."

The two of them worked together daily. They were part of a club where she didn't belong. As she listened to them talk about the ins and outs of things at Lucas Construction, things she would have known had she been working there since high school, Emma could feel the tension seething beneath her skin.

If she needed any kind of reminder about her own mistakes, this was it. She and her dad had always talked about working together some day. Even after his death, she could have been helping her mom run the company if she had not made the choices she had.

What was done was done. She could not change the past or the decisions she had made. That didn't stop her from resenting a woman she held responsible for so much of her pain.

"I better take off," Pam said after looking at her watch. "I'm already late. I told my friend I would stop by to see her a half hour ago."

"I'll see you later," Bryce said.

"I love what you've already done to the place," Pam said. "I can't wait to see the rest. I'm sure it will all be fabulous when you're finished. Everything you touch ends up so much better."

"Thanks," Bryce said, clearly pleased.

Emma again fought the urge to punch Pam in the face. And Bryce, too, while she was at it. He *was* doing a great job here but Emma had certainly helped. She had come up with most of the ideas and she was spending plenty of her free time after hours helping where she could.

After Pam *finally* left, Emma went to the front door and turned the sign to Closed, then locked it. If she used a little more force than usual, who could blame her?

When she was certain Pam couldn't somehow sneak back in, she finally turned to Bryce. "I wasn't sure if I would see you here today."

"I did say I would be here when I was done at the other project, I just wasn't sure what time."

"I know, but I also know how much work you're doing to wrap things up over there."

She had enjoyed discussing the other jobs on his schedule while they were working together on the renovation here. Bryce was obviously passionate about his work and she loved hearing his enthusiasm when he described it.

Okay, she loved any moment she could spend with him.

She was developing a serious crush on Bryce Kendall and she didn't know what she was going to do about it.

"I do have other projects with unavoidable deadlines but The Rainy Day Bookshop is still my priority. I want to help you get this done so we can open the café before the summer's over."

"So *we* can open the café?" she asked shortly.

"So *you* can," he amended. He gave her a careful look. "Is everything okay? You seem upset at something."

She was tempted to tell him everything. She even opened her mouth, then closed it again. She couldn't. She wouldn't betray the secrets she had kept for all these years.

"It's the rain," she said instead. It wasn't a lie, just not the entire truth. "I don't like rainy days. I haven't, since . . . well. Since I was a teenager."

His features softened with compassion, and she knew he was also thinking of her father. He must know, after working with her mother for so long, that rain had played a factor in the accident that had taken Gary's life.

He could not know the rest of it. No one did. Not even her mother.

Emma was the only one who knew that she and her father had been fighting, that she had been furious with Gary, so angry that she hadn't paid attention when he warned her the roadway could be slick.

She hadn't been speeding, but she also hadn't been as careful as she should have been, too busy telling her father off. As the vehicle lost purchase, she had forgotten all the things she'd learned about steering into a skid.

"I'm sorry," he said.

"It's one of the reasons I moved to Vegas. Desert. Heat. Not much rain."

"You couldn't pick two more different climates."

She had come to love the area around Las Vegas while she lived there. She had grown to appreciate the vastness of the desert, punctuated by spindly Joshua trees, and the fascinating red rock formations of the state parks outside of town.

Still, the coastal rainforests and remote beaches around Wood Briar would always be home.

Bryce eased out of his jacket. "I, for one, love the rain. I guess I have to, if I live on the Oregon coast."

"Why?" she asked.

He paused, brow furrowed as he gave her single-word question serious thought. She admired that about him, how he never answered quickly or glibly.

"So many reasons. What's better than watching the storm clouds come in over the water, that dramatic sense of anticipation as you wait for them to unleash?"

She had always loved that as well. She could remember when she was a girl sitting in her bedroom and watching the water turn dark and clouds gather. It was the perfect weather for curling up in the window seat of her bedroom and watching the storms while she immersed herself in her latest read.

She wanted to reclaim that cozy mood here in the bookstore. That was her goal, making the shop a warm, welcome haven against an outside world that could sometimes feel dark and lonely.

"What's your plan for tonight?" she asked

"I need to keep working on pulling off the old lath and plaster to return the wall to its original brick. Another few days and I should be done."

"I can help. Let me know what you need me to do."

He looked surprised at her offer. "I'm fine by myself, if you need to get back to Olive."

She shook her head. "It's fine. She and I spent all day together, since I didn't come in until a few hours ago. I had planned to work on organizing a few things but I can do that another day."

"Is Olive with your mom tonight?"

"Mom and Sylvia. They can't seem to get enough of her and Olive has them both wrapped around her finger."

"Not at all surprised. She's quite a charmer."

"Too much. She already thinks she runs the world, living with three women who all adore her."

"If Olive truly did run the world, we would all be much better off."

"Don't tell her that. You'll give her more ideas. Now, how can I help you?"

While the rain pattered outside, they worked together in sections, with him pulling away the drywall and her coming in after him to clean off any residue with a wire brush.

The bricks beneath were a weathered rose, like the faded petals of a long-forgotten Valentine's bouquet. They would look fantastic under the track lighting Bryce planned to install, especially behind the open-backed shelving they had already agreed on for this wall.

"This is looking so good. You were exactly right when you insisted we should use the original bricks in the design."

"It takes more work than if we simply repainted the drywall but the results will be worth it."

"I wish we could close the whole bookstore for a month, clear everything out and then remodel from the ground up. It would be so much easier."

"Doing the work mostly after hours is definitely more complicated, but at least you can continue to stay open during the remodel."

"For all the good that's doing us."

"Business has been slow?"

She grimaced. "Painfully. You would think a rainy day would bring more traffic in, since tourists usually don't want to spend time on the beach in this weather. But I think they've either left town altogether, are staying in their hotel rooms, or have driven up to Newport or Lincoln City."

"It does seem quiet everywhere in town right now. Don't worry. They'll be back."

"I hope so."

She continued the work, wishing she could brush away her own unsettled mood as easily as she brushed away the residue of years from the walls.

CHAPTER TWENTY

—

Bryce

SHE WAS THE MOST COMPLICATED WOMAN.

As he worked together with Emma in the quiet space while rain pattered outside, Bryce felt an inexorable pull toward her, the same one he had been fighting since they were kids.

Emma had always been so pretty and together when they were kids. Her hair had always been curled, her clothes neat and clean, her locker and backpack organized, without a paper out of place.

He remembered sitting near her in the lunchroom a few times and marveling that her packed lunches always seemed crammed with healthy, delicious food. Fresh apples, cut into slices that somehow magically never browned. Sandwiches on whole wheat bread, with the crusts cut off. Sometimes even vegetable soup on rainy cold days.

Bryce had free school lunch, of course. His mom always made him turn in the paperwork the first day of school. He wore clothes picked up at yard sales or Goodwill and his mom always cut his hair.

He considered himself fortunate if she decided to do it on a good day, when her hands were steady.

His life had always seemed far different from Emma's and he had envied her as much as he yearned for her, even before he knew what yearning meant.

While she had invariably been kind to him, she hadn't paid him any more or less attention than anyone else at school.

He could still remember when he learned about her accident, the fear when he found out she had been injured and the sadness when he found out her father had died. He had taken her flowers in the hospital but had left them at the nurses' station without leaving a note.

She had missed two or three weeks of school. When she returned, she had seemed a pale, subdued version of herself for the rest of the school year.

By the time summer ended and the new school year started a few months later, she seemed to have undergone a complete transformation. She was hard, angry, sporting several new piercings, a tattoo and an attitude to go with them.

Her friends seemed to have changed, too. She hung out with the hard-drinking party crowd and he heard through the grapevine she was dating a much older guy.

As he worked off a particularly stubborn section of drywall, he frowned at the memory of her odd reaction to Pam earlier. The air in the bookstore had been as cold as trying to surf the Pacific in January.

Emma definitely didn't like the Lucas Construction office manager. What was that all about? Why would she have so much animosity toward Pam?

He was friendly with Pam. They had worked together for years and he considered her hardworking and dependable. When he needed any kind of paperwork for a job, she was always quick to prepare it for him. He knew Rosie relied on her extensively.

Still, he had to admit Pam was not his favorite coworker. He had seen her be vindictive to subcontractors who encountered unavoidable difficulties and she liked to carry tales to Rosie that showed other coworkers in unflattering light.

He had also wondered at times whether she might not be

too close with a few of their competitors. He had seen her around town several times having lunch with Vic Blackwood, who had once been the acting head of Lucas Construction after Gary Lucas died, but who had left the company under a cloud a few years later.

Rosie didn't talk about it, but he suspected Vic had run Lucas Construction into the ground. Around the time he left, Rosie sold Stormhaven and turned the running of the bookstore to her mother so that she could take the helm of the construction company.

Now, several years later, Blackwood seemed to be thriving. Vic's company often competed with Lucas on bids and frequently undercut them, turning in completely unreasonable bids that resulted in substantial overruns. To see Pam around town being so friendly with the man seemed disloyal somehow.

Regardless of his concerns, he had avoided bringing them up to Rosie. How could he complain about Pam telling tales on coworkers when he was tempted to do the same thing?

Why didn't Emma like Pam?

He couldn't figure out any good way to ask her as they continued to work, mostly in a comfortable silence interspersed occasionally with questions about the renovation.

They had nearly finished the wall when he noticed Emma stretching her back and shaking out her arm muscles.

"We've made good progress tonight. More than I expected on my own. I'm good with what we've done."

"We only need another hour before we finish, don't we? Let's keep going."

He frowned. "You can't work at the bookstore all day and then stay until midnight helping me."

"I told you I didn't come in until four. You've worked a

longer day than I have. I know you've been putting in a full day at other jobs before coming here."

"That's different."

"How?"

He tried to think of an answer. "Because I'm used to it."

"This is my project," she said. "I'm invested in the renovation and I want to be part of every step. Or at least as much as I can."

He had to admire her grit. He expected that grit had carried her through some pretty dark times.

Together they worked to clean up the construction mess they had made, carrying the debris out to the large dumpster he had placed in the rear parking lot.

The rain had stopped for now and a few stars peeked out from behind the clouds. The air was cool, fresh, smelling of the sea and the night.

"Guess who came into the store yesterday?" she asked when they returned to the bookstore for one more load.

"Who?"

"Bailey Hunter. She looks exactly the same as she did in school."

Bailey had been their class valedictorian, crazy smart but never annoying about it. She was now an attorney in town, one he would definitely use if he were ever in trouble.

"Except she's now Bailey Lattimore," he said. "She married Jamie Lattimore a few years ago."

"Did she? I had no idea. She didn't mention it." She paused. "Are you and I the only two unattached people left in our graduating class?"

"Not even close. There are plenty of us. It only seems like it sometimes. I think those who stuck around town seemed to have paired up and settled down at a higher rate than those who left."

"*You* stuck around. Why haven't you settled down yet?"

He didn't have a good answer for her. Not really. He had dated a bit and even had a couple of serious relationships, but nothing ever quite felt right. Beyond that, his mom and her health issues sometimes seemed all-consuming. Between work and dealing with her on his own, he didn't have a lot of emotional bandwidth left to pour into a relationship.

He decided to give her the simplest explanation. "The usual reasons, I guess. I've never found the right person."

"Maybe because you work eighteen hours every day? Where would you fit in a relationship?"

"I don't keep that schedule all the time. Only when I'm in the middle of a project."

"Which I suspect is all the time."

She was not precisely wrong. He worked too hard, probably because he was always aware of a compelling need to prove himself. He never felt quite good enough, which he didn't doubt he could trace back to school years, when he had struggled so hard academically.

"What about you? If Olive's father hasn't been in the picture since before she was born, surely you must have dated during the intervening years."

"Not really. Nothing serious, anyway. I was too busy going to school, working and caring for her."

"I'm in awe you were able to juggle all of that. You're amazing, Emma. I've always known it."

She gazed at him, eyes filled with an expression he couldn't read. "I wish that were true. All I can see are my mistakes. All the chances I wasted."

"Your mistakes don't define you. They're part of your journey. Every challenge you have overcome, every struggle you have faced. They've all shaped you into the incredible woman you are today. Your strength, your resilience, your compassion. Those are what truly matter."

As he spoke, something shifted in the air between them. Emma's gaze softened, a mix of vulnerability in her eyes . . . and something else. Something that made his heart race. Before he could second-guess himself, question what the hell he was doing, he leaned in, unable to resist for another instant this woman who had fascinated him since he was a punk kid.

Their lips met, and it was everything he had dreamed of for years. She was soft and yielding against him, her lips tasting faintly of cherry lip balm. He felt her tremble slightly in his arms, and he pulled her closer, wanting to protect and cherish her always.

The world around them seemed to fade away, leaving only the two of them in this perfect moment he had longed for as long as he could remember.

At first, the kiss was gentle. He cupped her face with one hand, his thumb caressing her cheek as he savored the feeling of finally, *finally* being able to taste her, touch her. When she didn't pull away, he deepened the kiss, pouring years of longing into their embrace.

He felt her tremble slightly in his arms, and he pulled her closer, wanting to protect and cherish her always. Her hands came up to rest on his chest, and he could feel the warmth of her touch through his shirt. It sent a shiver down his spine, igniting a fire within him that threatened to consume them both.

As the kiss continued, he marveled at how perfectly they fit together. It was as if all the years between them had been leading to this. The taste of her, the familiar vanilla scent of her shampoo, the softness of her skin beneath his fingertips.

Every sensation was seared into his memory, a treasure he would hold on to forever.

Just when he thought the sheer wonder might overwhelm him, Emma broke the kiss, gasping for air.

"Whoa. Whoa. *Whoa!*"

He would have stopped at the first *whoa.* He eased away, his heart pounding, hoping desperately that he hadn't ruined this tentative friendship they had been building since she returned. Or any chance he had of something more.

Had he misread the signals? Moved too fast?

She looked as astonished as if he had suddenly sprouted wings and taken flight right out of the bookstore. Her eyes were wide, lips slightly parted, a flush creeping up her cheeks. He had never seen anything more beautiful.

He held his breath, waiting for her reaction, terrified he'd crossed a line they couldn't come back from.

"What was that?"

"I thought it was a kiss. A pretty great one, from my perspective."

She looked dazed and aroused but he could see the softness beginning to give way to a kind of stunned annoyance.

"What the hell, Bryce. We're friends. Why did you have to ruin everything by throwing sexy times into the mix?"

That kiss wasn't even *close* to the kind of sexy times he wanted with her. Bryce took a ragged breath, his body hard and aroused.

"It was only a kiss. It's not like we banged in the middle of the self-help section."

Though he couldn't help thinking he would have liked to do exactly that.

"Why? Just . . . why?"

He had to give her some kind of answer. His mind raced

through a half-dozen excuses but he finally decided on the truth.

"Because I've wanted to do that since you came back to town."

From the instant he first walked into the bookstore and found her, with her purple-tipped hair and her gorgeous tattoos and all that attitude, he had wanted *all* of her, with a fierce, ever-present ache.

She glared at him. "Shut up. You have not."

"Why does that seem so unbelievable to you?"

"Because I'm completely not your type."

"Says who?"

"Me. That's who." Her eyes grew shadowed and she moved away from him, much to his deep regret.

"If you kissed me as some kind of sick joke, I'm not laughing."

Would he ever be able to get away from his own past, when he had become the class clown to mask his own vast insecurities. He had spent all of his school years trying to make everyone laugh. Especially Emma Lucas.

"Do I look like I find any of this funny?" he asked, his voice low.

She studied him and he couldn't help wondering what she saw when she looked at him now.

Finally she looked away. "Whatever the reason, don't do it again. I'm not . . . I don't have time for this. *We* don't have time for this. We have to work together for the time being, until this project is renovated. This kind of . . . unnecessary distraction won't accomplish anything."

He could think of several things that kissing Emma might accomplish. Maybe he could finally get her out of his head, after all this time.

Somehow he doubted it, though.

"Don't kiss me again," she repeated, as if he didn't understand her the first time.

He felt his jaw tighten at her order. "Got it."

He turned and went back to work, the thing he was best at. They were both silent as they cleared out the rest of the debris. Only after they were both outside again, lights turned off, door locked and alarm set, did she finally speak.

"It was a great kiss, Bryce," she finally said, avoiding his gaze. "I don't want you to think I didn't enjoy it."

Was she trying to protect his feelings? Somehow that touched him almost as much as that kiss had. He wanted to kiss her again. She had expressly asked him not to, though, which frustrated the hell out of him.

"Good to know," he finally answered.

"And, okay, under other circumstances, I might be tempted to . . . you know."

Yeah. He knew entirely too well.

"We can't," she went on before he could answer. "You and I are not right for each other.

"Emma, you don't have to explain yourself. You don't want me to kiss you. I won't kiss you."

"It's not that I don't want you to. I do. We just . . . can't right now. Too much is at stake for me."

Was she trying so hard to prove something to her mother or to herself?

"Whatever your reasons, I understand. I won't kiss you again."

"It sucks that you're so decent."

The disgruntlement in her voice almost made him laugh. "I'm . . . sorry?"

"You should be. You would be much easier to resist if you

were the same person I thought you were in high school. Fun-loving, troublemaking Bryce. You're not. You're much more than that." She paused. "I can't afford any more mistakes and somehow, I suspect you would be a big one."

He didn't know whether to be flattered or hurt by that. He sighed. Did it matter? The last thing he wanted to do was make her life more complicated.

"Point taken. Let's forget it ever happened and move on to take care of the renovation."

How long had he been focused on the job at hand? he wondered after he climbed into his pickup and headed toward home. Probably since his dad left when he was ten.

He felt like he had been looking after his mom forever. In the old days, he had taken a job after school to pay some of the bills, had cleaned her up after she would come home drunk, would go grocery shopping with whatever spare change he could scrounge up.

Then, when he finally felt more stable, and she seemed to slow down her drinking and drug use, if not stopped it completely, the early signs of dementia had begun to show. It had been easy to put them down at first as general forgetfulness, a side effect from her years of hard living. But then, about four years ago, she had nearly burned down the house because she had forgotten to turn off the oven, then claimed she hadn't been the one to turn it on.

A week later, she had been given a nuisance citation for yelling obscenities at a couple of very young neighbor kids for simply riding their bikes down the sidewalk. Police had urged a mental health evaluation and the diagnosis of a rare form of early onset dementia had been shocking and heartbreaking.

The reminder of his mother did more than any of Emma's words to him why kissing her had been a mistake.

She was right, as much as he didn't want to admit it. Neither of them was in a good place for a relationship.

Right now, he needed to focus simply on his job, on making sure he did his best work possible on the bookstore renovation to give Emma the chance she desperately needed to succeed.

CHAPTER TWENTY-ONE

—

Emma

"DO YOU WANT SOME SCRAMBLED EGGS WITH YOUR CREPES?" Emma asked her grandmother.

Sylvia sat again in Rosie's kitchen, almost in an exact replay of the scene the day after she arrived.

This time, though, Emma hadn't overslept, mostly because she hadn't slept much at all. She had awakened with the sunrise, before anyone else, and sat for a long time on the porch, sipping her coffee and watching the Pacific.

When she heard everyone else moving around inside, she had offered to make breakfast and had decided on her favorite crepes, along with strawberries from her mom's garden.

"No eggs for me this morning. Crepes and that fake sausage you made is more than enough," Sylvia assured her.

"Can I have a strawberry, Mama?" Olive asked.

"You can have a few strawberries with your breakfast," she told her, ladling another crepe out of the omelet pan to add to the growing stack.

"Okay," Olive said cheerfully, returning with a furrowed brow of concentration to the important task of slicing the strawberries with the child-friendly knife Emma had provided.

Her daughter loved helping in the kitchen and Emma loved teaching her the basics of cooking healthy, nutritious meals.

"Do I really get to spend all day with you today?" Olive asked.

"All day," Emma said brightly. She had decided to take the entire day off on this beautiful Sunday. As much work as she had to do at the bookstore, she couldn't spend seven days a week there. It wasn't healthy.

Besides, it would give her a good excuse to avoid Bryce, whom she hadn't been able to get out of her head since their kiss a few days earlier.

She had good employees who were perfectly capable of handling the bookstore for a day. At her mother's urging, Emma and Olive were going to take a hike to a favorite secluded beach, where they could build sandcastles, go beachcombing and otherwise enjoy a beautiful sunny day.

Olive couldn't be more excited if Emma had told her they were going to Disney World. Another thing she adored about her daughter was Olive's sheer joy at simple pleasures. It was a good lesson for her. Life didn't need to be nearly as complicated as she tended to make it.

After finishing one more crepe, she carried the stack to the table, where her mother and grandmother were chatting.

"What's on your agenda today, Mom?" Emma asked. She wouldn't have minded her mother's company on her and Olive's excursion but couldn't bring herself to issue the invitation.

She needed time alone with her daughter. Besides, she didn't want Rosie to feel like every spare second had to be spent with her and Olive

"I need to work in the garden," her mother said. "With all the rain we've had, I'm afraid I've been neglecting it. The weeds are taking over again."

For the past two days, they'd had beautiful sunshine. The tourists were out in force and through the kitchen window she could see kites already in the air, even though the bigger winds wouldn't come up until late afternoon.

"Do you need some help? We don't have to go on a hike today. We could stay here and help you instead."

Rosie shook her head. "Don't be silly. Today is a lovely day to hike down to Hidden Beach. You've been working far too hard. You need to stop and breathe and enjoy our beautiful surroundings."

"We could help you for a few hours this morning and then all go to the beach this afternoon," she said.

"Oh, that would be lovely. I can't today, though. I really do need to catch up on the garden and also some work. Oh, and Pam is coming by later to drop off a book she wanted me to read."

Emma froze. It had taken all she had to be civil to her a few days earlier. She wasn't sure how much longer she could keep up the pretense.

"What time will she be here?" she asked carefully. She would make sure she and her daughter were far away by then.

Sylvia, she saw, had sent her a quick look. Her grandmother was the only person Emma had ever confided in. Even her grandmother didn't know all the details, but she knew enough.

"This morning, I believe. She's heading out of town to meet up with some friends. Pam has a very active social life. We're not at all alike in that respect."

"You could have an active social life, too." Sylvia gave her a chiding look. "How long have I been telling you to try the dating apps? They've done wonders for me."

"Grandma!" Emma exclaimed. "You're not really on dating apps, are you?"

Sylvia gave a sly look. "Sure I am. That's the best way to meet people these days, isn't it? You can't tell me you don't have a profile on one of those sites."

Emma could feel her face flush. "I absolutely *can* tell you exactly that. I'm not interested in dating right now. Maybe someday, but right now I have other priorities."

She sent a meaningful look toward Olive, who continued eating her food while occasionally slipping a bit of her plant-based sausage to Dottie, who had learned to sit patiently beside her chair for just these chances.

"You're a mother, but you're still a woman," Sylvia reminded her. "There's no reason you can't get out there more."

"When would you suggest I date? I'm working long hours at the bookstore and then I come home to my child. There's not a lot of room in there for a love life. Maybe someday."

Maybe she would find time for that after she managed to persuade her mother that she should be working at Lucas Construction instead of the bookstore.

She wasn't making much progress in that arena. Or any at all.

First things first, she told herself. She needed to earn her mother's trust by making the bookstore a success, then slowly ease her way into working at Lucas Construction instead.

They had nearly finished breakfast when the doorbell rang.

"Oh! That must be Pam," her mother said. "She's early."

Emma froze. She did not want to talk to Pam today. She thought she would be able to avoid her, but now that seemed impossible.

"I'll get it!" Olive scraped her chair back and raced for the front door.

One of her daughter's favorite things was answering the door. Emma remembered she had been the same way. She always loved seeing what new adventure might be waiting on the other side.

Rosie followed close behind her granddaughter. With any luck, Pam might drop off the book and leave.

Unfortunately, that wish wasn't granted. From the kitchen, she heard Pam greeting Olive and Rosie.

"Sorry I'm early. My plans changed and my friends decided they wanted to leave earlier than we had arranged."

"It's no problem. We're having breakfast. Come through and you can say hello to Mom and Emma."

"I'm Olive," her daughter said cheerfully.

"I know you are, honey. You are the cutest thing."

Emma focused on her crepes as Pam came into the kitchen.

"Sylvia, hello, my dear. You are looking so adorable. I love that T-shirt."

Emma's grandmother was wearing a shirt that said Still Raising Hell, Just at a Lower Volume.

"Thanks. I made it myself at the senior center. They have a screen printing class every month or so, and we are able to design our own."

"How fun."

"I can make you one if you want."

Pam shook her head. "No way. That's a one-of-a-kind for you. I don't want to steal your great T-shirt."

Emma suspected Pam would not be caught dead wearing anything of the sort.

"Would you like a crepe or two? They're delicious. Emma made them."

Emma fought the childish urge to grab the plate and hide it behind her back.

"I remember back in the day you loved to cook," Pam said. "Your dad always loved to pass around the cookies you made to everyone in the office. He was always so proud of you."

Emma's fingers tightened on her fork so she didn't stab Pam in the eye. She did not want to sit here at this table and listen to her talk about Gary.

"As delicious as I'm sure your crepes are, I have to pass this time. We're going out for brunch and I don't want to be too full. It's lovely to see you both, though."

Neither she nor her grandmother answered and after a startled pause, Pam turned to Rosie again. "I should go."

"Thanks for going out of your way to drop off the book. It could have waited until Monday."

"I know but I wanted to get it to you while I was still thinking about it."

To Emma's vast relief, the two women walked out into the foyer.

"Are you all right?"

Emma looked over at her grandmother.

"I can hardly stand to be in the same room with her. She came into the bookstore a few days ago, and it was all I could do to be polite."

If Emma did end up working at Lucas Construction in any kind of leadership capacity, one of the very first things she planned was to figure out a way to push out Pam, no matter what it took. There was no way she could work with the other woman.

Sylvia sighed. "You really need to tell your mom the truth."

"No. Absolutely not."

"You can't carry this burden on your own forever."

"I'm not telling her. It will break her heart."

"Maybe I'll tell her, then."

"Grandma, you can't. Let her mourn my dad in peace."

"It's eating you up inside."

"It's not. I'm fine."

"Tell your mother."

Before Emma could answer, Rosie returned to the kitchen. She looked between the two of them. "What do you need to tell me?"

Emma aimed a glare at her grandmother, who needed to mind her own business.

“Nothing,” she improvised quickly. “Grandma was saying I need to tell you exactly where Olive and I are going, in case of an emergency or something.”

“I know right where you’re going. I’m the one who suggested it, remember? You’re heading to Hidden Beach.”

“That’s right. And while we’re there, we’ll probably make our way to Sea Glass Beach, since it’s not that far of a walk.”

“Olive will love that. Well, make sure you keep your phone with you. You should still have good reception.”

“I will. We’ll be fine, I’m sure. Come on, Olive, let’s go get our gear.”

Her daughter took care of her plate and silverware, setting them in the sink to be loaded into the dishwasher, then skipped down the hall with Emma.

Would Sylvia carry through on her threat to tell Rosie the truth about what had happened the day Emma’s father died? Emma didn’t think so. Sylvia could have told Rosie at any point over the years yet had chosen to honor Emma’s wishes.

She had to keep her fingers crossed her grandmother would continue to stay silent.

CHAPTER TWENTY-TWO

—

Rosie

HER DAUGHTER WAS HIDING SOMETHING. IT WAS NOT THE first time she had received that impression. And whatever it was, Sylvia knew the details.

"What was that really about? What does Emma need to tell me? And don't make up some BS story about giving me her itinerary for the day."

Her mother gave her an innocent look that didn't fool Rosie for an instant. Sylvia was a lousy liar.

"Just as we said. We were talking about Emma and Olive's hike. They will have to enjoy the beach on my behalf, too. I'm afraid it's going to be a long time before I'll be able to do any hiking," she said, her features suddenly morose.

Was her mother trying to distract her by reminding her about her injuries? She wouldn't put anything past her.

Rosie frowned. "The doctor says you're healing very well. You told me he thinks you'll be able to start weight-bearing again in a few weeks."

"Well, if you want me to, I can milk this injury longer, especially if it keeps our Emma and Olive here."

Rosie sent a swift look to her mother. "Is that what you've been doing?"

Sylvia gave her a mischievous look. "The doctor said a week ago that I could start putting weight on my ankle again."

No. She wanted more time to convince her daughter to stay!

Some of her distress must have been clear on her features.

Sylvia covered her fingers with her hand. "You know, we don't need to use my ankle injury as an excuse to keep Olive and Emma here."

"I'm not so sure of that."

"When you first told me you wanted to ask Emma to stay while my ankle healed, I felt like you were putting me out to pasture. After she arrived, I realized what a brilliant idea it was. She and her daughter need to be here."

"I agree."

"She seems to be doing a great job. All my friends are buzzing about the changes she's making at the bookstore. I need to get down there myself and see them."

"Are you . . . upset that she's changing things?"

Sylvia made a face. "Why would I be upset? That place needed shaking up. If she's got the energy for it, more power to her. I'm more than happy to step back and give her a chance to shine."

"I'm not pushing you out, Mom," Rosie said carefully. "I'm so grateful for all your help. You've kept the bookstore going all this time and I can never thank you enough."

"Don't be silly. I loved it. Who wouldn't love working at a bookstore?" Sylvia said. "Maybe after a few months, I'll see if Emma might be willing to give me a job there, just for fun. That way I can take time when I want to travel, without all the responsibility."

Had she been holding her mother back all this time from doing what she wanted by asking her to run the bookstore? She should have sold The Rainy Day Bookshop years ago but her mother would never hear of it whenever Rosie brought it up.

"If I worked there a few afternoons a week, I could still hang out with customers, which is my favorite part. I could do without any of the management responsibility. I'm more than happy to pass all that nonsense along to Emma."

Rosie felt a deep relief. She had been trying to figure out how to gently talk to her mother about her desire to keep Emma there longer than the summer.

"I love you, Mom. I know I don't tell you that nearly often enough."

"I love as you as well, my dear," Sylvia said, taking another bite of her crepe.

Their relationship had not always been easy. Sylvia had argued long and hard against her marrying Gary at such a young age and tying herself down to one place. Rosie knew she carried some lingering resentment for that as well as for the nomadic nature of her childhood that prevented her from establishing any roots.

Still, she always knew her mother had her best interests at heart. Just as Rosie had Emma's.

She frowned, remembering what had started their conversation. "I really wish you would tell me what you and Emma were talking about."

Sylvia looked unconcerned. "And I wish I could still do the splits. Too bad we can't always have what we want."

She sighed, recognizing her mother's obstinacy.

She wanted to ask Emma again when she and Olive came back downstairs while Rosie was clearing up the kitchen, but she didn't have the nerve. She didn't want to risk anything that would damage the fragile peace they had built.

"We're going on our hike," Olive announced, looking exactly as Emma had at her age, feisty and adorable.

"I hope you have a wonderful time," Rosie said, drying her hands so she could hug her granddaughter.

She had a fleeting wish that she had changed her mind and

agreed to go with them, but she quickly squelched it for the same reasons as before. She really did need to weed her garden and Emma needed time alone with her daughter.

"Maybe we will find some shells. I want to find a purple one."

"I hope you do." She hugged her again and then on impulse hugged her daughter. Physical affection had been limited between them since Emma's return. Rosie hadn't wanted to overwhelm her daughter by being too effusive in her affection.

As she felt Emma hug her back, first awkwardly and then more genuinely, her heart seemed to give a happy little flip. She could not ask for anything more than to have these two people she loved so much back in her life on a daily basis.

She would do whatever necessary to keep them close.

CHAPTER TWENTY-THREE

—

Andrew

THIS WASN'T A BAD WAY TO SPEND A MORNING, ANDREW thought as he adjusted Finn's helmet, double-checked Zara's, and put on his own.

The morning was sunny and bright, with the air smelling fresh and clean from all the rain and sunlight gleaming on the water. A few more days like this and he might begin to think living here in Oregon hadn't been the worst idea ever.

"Okay. Ready to do this?"

The kids grinned at him.

"Yes. Let's go," Zara said.

They took off with Finn in front. Zara followed behind him on her pink mountain bike and Andrew took up the rear so that he could keep a careful eye on both of his children.

He loved bicycling. In LA, this had been one of his favorite exercises, taking his bike down to the beach paths and riding up and down the coast. This wasn't quite the same as a good, hard workout. He had to ride at a pace slower than a snail stuck in peanut butter and maintain a careful eye on them at the same time, but he enjoyed it nonetheless.

"Do you have the package, Z?" he asked his daughter.

She gestured to her basket. "I've got it here. It's all wrapped up."

Andrew was aware of a tingle of awareness as they biked several houses down on their way to Rosie's place.

He had only seen her sporadically since the party. She had stopped at Stormhaven a few times to check on the progress, but he had either been away from home or up in his office.

He wasn't sure how but since she had taken over managing his renovation, the pace of the work seemed to have accelerated dramatically. At this rate, he hoped the house would be done in the next month, right around the time his book was due to his publisher.

"I hope she's home," Zara said.

"If she's not, we'll simply keep bike riding and stop on our way back."

Their plan had been to head to a park on the other side of town they hadn't yet visited, one he had heard had a fun playground as well as an easy path down to the beach.

Mostly, he wanted to take advantage of the nice weather to explore their surroundings. They crested the hill toward Rosie's house and drove up her driveway. As they did, several chickens scurried out of their way.

"I hope Dottie is around," Zara said. "She's the funniest dog."

Rosie's little Dottie might quite possibly be the ugliest dog Andrew had ever seen, with her wispy fur and squat body, but somehow she was still adorable in spite of it. Or maybe because of it.

"I get to ring the doorbell," Finn said, carefully grabbing the package out of Zara's basket with both hands.

"Not if I get there first," Zara said. She raced up the porch steps, but before she could ring the bell, Andrew heard a sound from around the side of the house.

Someone was singing. It was Rosie, he realized, singing along to a nineties pop group he remembered well, in a sweet alto voice.

He didn't want to surprise her, but if she had headphones on, she wouldn't hear them anyway.

"Guys, it sounds like she's in the backyard. Let's go around and find her."

His children eagerly agreed and headed in that direction. The chickens seemed interested in their goings-on and followed close behind them. Zara was nervous about them, but Finn seemed completely comfortable.

When they rounded the house, they found her kneeling by one of her flower gardens, pulling weeds and deadheading old blooms.

"Hi, Rosie!" Finn exclaimed. She didn't hear, so the boy moved closer. "Hi, Rosie!"

She squealed and whirled around, dropping her hand tools in the dirt. "Oh my word! You scared the life out of me."

"Sorry," Andrew said. "We tried to make noise so you'd hear us, but you seemed preoccupied."

A hint of color crawled up her cheeks. She looked fresh and lovely, so pretty he wanted to simply stare at her.

He was fiercely drawn to her and wished he dared pull his phone out and take a picture of her, right here in her garden, surrounded by flowers and sunshine.

"We brought you a present," Finn said. "I made it myself."

"A present! That's so kind of you." She rose with a puzzled expression.

"This is completely Finn's idea. He did all the heavy lifting. Zara and I just rode along."

"Thank you," she said, still looking confused as she accepted the hastily wrapped gift Finn handed to her.

"At art camp, we had to make a sculpture from clay. I didn't know what to make and the teacher said I could make something for someone else who did something nice for me."

"Okay," she said slowly, looking no less baffled.

He beamed at her. "You helped my dad find my Darth Vader minifig when I lost it at the party. I was so sad and I thought it was gone forever. My dad said you are the one who first saw it in the grass and that you looked for a long time."

Rosie's expression softened with pleasure. "That is really kind of you. I can't wait to see what you made."

He beamed with pride as he handed over the small bundle. Andrew wanted to tell her to keep her expectations low, but he would never say anything to hurt his son's feelings.

He had to hope she could understand the emotion behind the gift. Something told him Rosie was the kind of person who would never denigrate a child's offering, no matter how humble it might be.

As he had hoped, she unwrapped the bundle as if it were a priceless antique. When she saw the misshapen clay trivet Finn had made, embedded with shells they had picked up on the beach, her features lit up.

"It's beautiful," she exclaimed. "How did you know I needed exactly this in my kitchen?"

Finn beamed. "I didn't know. I just made it. We found those shells ourselves. Since they were broken, my dad said we could keep them."

"I love the way you made them in a circle around the edge. That's very creative."

"I made one, too," Zara said. "Dad's going to keep mine. It's bigger, but I don't think my shells looked as good as Finn's did."

He wanted to hug his daughter for going out of her way to praise her younger brother. As annoyed as Zara could sometimes get with Finn, she loved him and would be the first to protect and defend him.

"What are you doing?" Zara asked. "Why are you pulling up your plants?"

"I'm not. I'm pulling up the weeds. They are starting to take over because of the rain. I want to plant some new flowers in my beds, but I have to get the weeds out first."

His children looked so intrigued by the process, he had to

wonder if he had never weeded with his children. The answer came easily. No. When would he have? In California, they had lived in a gated neighborhood where the grounds were taken care of by a company. Tracy had kept flower baskets but she had been too frail to do much gardening the last year of her life.

"Where is Dottie?" Finn asked.

"I'm afraid she's not here. My daughter and granddaughter took her for an adventure today. They were going on a hike to Hidden Beach. Have you been there yet?"

"No," Andrew said. "Never heard of it."

"Oh, you need to take the kids someday. It's about a mile hike from the trailhead, and then you come to a beach that very few people go to. You usually have it mostly to yourself, with only two or three other people. If you hike down the beach another half mile or so, you'll find a beach that has the most magnificent sea glass."

"Why?" Finn asked, his favorite word.

"It's a long story but a long time ago, people threw their trash over the side of a cliff nearby and down to the beach. The beach has been cleaned up but over time the ocean has taken all the glass from those bottles and jars and smoothed it over to make sea glass."

"So the sea glass is garbage?" Zara asked.

"Some of it might have started that way. But now it's like beautiful, colorful stones."

"Can we go there?" she asked Andrew with a pleading look. "Our art teacher said we could make another trivet at home and put sea glass in it instead of shells. She gave us the directions in our packet."

"That does sound fun," he said. "Not today, though. We're on a bike ride now, going to Orca Park."

Zara's features fell. "I'd rather go find sea glass. Can't we do that instead?"

He really needed to work on teaching his daughter to embrace the present instead of always looking ahead. He feared that was a habit she had picked up during her mother's illness. They were always looking toward the next doctor's visit, the next surgery, the next chemotherapy treatment.

He needed to remind himself of that, too. His children were growing up far too quickly and he needed to savor days like this.

"Can we help you plant your flowers before we go to the park?" Finn asked Rosie.

Rosie sent Andrew a quick look, and he could tell she was gauging what he wanted her to say. He supposed they could plant a few flowers if his kids would enjoy it.

He gave her a noncommittal shrug, and she smiled at the kids.

"You want to plant flowers instead of going to the park?"

"Yes!" Zara exclaimed, much to his surprise. "We can plant flowers first then go for a bike ride."

He was not about to discourage his children from helping someone else, especially if that meant he would be able to enjoy more time in Rosie's company. Win-win, all the way around.

"Great idea," Andrew said. "We can spend a few moments weeding and planting some flowers, then we'll head to the park."

The children exclaimed with delight.

"I might even have a few extra pairs of gardening gloves," Rosie said. "Let me go put my lovely new gift in the kitchen and I'll grab them for you."

The children laughed at the chickens pecking around until

Rosie emerged from the house with two pairs of small gardening gloves and one pair of large leather work gloves.

"You'll have to show us what to do. I don't want to pull up your prize pansies or something," he said.

She pointed out a few of the more common weeds for them to identify. "If you're in doubt about whether something is a flower or a weed, you can always ask me."

The children took to gardening with far more enthusiasm than he might have expected. They seemed to be enjoying themselves as much as they might have at the playground.

Together they finished clearing out one small bed and were working on a second one when Rosie's mother came out of the tiny cottage where she lived, hobbling on her crutches. Sylvia looked delighted to see them all.

"Someone is having a party without me," she said.

Zara giggled. "Not really. We're helping weed so you can plant some new flowers."

"I'm afraid my planting days are still a few days away," Sylvia said, gesturing to her crutches.

"We're helping *Rosie* plant flowers, Miss Sylvia. Not you."

He was about to chide Finn for the familiarity when he remembered that Sylvia was good friends with his mother. The children must have spent more time with her than he realized. They all seemed comfortable with each other.

"Oh, that makes more sense," she said with a teasing grin. "Do you happen to belong to those fancy bikes I saw out front?"

His son nodded. "We're going on a bike ride to Orca Park when we're done helping."

"That sounds fun. Let me guess. The purple bike is Zara's and the big red bike is Finn's."

"No!" Fin chortled. "The red one is my dad's. Mine is the green one."

"Oh. I thought maybe the green one was your dad's."

Finn apparently thought it was hilarious to imagine his father riding the little green bike that was about half the size of Andrew's.

Rosie smiled, and Andrew could only assume she was creating a mental picture of him trying to work the pedals of the diminutive bike with his gangly legs.

"You won't believe this, but I just made a fresh batch of cookies. Would anyone out here want one? If it's okay with your dad, anyway."

"I would!" Finn exclaimed.

"I could use a cookie," Zara said more sedately.

"The only problem is that I can't carry them out here with these crutches. Why don't you both come help me? Maybe you can also carry some lemonade out to your dad and Rosie."

The children were enthusiastic about another opportunity to help, especially if it meant cookies. They followed Sylvia, chattering away to her about the present Finn had made for Rosie and about the art camp they had attended.

After they left, Andrew was painfully aware that he was alone with her. Well, alone except for her chickens, a few dozen birds singing in the treetops and countless bees buzzing from flower to flower.

"You really don't have to help me. I appreciate the gesture, but I didn't have that much left to do. When they come back, we can plant a few token flowers and you can be on your way."

"I don't mind," he said and was more than a little startled to realize he meant the words. He found something quite enjoyable about being in this beautiful yard on a sunny afternoon, the scent of roses and irises mingling with the sea air.

"I really wanted to thank you," he said. "Not only for helping me find Finn's toy the other night but for the way you have cracked the whip on all the subcontractors. The progress has been unbelievable."

"I can't take all the credit for that. Bryce had everything in hand and was working hard to move things along. But I will admit, sometimes the subs work faster when the boss lady tells them she won't hire them for anything else unless they drop everything and get this done."

She had done that for him? He was both touched and gratified. "Thank you," he said. "The kids are anxious to move into the house."

"I'm sure they are. I hope we're on track to be done in about three more weeks."

Even faster than he had hoped. "I can't tell you how happy that makes me."

"How is everything else going?" she asked, picking up her weed pile and carrying it to a nearby wheelbarrow.

"It's good. The kids have been enjoying their various day camps. We've got one more this week, then I'm not sure what we'll do." He paused, slanting her a sideways look. "I could use some advice, actually."

"Oh?"

"I would like to hire someone to be a nanny-slash-housekeeper. Do you know anybody in the area you could recommend?"

She pursed her lips, considering. "Are you looking for a live-in nanny?"

"No. I was hoping for somebody who could mainly help keep the house clean, cook a few meals, pick up the kids, and be with them for a few hours in the afternoon. Maybe three or four hours a day max. Maybe more, if the need arises."

"When do you want them to start?"

"When the house is done. My publisher wants me to go on

a book tour in a few months. My mom could handle the children by herself but it's a lot to ask. I was hoping I could find somebody before I leave who could help her out."

"I can't come up with any names off the top of my head, but I'll give it some thought. I do have a couple of workers whose wives have talked about doing something outside the home, especially now that their kids are in high school. Let me ask around."

"Thanks."

"What did you do for childcare in Los Angeles?"

"We had a housekeeper who started right before Tracy was diagnosed with cancer. Vivian was a rock. We would have been lost without her before and after Tracy died. But she quit about six months ago. Her granddaughter was born with some health challenges, and she wanted to move closer to her daughter in New Mexico to help her out."

"That must have been rough for the kids, to lose their mom and then someone else they had been close to."

"Yeah. It didn't help at all that we also lost everything familiar to a wildfire."

Her eyes were soft with a compassion he wanted to lean into. "No wonder you picked up and moved, buying a house on a whim."

"It wasn't really on a whim. My mom was here."

"Yes, but you bought the house without even seeing it in person."

"Not my smartest move," he agreed. "I think it's working out, though."

"You are an eternal optimist, Andrew Morgan."

He laughed. "I do believe you are the first person in my life who's ever said that to me. I'm usually a cranky, glass-half-empty kind of guy."

"I doubt that. You couldn't write books about conquering evil and saving the world if you weren't somewhat of an optimist."

"An optimist who writes like he's never even met a woman?" he said with a grin.

She groaned. "If there were ever five minutes of my life that I would like to scrub out of the permanent record, it would be those."

"I'm sorry. I shouldn't keep teasing you about it."

She studiously looked down at the weeds she was yanking from the ground. "If you must know, I'm listening to the series on audio again. I am either in a different place in my life—or perhaps knowing you personally changes my perspective—but I'm very much enjoying them."

He felt ridiculously flattered and also lost for words. "I'm so glad," he finally said.

"I'm starting from the beginning of the series and listening straight through. I'm beginning to see why they're so popular. And it's very obvious you *have* met a woman."

Her gaze met his and the air between them seemed to crackle and spark. Andrew found himself leaning closer, drawn inexorably to this particular woman, whom he found warm and kind and irresistible.

Her breath caught and her gaze flickered to his mouth. Andrew could have sworn time stood still. He tilted his head, about to close the distance between them when he suddenly heard children's laughter drawing nearer.

He managed to ease away from her an instant before the children came around the hedge.

"We have cookies and lemonade," Finn announced. He held the cookies on a plate while his sister walked carefully toward them, balancing two glasses.

Andrew reached for the lemonade and swallowed a long drink, wishing the iced liquid could cool the blazing desire that had built up in the few short moments the children had been gone.

"It's good, isn't it?" Finn demanded.

"Delicious," he assured his son.

Rosie, he saw, was taking several long swallows as well. Her face looked flushed, her eyes bright.

"Do you want a cookie?" Zara asked.

"I'll pass," Andrew said gruffly. "If you do want to help Rosie plant some flowers, we should probably do that so we can get to the park."

The kids' faces didn't look as if they wanted to leave but they put on their gardening gloves again and knelt to help.

After a charged pause, Rosie gave them instructions and while the three of them discussed the annuals she was using for color in the garden, Andrew continued to yank out stubborn weeds, wishing he could yank out his attraction to Rosie as easily.

He could think of a dozen reasons why he should completely ignore the way his pulse leaped around her and his skin prickled with awareness.

He liked Rosie Lucas immensely. She was kind, funny and intelligent. She had a way of making everyone around her feel at ease, and she seemed to genuinely care about his children.

Plus, she was even more lovely than her garden on a sunny day, with a smile that left him lightheaded.

When the children had each planted six or seven small starts, he rose, brushing dirt off his pants.

"We need to get going," he said.

The kids groaned in unison but to his relief they didn't argue.

Rosie stood as well, her expression warm and genuine. “Thanks for the help today,” she said. “You’ve made a huge dent in my never-ending battle against these weeds.”

“Anytime,” Andrew replied, even though he knew he should grab his children and ride out of this lovely garden as fast as they all could pedal.

Despite the confusing feelings swirling inside him, he couldn’t deny that he enjoyed spending time with Rosie. As they said their goodbyes and he herded the children towards their bikes, Andrew found himself already looking forward to their next encounter.

He knew he should probably keep his distance, but something told him that staying away from Rosie Lucas might be easier said than done.

CHAPTER TWENTY-FOUR

—

Emma

EMMA INHALED THE SCENTS OF DAMP EARTH AND PINE AND sea, Olive's hand in hers as they navigated the winding forest trail. She loved this area, from the rugged cliffs to the offshore formations to these lush forests overflowing with ferns. This was her childhood.

"It's so green!" Olive said. Her daughter walked slightly ahead of her, with Dottie on the leash. They had borrowed the dog from her mother, mainly because Olive adored her.

"There are a million kinds of green, aren't there?"

"It looks like a fairyland. Do you think there are fairies in the forest?"

Olive had become fascinated with fairies since they arrived in Oregon, in no small part thanks to Sylvia. Emma's grandmother had created a spot near her cottage that she called her fairy garden, filled with tiny structures and whimsical buildings. Her grandmother had even attached a small door to a tree growing near her place, claiming that was the fairies' house.

"I wouldn't be at all surprised. It looks exactly like the place a family of fairies would live, doesn't it?"

"Do you think there will be mermaids, too, when we get to the beach?"

"We'll have to watch for them," Emma answered.

Was it wrong of her to encourage her child's vivid imagination and fantasy life? She couldn't think why it would be. There would be plenty of time for Olive to come to the sad realization that the world could be a hard, unrelenting and unforgiving place. For now, let her have her flights of whimsy and joy where she could find them.

This had been exactly what Emma needed.

As they continued the short walk toward the beach, accessible only by this trail, Emma felt weeks of stress slide off her shoulders. It was hard for her to think that perhaps she'd made a mistake coming back to town when this morning seemed so pure and lovely.

They continued along the path, Olive's excitable chatter punctuated by the distant cry of seagulls. Towering firs and hemlocks stretched skyward, their branches creating a verdant canopy that dappled the forest floor with shifting patterns of sunlight and shadow.

The path narrowed, winding between moss-covered rocks and gnarled tree roots. Emma lifted Olive over a particularly tricky section, her daughter giggling as she was momentarily airborne.

They were not the only ones on the trail. This was a fairly popular hike. She nodded in passing to another couple she vaguely remembered from her time living in town. If she wasn't mistaken, the man was a teacher at the community college up in Coos Bay. Or he had been a decade ago, anyway.

"Nice day, isn't it?"

"It's great to have sunshine after so many weeks of rain. I forgot how much it rained in Oregon."

"Enjoy your morning," the woman said.

Olive wanted to look at every plant and tree and flower they passed. Those she didn't want to examine, Dottie did. After several more steps, the terrain began to change from forest to sand dune.

They walked through a small grove of trees, and finally, the ocean spread out below them.

"We're here! We made it!"

Olive looked delighted, almost as if she hadn't really believed Emma when she said they would be going to the ocean. There were a few other people there on a beautiful summer morning. She would have been surprised had they been the only ones who decided this was the perfect day to enjoy this magical spot.

She saw a young family playing in the sand, a couple around her age who were taking photographs and videos of each other, and two sets of older couples who appeared to be tourists.

"Hey!" Olive exclaimed. "That's my friend Bryce."

Emma jerked her gaze in the direction Olive pointed and felt her heart give a silly little lurch. On the far side of the beach, she also saw a man throwing a ball to a silver dog.

In an instant, she was back in her bookstore the evening he had shocked her with that kiss. She hadn't been able to stop thinking about it since.

What were the odds that she and Olive would hike to the very same beach as Bryce and Pearl, simply by chance?

She was tempted to grab her daughter and hurry back up the trail but it was too late now, especially after Olive waved vigorously and raced toward him.

"Hi, Bryce!" her daughter exclaimed.

He looked up at his name and Emma saw a mix of emotions cross his gorgeous features. First delight, followed quickly by wariness.

"Look who's here! Two of my favorite people," he said as they reached him.

"And Dottie," Olive reminded him.

"And one of my favorite dogs. What are you guys up to?"

"We came for a hike. Grandma said we should come here."

Bryce raised an eyebrow. "That's funny. She suggested the same thing to me, too."

So it wasn't at all a coincidence that they found themselves on the same beach. Emma was instantly horrified.

Her mother had orchestrated the whole thing. She been dropping hints for days about how fun it would be to take a hike to Hidden Beach and how much Olive would enjoy it.

Had she been giving the same advice to Bryce?

No doubt Rosie thought throwing Emma together with her second-in-command might spark a romance, which in turn might compel Emma to stick around in Wood Briar longer.

She did not need her mother interfering in her love life. She was screwing it up just fine on her own.

Her gaze met his and she could see he had come to the same conclusion. How mortifying. She could do nothing about it now but she fully intended to have a long talk with Rosie when they went home.

She forced a sunny smile. "It's beautiful here today," she said.

"We're looking for mermaids," Olive informed him.

"Are you?"

"Have you seen any?"

"Not yet. Maybe Pearl scared them all away."

"Are mermaids afraid of dogs?" Olive asked.

"I'm not sure," he answered in a serious tone. "I've never had the chance to ask one."

She giggled. "I got a new sandcastle bucket and shovel. Want to see it?"

"Um. Sure."

The bucket was dangling from Emma's backpack with a carabiner. She obediently swung her bag to the sand and pulled off the pink bucket and its matching purple shovel.

Olive showed it to Bryce, who gave it due appreciation.

"Looks like a good one," he said. "You can make a great sandcastle with that."

"Grandma Sylvia says if we build a sandcastle, maybe the fairies will come visit."

"Fairies and mermaids. I had no idea Hidden Beach was so exciting."

"You build houses like Grandma Rosie. Can you help me build a sandcastle for the fairies?"

Emma frowned. "I'm sure Bryce and Pearl have plans today. I'll help you build a sandcastle."

"But you're not a builder like Grandma Rosie and Bryce. It has to be a good one or the fairies won't like it."

"They are pretty picky, I've heard," Bryce agreed. "I bet with that bucket you and your mom can build a great one. But I'm happy to help."

Emma wanted to tell him he didn't need to do that but Olive looked so thrilled, she didn't have the heart to be the cranky mom here.

Bryce led them to a spot near the water's edge, where the sand was damp and perfect for building.

"All right, builders," he said, kneeling down. "Let's start with a strong foundation."

He showed Olive how to pack wet sand tightly into the bucket, then flip it over to create the first tower. Emma watched, impressed by his patience as he guided Olive's small hands. Pearl sniffed around the sand excitedly while Dottie nestled onto the beach blanket Emma spread near their structure and observed the proceedings for a few moments before she fell asleep.

As the three of them worked together, Emma found herself fully engaged, shaping windows and turrets while Bryce focused on the main structure.

After they had been building for a while, a girl about Olive's age approached, her eyes wide with curiosity.

"Can I help?" she asked shyly.

Olive beamed, immediately handing her a spare shovel. "We're building a fairy castle. I'm Olive. What's your name?"

"Lily," the other girl said, settling down next to Olive. In the magical way of children, the two girls were soon chattering away as if they had known each other for years.

Lily had the idea of building a moat and lining it with seashells and driftwood, so they worked together gathering up supplies, their laughter mingling with the sounds of the waves.

Emma caught Bryce's eye, sharing a warm smile at the unexpected friendship blooming before them.

"Thanks for getting her started," she said.

"Happy to help. It's been a long time since I built a sandcastle."

She thought he might offer a farewell and resume throwing a ball for Pearl. Instead, he eased down on the blanket beside her, long legs stretched out before him.

He wore khaki shorts and a light blue T-shirt with a surfboard on it. She could see his muscles outlined by the thin material of his shirt and immediately pulled out her water bottle to take a long swig.

What was it about Bryce that left her feeling lightheaded and off-balance every time they were together?

Maybe the fact that he had kissed her until she couldn't think straight. And she really wanted him to do it again.

He lifted his face to the sky and she had a sudden wish that she could see the hazel of his eyes behind his sunglasses.

"After a week of rain, a day like this feels like a gift."

"Agreed."

He smelled delicious, of sand and sun and *life.* Emma

wanted to sink into him but she was only too aware of her daughter and her new friend playing six feet away.

"What else are you up to today?" she asked. "Are you visiting your mom?"

At his shrug, the bare skin of his lower arm brushed against hers and she had to suppress a shiver, fighting with all she had not to move away a few inches.

"I'm driving up later tonight to have dinner with her at the care center. I try to do that most Sunday evenings. I'm not sure if she's even aware I'm there but I still go."

He was such a good son. Her admiration for this man seemed to grow every time she talked to him. Most guys she knew would have been quick to run away from an emotionally fraught situation like dealing with a parent with dementia. It would have been easy to put his mother in a care center and forget about her. Yet Bryce had stepped up and was doing his best to be a dutiful son, making regular visits and dropping everything to be at her side after her fall a few weeks earlier.

If her mother were in a similar situation right now, would Emma be as dutiful and loving as he was? She wanted to think so, but she wasn't sure.

She was finding it very hard to resist him.

"Are you able to have any other life besides work and taking care of your mom?" she asked. She certainly didn't feel like she did. Her life right now consisted of caring for Olive and devoting all her remaining energies to the bookshop.

"Sure I do," he said. "You already know I read a lot. Well, I listen to audiobooks, anyway. I usually take Pearl for a run in the morning before I head to work, then we try to squeeze in a quick hike or walk in the evening. Sometimes I go to the gym, though not as often as I should."

Why did he bother going to the gym at all when he had

such a physically demanding job? The man never seemed to stop moving.

She had a sudden memory of watching him haul in lumber for the renovation. He had hardly even seemed to notice the weight.

Her stomach felt shaky, as if she were teetering on a slippery log trying to cross a chasm. She couldn't seem to stop thinking about how wonderful she had felt to have his arms around her, his strength surrounding her.

"What about your love life?" she dared ask.

She had asked him the other day why he hadn't settled down and she only realized after their kiss that he had deftly changed the subject without giving her any information at all.

"What about it?" he asked, his tone wary.

"How do you manage anything like dating, in the middle of caring for your mom?"

"I'm not caring for my mother all the time. Even when she lived at home with me, we had caregivers who helped."

"Still, I'm sure it's a big burden. That's a lot of responsibility on your young shoulders."

No matter how broad they might be.

"I date. I'm not currently seeing anybody on a regular basis, but I've had a couple of serious girlfriends over the past few years."

Who? Anybody she knew? She wanted to ask but wasn't sure she wanted to know the answer.

"What happened? Why didn't any of those serious girlfriends turn into anything more?"

"Why are you so interested?" he countered.

She felt her face flush and hoped he couldn't see under the floppy beach hat she had to use because of her coloring.

"Curious. That's all."

"You know how it is. One reason you date people is to see

if you fit together for the long haul. Neither of those relationships did."

"Why not?"

He didn't answer immediately. "One of them fell in love with another guy, a coworker," he finally said. "The other one wasn't crazy about the situation I was in."

"What situation? Your mom?"

He nodded. "This was a year or so ago. I can't really blame her. I had to back out of a hiking trip in Canada we had been planning for months because things were coming to a head with my mom. Her condition was progressing quickly and her needs were becoming too much for the assisted living facility she was in prior to her current care center. It wasn't a good time. My girlfriend at the time was overwhelmed by it all."

She was outraged on his behalf. "That's awful. Who was it? Anybody I know?"

He sent her a sidelong look. "Again. Why do you want to know?"

"So I can ban her from my bookstore for being a horrible person."

He shook his head. "You don't know her. Carly isn't from here. She lives in Eugene. Long distance wasn't really working out either."

"Still."

"And she's not a horrible person. Over the years, I've learned I can't judge somebody else's reluctance to put themselves in a tough situation, for whatever reason."

Emma could. And did. She wanted to find this Carly and punch her in the throat for hurting a good man.

"My mom's situation made her frustrated and uncomfortable. But that's not the only reason. There were other problems between us."

He gazed at the girls, who were now pretending a couple

pieces of twigs were people living in their castle, then back at Emma. If she wasn't mistaken, a hint of color crawled up his neck. But maybe it was the beginnings of a sunburn.

"Carly was finishing up law school with plans to be a criminal defense attorney. She knew what she wanted and I think she was looking for somebody . . . smarter."

Emma stared, aghast. "Are you kidding me? All the more reason I need to ban her from my bookstore if she ever comes in. I might ban everyone named Carly. You're one of the smartest people I know."

"You don't have to patronize me, Emma."

"I'm not! Trust me, I've met a lot of not-smart people in my life, not to mention people whose life choices have taken away even more brain cells. As I've watched you work on the bookstore renovation, I've been amazed at what you do. You're precise, you're detailed, you're a creative problem solver. You're bringing things together in ways I never could have imagined."

"That's different."

"It's not. It takes math to figure out the angles of cuts, the layouts, the construction materials you're going to need. Most people find that difficult but you handle it like it's second nature."

He looked pleased at her words but she felt compelled to go further.

"And you're incredibly well-read. You've told me some of the audiobooks you listen to when I've asked. History, philosophy, science. You're constantly learning, constantly growing. Just because school didn't come easily to you and you didn't go to college doesn't mean you're not smart. You've learned to adapt and to succeed, and that takes a kind of wisdom and intelligence no silly law student could ever have."

He looked at her for a long moment, a flicker of something deep, something real, in his expression. Emma caught her breath, her heart pounding, and she couldn't help wishing they were alone back in her quiet bookshop instead of here on this beach, surrounded by strangers.

CHAPTER TWENTY-FIVE

—

Bryce

BRYCE COULDN'T SEEM TO TAKE HIS EYES OFF EMMA.

He wanted to think she was only being kind, as she had always been in school, but her words seemed to ring with conviction. He remembered now that Emma had always known how to make him feel seen, even when he'd been a punk kid begging for attention.

He used to think he was dumb, plain and simple. School had been such a struggle, a long, slow march through confusion and frustration. But she was right. Since then, he had discovered he simply learned differently from other people.

Hearing Emma defend him with such surety made something deep inside him stir.

He wanted to kiss her again. The urge was strong enough to make him clench his fists. He couldn't. Not here. And not again. She had asked him not to and he wouldn't go against her wishes.

Instead, he looked out at the glittering water and shifted the conversation away from himself. "What about you. I know you dropped Olive's father before she was born. Sounds like a smart move."

"The best thing I ever did."

"Has there been anyone else since then?"

"I don't have time for that right now." She gestured to her adorable kid, who was giggling with her new friend while Pearl and Dottie kept watch. "I have a preschooler who deserves all of my attention. She doesn't need the chaos of men coming in and out of our lives."

He frowned. "So you don't intend to date ever again?"

"I haven't ruled it out completely. Maybe in a few years. It's not my priority right now. I . . . have a lot to do first."

"Like what?"

When she finally spoke, she met his gaze, hers fixed with a mixture of determination and nervousness.

"I want to work for Lucas Construction."

He looked at her in surprise. "Doing what?"

"Whatever I can at first. Anything. But eventually I want to do what my mom does. Manage projects and help run the company. Does that sound crazy?"

"No. Just surprising. I had no idea you were interested in construction."

He should have realized, though. She had been intensely involved in the renovation of the bookstore, asking him questions about everything he did and pitching in whenever she could. She was obviously interested in every aspect of the project. He thought it was because she wanted to make sure the renovation went well. Now he could see the process interested her as much as the finished project.

"I have always loved it. I used to love going out on jobsites with my dad. There was something magical in seeing something go from an idea on paper to an actual building where people could live, work, play. He used to talk about the day when I could join him at the company. My dad never cared that he didn't have a son. He wanted me to be a partner."

"Have you told your mom what you want?"

She shook her head. "I feel like I need to prove myself at the bookstore first."

"Is that really necessary? She's your mom. She wants the best for you. If you would rather be working at the construction company than the bookstore, I'm sure she can figure something out."

She shook her head. "Not yet. I shouldn't have told you. Please don't tell her what I said."

"I don't get it. Why not? I'm sure she'll be happy to see you take an interest in the family company."

"Things between my mom and me are . . . complicated. You know that."

"I know that your mother blames herself for the years you were gone. She thinks if she had been a better mom to you after your dad died, you wouldn't have felt the need to run away."

She inhaled sharply. "That's not true. Not true at all. She doesn't really believe that."

He didn't answer, though he had heard Rosie say those very words. He didn't think she had meant for him to overhear but she had been talking to Sylvia one day in the bookshop when he had been there. His ears inevitably perked up when Emma's name had been mentioned.

Maybe he shouldn't have been quick to share what he overheard with the woman in question.

"It was never my mom's fault I left. Never. She did nothing wrong. I'm the one to blame. I made stupid, stupid decisions and screwed up my whole life."

"Not your whole life," he said, inclining his head toward Olive.

Her features softened, as they always did when she saw her daughter. "Not everything," she agreed.

As if she knew they had been talking about her, Olive ran over to them and plopped onto the blanket. Her new friend had returned to her own family, he saw, and they were packing up their things to leave the beach.

As Olive hugged her mother, Bryce watched the two of them and felt something hard lodge in his chest, an awareness he could no longer escape.

He was in love with Emma Lucas.

It wasn't a big surprise to him, since he'd loved her in some form or other since they were kids.

Even as he acknowledged this to himself, Bryce felt a pang of sadness. Emma had made it clear she wasn't interested in a relationship with him or anyone else and he knew he had to respect her wishes.

Still, he couldn't help imagining what it would be like to be part of their little family, to wake up each morning beside Emma, to help her raise Olive.

The longing was almost painful. But Bryce knew he would rather have Emma in his life as a friend than not at all. He would cherish these moments, these glimpses of what could be, even if they never became reality.

"Mama, I'm hungry. Can we have lunch now?"

Bryce knew that was his signal to grab Pearl and head back to town.

He didn't want to. He didn't want his time with Olive and Emma to end.

Her daughter was right. The beach was magical. He wanted to stay here, just the three of them, and enjoy the sunshine, the sound of the waves, and the tingle in his veins he got whenever he was around Emma Lucas.

He rose, brushing sand off. "I hope you guys enjoy your lunch."

"You should stay and have lunch with us," Olive said, in what sounded more like an order than a suggestion.

"That's very kind of you, sweetheart, but you and your mom didn't know you were going to be bumping into me when you packed your lunches today. You probably didn't bring along enough lunch for all three of us."

"I actually did," Emma said, looking embarrassed. "I made an extra sandwich in case one fell in the sand or something. I've learned with Olive it's better to have a contingency plan, especially when it comes to food. It's not much, only ham and cheese sandwiches, but we do have pasta salad and cookies we picked up at the bakery in town."

"How can I say no to cookies?" he said, then settled back down on the blanket to rejoin them.

Years from now, Bryce knew he would look back on this day as one of the most enjoyable of his life.

The day was gorgeous, the setting serene. A few other people came and went from the beach as they enjoyed their lunch but for the most part they had it to themselves except for the occasional seabird that toddled along the water's edge.

Olive was adorable, full of sass and funny observations about the world. She had stolen his heart the first time he met her in the bookshop and she seemed destined to leave a permanent imprint there, along with her mother.

What was he going to do about this love he could no longer deny?

Emma had made it abundantly clear she wasn't interested in a relationship, and he certainly did not want to be the guy who couldn't take a hint, especially when it had been delivered to him in unmistakable terms.

Despite her words, he knew something simmered between them, even if she didn't want to acknowledge it. She seemed as aware of him as he was of her. He saw it in the faint color that sometimes brushed her cheekbones when she looked at him, in the way her fingers trembled if they inadvertently touched, in the way she would catch his gaze and then look quickly away.

Was she remembering the kiss they had shared? Or was she determined to put it out of her head?

He had dreamed about having her in his arms again, about long, delicious days like this one, filled with laughter and conversation and that sizzle of awareness under his skin.

After lunch, they packed up her blanket and the picnic supplies and decided to walk around the point to take advantage of low tide and walk to Sea Glass Beach.

He took her backpack from her, much to her disgruntlement, and they made their way around the rocks to the beach.

As soon as they rounded the point, the beach came into view, stretched out like a glittering tapestry. Sunlight danced across the colorful fragments, transforming the coastline into a kaleidoscope of blues, greens and the occasional flash of amber.

"It's magic! Like mermaid jewels," Olive exclaimed.

"It is," her mother agreed.

"I know we can find some purple glass for Grandma here."

"We might, but if we do, we can't take it home," Emma told her in an apologetic tone.

"Why not? Grandma said we're supposed to take the sea glass off the beach if we find it."

"See that sign?" Emma says. "It tells people not to remove the sea glass from this particular beach. If you find it on other beaches, like the one by Grandma's house, you can take all you want because it's not a natural part of the shore. It's only there because of people throwing trash in the ocean. But here, all the different colors of sea glass are what makes it so beautiful."

"There's a bazillion pieces of glass. I can take one, can't I?"

"If everybody who came here took some of the sea glass away, soon there wouldn't be any left for other people to enjoy," Bryce said.

She gave a pouty expression but seemed to understand.

"Let me take your picture," Emma said, pulling out her phone.

Bryce reached for his phone as well to capture this memory, the two dogs cavorting above the high water line, where they couldn't hurt their paws on any jagged edges of glass, and these two people who had come to mean so much to him.

He knew he would treasure these memories forever.

As they walked along the shore, Bryce found himself lost in thought. Each piece of sea glass told a story of the ocean's patient polish. He bent down to pick up a deep cobalt piece, holding it up to the light. The edges, once sharp and dangerous, had been smoothed by time and tide into something beautiful.

Like the glass, Emma had been tossed by life's turbulent waves, weathered by storms of heartbreak and loss. Yet here she stood, not broken, but transformed. The harsh edges of her past had been softened, leaving behind a woman of remarkable strength and beauty.

Her infectious laughter, mingling with Olive's giggles, rang out across the beach. Bryce marveled at how she had emerged from her trials somehow polished into something even more beautiful.

The thought filled him with a profound tenderness and a surge of protectiveness. He vowed silently to be the shore for her, a safe haven against whatever waves might come. Even if she didn't want him to be that yet.

"We should probably head back," she said after they had

wandered the beach for nearly an hour. "The tide's going to start coming back in. I would hate to be trapped here."

Bryce would love to prolong the rest of this day, though he understood she would worry about her daughter being in the sun for too long and exposed to the elements.

He gathered the dogs' leashes and they made their way back around the point, scrambling over rocks.

Olive was tired, he could see, so Bryce handed the leashes to Emma, then picked Olive up to give her a piggyback ride. She curled up against his shoulder, her head nestled in the crook of his neck with a trust that made his throat feel tight and achy.

He was almost certain she fell asleep as she cuddled against him without a sound except her slow, even breathing.

In the parking lot, Emma led the way to the battered car that he had seen before in the bookstore parking lot. She opened the rear door and he carefully deposited a still-sleeping Olive in her car seat, where she leaned her cheek against the headrest without opening her eyes.

After Emma secured her seat belt, she turned to him. "That was fun. Thanks for carrying her."

"Thanks for letting me spend the afternoon with you."

"I don't think we *let* you do anything. We kind of made you. Olive can be very bossy when she wants to be."

"Good. She'll go far in life."

"I hope so."

"She's an adorable girl, Emma. It's impossible to be unhappy when you're around Olive."

She sent him an appraising look. "Do you consider yourself unhappy?"

He mulled her question. Did he? Yeah, things with his mom could be tough but for the most part, he enjoyed his life.

He had a challenging job he loved and friends he could always count on when he needed them.

Still, he had to admit he sometimes felt like something was missing.

"Not unhappy, though maybe not quite . . . content. Does that make sense?"

"Yes," she answered, her voice low. "Perfect sense."

Did she feel the same? Was she lonely sometimes?

Their eyes met and Bryce felt the air between them change. The empty trailhead parking lot faded away, leaving only Emma, bathed in the late-afternoon sunlight. Without conscious thought, he found himself stepping closer, drawn by an invisible force.

"Emma," he whispered, his voice barely audible over the distant crash of waves and the breeze in the treetops.

She didn't back away. Instead, her gaze flickered to his lips, then back to his eyes. It was all the invitation Bryce needed. Slowly, giving her every chance to pull away, he leaned in.

Their lips met softly, tentatively at first. Emma tasted of sunshine and lip balm, with a hint of cinnamon that reminded him of the cookies they'd shared earlier.

The scent of sunscreen lingered on her skin, mingling with something uniquely her. Bryce's heart raced as the kiss deepened, becoming more urgent, more needy.

His fingers found her waist, pulling her closer as her hands slid up his chest to rest on his shoulders.

Bryce wanted to lose himself in her, to keep kissing her forever. Each brush of her lips sent sparks through his body, igniting a fire he'd long tried to ignore.

But even as he reveled in the kiss, a small part of his mind reminded him of reality. Emma wasn't ready for this, for them. With immense effort, Bryce slowly eased away, his breathing ragged.

As their eyes met again, a mix of emotions swirled in Emma's gaze—desire, confusion and a hint of fear.

"I thought we said we weren't going to do that anymore," she murmured, her voice husky with lingering desire.

He gave her a long, slow look. "When I'm with you, Emma, I can hardly think of doing anything else."

She sent him a startled glance, and he saw color flare on her cheeks. After that kiss, did she really not have any idea how attracted he was to her?

Even if she didn't know the deeper feelings he was only now admitting to himself, she had to have some clue that he wanted to go on kissing her forever.

"I always had a crush on you in school. You knew that, right?"

She stared at him, eyes wide. "No! You had a funny way of showing it. You were always teasing me. I always felt like you were laughing at me for not being as cool as you and your friends."

"I was never laughing at you. If I teased you, it was out of sheer jealousy. I wanted you to smile at me instead of smiling at everybody else in school."

She swallowed hard, looking stunned.

"I planned to ask you to the junior prom. I was trying to get up my nerve and then . . . well, then your dad died."

"And my whole world fell apart," she said quietly.

"Yeah. You were in the hospital first then had his funeral and everything. I knew a stupid school dance would have been the last thing on your mind."

"Probably," she admitted.

"If things had been different, would you have gone with me?"

She appeared to consider the question. "I don't know," she said, honesty in her voice. "I might have thought you were too wild for me back then. You scared me, if you want the truth."

"Do I still scare you?"

Her gaze flickered to his mouth. Her lips looked swollen, her features flushed, and he ached to taste her again.

"For very different reasons," she murmured, then immediately looked as if she regretted saying anything.

"I need to go. Today was fun. I'm glad we bumped into you, even if I am afraid my mom might have orchestrated the whole thing."

"Seriously?"

"Don't you think it's a coincidence that she suggested hiking to Hidden Beach to both of us separately?"

"Why would she do that?"

"My mom wants me and Olive to stay in Wood Briar. I suspect she wants to push the two of us together in hopes that if you and I . . . start something together, I would have more incentive to stick around."

If only he had that kind of power over her decisions.

"Your mom's pretty crafty. But I'm glad we ran into each other, too, regardless of how it happened."

Emma nodded, her eyes meeting his briefly before she turned to her car. Bryce watched as she carefully checked on Emma then settled into the driver's seat.

Unable to resist, he leaned in before she could close the door and kissed her on the forehead.

"Drive safe."

She nodded, closed her door then started her engine.

Bryce stood rooted to the spot as her car pulled away, watching until it disappeared around the bend. The weight of his feelings pressed heavily on his chest.

He wished things could be different, but he knew he had to respect her boundaries.

As the sound of Emma's car faded into the distance, Bryce

let out a long sigh. He turned to walk back to his own vehicle, his mind replaying the kiss they had shared and wondering if there would ever be a chance for more.

Despite the ache in his heart, he couldn't help but feel a glimmer of hope. For now, it would have to be enough.

CHAPTER TWENTY-SIX

—

Rosie

ROSIE STOOD IN THE LARGE KITCHEN OF STORMHAVEN, LOOKing around in wonder.

"Oh, Kyle, this cabinetry is amazing. Thank you so much for putting a rush job on it as soon as everything finally came in."

Kyle Porter, one of her favorite local contractors, nodded. "Happy to do it for you, Rosie. I'm sorry it took us so long to make it work with the supply chain disruption and our busy schedule."

"The results are worth the wait," she said. "It all looks fantastic. I knew it would be. You do such great work."

"You're making good headway here. Won't be long, maybe another few weeks, and this old place might be livable again."

"I hope so," she said. "I know Mr. Morgan and his children are eager to move in."

Kyle shook his head. "I still can't believe I'm installing cabinets in a house for Andrew Morgan, the creator of my kids' favorite movie."

"Your kids are into The Starbound Chronicles?"

"They're crazy about the whole series. We've seen the movie a dozen times, and my kids are always playing the video game. I'll admit, I've even played it myself a time or two. We're excited to see the second installment. It will be even more fun now that Mr. Morgan lives here in town. I wonder if the movie theater will host any special screenings."

"That's a good idea. Maybe someone should mention it to Harriet Bell, though I'm guessing someone already has."

Harriet owned the only movie theater in town, a three-screen ancient movie house that still sold the best popcorn in town. Sometimes Rosie and her friends went for that alone.

"It's fun to know the creator of The Starbound Chronicles is such a nice guy, too. He's talked to me several times in the past three days that I've been doing the cabinets throughout the house, asking if I have everything I need."

"Did he?"

"I thought I would be nervous and a little starstruck around him, but he has a way of making you feel at ease, you know."

Were they talking about the same person? Every single time she saw him, Andrew left her feeling unsettled.

"And his kids seem nice, too," Kyle went on. "My youngest has been in drama camp with them. She and Zara have kind of become friends, which Lucy thinks is the coolest thing in the world, to know the daughter of one of her favorite authors."

As if on cue, the door opened and Zara and Finn raced in, followed closely by their grandmother. They all stopped and looked around at the kitchen with expressions of delight.

"Is the kitchen all done?" Zara asked.

"Almost," Kyle said. "Just have to put in the countertops and a few other details. It's getting there."

"Yay!" Finn exclaimed. "I can't wait to have my own bedroom again."

"Me, too," Zara said.

"This looks great," Nancy said. "Even better than the cabinets you did for me. Good to see you again, Kyle."

"What have you guys been up to today," the man asked.

"I just picked them up from drama camp," Nancy said.

"We're doing a play," Zara said. "It's called *The Karate Princesses.*"

"Wow. That sounds fun," Rosie said. "Do you have a part?"

"We both do," Finn said proudly. "I'm a karate guy."

He kicked the air and moved his hands like he was fighting an unseen opponent.

"And I'm one of the princesses," Zara said.

"It sounds lovely," Rosie said.

"You should come," Finn said. "You could bring Olive, too."

"When is it?"

"Friday, down at the community center. At 6:00 p.m., I believe," Kyle answered. "Lucy has been so excited about it. They're putting the whole thing together in only a few days. She did the same camp last summer and loved every minute of it."

"That sounds really fun. I can't make any promises, because I'll have to see what my Friday is like, but I'll definitely try," she answered.

She was charmed by these two cute children. Despite the pain of losing their mother and their home within only a few years, they seemed like great kids, curious and friendly.

The children told her all about their play while Kyle excused himself to take a phone call.

As he left, Andrew walked in. He looked rumpled and tired, his hair slightly messy as if he had been dragging his hands through it, and his shirt was wrinkled.

Despite that, Rosie had to catch her breath. Why did she always forget how gorgeous he was whenever she hadn't seen him for a few days?

"We were coming to see you," Finn said, launching himself at his father, who scooped him up in a tight hug.

Zara followed her brother, and Andrew reached out with his free hand to draw her close.

The clear love in their small family unit touched her. Yes, he was incredibly sexy in his rumpled creator persona but she somehow found his clear affection for his children even more attractive.

"Grandma said we could interrupt your writing for five minutes to tell you we both got parts in *The Karate Princesses*," Finn informed him. "I'm one of the karate guys."

Finn slid down out of his father's arms to repeat his fancy martial art moves, earning a smile from Andrew.

"Impressive. What about you, Z?"

"I'm one of the three princesses. We have to save our whole kingdom from some bad guys who want to take it over."

"I'm not a bad guy, though," Finn assured them all. "I help the princesses."

"That's a relief," his father said.

"Rosie said she might try to come. And maybe Olive, too," Zara announced.

"I hope I can make it," Rosie said, determined to juggle her schedule, if at all possible. How could she disappoint the children?

"Okay, you two," Nancy said. "You told your father your exciting news. We need to go practice your lines and let him get back to work."

"I'm nearly done for the day. I have a marketing phone call in a half hour, then I'll be home after that. Thanks for picking them up, Mom."

He kissed his mother's cheek, then turned to Rosie after his family left the kitchen.

"It was very kind of you to agree to go to the play, but you really don't have to. I'm sure you have other plans."

What other plans? The ever-present yard work? Her social life was not exactly packed right now.

Maybe she ought to look into the dating apps, as her mother had recommended. Maybe that would help her get over this silly crush on her neighbor and client.

"I believe I will have Olive all that night since her mother will be working late at the bookstore. I think she would love to see it, especially because she considers Finn and Zara her friends. They've been so kind to her. She and I can make a night of it and maybe go to dinner after the show."

She almost invited him and the children to join her but at the last minute common sense intruded.

"Sounds lovely," he said with a warm, slightly distracted smile that made her remember his mouth on hers.

She quickly drew herself back to the job at hand. "Actually, I was hoping I would run into you. I didn't want to interrupt your work, but I do need to talk to you about the tile in the third-floor guest bathrooms. Do you mind taking a look with me?"

"We can look, I suppose, but I know nothing about bathroom tiles."

She was fiercely aware of him as they walked up the two flights of stairs to one of the guest bathrooms.

"Your designer picked these small period subway tiles in the shower surrounds but this particular kind is back-ordered," she said. "Eddie, the tile subcontractor, is suggesting two alternatives to choose from. I've sent photos to Yvette and she said either one would work and that you can choose which one you like best."

She held out the sample boards for his perusal.

Andrew made a face. "Do you really think I care what kind of tile we end up with in these two bathrooms? I will probably never even use either of them."

"You might. Who knows? Maybe five years from now, you

will walk into one of them, look around and decide you hate every inch of it. Then you'll have to pay someone to come and tear it all out again."

"I can one hundred percent guarantee that is not going to happen. I am more likely to take up competitive yodeling in the Swiss Alps. Why don't you decide? Which one would you pick if this were your house?"

He winced as soon as the words were out. "I'm sorry, Rosie. I totally forget this once *was* your house."

She gave him a reassuring smile. "You don't have to apologize. I had to let go of my dreams for this house a long time ago."

"But what if you hadn't? Which one would you choose?"

She looked at the two samples, holding them up against the paint swatch. "If this were my house, I would probably go with this one, with the gray marbling. I think the other one is too dark for me, but that's my taste, not yours."

"Gray it is. I trust you, Rosie."

"I suppose that's a good thing, since I'm now managing your construction project."

"Even if you weren't, I think I would trust you. You obviously have good taste. Your house is very warm and comfortable. The few parts I've seen, anyway."

She had a sudden stray wish that he had seen her bedroom.

As soon as the thought entered her mind, Rosie felt her face heat. What on earth was the matter with her?

"Are you ready for tonight?" she asked quickly.

He grimaced. "Thanks for reminding me. I've been trying all day to put it out of my head so I can actually get some work done."

"It's not a big deal. I promise. We're not scary. And everyone is so happy that you agreed to come speak to our book club. The Wood Briar Sea Witches only has about twenty members—not all women, actually. Only about fifteen or so can make it with any regularity to our meetings."

"That shouldn't be so bad, I suppose."

"Although," she warned, "I do expect we'll have more than that tonight. You're a pretty big deal and several of our members were upset they couldn't meet you at the neighborhood party. Oh, and on our text chain, a few people have said they are planning to bring along a friend who loves your book."

"You're not really helping put my mind at ease."

"I'm really sorry to stress you more," she said. "You have no reason to be nervous. If it's any consolation, there will be plenty of friendly faces. My mom goes to the book group. And you met Mei Lin and Nina and several other members at the neighborhood party. Emma is coming as well. You know how much she loves your books."

"I'm sure I'll be fine. It's the lead-up to an event that gives me a few twinges of nerves. It doesn't take long for me to become so busy talking about books that I forget my anxieties."

"I don't understand why you would be nervous at all. Like I said, we're a small, friendly group and you're a celebrity writer. Everyone loves your books."

"I've had a couple of bad experiences. Right after my first book came out, one of my university professors invited me to come and speak to his Fiction Writing 101 class. I was flattered, to be honest, but when I arrived, he spent the whole hour talking about how commercial fiction like mine was ruining *real* literature."

"That's terrible!"

"I tried to put it down to professional jealousy. He had been trying to sell his own literary fiction for years, with no luck. I imagine it must have burned to see me find success so readily. I was a dumb kid who really had no idea what I was doing. Not only did my debut novel find a publisher, but it also hit some bestseller lists."

"I can promise, no one will be treating you with anything but respect and admiration tonight. I'm sure it will all go to your head."

He laughed. "I doubt that. That's the funny thing about writers. I imagine there are a few who are overflowing with confidence and hubris, certain that every word out of their pen is sheer magic. They're in the minority. Most of us who create still feel like imposters most of the time, waiting for everybody else to figure out we're talentless hacks."

This rare glimpse into his mind fascinated her. Okay, everything about this man fascinated her.

"The rest of the world strongly disagrees with that," she said. "You'll see tonight. You have the address, right?

"Your friend texted it to me."

"It might be hard to find. Barbara West lives on a cul-de-sac in a secluded beachfront neighborhood outside of town. Sometimes GPS doesn't always get things right around here. Text me if you have trouble and I'll try to direct you. In fact, we could go together, if that would be easier."

As soon as the words were out, Rosie wondered what on earth she was thinking. She did not need to spend more time alone with him.

Right now, she definitely did not trust herself around Andrew Morgan. If she wasn't careful, she was going to end up doing something stupid that she couldn't take back. Like fall head over heels for him.

"Sure. That would be great," he said.

She had no choice now. Might as well roll with it.

"At least that way you can be sure to see at least one friendly face. I can hold your hand if you get too nervous," she teased.

"Something to look forward to, then," he said, his voice low and amused.

She swallowed hard and had to look away, not sure if he was sincere or teasing her back.

"The book club starts at seven. Why don't I pick you up at twenty minutes to seven? That gives us plenty of time to make it to Barbara's house without being the first ones there."

"Perfect."

His cell phone rang and he gave her an apologetic look. "Sorry. This is the call I've been waiting for."

"Go ahead. I'll see you this evening."

He smiled in response and answered his phone. As he headed up the stairs to his attic office, she could hear him speaking in a brisk, businesslike tone that did funny things to her insides.

Face it, she thought. Everything the man did affected her like that. Whether she liked it or not.

CHAPTER TWENTY-SEVEN

—

Andrew

"THANKS FOR PICKING ME UP," ANDREW SAID AS HE SLID INTO the passenger seat of Rosie's late-model Volvo SUV. "I should have offered to drive. I didn't think about it."

"It makes more sense for me to drive. I know exactly how to get to Barbara's house."

Her car smelled like her, of springtime and flowers and lemons. Delicious.

"You don't have Emma or your mom?" He gestured to the back seat, empty except for a covered platter.

Rosie shook her head. "No. Em had a problem at the bookstore so she's going to be late. And Emma's picking up her grandmother on her way, since her car is easier for my mom to get in and out of."

"What about Olive?"

"One of the employees at the bookstore agreed to babysit her. She's at the house now."

"She's a really cute kid. You must enjoy having her live with you."

Rosie's features softened with a radiance that sent a funny quiver through him. "It's a dream. I'm sure your mom feels the same way about having your kids close. Some day you'll understand that, when you have grandkids. It's an entirely different kind of love."

"Is it?"

"Raising kids is like having to tend a garden you planted yourself. It's hard work, full of worry and responsibility. But loving a grandchild? That's like walking into a beautiful, wild meadow that's already in bloom. You get to marvel at its beauty without the burden of having cultivated it yourself. That probably sounds silly."

"It sounds lovely," he assured her.

"It's a love that's just as deep, but lighter somehow. You see all the joy and possibility without feeling the weight of knowing you're quite possibly shaping their entire future. It's a second chance to savor childhood, this time with the wisdom to know how fleeting and precious these moments truly are."

She had changed clothes from the jeans and work shirt she had been wearing earlier. Now she wore a pretty sundress with a matching sweater over it against the chill of the coastal evening.

She hardly looked old enough to have a daughter, let alone a granddaughter. If he were a smooth, slick kind of guy, he might be able to figure out a way to communicate that to her without sounding smarmy.

Instead, he kept his mouth shut, wishing he were better at this sort of thing.

He had never been much of a womanizer. After his first few books came out and he started to get a fan following, he had plenty of women proposition him at signings or book events. Though he did know a few other tomcat authors who leveraged their quasi-celebrity status to take advantage of their fans, that had never appealed to him.

He had only one serious relationship before he met his wife, with a woman he had known in college and met up with again while he was writing his first book. She had been a chef and the two of them had lived together for two years. The food—and the sex—had been great but Soledad hadn't wanted to commit, too married to her career.

When she left him for the owner of the restaurant where she worked, he hadn't really been brokenhearted.

Two years later, he had met Tracy in a meet-cute straight out of a romance novel. On a rainy afternoon, he had been finishing up meetings in New York with his publisher when they had both jumped into the same cab. She had been an editor at the same publishing house—not *his* editor and not even his imprint, but she had known and read his books.

One thing led to another and he had asked her out for drinks that turned into dinner. Before he quite realized how it happened, they were taking turns flying between his place in Los Angeles and hers in New York City.

Their relationship had seemed easy and comfortable from the very beginning and it had seemed a natural progression when he proposed. Since he could write anywhere, he had fully intended to move to New York, but Tracy had been frustrated with her job and wanted to strike out on her own as a freelance editor and literary agent. She had been the one who pushed for them to buy a house in the hills above Los Angeles and settle there, where they could raise the children they both wanted.

He never would have imagined back in those heady days of starting their lives together that a decade later, he would be a widower raising those children on his own, that they would lose their cherished house in a fire, or that he would upend everything to move himself and his children to a crumbling house on the Oregon coast.

Tracy would have loved it here, he thought. She would have found peace knowing Zara and Finn were safe, happy and loved, that they were living close to their grandmother and were making new friends in this community that had already embraced them.

He suspected that Tracy would have loved Rosie, too. The two of them would have gotten along great, bonding over their shared love of books.

"Almost there," Rosie said, tugging him out of his thoughts.

"Sounds good."

"I think you'll like everyone. The Sea Witches have been meeting in some form or another for about twenty years. People come and go, but the core group of about ten of us have been there forever. We're pretty eclectic in our reading choices. We like everything from sci-fi to historicals to nonfiction. It depends on who is hosting the group that month. They get to pick what book we read."

"In my experience, book clubs are only peripherally about the books. Is that the case with yours?"

She laughed, a sound that rippled through her vehicle.

"Guilty," she admitted. "We do talk about the book for a nominal portion of the book club. The rest of the time is spent visiting, catching up on our families and what's happening in our lives. They're a fascinating group. Barbara, for instance, recently got back from a monthlong cruise around Japan. I can't wait to talk to her about what she saw. My other friend Shara is trying to adopt a child through the foster system, since she and her husband haven't had any luck conceiving. I haven't had a chance to talk to her about the status of their application. We've supported each other through all kinds of things—divorce, problems with our kids, loss of our spouses."

"They must have been a big help to you after your husband died."

She nodded and grew silent. "Amazing. I would have been lost without them. And my mom, of course." She sent him a look across the width of the vehicle. "Did you have someone to help and support you when your wife died?"

"My mom, of course. She came to live with us after Tracy

was first diagnosed. I also have a couple of good friends. We've been tight since we were in boarding school together. They're more like brothers to me."

"Where are they now?"

"Pete lives in Palm Beach. He's an attorney. Jonas is actually in Africa working for an organization that helps villages access clean water."

"A worthy cause."

"The two of them couldn't be more different but they were still both rocks in their own way."

"Boarding school," Rosie said in a surprised tone. "I'm not sure I would have taken you for a boarding school kid."

The first few years, he had hated every moment of it. He had desperately wanted to go home but of course his father wouldn't allow it.

"My dad would never have considered anything else for his sons."

"Sons?"

He frowned, wishing he hadn't let that slip. He either had to ignore the question or talk about a topic he usually tried to avoid.

He found he didn't mind sharing that part of his life with Rosie, for reasons he wasn't sure he was ready yet to analyze.

"I had an older brother. Will. He was two years older than me. He died when I was eight."

She shifted her gaze from the road and he saw her green eyes looked murky with compassion. "Oh, Andrew. I'm so sorry. I had no idea. I'm not sure your mother ever mentioned her other son."

He wasn't surprised by that. Nancy had done all her grieving inwardly. Will's death had devastated what had already been a dysfunctional family.

"He drowned," Andrew said, his clinical tone at odds with

the grief that still felt raw. "Every summer we would go to a family cabin on a lake. He went out for an early morning swim one day without permission and . . . never came back. He was a strong swimmer but they think he had a leg cramp or something."

"How terrible for your family."

"It was rough."

He remembered that time vividly, waking up and being angry that Will must have gone swimming without him. He had rushed to the lake to yell at him, only to find his brother floating twenty yards from the shore.

He had screamed and screamed his brother's name and could still recall how his father had shoved him aside as he dove into the water.

"Your parents still sent you to boarding school? I wouldn't have wanted to let you out of my sight."

"It was our family's way. Will had started the year before he died. Then it was my turn."

"Was it as horrible as people say?"

"Not really. Parts of it were. I missed my mom."

"Not your dad?"

Andrew thought of his brusque, distant father who seemed to become even more so after his brother's death.

"We didn't have a close relationship." Or one at all, really. "He was very busy with work. He was an investment banker with a lot of important clients. His work responsibilities didn't leave much time for him to play catch in the backyard."

She gave him a long look, as if his words explained something she'd been trying to piece together in her mind.

"So you turned to books."

Nailed it. "Yeah. Will was the gregarious one. I was happier curled up with a stack of library books."

"Same. I don't have the trauma of losing a sibling in my past, but I think I told you my family moved around a lot when I was young. I wasn't great at making friends but it's hard to feel lonely when you've got a world of book characters to keep you company."

Oh, he liked this woman. He could easily see himself falling hard for her if he wasn't careful.

"I think it's even more remarkable, then, that you've chosen to be an entirely different kind of dad than your own."

"What do you mean?"

"I was thinking this afternoon what a great father you are. From my perspective, everything you do seems to be aimed at ensuring you're making the right choice for your kids."

Andrew knew he did not deserve her praise. Most of the time, he felt he was completely fumbling through this single father thing, like a sailor navigating through uncharted water with a broken compass. Every day brought new challenges, unexpected storms and hidden reefs that threatened to sink the whole damn thing.

Still, it was nice of her to say.

"I try. My kids are my greatest gift."

"I get that. Emma was mine. We tried for about five years to have a second child with no success. I wish I had done what Shara and John are doing and gone the adoption route."

"Why didn't you?"

"Multiple reasons. We tried all the fertility treatments without success. I had a couple of miscarriages that were devastating for both of us. We finally decided around the time Emma turned seven that we were spending so much time and energy trying for another child that we were wasting our chance to savor the one we already had."

"Sounds very wise."

"I don't know about that. But I don't really regret it," she said as she pulled up to a house in a secluded cove he never would have been able to find on his own.

When he saw the line of other cars parked in the neighborhood, Andrew was annoyed to feel a quiver of nerves again. He knew he had absolutely no reason to be nervous. Readers were his people. Even if they weren't huge fans of his books, they all shared an appreciation for the power of the written word.

Too late to back out now. He might as well roll with it. As he climbed out, Rosie opened the rear door, reached in and emerged with a bottle of wine as well as the covered tray he had noticed earlier.

"My lemon bars," she informed him. "We sign up each month to bring either appetizers or desserts."

"I didn't realize there was food."

"Small bites, mostly. Though I've had a busy day and I didn't have time for dinner. Or much lunch, come to think of it. I hope I can nibble enough through the evening that my stomach won't growl in the middle of the book club."

"Let me carry something for you," he said.

She handed over the tray of lemon bars and led the way to the front door of what looked like a large, modern beach house with soaring windows and elegant landscaping.

A small sign on the door bid new arrivals to come straight in, so Rosie pushed it open. As soon as they walked inside, everyone greeted them with enthusiasm.

Andrew counted a few more people than he was expecting. Maybe thirty?

As she had done at her neighborhood party, Rosie made the rounds, introducing him to everyone. He knew he would never remember anyone's names and was touched when their host, a tall, stately woman, pulled out a marker and adhesive name tags for everyone. He knew it was only on his account as these people must all know each other.

It was clear that Rosie was enormously well respected in town. He had noticed it during her party and it was even more apparent here, surrounded by a smaller group of friends.

As the group chatted prior to the actual start of the meeting, Andrew found himself pleasantly surprised by how much he was enjoying himself. Everyone was gracious and welcoming and their enthusiasm for his work was both flattering and invigorating.

Every so often, his gaze would drift to Rosie, catching the way her face lit up when she smiled or how she leaned forward, completely engrossed as she listened to someone speak to her. Her genuine interest in others was magnetic, and Andrew found himself increasingly drawn to her gentle strength and easy grace.

He marveled at how she could make everyone, including him, feel so at ease.

He liked her, more than he had liked anyone in a very long time.

CHAPTER TWENTY-EIGHT

—

Emma

"I'M SORRY WE'RE GOING TO BE LATE TO THE BOOK CLUB, Grandma."

Sylvia made a dismissive gesture. "Don't you worry about that. Being late gives us the perfect chance to make an entrance, which you know is my favorite thing in the world."

Emma had to smile, even after the long, arduous day she'd had. She adored Sylvia, who looked particularly charming tonight wearing a dress in kaleidoscopic colors, along with dangly earrings and multiple bangles at her wrist.

"Did you get our Olive settled with the babysitter?"

"Yes. She was excited to have her. She's quite familiar with Maya from seeing her at the bookstore. Maya's always great to read to her when she has a minute free between shelving books. I think they'll have fun."

As usual, she hated leaving Olive yet again, though they had spent all morning together. Still, Emma had vowed to herself that after tonight, she wouldn't go to another social event without her daughter for at least a month.

As soon as the bookstore renovation was done, she planned to reduce her hours to spend more time with Olive. For now, she brought her daughter into the store with her as much as she could and always had Josie, her mother and Sylvia as backup.

How could she miss out on the chance to hear Andrew Morgan talk about his books? She had her own copies of The Starbound Chronicles in her bag and hoped he would agree to sign them.

"How's the renovation going?" Sylvia asked as Emma drove toward the cove where the book group was meeting.

"Slow but steady. Bryce is a good worker."

"And he's not bad on the eyes, am I right?" Sylvia asked with a twinkle.

Emma sighed. Not at all. If he was only good-looking, she would find it much easier to resist him. But Bryce was so much more and she was having a tough time reminding herself she didn't have room in her life for a man right now.

"Oh, he's fine, I guess," she said casually.

If you're into big, muscular construction workers who are also well-read.

And who wouldn't be? Emma rolled her eyes at herself. Was she crazy to keep him at arm's length? It was obvious he was interested in her, and she certainly was attracted to him. Every time she thought about him, she was aware of a breathless feeling.

"He's a great guy," Sylvia said. "Hardworking, conscientious. You could do a whole lot worse."

Yes. She was fully aware. She had dated enough losers to know when a man was the very opposite of one.

"Not in the cards," she said to Sylvia. "I'm much too busy right now with the bookstore and Olive and trying to figure everything out."

To her relief, Sylvia didn't press the issue as she helped navigate to a part of town Emma wasn't familiar with, a development of newer beach houses.

She didn't know the woman hosting the book club. Apparently Barbara West was a relative newcomer to town. Thanks to Sylvia's directions, they soon arrived at their destination.

"These are nice houses," Emma said, admiring the way they seemed to blend into the landscape.

"Your mom is very proud of them. Lucas Construction was the builder on all of them. That's how she and Barbara became friends. Your mom was the project manager on Barbara and her husband's house."

These were definitely higher-end custom-built homes. Lucas Construction had done a great job, from what she could see on the outside.

She found a parking space between a small SUV and a flashy convertible, then moved around the side of the car.

"I can do this," Sylvia said as Emma opened the door and reached a hand in to help her grandmother out. "With this walking cast, I mostly just need a cane. I'm getting along much better now."

Emma had noticed and wasn't sure what to think about that. "I'm so glad you're feeling better. Whenever you feel like you're ready to come back to the bookstore, I can step aside. I'm sure I could find something else in town to do."

Perhaps she could persuade her mother that she wanted to start at the bottom at the construction company.

Sylvia snorted. "Don't be silly. The last thing I want is for you to step aside."

"You don't want to come back to the bookstore?"

"Not to run the place. You are exactly what The Rainy Day Bookshop needed to shake things up, someone with more energy, enthusiasm and ideas than I could ever find, especially at this stage of life."

"I hate feeling like I showed up in town and pushed you out of doing something you love."

"Don't be silly. I was more than ready to quit. If I hadn't been, do you really think a silly broken leg would have kept me on the sidelines?"

Emma narrowed her gaze at her grandmother. "Then why am I here?"

Sylvia shrugged. "You needed to be home and this broken ankle was as good an excuse as any."

Emma frowned as she helped her grandmother up the two steps to the front door. "Are you telling me you orchestrated this whole thing?"

"Not the broken ankle. That was real, unfortunately. But I'm glad things happened as they did. You and Olive needed to come home."

Since she couldn't argue, she only gave her grandmother a chiding look. "I like making my own decisions for my life. You could have asked me to come back even before you broke your ankle."

"Would that have made a difference? You only came home because you thought it was an emergency. Admit it."

She could not disagree. "You are a rascal, Grandma," she said.

Sylvia only laughed. "I know, but you love me anyway."

She hugged the older woman, smelling her familiar scent of roses and sandalwood that immediately took her back to being a girl cuddling beside her grandmother while Sylvia read to her.

"You're lucky you're so lovable."

Sylvia laughed, a low, husky sound. "Don't I know it?"

There was a sign on the door that bid visitors to enter. Feeling odd about walking into a stranger's home, Emma knocked softly before she pushed open the door. A sleek, well-groomed woman beamed at them.

"Hi, Sylvia. And you must be Emma. You look like your mother. Come in."

She ushered them into a large open room packed with people, some she recognized and others who were unfamiliar to her.

"Have we missed listening to our sexy new author?" Sylvia asked.

Barbara chuckled. "He hasn't officially started talking. You have time to come and grab something to eat. We have tons of food. Pam brought croissant chicken salad sandwiches, and they are absolutely delicious."

Emma stiffened. Pam was there? She hadn't realized the other woman was part of the book club.

She should have asked her mother for the guest list. She had absolutely no desire to socialize with her.

She couldn't back out now, though. They were here and she had to stay so she could drive her grandmother back home.

"That sounds good. I'm starving," Sylvia said. She hobbled over to a table that had been set up in the open-plan kitchen, which had two large islands that were covered with food platters.

The people of Wood Briar certainly never wanted anyone to go hungry.

The book group was a large, eclectic mix. Some of the women were her grandmother's age, but she was happy to see a few that were her own.

Her mother was engrossed in conversation with several other woman and Emma was struck by how put-together her mom looked. Rosie wore soft-gray trousers and a silk blouse that brought out the green in her eyes. She looked every inch the successful businesswoman she'd become.

She was lovely, Emma thought, not for the first time. At forty-five, Rosie had decades of life ahead of her. She could easily find another relationship, start a new chapter in her life. So why hadn't she?

The question nagged at Emma. In all the years since her father died, Emma wasn't sure Rosie had dated anyone. Sylvia had never mentioned it to her, anyway.

Had Rosie put her own life on hold all this time? The

thought made Emma's chest tighten with a mix of guilt and concern.

Her mother must have sensed her scrutiny. She looked up and smiled, maneuvering through the crowd to hug Emma.

"I'm so happy you made it! Was Olive all right with the babysitter?"

"She and Maya were having a lovely time when I left. Olive was thrilled because Maya brought a bunch of craft supplies. I think she will be very entertained."

"Oh good. You need to grab something to eat. There are a few vegetarian options. I was worried about that, but it looks like somebody brought a veggie plate, and there are some croissants that don't have the chicken salad on them."

"Mom, I'm fine. You don't have to fuss over me."

Rosie looked slightly put out, and Emma regretted her tone. When would they relax around each other? Would they ever, or were the scars between them too deep for them to ever completely heal their relationship?

"This is a big crowd. How's Andrew doing?"

To her surprise, she saw a faint hint of color climb her mother's cheeks.

"He's fine. I believe he's over there being cornered by Susie and Betty Phillips."

She followed the direction of her mother's inclined head and found Andrew surrounded by several women—including Pam Clarke, she saw with annoyance.

As if he somehow sensed them talking about him, Andrew looked up. His gaze seemed to unerringly find Emma's mother and his polite smile widened into something that looked much more genuine. Rosie smiled back, then looked away, the flush on her cheeks climbing higher.

Well. Wasn't that interesting?

Was something going on between her mother and Andrew Morgan?

The man really was good-looking, for an older guy. He had brown hair with only a trace of gray and a long, lean frame.

And he seemed to be looking at her mother with a definite light in his eyes.

Emma was not sure how she felt about that.

Andrew seemed like a very nice guy. They had lots in common, too, especially their love of books.

She wanted to ask her grandmother if she had noticed anything between the two of them, but Sylvia was talking to a couple of other women she didn't recognize.

Her stomach rumbled, so Emma hurried to the kitchen. An assortment of appetizers and sweet treats presented a tempting display. She filled up her plate with vegetables and relented enough to grab one of the small croissants.

Pam might have brought them but she obviously hadn't made them herself. She likely had purchased them from the bakery in town. That somehow made it okay for Emma to eat one, though she had to wonder if she was rationalizing.

Emma nibbled on a cucumber slice as she walked across the room to chat with Candace Early, the town librarian. She had always been kind.

"Emma! I'd heard you were back in town and running your mom's bookstore. I'm sorry I haven't had a chance to come in yet. It's so great to see you. You look fantastic."

Did she? Emma felt exhausted most of the time and was fairly sure her appearance reflected that.

"I love that tattoo." A younger woman whose name tag read Lindsay pointed to the moon and heart on Emma's forearm with the cursive "To the moon and back."

Emma smiled. "Thanks. It helped me get through some tough times."

"I have a tattoo," the librarian said.

Emma gazed at the quiet woman, surprised. "Do you? What is it?"

To her delight, Candace pushed up her sleeve to reveal a tattoo on her upper arm of an open book with planets rising out of it.

"Oh, that's perfect!" Emma exclaimed. "I love it."

"Mel was quite astonished when I came home with it after I went on a girls' trip with my sisters to Seattle. Now he likes it, though."

Before Emma could respond, their host tapped a spoon against a glass to catch the group's attention.

"Everyone, please take your seats. I know we love to chat but we're going to be here all night if we don't get started."

Somehow, miraculously, there were enough seats for them all. When everyone seemed to settle, Barbara cleared her throat and spoke.

"It is my great honor to welcome our special guest, who is also our town's newest resident. We're so pleased to have the amazing Andrew Morgan with us. If you have not read his books, you are definitely missing out. They're full of adventure, intrigue, great characters and fabulous writing. Andrew has kindly agreed to give us a short reading from his latest book that will be coming out next month and then he is happy to answer some questions. I thought we could maybe have a short Q and A for ten or fifteen minutes to ask him about his process."

Andrew, Emma saw, didn't look particularly happy to be the center of attention but he gave a polite smile. Emma glanced at her mom and saw Rosie offer a bright, encouraging smile. As if some secret message passed between the two of them, the corner of Andrew's mouth lifted and he straightened slightly as he moved to the front of the room.

As Emma listened to him introduce himself and his book, she was struck again by what a handsome man he was. He would be perfect for her mother.

If Rosie could maneuver behind the scenes to throw Emma and Bryce together by sending them both to the same remote beach, Emma should be able to do something similar for her mom and Andrew Morgan.

She listened with fascination to his reading, a continuation of his Starbound Chronicles. She couldn't wait to read it and wondered if she could finagle an advanced reader's copy out of him for the bookstore.

She had already ordered one hundred copies for the store and would love to persuade him to come and sign some of them for her.

Even better would be a book launch event where he would sign them for the public. She would have to work on that while she tried to come up with some creative way to push him together with her mother.

After he finished his reading, he answered a few questions about how he started writing and why he chose to write the kind of books he did. Barbara cut off questions after twenty minutes and everyone continued socializing.

Emma was glad she had made the effort to find a babysitter for Olive and carve time out of her schedule to come. Besides the chance to listen to a fascinating author she admired, she had been able to chat with several people she knew, and she had made a few new friends.

Through it all, she had been able to avoid Pam—until the end of the evening, anyway.

After three glasses of sparkling water, Emma found herself in need of a bathroom break. Barbara pointed her down a hallway and around a corner to a guest bathroom. As she headed that way, the door opened and someone came out.

Pam.

The two of them were alone in the hallway, and Emma had nowhere to go. She braced herself to be as polite as humanly possible.

Pam gave her a bright smile. "Emma, darling. I feel like you've been avoiding me all night. I'm sure I'm imagining things, but it felt like every time I tried to approach you, you moved to the other side of the room."

Oh, she'd noticed that, had she? Apparently, Emma had not been as subtle as she had hoped.

"Is everything okay?" Pam pressed.

No. Everything was not okay.

"Sure," she mumbled. She would have moved past the woman and locked the door of the bathroom, but Pam held out an arm.

"I get the impression you're mad at me for something. What did I do? I would love to clear the air."

Emma thought about lying to her, making nice and being polite. But the scene Andrew had read that featured his main characters digging deeply for courage to face their foes against overwhelming odds seemed to resonate in her head.

She did not need a confrontation with Pam tonight, but she was also not in the mood to lie simply to be polite to this woman.

"I saw you that day."

Pam stared at her, eyes wide and confused. "You saw what? What day?"

"The day my dad died. I saw the two of you together."

Pam's face seemed to lose color and her jaw sagged. "You . . . what?"

Emma nodded. "I was supposed to meet Dad at four so he could take me driving after school. We had some kind of school assembly that day so I decided to leave early and surprise him."

She had been the one surprised, though.

The memory of all she had seen and heard burned in her mind, hot and shameful.

Pam seemed to turn another shade paler.

"Imagine my surprise when there was nobody at the front desk to meet me. I could hear sounds coming from his office. I didn't want to disturb my dad but I wanted to let him know I was there. The door was slightly ajar and I saw the two of you there on his sofa. You certainly weren't going over the payroll. You were all over him."

Now a hot tide of color seemed to wash over Pam's features, leaving her skin splotchy. "I'm sure you misunderstood what you saw. You were only a girl and it was a long time ago."

"I didn't misunderstand anything. I know what I saw. You were making out. How long had you been going after my dad?"

"You don't know what you're talking about," Pam said, her voice icy.

"I know what I saw. I have no idea how you have managed to hide the truth from my mom for all these years. If she had any idea you were screwing her husband, I know she would never have let you stay working at Lucas Construction."

A host of emotions seemed to cross Pam's features. Embarrassment, unease and the beginnings of anger. "We never slept together."

"That's what my dad said, too. I didn't believe him any more than I believe you."

Pam now looked like she wanted to rush past her back to the party but Emma remained in her way. Now that the words had spilled out, she couldn't seem to hold back her scorn.

"What kind of person sleeps with the husband of someone who was supposed to be her friend? A friend who has continued to employ you and pay you very well for the past ten years."

"I don't need to listen to this." Pam again tried to push past her but Emma stood firm, ten years of pain and anger spewing out as if she had ruptured a pipeline.

"What did you hope to achieve? Did you really think my dad was going to leave my mom? He loved her."

Pam drew in a sharp breath, her gaze hardening. "Your mother was never the woman Gary needed," she hissed, her voice low and intense. "He needed a partner. An equal. Rosie didn't care about Lucas Construction. She didn't care about anything but her stupid little bookstore and about buying Stormhaven. She wasn't there for him. *I was.* I was the one staying late with him to work on bids, advising him on personnel issues, spending my weekends dealing with bank paperwork."

Her mom *had* been a little distracted around that time, Emma remembered. And her parents had been bickering more than usual. Had Pam swooped in to take advantage of the opportunity when her parents were going through a rocky time?

"Your dad had feelings for me," Pam went on, her voice still low. "He *was* going to leave your mom, and we were going to run the company. Together, we would have been unstoppable. We were talking about having a future together. We would have had a great one, too."

She narrowed her gaze, skewering Emma with a look of deep antipathy. "Until you had to go and ruin *everything* by killing him."

Emma nearly reeled in the face of the other woman's vitriol. She felt dizzy, lightheaded, as all her own guilt and pain coalesced.

She curled her hands into fists, wanting to smack Pam right

in her furious face. She wanted to hit out, to run from the house, to go get wasted or high or any of the old things she once used to escape.

"It was all *your* fault," Emma hit back. "We were fighting about *you* right before I hit the slick patch and drove off the cliff."

"That doesn't make it my fault. You were behind the wheel."

"I told him I had seen you together. Do you want to know what he said?"

Pam looked as if she wanted to cover her ears with her hands. Her gaze flitted down the hallway but Emma didn't turn around, too busy finally, *finally* spilling out all the ugliness of that day.

"He said it was only a harmless flirtation. Meaningless. You were lonely and he was flattered by your attention. He said he felt sorry for you, that he lost his head, but that it meant nothing and would never happen again."

"Of course that's what he said. He wasn't going to tell the truth about what we felt for each other to his fifteen-year-old daughter."

Wondering about that had haunted Emma for all these years. Had her dad been lying? Could his and Pam's relationship have been deeper and more important to Gary than he claimed?

She would never know. She only knew that her father died that day but she had also lost her idealized image of him as a loving father and husband.

She felt shaky and sick and wished she had never started this, that she had turned back around and rushed away as soon as she saw Pam come out of the bathroom. The same way she had rushed away that day in the office when she had found them together, only to come back inside, this time making noise and calling out to alert them to her presence.

Pam made a move to rush past her but Emma had one more thing to say. She drew in a breath and faced this woman who had caused irreversible harm.

"Even if you were having an affair with him that had been going on for years under my mother's nose, my dad loved us. He never in a million years would have left my mother for someone like you."

"You keep telling yourself that, honey."

"Wh-what?"

At the new voice from the end of the hallway, Emma turned and felt any blood remaining leave her face.

Rosie stood staring at both of them, her features pinched, haunted.

How much had her mother overheard? Her stomach roiled as every bite she had eaten that evening threatened to rise up again.

"Mom."

"What are you saying?" Her mom was looking at Pam. "You and Gary had an affair?"

Pam said nothing, looking as if she would rather be anywhere else on earth.

"This isn't the place or time for this, Mom. Let's talk about it when we get home."

"No. I want to talk about it now."

Her mom was shaking, she saw. Emma stepped forward and would have taken Rosie's arm but her mother held her hand out as if pushing away a tidal wave of pain.

"Gary wouldn't have betrayed me. We . . . we loved each other since we were in high school."

"People change," Pam said tightly. "Their needs change and sometimes they no longer want the same things they did when they were teenagers. I used to love fruit-flavored bubble gum but then I grew out of it."

Okay. Emma *was* going to punch the bitch.

Rosie looked devastated, as if this entire beach house she had built for Barbara West had collapsed around her.

Emma narrowed her eyes at Pam. "And sometimes they realize what they want and need has been right in front of them the whole time and that everything else is a pathetic attempt to fill a void that didn't need to be there in the first place."

Pam gave her one last look of loathing and then pushed past both of them to return to the party. A moment later, she heard a door shut and assumed Pam had left.

Meanwhile, Rosie was staring at her out of eyes that looked bruised, betrayed.

"You knew about . . . about your dad and . . . her?"

Emma swallowed, closing her eyes. She had never wanted this day to come. She had hidden the truth for a decade, unable to truly grieve her father's death properly because she was so full of anger toward him.

She could never accept her mother's attempt to comfort her after Gary died because Emma was so afraid of Rosie finding out the truth.

"All this time, you knew and you didn't say anything to me?" Rosie pressed.

Emma released a shaky breath. "There wasn't anything to say, Mom. Not really. I had no idea what was truly going on between them. I only know what I saw."

"Which was what?"

She couldn't lie. Not now, after all this time. "They were on the couch in his office. The one where I used to sit and do homework while he would make phone calls. They were both dressed but . . . they were making out. I'm sorry, Mom."

"Why didn't you tell me?"

Emma closed her eyes, unable to look at her mother as she

spoke the truth that had haunted her all this time. The truth she had tried to escape with booze and drugs, the truth she had been trying to run from when she left Wood Briar.

She and her mother had fought about every single thing back then except this. The one inexorable fact beneath everything else.

"Because an hour later he was dead and it was my fault. We were fighting about *Pam* and I wasn't paying as much attention to the road conditions as I should have been and neither was he. And as a result, I killed him."

CHAPTER TWENTY-NINE

—

Rosie

ROSIE HEARD HER DAUGHTER'S HARSH WORDS FROM A LONG distance away but it took her several seconds to register them through her shock.

An hour later he was dead and it was my fault . . . I killed him.

"It was an accident," Rosie said, her voice as firm as she could manage around the horror that was only now beginning to feel real. "Completely an accident. It was only bad luck that you hit that patch of wet road and spun out right where the railing was weak."

This couldn't be happening. Rosie felt as if the very foundations of her world had crumbled.

This had to be a mistake. Gary wouldn't have cheated on her with anyone, especially not Pam.

Would he?

Rosie felt like she was going to throw up. She was going to be sick all over Barbara's lovely tile flooring they had spent two weeks installing.

"Come on, Mom. Let's go home. We can talk about this there."

That made the most sense. They were in the middle of a party. A party with thirty-odd people who did not need to be part of this airing of dirty laundry.

Pam.

Could Gary have been sleeping with Pam? The woman who had been a rock for Rosie since his death, who had stepped up to help run things with Victor Blackwood when

Rosie had been too numb with grief and shock to think about Lucas Construction?

She felt betrayed on every single level.

How was she going to go back in there to the rest of the book club and pretend that nothing was wrong, when she felt as if she had shattered into a million pieces?

For ten years she had grieved Gary. Had she been grieving a mirage?

He had been the love of her life, the yang to her yin, the other missing piece of her. From the time she was seventeen years old, she had loved him. When she found out she was pregnant with Emma, it had been an easy decision to marry him. They had adored each other.

Yet apparently he had betrayed her on that final, monumental day.

She didn't know how to absorb the blow but she could see from the pale, stiff set of Emma's features that it must be true.

What was she going to do? She wanted to flee but she was supposed to give Andrew a ride home. She wasn't sure she could even talk to the man right now, when her emotions were in such turmoil.

As if sensing her thoughts, Emma stepped forward. "Let me gather Grandma, and I'll meet you at the house. I can get Olive to bed if she's not already asleep and I will tell you the truth about what happened that day, at least what I know."

She nodded numbly, drew in a sharp bracing breath and returned to the book club meeting.

Somehow Rosie made it through the next few moments, feeling as if all the broken pieces of herself were being held together by sheer grit.

She was trying to arrange a ride home for Andrew when he

overheard her asking a couple of her friends if they could drop him off at Stormhaven.

"I don't need to stay," he said. "I can leave now."

She frowned through facial muscles that felt strained and achy. "Are you sure? I don't want to take you away if you're having a good time."

He gave her a careful look and she saw concern in his dark eyes. Apparently she wasn't as good at hiding her shock and dismay as she hoped.

"No, it's fine. I'm ready to go. More than ready."

"All right. I just need to get my things."

She found her purse in the closet where she had left it, grabbed the empty plate that had once contained lemon bars and somehow managed to extricate herself from the party, giving monosyllabic answers to everyone who wished her good evening.

She was still fighting back tears as she made her way to her car and unlocked it with hands that trembled.

She had to hope Andrew didn't notice. "I'm really sorry to drag you away from the party," she said, starting the car when he slid inside.

"Why? It was wrapping up anyway. I'm happy to leave."

She made some kind of sound, she wasn't sure what, as she pulled out into the street and headed back toward their neighborhood.

She could feel Andrew's scrutiny through the darkness. "What is this about, Rosie? What happened? Everything seemed to be fine but now you look like you were smacked in the head by a two-by-four."

"I'm fine."

She couldn't tell him. Not when she was still trying to come to terms with the shocking information herself.

"The book club went well, don't you think?" she said in an artificially bright voice. "Everyone there was so happy to meet you and to talk about your books."

"I enjoyed myself more than I expected to," he admitted. "Wood Briar seems like a very welcoming place."

"It is. I saw you talking with Samantha Taylor. She's a dear friend with kids around the same age as Zara and Finn. You two would be a good couple."

It was the only distraction she could come up with right now, with her emotions so tangled and raw.

"Are you really trying to set me up with one of your friends?"

She tightened her hands on the steering wheel. "Not exactly. I was only spilling the tea that she's available. If you're interested."

"I'm not."

"Well, you could do far worse, if you were," she answered, grateful to focus on something else. "Sam is a smart, funny, warm woman. And a terrific mom to her kids."

"Now you sound like my mother."

Ouch. She was older than him by at least a few years. And, yes, she was a grandmother. But she was a young grandmother, wasn't she?

Somehow she managed to compartmentalize what she had overheard so she could speak politely to Andrew about other things. The children's play coming up, the construction project, the rain that was forecast for at least a few more days.

She knew she was babbling. The words seemed to spill out of her, but she didn't care. Better to focus on anything else right now.

It was only a few moments but it felt like forever before she finally pulled up to the carriage house at Stormhaven. "Here we are. I hope you have a good night."

To her dismay, he made no immediate move to get out of the vehicle. Instead, he turned to face her, studying her features in the dim light from her dashboard.

"You've done a pretty good job of hiding it, but I can tell you're still upset. Is there anything I can do?"

Her throat closed up at the concern in his voice and she barely fought down a sob.

"It's been a rough night," she admitted. "But I'll be fine once I get home."

At the last word, her voice finally broke, and the tears she had been shoving down began to spill over, much to her horror.

Oh, she hoped he couldn't see them in the darkness.

"Are you sure?"

No. She wasn't at all sure. She didn't think she would be okay ever again.

"I found out tonight that my husband was cheating on me before he died."

Her hand gripped the steering wheel, and she could not look at him, appalled that the words had somehow burst out of her, despite her best efforts to hold them in.

She saw compassion and concern in his expression. "Oh, Rosie. I'm sorry. You really didn't know before tonight?"

She shook her head, reliving the horror of hearing Pam and Emma fighting.

Even if you were having an affair with him that had been going on for years under my mother's nose, my dad loved us. He never in a million years would have left my mother for someone like you.

"If it's true, apparently I'm the most naive woman in the world."

"Is there a chance it might not be?"

"An hour ago, I would have told you there was no chance in hell Gary was cheating on me. Now I don't know what to think."

"What happened? What makes you even suspect it?"

"Emma believes it. I don't know anything but that. I overheard her fighting with the other woman about seeing them together the day he died."

"Oh wow. That's rough. She was, what, fifteen when he died?"

"Yes."

Her poor Emma. She completely changed after the accident, going from a bright, happy young woman to a surly, angry stranger. Rosie had always assumed it was because of her own injuries and her grief over her father's death. That was enough, wasn't it? Now she had to wonder if there was more to it, if she also had been carrying the overwhelming weight of this secret.

"Apparently she's known all this time and she never told me."

"The other woman was obviously someone in your book club."

That crushing sense of betrayal pressed in again and despite her best efforts, Rosie finally couldn't contain a sob. He made a low sound and reached for her and she leaned against him across the console, seeking the comfort and strength of his arms.

After indulging for a few moments while rain clicked against the roof of her car, Rosie forced herself to ease away.

"I'm so sorry. You didn't need this tonight."

"Neither did you."

"You asked me if the other woman is in the book club. Not only is she in the book club but she works for me. Until tonight, I thought she was one of my dearest friends. All this time, she's been lying to me. Am I the dumbest woman in the world?"

"You're far from dumb," he assured her. "Or naive. There's nothing wrong in trusting people. You had no reason to do otherwise."

She was suddenly immensely grateful for this man who had stepped in to comfort her even though he didn't know the situation or any of the players except her and Emma.

He was a good man. A kind one. When he reached to squeeze her hand, she twisted her fingers through his, finding enormous comfort in that simple touch.

"Which one is she? Did I talk to her?"

"Yes. She chatted with you a few times. Pam. Streaky blond hair. Fake eyelashes. She was wearing the gray top with the green jacket."

"Oh right. I remember her now. And you said she works for you?"

She nodded and released a heavy breath. "She has been my right hand since Gary died. She handles all the financial details of the business and so much more. She's the office manager, she does the payroll, she keeps my calendar. I've talked to her nearly every single day of the last ten years. How could she come in day after day, month after month, year after year without revealing one hint that she wanted my husband?"

Rosie curled her fingers in his. Pam had grieved after Gary died, she remembered. She had seemed lost for months. At the time, she had been recently divorced from her second husband and Rosie had assumed it was a combination of losing her marriage and losing her boss, a man she respected.

"For a few years after Gary died, I was too battered by grief to pay much attention to the construction company. I didn't care about any of it. Pam basically ran things, along with Gary's second-in-command at the time of his death."

Had Vic Blackwood known Pam and Gary were having an affair? How deep had the betrayal run?

She felt another sob threaten and was almost successful in swallowing them down. He heard, though, and pulled her back into his arms.

"I'm sorry," she said again after a few more minutes. "I bet you're wishing you had driven yourself to the book club."

"Not at all. I'm glad I could be here when you needed someone. Better me than someone else."

"Why is that?"

"I don't know any of the parties involved, so I don't have any preconceived ideas about what is or is not true."

"I think it must be true," she whispered. "I could tell Emma was keeping something from me, even back then. She was hurting so badly after Gary died, and I didn't know how to comfort her."

"I'm sure you did your best."

She shook her head as a fresh wave of pain washed over her. "I didn't. I was so lost in my own grief, I wasn't the mother she needed. I thought she blamed me for that, but now I wonder if there was more to her anger."

"You won't know until you talk to her."

She didn't want to. She wanted to get back in her car, drive up the coast, and keep on going. Washington State was lovely this time of year. So was Canada. She would drive and drive until the road ran out.

It was a wildly tempting idea, impossible as it might be. She wanted to escape all of this.

Another horrible thought occurred to her. "How am I supposed to face Pam in the office tomorrow?"

The idea of it made her feel nauseated.

"You can always fire her. Send her an email and tell her to pack up her things and get out."

Much to her shock, since she wasn't sure she would find anything funny ever again, she gave a rough laugh at his firm response. "I'm not sure I can do that. She's the human resources manager, too."

"Fine. Give her two weeks' notice, along with two weeks' paid leave so you don't have to see her disgusting face."

This time her laugh sounded more genuine. She squeezed his fingers again, grateful beyond words for this man she had dragged into the emotional tornado of her life right now.

"Thank you for talking me down off the ledge."

"What are you going to do?"

She looked out the windshield at the raindrops making rivulets against the glass. Beyond them, she could see the crescent moon like Emma's tattoo, shining through the clouds.

Love you to the moon and back.

She drew in a breath and eased back to the driver's seat.

"I suppose I need to talk to Emma first to find out what she knows. Then I need to figure out if I can ever stand to see Pam again."

CHAPTER THIRTY

—

Andrew

POOR ROSIE. SHE WAS COMPLETELY DEVASTATED, NATURALLY. Any woman would be.

"Why didn't Emma tell me, all this time?" Her voice vibrated with emotion. "How could she keep this a secret for a decade?"

"Because she was trying to protect you. That's my guess, anyway."

"I didn't need protection. I needed the truth."

"Why? What have you gained by knowing that your husband might have cheated on you?"

"Nothing," she admitted, her voice edged with sorrow. "And I'm afraid I've lost so very much. I thought we had a perfect marriage."

"There is no such thing as a perfect marriage. There are only imperfect people trying their best to make it work and hopefully growing stronger together in the process."

She sighed. "You're right. I know you're right. It's easy when someone is gone from your life to idealize everything you had together. Thank you for the reminder."

"You're welcome."

"I didn't mean to dump all this on you, but I'm actually glad I did."

"Oh good. I hope this proves to you once and for all that not only have I *talked* to women before but I can sometimes offer a halfway decent shoulder for them to cry on."

She gave a rusty-sounding laugh. "Absolutely. You're a sensitive, compassionate person and writer. Believe me, I'll tell everyone I know. Next time you overhear me talking about you in a bookstore, that's probably exactly what I will be saying."

They shared a laugh and he was relieved to see she seemed to have lost that haunted, lost look she had worn the entire drive here.

"Good night, Rosie. Call me if you need to talk, even if it's the middle of the night."

"I will."

To his surprise, she reached across the width of the vehicle and kissed his cheek. The intoxicating scent of her, citrus and flowers and Rosie, tantalized him and the fierce desire to shift slightly for a real kiss almost overwhelmed him.

So much for being a sensitive male. She was going through a life crisis and all he could think about was pulling her into his arms, tasting her sweet mouth again, feeling that petite, curvy body against his.

Could he be any more of a cliché?

He forced himself to ease away.

"You really have been lovely. You're right, it helped that you don't know any of the particulars or the people involved. Thank you."

"You're welcome. Good night," he said again. "Do your best to sleep. I know your brain will probably be going a million miles an hour but you'll be able to process all of this much better in the morning."

"Good advice, but I doubt I'll be able to follow it," she answered.

He opened the car door, grateful for the misty rain that cooled his skin and his overheated imagination, and hurried toward his temporary apartment, wondering how he had become so embroiled in her life—and why that didn't bother him at all.

CHAPTER THIRTY-ONE

—

Emma

WHAT HAD SHE DONE?

A half hour after her horrible confrontation with Pam—and the even worse moment when her mother had stumbled onto the conversation—Emma still couldn't quite believe the evening had played out so horribly.

One hell of a book club, she had to admit, as she helped load her grandmother back into her passenger seat.

When she had parked in this spot earlier in the evening, she never could have imagined that scene in the hallway with Pam or that all the ghosts of the past would come pouring out, after all this time.

It was the worst possible luck that her mother happened to come down the hallway toward the powder room at that particular instant.

If only Emma could have jumped back in time ten minutes, she would have waited to head for the bathroom herself until she was certain Pam was nowhere in sight. The whole ugly mess could have been avoided.

"Okay, out with it," Sylvia said bluntly when Emma climbed into the driver seat. "What the heck is going on? Your mother left in a rush with her sexy author, and now you're hustling us home like you just stuffed Barbara's polished silver in your purse and are trying to make a fast getaway."

"No stolen silver," she assured her grandmother. "I'm sorry if I dragged you away when you weren't ready to leave yet. I just . . . couldn't stay."

She started the car, hoping her grandmother would let the matter rest.

She should have known better.

"Something's happened," Sylvia said as Emma pulled out into the street.

She thought about denying it, but what was the point? Sylvia would find out eventually. Emma nodded, feeling tears burn as she drove toward their house.

"The worst something," she admitted. "Mom knows about Pam."

"How did *that* happen?"

"She overheard me fighting with her. I thought we were being quiet, but Mom happened to stumble into the hallway where we were busy having it out. And at the worst possible moment."

"Finally!" Far from looking horrified, as she should, Sylvia looked relieved. "It was high time you told her the truth."

"I didn't *want* to tell her the truth. I never wanted her to know."

"I know you didn't. If you had followed my advice, you would have told her a long time ago."

"Why? What possible benefit would come from Mom knowing Dad might have been having an affair and at the very least he was making out with another woman an hour before he died?"

Sylvia was silent. When she spoke, her voice was quiet and filled with a compassion that made Emma want to cry.

"For a decade, my daughter has been grieving your dad like he was some kind of saint. Gary was a good man, don't get me wrong. But clearly he was human, too. He made mistakes. Maybe hearing the truth will finally help your mom move on."

"And maybe it will only hurt her and cause a whole new kind of grief."

"Maybe. That's up to Rosie, I guess."

"I wish I'd had a chance to tell her under better circumstances."

"You've had ten years, honey. I've been trying to convince you to tell her since I found out myself."

Emma had tried to keep the truth from everyone, including Sylvia. She hadn't wanted to tell her grandmother either. Better if she hadn't. But one night about a year after her father died—a few months before she had run away for the final time—everything had spilled out.

She had been hanging out at Orca Park with friends, drinking, smoking a little weed, when they'd been caught by the police. She and her friends had been arrested, since they were all sixteen at the time. She could still remember the mortified fear.

As wild as she had been that last year, Emma had escaped any brushes with the law until that night. Knowing she couldn't call her mom to get her, in desperation she had reached out to her grandmother. Sylvia had rushed down to the station, of course. Emma never would have expected anything else.

After they were back at Sylvia's place, her grandmother had been supportive but blunt when she told Emma she needed to get her act together or this wouldn't be the last time she ended up in trouble with the law.

Emma remembered bursting into tears of humiliation and pain. As her grandmother held her, gently asking what was wrong, all of Emma's turmoil—the months of pain and guilt and grief—tumbled out. Before she quite realized she had done it, she was spilling everything to Sylvia.

"I couldn't tell her," she said now to her grandmother, as she had said that night. "She was grieving Dad so hard, and I couldn't make things worse for her. I had killed him. I couldn't ruin his memory, too."

Her grandmother made a small sound of disgust. "First of all, you did not kill your father. I've told you that more times than I can count. It was an accident."

Intellectually, she might know the accident hadn't truly been her fault and that only sheer luck had saved her from dying alongside her father in the wreck.

That didn't ease the guilt that ate away at her like termites in a pine forest.

"Second, you keeping the truth from your mother has only driven a wedge between you that widens with each passing year. All you've achieved by your silence is further pain on both sides."

She closed her eyes, knowing the truth of her grandmother's words.

"She's never going to forgive me."

"Don't be ridiculous." Sylvia's voice was crisp and no-nonsense. "My daughter is a sharp woman. She will understand, if you give her the chance."

"You should have seen her face. She was devastated."

"Of course she was. Pam, that two-faced bitch, has spent a decade wiggling her way into Rosie's good graces, becoming indispensable in the process. I tried to warn Rosie to be careful of her intentions, but my daughter didn't listen to me when she was a girl and she doesn't listen to me now that she's over forty. What is it about the women in our family not listening to their mothers? I hope to God that pattern ends with you and Olive."

Emma smiled, much to her surprise.

Her smile faded as they approached her mother's house. The looming confrontation pressed in on her and she wanted desperately to drop her grandmother off, grab Olive and drive away.

She had spent ten years trying to escape. It was past time to face the past, no matter how difficult.

After driving to Sylvia's cottage, she helped her grandmother into her house, despite the older woman's insistence she didn't need a hand. After bidding her grandmother good-night, Emma kissed her cheek and headed for the main house, her nerves frayed and her stomach in knots.

She caught Maya trotting down the front steps.

"Hi, Emma. Your mom already paid me."

"Oh good. How did it go?"

She couldn't even use the excuse of having to drive the babysitter home to avoid the conflict, since Maya had driven there herself.

"We had tons of fun. Olive is adorable. She loved playing with filters on my phone. I'll text you a few of the photos we took."

"Thanks."

"She went straight to bed when I told her it was time and she's been sound asleep for about an hour."

Emma had screwed up many things in her life. So far, Olive was turning into the very best thing she had ever managed to produce.

After thanking her again, she went slowly inside.

As she feared, Rosie was waiting for her, perched on the edge of the sofa.

Emma took her time taking off her rain jacket, hanging up her bag, removing her shoes, before finally facing her mom.

She gave an exaggerated yawn. "Well, It's been a long day,

and I've got to head to the bookstore early tomorrow, so I think I'm going to head straight for bed."

It was worth a shot, anyway.

Rosie glared at her. "Oh no, you don't. You can't run away like that. That's what you did last time, isn't it? You ran away because you didn't want to talk to me about this."

Emma shifted. "I ran away for a lot of reasons, Mom. This house had become a battleground. We were fighting about everything. I hated your rules and you hated just about everything about me."

She hadn't meant to say the last part. The words slipped out, leaving her mother looking devastated.

"I did not hate anything about you. I loved you. You were . . . my everything."

"I didn't want to be your everything. I didn't deserve it."

Her mother stared at her, looking scrubbed raw with emotion. "Oh, Emma. I'm so sorry I wasn't a better mother to you during that time."

"You were fine. I was a mess."

"We were both a mess," Rosie said. "But I was the grown-up. You were a child. I should have been able to put aside my grief to support you. I wanted to but . . . everything I did with you seemed to be wrong."

"I was impossible. I know I was. I'm sorry," Emma said quietly.

"A wise friend recently reminded me that grief is like the ocean, some days calm, other days stormy and ugly. But in time, you figure out how to navigate the waters."

Emma nodded. She had spent far too long dog-paddling in place.

"Tell me about tonight. I know you don't want to talk about it but I need to know. I only heard the tail end of that conversation. I would like to hear all of it."

Emma again fought the urge to escape up the stairs, to find the peace she always did with her daughter. She couldn't. Not now. Rosie wanted to know the truth about that day.

Sylvia's words rang in her ears. *You keeping the truth from your mother has only driven a wedge between you that widens with each passing year. All you've achieved by your silence is further pain on both sides.*

"I don't want to talk about it again," she admitted. "I would rather forget the whole thing happened."

Her mother gave her a look filled not with the anger she might have expected for her secrets but a compassion that made Emma want to weep.

"You can't forget, though. Can you?"

She shook her head, miserable at heart. She didn't want to rehash the past with her mother, the past that had haunted her for a decade.

"What happened?" Rosie pressed.

She released a breath, knowing the time for secrets was well and truly past. "I was early for our appointment to go driving together, about an hour earlier than Dad was expecting me. I heard two people in his office and started to go in when I realized who they were and what they were doing. They were on the sofa. She was in his lap. They were making out."

Rosie drew in a sharp breath, her face pale again. "Are you sure you didn't misunderstand what you saw?"

"This is one of the reasons I didn't want to tell you, Mom, because you always want to look for the best in people. There was no *best* in this situation. They were all over each other."

She hated that she had to talk about this. More, she hated that was one of her last memories of the man she had adored. The man who had coached her soccer team, who never complained about helping her with math homework, who loved to take her hiking and biking and tide pooling.

"What . . . what did they say when you interrupted them?"

"I didn't give either of them a chance to say anything. Not then, anyway. I ran out, afraid I was going to puke. When I calmed down, I went back into the office, making a lot of noise that time and calling his name so they knew I was there."

"You were fifteen. You could have misunderstood what you saw." The desperation in her mother's voice made her heart hurt.

"I did not misunderstand. I know what I saw. More than that, Dad confirmed it when I confronted him about it."

"You . . . you talked about Pam with him?"

"I wasn't going to. I wanted to forget everything. But we were driving along the cliff road and he turned the radio on. Some old song came on and Dad made a big point of talking about how it was one of your favorites and how the two of you danced to it together at your prom. And I just . . . lost it."

She had hurled bitter, angry words at him, telling him she had seen him and Pam on the couch in his office. She told him she couldn't believe he would ruin all their lives because he had a thing for his secretary. How could he betray Rosie like that? Now they would get a divorce and Emma would have to shuttle between their houses and they wouldn't be able to renovate Stormhaven after all and Emma was going to be miserable.

It had all been self-absorbed. How his disgusting behavior was going to impact *her* life. She supposed that was not an unusual reaction for a teenager but it made her cringe now.

Her father had been devastated. She could still replay the conversation in her head.

"It was one kiss, that's all," her dad had insisted.

"How stupid do I look? That was not a kiss between people who'd never kissed each other before."

"Okay. We've kissed a few times, but that's all. It's never gone beyond that. I won't let it. I love your mom."

"How can you even use that word? If you loved Mom, you would not have any desire to be bumping uglies with your secretary."

She had been so very angry and hadn't been paying attention to the road. The next thing she knew, the car was spinning out of control, heading for the guardrail and then flipping over it, rolling down and down and down.

Her father hadn't been wearing a seat belt. He must have taken it off in the split second the car started to spin in a vain attempt to grab the steering wheel and wrestle the car back onto the road.

He had been thrown out while she had hung suspended by her seat belt when the car came to rest upside down.

The most horrible minutes of her life had been seared into her memory.

She was crying, she realized now, yanked back to her mother's living room with its comfortable furniture and lovely watercolors.

To her dismay, Rosie stepped forward and wrapped her arms around her. The warm, familiar scent of citrus and flowers surrounded her, comforted her, sending more tears spilling out.

"Oh, honey," her mother murmured. "You have carried this burden by yourself all these years. I'm so, so sorry you didn't feel like you could share it with me. I wish you had."

"You loved Dad so much. You were shattered when he died. Completely lost. How could I tell my grieving mother that her husband was possibly having an affair with his secretary?"

"So you carried the burden by yourself for all this time,"

Rosie said gently. "Is that the reason for everything else? Why you seemed to completely pull away from me after your father died?"

Emma could not come up with the right answer. It was part of the reason, certainly, but she also had constantly felt as if her mother blamed her for Gary's death. Whenever she would catch Rosie silently crying while she washed dishes or worked in the garden, Emma's guilt would eat away at her like acid.

"That time was such a blur, if you want the truth. I was so angry at everything. I was dealing with all the usual teen things that fifteen-year-old girls have to face along with my own recovery after the accident. Hormones, acne, PMS. And I was so angry at Dad, too. I missed him so much, at the same time I wanted to go on yelling and yelling at him."

"Sounds like a perfectly reasonable reaction. I want to yell at him right now, too. If he were here, he would definitely be hearing some choice words."

To her shock, Emma felt a giggle welling up amid all the tears. Her mother gave a tiny smile and hugged her again. Emma leaned her cheek against her mother's and felt some of the massive ball of mingled grief and anger begin to untangle.

"Can you ever forgive me?" she whispered.

Rosie eased away and gave her a stern look. "Oh, honey. There's absolutely nothing to forgive. You did nothing wrong. Even by keeping the truth from me, I can see you were only trying to protect me."

"Are you . . . completely wrecked?"

Her mother appeared to consider this. "Completely? No. I'm devastated, if you want the truth. I thought our marriage was perfect. I thought I was the best possible wife and that your father would never have any reason to turn to another woman. It's going to take some adjusting for me to accept that perhaps we weren't perfect. That *I* wasn't perfect. Perhaps all this time I've been looking at things through the wrong lens."

"You mean Rosie-colored glasses?"

It was something her father had often said, a phrase that had become something of a family joke.

Rosie always tried to see the best in people. Emma didn't know how she would be able to do that in this situation, though.

"What are you going to do about Pam?" she finally asked.

Her mother's features hardened. "I don't know. I will have to figure that out. I'm not sure I can work with her, knowing that she was willing to betray me with Gary and then hide it from me for a decade, going on as if nothing ever happened."

"I can step in to help out at the construction company, if you want me to," Emma said, then held her breath, wishing she hadn't said anything. This wasn't the time, when their emotions were all on edge.

Rosie gave her a look of surprise. "You? But what about the bookstore? Aren't you happy there? You've done such a good job. I'm so thrilled at all the changes."

"I have enjoyed the challenge of giving the place a refresh. I would be happy there for several more months while we fully implement things." She caught her breath, again wishing she hadn't started this now. "But . . . eventually I would like to have a role at Lucas Construction. It's the main reason I agreed to come home, if you want the truth."

"Oh, honey. I had no idea."

"We can talk about this another time. Just know that if you need my help at the company, I'm ready. We could always hire someone else to run the bookstore. Or I could hire Maya and Jenny to be assistant managers and turn many of the responsibilities over to them, which would free up my time to help you."

"This is a lot to think about. I don't even know what I'm doing about Pam yet."

"I know. Not the greatest time to bring it up, but it's been on my mind a lot since I came back and I . . . I wanted to let you know. No more secrets, Mom. I promise."

Her mom hugged her again and this time, Emma felt the years of tension and misunderstanding melt away. As they held each other, a comfortable silence settled between them, filled with unspoken forgiveness and renewed love.

When they finally pulled apart, Rosie's eyes were glistening with tears, but her smile was warm and genuine.

"No more secrets," she agreed softly. "We've lost so much time, Emma. I don't want to waste another day."

Emma nodded, feeling a weight lift from her shoulders. "Me neither, Mom."

Rosie reached out and tucked a strand of hair behind Emma's ear, a gesture so maternal and familiar that it made Emma's heart ache with a bittersweet joy. "I'm so proud of the woman you've become, sweetheart. Your father would be, too."

As they stood there, bathed in the soft moonlight streaming through the windows, Emma felt a sense of peace she hadn't experienced in years.

The road ahead might not be easy, but for the first time in a long time, she felt hopeful about her relationship with her mother. They had taken the first steps towards healing, and together, they would face whatever challenges lay ahead.

CHAPTER THIRTY-TWO

—

Rosie

AFTER A SLEEPLESS NIGHT, ROSIE STILL DID NOT KNOW WHAT she would do about Pam. She had to face the woman. She couldn't escape it. She foolishly wanted to call into the office and say she would be working at jobsites all day so she could avoid any difficult conversation.

She finally rose at dawn and went out to gather eggs, finding peace in talking to her girls. After the chickens were fed, she saw a few weeds coming up again in the flower bed she had cleared with Zara and Finn, what felt a lifetime ago.

She began ripping them out with more enthusiasm than strictly necessary, enjoying the chickens scratching around her and Dottie sniffing at the weeds she pulled.

After the rain of the night before, the storm clouds had blown away, leaving a glorious morning. She could see miles out to sea, where a couple of fishing boats were heading out for the day.

Rosie wished she could stand and watch the waves all day.

This all still felt like a nightmare that she couldn't awaken from. Had her entire marriage been a lie? Had Pam been the only one or had there been a long line of women that Gary had flirted with, kissed, possibly more?

She couldn't believe it. Her husband had loved her. She was certain of it.

She was dumping her load of weeds into the green waste container when a car pulled into her driveway. Rosie glanced at her watch. It wasn't yet 8:00 a.m. Who would be here this early?

She walked around the house and felt her breath catch when she recognized Pam's luxury convertible.

Her employee walked out looking years older than she had the night before. Her hair wasn't fixed in her usual sleek style and her makeup appeared to have been applied with a shaky hand.

Rosie did not want to do this right now, not after she had spent the past hour trying to attain some measure of calm. Apparently, she wasn't going to have a choice, though. Pam moved toward her with a determined set to her jaw.

"I wanted to talk about everything this morning before work. The office is not the place," the other woman said bluntly.

Rosie gripped her trowel more tightly. "Where is the best place to have a discussion about one of your closest friends betraying you with your husband?"

Pam's jaw tightened. "Don't be that way, Rosie. We are two adult women, well past being silly girls fighting over a guy."

"Excuse me, but the guy in question is not some quarterback of the football team. He was my husband of sixteen years. I can't believe that you would do this to me."

Pam straightened and glared at Rosie. "I'll remind you that I did not make vows with you. The one you should be mad at is Gary."

"I am. Believe me, I am. But I'm also furious with you. I don't want to look at you right now. Why don't you take the rest of the week off?"

Rosie wasn't at all certain she could fire Pam for whatever might have happened between her and Gary a decade ago. She would have to talk to the company attorney. Pam was exactly the sort to sue for breach of contract and drag Lucas Construction through an ugly court battle.

But at least a few days might give her breathing room to process everything and come up with a plan.

"That won't be necessary," Pam said stiffly. "I came over this morning to hand in my notice. I've been thinking about it for a long time, if you want the truth. You are not easy to work for, Rosie."

"Ouch." She thought she had been an excellent boss. Her other employees seemed to have no complaints.

"It doesn't have to come to that," she said, though she wasn't sure her words were true.

"It's already come to that. I'm not going to work in a place where you are going to sit in judgment of me every single day when I come into the office. I've had many other great offers over the years and turned them down out of loyalty to you."

Rosie almost laughed outright at that but managed somehow to swallow it down.

She remembered what Andrew had suggested and decided to take his advice. "You have accrued plenty of personal leave. Spend today tying up any loose ends from home and you can start your leave tomorrow."

"I'm the backbone of your whole operation. You know that as well as I do. The whole company is going to fall apart without me."

Rosie very much feared Pam was right, though she intended to fight like hell to make sure that didn't happen, as she had after Gary's death.

"You have been an invaluable part of the company," she said.

Pam looked as if she had more to say but she finally turned to go. Before she returned to her vehicle, she threw out one more conversational grenade.

"I did care for Gary, just so you know. I loved him. And he loved me."

She didn't want to hear this. Rosie fought the urge to clap her hands over her ears.

"How long had your affair been going on?" she finally asked, through lips that felt stiff and unnatural. She didn't want to ask, but the words came out anyway. She needed to know how clueless she had been.

Pam looked away. "Not long. A few weeks."

A few weeks too long. Rosie felt queasy again.

"We never slept together, for what it's worth. Though it would have happened sooner or later, I'm sure. I don't know if you could even call it an affair."

He had kissed this woman, though. Shared things with her he hadn't with Rosie.

"I think in those last few weeks Gary was a man tormented, trying to figure out how to have what he truly wanted—me—without hurting you in the process."

Rosie assumed Pam told her that as some kind of consolation prize but the words actually made her feel worse. She might have found her late husband's betrayal easier to handle if it had strictly been a physical relationship, with no emotions involved.

Knowing he might have truly cared for Pam and might indeed have been planning to leave Rosie felt so much worse.

The weight of this revelation, ten years in the making, threatened to crush her. She wanted to scream, to lash out, to demand more answers, but found herself paralyzed by the enormity of it all.

With one more hard look, Pam climbed into her vehicle and drove away, leaving Rosie standing by her flower bed, trowel still in hand.

Rosie returned her supplies to her gardening shed and walked slowly up the stairs to the house she and Gary had renovated together, feeling as if the carefully tended narrative of her marriage had burned to the ground overnight.

Had their love been a lie? Or worse, had it been real, only to be discarded so easily for someone else?

She fought tears as she grappled with this new reality. But beneath the pain and betrayal, a small spark of something else began to ignite.

Determination.

She had rebuilt her life once after Gary's death, learning to run the company alone. She would do it again without Pam.

This time, she would rebuild on a foundation of truth, no matter how difficult it might be. Rosie took a deep breath and headed into her bedroom to shower and change for the day.

She had a company to run, a daughter and granddaughter to love, and a life to reclaim—one that was entirely her own.

CHAPTER THIRTY-THREE

—

Andrew

THIS DEADLINE WAS GOING TO KICK HIS BUTT.

The next time he decided to pack up and move his family eight hundred miles away when he was so close to a hard and fast deadline, Andrew needed to tell his future self to get his ass in gear.

He had turned his phone on Do Not Disturb so that he could have an hour of uninterrupted work time, but he couldn't seem to make his brain cooperate. His thoughts kept going back to the evening before, to Rosie's ravaged features as she told him about the shocking revelations she had learned that night.

He couldn't imagine what she must be going through. He had wanted to call or text her a dozen times that morning to see how she was doing but hadn't been able to think of anything that didn't feel like hollow words of comfort.

How was she? Still reeling?

He picked up his phone again, then set it back down and forced himself to return to work. He could probably focus better if he shut the door, but he couldn't bring himself to do it. Rosie had mentioned she might be stopping by again. If she did, he wanted to be sure not to miss her.

Somehow Andrew managed to muddle through revisions on one chapter and started working on the next when he saw a familiar Lucas Construction truck pull up in front of the house. A moment later, she climbed out and came inside.

Andrew saved his manuscript and rose abruptly. He was due for a break anyway, wasn't he?

He hurried down the stairs, following the sound of her voice. He found her talking to the two carpenters who were doing the final framing in the kids' bedrooms and hanging the closet doors.

When he poked his head in, she gave him a half smile. "Oh, hi. I'm sorry if we disturbed you."

He decided not to tell her she had been disturbing him since he first met her in her bookstore.

"I was waiting for you. I could have shut my door and put on my noise-blocking headphones, but I was hoping to get the chance to check on you today, if you stopped by."

She sent a quick look at the carpenters, clearly averse to sharing her personal life with her subcontractors. He waited until after she finished talking with them and moved out into the hallway before he gave her arm a comforting squeeze.

"How are you? Did you get any sleep at all?"

She gave a rough laugh. "Not much. Does it show?"

She had dark smudges beneath her eyes and she seemed more fragile than usual, but other than that, she still looked vibrant and lovely.

"Not at all. That was sheer speculation on my part." He didn't tell her that *he* also had not slept well, too concerned for what she must be going through.

"Well, your speculation is spot-on. I'm not sure I slept at all. I couldn't seem to shut everything down."

"Understandable."

"I spent the morning yanking out weeds, which always helps me work out my big moods. I had just settled down when Pam showed up."

"At your house?"

Rosie nodded, her mouth tight. "She wanted to have it out somewhere that wasn't the office."

"How did that go? Do you need me to help you hide a body?"

She laughed, then blinked as if surprised at the sound. "No. I wish. I wanted to sic my chickens on her, but they weren't cooperating. Even Alfredo, my mean rooster, stayed away."

"Sounds like you need to train them better."

She smiled again. "I'll work on that. I didn't even yell. We actually had a moderately civil conversation."

"You're a better person than I could be."

"I'm really not. I planned to figure out how I could fire her, if you want the truth, but she quit before I could. I'll admit, I'm disappointed I didn't get the chance to act first."

"The end result is the same, though. You don't have to go on working with her."

"I suppose. Firing her would have been more cathartic but it's done now. I did take your advice and told her to work at home today wrapping up any exit details and take her personal leave time starting tomorrow."

"Smart."

"She said she had other offers and was ready to move on anyway. I'm sure she will end up working for one of my competitors. At this point, I don't care. I'm just relieved I don't have to see her in the office."

"That would have been excruciating."

She nodded and moved to the floor-length window on the stair landing that overlooked the ocean. "She told me they were in love but at the time of his death, their affair had been strictly emotional."

"Do you believe her?"

"I don't know what to believe anymore. It doesn't make much difference, does it? An emotional affair almost feels like more of a betrayal than a purely physical one."

He could see that, though he expected some men wouldn't be able to grasp the subtle difference.

"What was he not finding from me? What was I not doing to make him feel loved and appreciated so that he had to turn to someone else?"

The despair in her voice broke his heart and made him want to smash something. "This wasn't about you, Rosie. Gary's choices were his own."

She sighed. "It's easy to say that, but I look back at how things were in the year before he died and we hardly saw each other. He was working long hours at the construction company, I had bought the bookstore. And then I complicated everything by persuading him that we had to buy this house. I added so much pressure, financial and emotional, to our marriage. How can I blame him for turning to someone else?"

He moved closer, wishing he could take away this pain. "Unfortunately, we can't ask him. He's not here. Your mind can come up with a million different reasons why he might consider turning to another woman but you can never know the truth. You don't need to torture yourself by trying to figure it out."

She sighed. "I know. I need to stop. It's not that easy."

"You didn't even know any of this twenty-four hours ago. It will take time to come to terms with everything."

She nodded, giving him a tentative smile. The afternoon sun coming through the windows lit up her features and he had a tough time looking away.

"Thank you for being a listening ear. I don't have anyone else to talk to about this. I can't really discuss it with Emma and I don't want to talk about it with my mother. The three of you are the only ones who know and I don't really want to tell any of my other friends that Gary was having an emotional affair with Pam when he died."

"Understandable."

"You really have been amazing," she said. "Thank you. The last thing you need right now when you're trying to finish a book is me spraying you with a fire hose of my emotional trauma."

He smiled at her imagery. "I actually really appreciate the distraction."

"The book isn't going well?"

"It never is at this stage. This is always when I wonder what I'm doing and why I'm fooling myself to think I can ever manage to write a book that anyone would be interested in."

She gave him an empathetic smile. "I know it's not at all comparable, but I feel the same way every time we take on a new building project. I look at the architectural renderings and consider everything ahead of us and it always feels impossible."

"Yes. That."

"It's not quite the same. You're trying to come up with everything out of your own imagination. But a big project is a big project."

"True enough."

"Other than my own emotional trauma, I really do think the book club went well. I've heard from several of my friends today telling me how charming and approachable and kind you are. No one quite expected that."

"Given my tough persona."

She smiled. "Well, you do have something of a reputation for being remote and standoffish. Unless we're talking about your red carpet appearances with Willow Voss, anyway."

He made a face, embarrassed at the reference to a time in

his life he would prefer to forget. "You know that whole thing was mostly made up by the tabloids, right? I went out with her a few times, that's all. I did like her and so did the kids but I wasn't in the market for an ambitious actress looking for publicity and she wasn't looking for an introverted, too-serious widower with a couple of kids."

"Then she's a fool."

Rosie immediately looked as if she wished she hadn't said anything.

He wanted to kiss her again, right there on his second-floor landing, in the middle of hammering and power tools and chaos. Not the time, he reminded himself.

"I should go," she said. "I only dropped by to check on things with the carpenters."

"I'll walk you out. I could use some air."

They made their way through the house that slowly seemed to be coming together. In another few weeks, the Stormhaven renovation would be done and Andrew would no longer have her occasional drop-in visits to anticipate. It was a bittersweet prospect. He wanted the house to be done but he didn't want to lose this connection to her.

When they reached her pickup truck, he opened the door for her.

"I'm sorry for what you're going through, Rosie," he said before she climbed inside. "Don't beat yourself up about something you can't change."

"Thank you. I appreciate that. I'm sorry again that I interrupted your work."

"Don't be. I've been waiting all day for you to come by. I told myself it was mainly because I wanted to know how you were doing after last night, but the truth is, I mostly wanted to see you."

Andrew watched as Rosie's eyes widened, her lips parting slightly in surprise. She seemed to struggle for words, clearly caught off guard by his candid admission. Her cheeks flushed, and he could see the uncertainty in her gaze, as if she couldn't quite believe what she was hearing.

This wasn't the time to kiss her, he reminded himself. She was struggling with this personal crisis and didn't need more complications. But he seemed powerless to resist. Before he could second-guess himself, Andrew leaned in, gently cupping her face with one hand.

Their lips met, and suddenly the world around them and all his rationalizations faded away. The kiss was tender at first, almost hesitant, but it quickly deepened as all of his pent-up attraction and longing poured out.

Andrew felt a surge of emotions he hadn't experienced in what felt like forever. The softness of Rosie's lips, the warmth of her body as she pressed closer, it all ignited a fire within him that he thought had long since burned out. He wanted more—so much more. He longed to pull her even closer, to explore every inch of her, to show her how much she meant to him.

As the kiss intensified, Andrew's mind raced with possibilities.

Sometimes his overactive imagination offered both perks and drawbacks.

He could too easily imagine lazy Sunday mornings spent tangled in sheets, stolen afternoons when she distracted him from his work or he visited her on jobsites, building a rich, beautiful, rewarding life here in Wood Briar together.

For now, he wanted to lose himself in the softness of her mouth and the intoxicating heat they seemed to generate together without even trying.

CHAPTER THIRTY-FOUR

—

Rosie

ROSIE'S HEAD WAS SPINNING. ONE MOMENT SHE HAD BEEN caught off guard by Andrew's confession, and the next, she found herself lost in the most passionate kiss she'd experienced in years. His strong arms encircled her, making her feel safe and desired all at once.

She hadn't realized how much she had been craving this connection until now. The tenderness in Andrew's touch, mixed with the obvious desire she could feel radiating from him, was intoxicating. All her worries about Pam, about Gary's betrayal, about the company melted away, leaving only the sensation of Andrew's lips on hers and the promise of something new and exciting on the horizon.

Rosie lost herself in the kiss, the strength of his muscles against her, his hands pressing her toward him.

What was it about this man that seemed to work its way through all her defenses? For ten years, she had used her grief as armor, telling herself she would never find anyone else like Gary.

She had compared every guy she went out with to her husband, and they'd all come up short.

Now, as she lost herself in Andrew's kiss, some part of her wondered if she had been wrong this entire time. Maybe finding out Gary hadn't been the perfect husband would finally give her freedom from those unrealistic expectations and allow her to find room for someone else in her life.

They might have continued that way, wrapped in each

other's arms and lost to anything else but she heard the door to the house open.

She jerked away from him, her heart racing and her body on fire, praying whatever worker was coming out of the house hadn't noticed them.

She wanted Andrew more than she wanted anyone or anything in years. She managed to catch her breath, though she was quite sure her features were still flushed when she saw one of the painters trotting down the porch steps.

"Oh good. You're still here. I wanted to check to make sure we're on the same page, that all the door and window trim will be the same color, no matter what color we're painting the bedroom."

She could hardly make any part of her brain work. How was she supposed to advise the painters on anything right now, except her own frenzied heartbeat?

"If that's what the designer specified, then yes. But I'll come take a look before I leave."

He nodded and headed back inside, leaving her with Andrew.

What was she going to do about this attraction for him? She could tell herself this was foolishness, but she still wanted to step right back into his arms.

"I hope you don't think I kissed you out of pity," he said. "I've been wanting to do that again ever since the first time."

His words sent heat arcing through her. Oh, she had, too, even as she knew it was impossible. *They* were impossible.

"This is crazy, Andrew. What are we doing?"

He lifted his mouth in a half smile. "If you have to ask, apparently I wasn't doing it right."

She made a face. "Oh, be quiet. You know you were doing nothing wrong. That's not what I meant. None of this makes sense. I'm very attracted to you, but I won't have an affair with you. It would never work."

"Who said I wanted an affair?"

Her face flamed again and she wanted to disappear. Had she totally misconstrued that kiss? "Right. You go around kissing all your contractors."

"Nope. Only you. I'm attracted to you as well, Rosie. I would think that's fairly obvious. More than that, I like you. I would be interested in seeing if there might be more than simple attraction. That doesn't mean we need to jump into bed or that we need to swear undying love for each other right now. I would simply like to get to know you better."

She didn't know how to answer him. It sounded wonderful. She would love the chance to see if this attraction could turn into something more.

Why couldn't they date? Unfortunately, she could immediately think of a dozen reasons, starting with the house behind them.

She sighed, already regretting what she knew she had to say. "We both know this isn't the right time for either of us. You have your deadline, the book tour, your children, the house."

He gave a short laugh. "Yeah. My life is barely contained chaos. Thanks for the reminder."

"Mine is no better. Even before everything happened last night, I had my hands full trying to juggle my mom, my daughter, my granddaughter, the construction company. And now I have to replace someone who before yesterday I considered one of my most valuable employees. All while trying to finish your renovation."

"I think you're trying to come up with excuses because you're scared, Rosie."

She opened her mouth to argue instinctively but closed it again.

She considered his words. "Maybe you're right. Maybe I am scared. But that doesn't change the fact that our lives are complicated right now."

Andrew nodded slowly. "You have a point. We both have a lot on our plates. And for what it's worth, you terrify me."

She wasn't sure how she felt about that, though she couldn't deny she liked the idea.

"So what do we do about it?"

Andew sighed. "How about this. We don't make any decisions right now. Let's get the house done and I'll finish my book. When things have settled down a bit, we can revisit this conversation."

Rosie felt a mixture of anticipation and regret. She conversely wanted to tell him she wasn't sure she could wait that long.

"That sounds reasonable."

"No pressure, no expectations. We'll see where we are then and in the meantime there's no reason we can't get to know each other better as friends."

"Friends," Rosie echoed, feeling both heartened and somewhat deflated at the prospect. "I can do that."

"Okay. I think we need one more kiss to seal the deal."

Though she knew it would only make the waiting harder, she couldn't resist stepping into his arms again and lifting her mouth to his.

When he finally lifted his head, they were both breathing hard.

"Promise me you'll finish the house fast."

She gave a husky laugh. "I can only push the subs so hard but I'll do my best. What about your book?"

"You're better incentive than if my publisher were standing over me, cracking the whip. Believe me, I'm not going to have any trouble writing authentic love scenes right now, with the way you've sent my imagination into overdrive."

She laughed, feeling worlds better than she ever expected to today. She eased away from him. "I'd better go or John will be wondering what happened to me."

She hurried inside the house. When she was safely inside, she leaned against the wall to catch her breath, her hand pressed to her mouth, aware of a flutter of excitement for what the future might hold.

For now, though, she was content to leave things open-ended, knowing they had time to explore these new feelings when the time was right.

CHAPTER THIRTY-FIVE

—

Bryce

SOMETHING WAS GOING ON WITH EMMA.

As Bryce carried in another load of lumber for the open shelving he was building in the extension, he caught her once more staring into space, her features tight and troubled.

Even with her uneasy expression, he couldn't seem to stop looking at her. From her purple-tipped hair to her piercings, to her ink, Emma gave the appearance of a tough girl but he knew it was all an illusion, the masks she wore to hide the vulnerable woman inside.

He found her breathtaking and wished he had a better ability with words so he could tell her so.

The bookstore was busy on this rainy day, filled with tourists and locals alike. Only one other employee was working today, Maya Thompson, who grew up near him. She was about four or five years younger than Emma and worked for the bookstore when she came back to town from college during the summer.

He wanted to ask Emma what was wrong but she seemed to go out of her way to avoid him, striking up conversations with Maya or a customer whenever he tried to approach.

His opportunity to talk to her finally came after he had made a trip outside to his truck in order to grab a tool he had left out there. When he came back inside, he found her standing in front of one of the bookcases he had redone, her mouth set and her features in turmoil. She didn't seem aware of him.

Maya, he saw, was speaking to the only customer currently in the store, so he decided he probably wouldn't have a better chance to ask Emma what was wrong.

"Hey, Emma, could I steal you for a minute? I could use some advice about something."

That seemed to jerk her back to awareness. With a wary look, she followed him into the extension.

"It's looking so good in here. How much longer until you think you'll be done? I've been on a wild ordering binge to fill all the new shelves."

"Close. Another two weeks, maybe?"

"Thank you for working so hard on it." Her polite smile didn't reach her eyes. "What did you need help with?"

"I wanted you to tell me what's bothering you."

She gazed up at him in surprise. She swallowed but looked quickly away. "Nothing. Everything's fine."

"Really? Because you've been distracted since I got here."

She shook her head. "You're imagining things. If that's all, I need to get back to work."

He couldn't force her to tell him, he knew. Still, he wished she trusted him. "Okay. If you change your mind and want to talk, I'm here."

She studied him, then leaned back against the brick wall they had stripped, eyes closed with complete exhaustion.

"I didn't sleep well last night. I'm a mess."

He wanted to tell her she was beautiful, as always, but he sensed that wasn't what she needed right now.

"What happened? Was the book group meeting a complete disaster?"

She hesitated then finally sighed. "The meeting itself was good. Andrew read from his new book and it was wonderful. I can't wait to read it. Everything went great until . . . until my mother accidentally found out something I've been trying to keep from her."

He waited for her to continue. When she didn't, he frowned. "You can't leave me hanging like that."

"I don't really want to talk about it."

He nodded. "Okay. I'm sorry I pushed. None of my business. I don't like to see you looking so distressed. Since you're here, would you help me measure again for these shelves? I want to be sure before I start cutting boards."

He had absolutely no need for her help since he already had checked and double-checked, but he sensed she needed something to distract her.

She obediently held the tape measure for him and he made a show of comparing the numbers on the tape to what he had already recorded in his phone.

When they finished, she spoke in a low voice he almost couldn't hear.

"The day we had the accident, I found my dad kissing someone who wasn't my mom."

Bryce's chest ached at her tormented expression. She sounded as if she had carried the pain for a very long time.

"You knew but your mom didn't?"

Emma shook her head. "I couldn't tell her. Especially not after he died. It would have destroyed her."

Bryce could only imagine how Emma must have struggled with the secret. He hadn't known her father at all but from everything he'd heard about Gary Lucas, the man was a saint. Everyone at Lucas Construction had nothing but wonderful things to say about him. Pam especially couldn't sing his praises enough.

Suddenly all the pieces fell into jarring place. "Is that why Pam quit today?" he asked, before he could think better of it.

Emma stared at him. "She what?"

He immediately wished he hadn't said anything, in case he was dreadfully wrong. "That's what I heard, anyway. One of the other project managers texted me earlier today. He said she's put in her two weeks' notice but won't be back in the office at all. It seemed like it came out of the blue."

"I had no idea! My mom didn't tell me. But I haven't really talked to her today, I guess. She was out on a jobsite all morning and I've been here all afternoon."

"Nobody was expecting it. But I guess if Pam was the one having an affair with your dad and your mom found out, it's no wonder she left."

"I never said it was Pam," she said, but both of them knew he was right, especially when she covered her face with her hands. She didn't cry but he could see her shoulders trembling and knew she was holding back a sob.

Aching for her, he reached out and pulled her into his arms. She resisted for only a second or two before she sagged against him, her arms sliding around his waist.

"Catching my dad making out with another woman was the most horrible moment of my life. For about an hour, anyway, until the *truly* most horrible moment of my life happened on the cliff road."

"Oh, Emma. I'm sorry."

"We were fighting about Pam when . . . when the accident happened. I told him he disgusted me. Those were the last things I ever said to him. How much I despised him."

Now she did sob, a small, strangled sound that hit him harder than full-blown weeping might have.

"I didn't. I loved him. But I was so angry at him for a long time."

"It's understandable. It must have felt like a betrayal."

He could certainly relate. When his father had left his mother, Bryce had wanted to kill the man.

"I could never tell my mom. She loved him so much. I knew it would have devastated her to find out he was cheating on her."

"But she found out anyway."

"Last night I was fighting with Pam about what happened that day. My mom overheard. You should have seen her. She looked like she was the one who just crashed her car down a mountainside."

"You should never have held it inside for so long."

"What was I supposed to do? My dad was dead. What would have been the point in telling her? If he had lived, maybe they could have worked through it. Maybe he never even would have had an affair with Pam. He claimed they had only kissed, nothing more. Maybe that's true. Maybe it never would have gone any further than that. We'll never know, will we? Because I killed him."

He pulled her back into his arms. "Hush. You did not. You were fifteen years old. You weren't responsible for any of it. The accident was exactly that. An accident."

"An accident that might not have happened if I hadn't been so self-righteous and self-absorbed."

"You can't know that. You're lucky to be alive. I wish you could focus on that instead of your guilt that is completely misplaced."

"I didn't want to be," she admitted. "For a long time, I thought it would have been better if I'd died instead of my dad."

"I would have hated that."

He remembered hearing about the accident when they were in school and how sick it had made him. Literally. He had puked up his guts.

Of course, there was a good chance he'd been hungover at the time. That wasn't an uncommon state for him back in high school when it was much easier to bury his feelings than try to deal with them.

Those habits had been tough to break. Even now, there were times he wanted to forget everything and get hammered down at the Rusty Anchor.

He, of all people, knew how infidelity on the part of a loved one could rupture a person's confidence and sense of self. His mother never recovered from her pain and rejection at being abandoned by her husband, even though Bryce's father had never been any great prize.

He couldn't really fault Emma for trying to spare her mother that kind of pain, especially when Rosie was already struggling with the even more devastating grief of her husband's death.

Knowing that she had carried the burden alone for a decade filled him with an almost unbearable tenderness.

"I would have really hated losing you, Em." He pushed a loose strand of hair away from her delicate, fragile features and leaned forward, the intoxicating scent of her washing through him.

"I'm glad you're here. That we're here together."

Bryce leaned in slowly, his gaze fixed on hers.

Their breaths mingled for a heartbeat before he closed the distance, pressing his mouth to hers in a soft, heartfelt kiss. Emma's eyes fluttered closed as she seemed to sag against him, her hands sliding up to rest on his chest.

He cradled her face gently, his thumb caressing her cheek as their lips moved together. The world around them faded away, leaving only the warmth of their connection.

CHAPTER THIRTY-SIX

—

Emma

EMMA'S HEART RACED AS SHE SLOWLY OPENED HER EYES TO find Bryce's intense gaze fixed on her. The tenderness of his kiss had completely destroyed her defenses, leaving her raw and vulnerable.

She struggled to form coherent thoughts, overwhelmed by the rush of emotions coursing through her. Part of her wanted to pull him close again, to lose herself in the comfort and passion of his embrace. But another part—the cautious, guarded part that knew better—whispered urgent warnings.

"Bryce," she began, her voice barely above a whisper. But what could she say? That the kiss had shaken her to her core? That she didn't deserve this kind of happiness?

Instead, Emma took a shaky breath, trying to steady herself.

"You matter to me, Emma. You always have." His voice was low, gruff and slid down her spine like he had traced each vertebrae with his fingers.

She found herself lost in his eyes, seeing an emotion there that both thrilled and terrified her. "I don't know what to say."

No. She didn't deserve to have someone good and honorable like Bryce kiss her with such tenderness. The weight of her past pressed down on her. Running away, the hard life she'd lived, having a baby at barely twenty-one with no dad in the picture. All the people she had hurt along the way.

Bryce deserved someone good and true. Someone whole. Not her.

Summoning every ounce of willpower, Emma pushed him away. "I should get back to work."

The raw emotion in Bryce's eyes pierced her heart. "We need to talk about this."

"No. We really don't."

"You can't keep running away from me. I have feelings for you. I had a crush on you when we were kids, and since you've been back, that crush has become something much more."

Emma wanted to plug her ears like a child and flee the room. She had spent so long hurting other people. She couldn't bear to hurt Bryce, too. But she knew pushing him away was best for him in the long run, even if it was killing her inside.

She forced herself to think of all the reasons they couldn't be together. He deserved a woman unburdened by the pain and trauma she'd endured. She couldn't saddle him with all her baggage.

She also couldn't step into any role at Lucas Construction that might push him out or take away an opportunity from him. He had earned it. He deserved it. She had done nothing but be born a Lucas.

She would continue working here at the bookshop for now and then figure something else out. It was the only thing she could do.

"It is true that I'm attracted to you. You grew up into all . . . this." She gestured at him, trying to keep her tone light. "Any woman would be lying if she said she wasn't attracted to you. And I'm grateful for your friendship and all you've done to help me with the renovation. But that's all it is. Nothing more. That's all it can ever be. I don't . . . I don't want anything with you."

It was so untrue. In this moment, she wanted everything

about him. He was a good man who loved his mother, and she was not a good person. She had been selfish and self-centered, hurting her own mother so deeply.

“You aren’t a very good liar, Emma.”

Wrong. She was a great liar. She’d been lying to herself to think she could ever have this.

“I’ve got to get back to work. Thanks for being a shoulder.”

She could see the hurt in his eyes, and it tore at her. But she didn’t know what else to do.

“Anytime,” he murmured.

As Emma headed back to the other room, she added one more thing to the long list of reasons to be upset with herself.

She was doing the right thing, wasn’t she? Even if it felt like she was tearing her own heart out in the process.

CHAPTER THIRTY-SEVEN

—

Rosie

BY FRIDAY NIGHT, THE SHOCK OF HER DAUGHTER'S REVELAtion had begun to ease, and Rosie had come to accept her new normal.

Pam's exodus had left everything in a complete disaster. The records were tangled and her notes were in a shorthand that no one else could read but Pam. Rosie knew it would be months before things were sorted and back on track.

She would worry about how she would clean up the mess another day. For now, she planned to enjoy an evening's entertainment with her daughter and granddaughter, watching a children's play about some karate princesses.

"Thanks for letting me tag along with you and Olive on your date," Emma said as Rosie pulled up to the town's performing arts center.

"I'm delighted to have you," she told her daughter honestly. "I love any chance to spend time with you."

Even with all the chaos surrounding Pam's departure from the company, Rosie found peace, at least, in knowing that she and Emma seemed to have made great strides in healing any lingering rift between them.

Now that the truth was finally out between them, Emma seemed free to talk to her in a way she hadn't been before. They had stayed up late the other night going through home movies, laughing about some memories, crying a little about others. They were finally finding their way through the darkness.

She couldn't say everything was perfect. Though Emma had finally told her the truth about Gary, her daughter still seemed subdued, even sad at random times.

Rosie had asked her a few times if everything was all right and each time Emma would assure her she was simply tired from trying to wrap up the renovations at the bookstore.

She suspected something else might be going on but hadn't wanted to press her daughter. If something else truly was bothering her, Emma would tell her when she was ready.

She had also been surprised that Emma seemed to have changed her mind about coming to work for Lucas Construction. When Rosie had suggested perhaps Emma could arrange things at the bookstore, as she had suggested, to enable her to come into the construction company a few days a week, Emma had declined.

I think I'll focus on Rainy Day for now, she had said. Rosie had decided not to push the matter. If Emma wanted to have a bigger role in the company, she would have to speak up. Rosie wouldn't pressure her.

When the three of them walked into the smaller of two auditoriums in the town's performing arts center, her gaze instantly seemed to find Andrew. He and his mother sat on the second row, with several seats open next to him.

Rosie's mind instantly flashed back to those delicious moments when he had kissed her. How lovely it had been to share her burdens with someone else, to lean on him for comfort and support when she had been feeling overwhelmed.

For so long, Rosie had struggled through everything alone. She had forgotten how wonderful it felt to share her fears and her pain with someone else for a while.

Simply seeing him again in the auditorium, hair slightly messed as he gazed at her with a smile of welcome, sent butterflies spiraling through her.

Nancy waved vigorously to them and gestured to the empty seats beside them. Rosie knew she ought to pick a seat somewhere else, somewhere far away from Andrew Morgan, with his afternoon shadow and his comforting shoulders and the scent of pine and new books that clung to him.

"Oh look. There's Nancy and Andrew. Looks like they have room for us on their row," Emma said, plucking the choice out of Rosie's hands.

Resigned, Rosie made her way down the steps toward their row, waving to a few people she knew. Somehow, she wasn't sure how, she ended up seated next to him, with her granddaughter beside her and Emma on the other side of Olive.

Great. How was she supposed to remind herself of all the reasons she and Andrew couldn't be together when all she wanted to do was lean into him and enjoy this?

"Hi there." He smiled in greeting, and Rosie told her ridiculous heartbeat to settle down.

"Hi."

"I was wondering if I would see you tonight."

"How could I miss a play about karate *and* princesses? I told the children I would try to come. I didn't want to disappoint them."

"If you hadn't come, *I* would have been disappointed as well."

His voice, low and intent, left her feeling ridiculously giddy. She had a sudden clear conviction that if she wasn't careful, she was going to lose her heart to this man—if it wasn't already too late.

"I've been watching for you at the jobsite, but you haven't come by Stormhaven for a few days."

"I haven't had much chance to leave the office since Pam left. I've been doing her job and mine. Things are in a bit of a muddle."

"I'm sorry. That must be stressful for you. How are you coping?"

"I'm figuring things out. I keep telling myself it's better than the alternative of having her still there. I've posted for a replacement on some job-sites and we've already had a few decent applications come in."

"Then you get to go through the fun of trying to hire the right candidate."

"There's always that. How's the book?"

"Coming along. I'm finally making progress." He gazed at her with a meaningful look. "It helps to have some incentive to stay in the chair."

Rosie could feel her cheeks heat, remembering his words after he had kissed her the other day.

He couldn't really mean it, could he?

She thought for sure he would have come to his senses by now.

Before she could answer, the house lights dimmed, music began to play and Jane Baxter, who ran the community theater as well as the children's drama camp, took the stage to introduce the play.

Rosie settled back into her seat, fiercely aware of Andrew beside her. Each time he smiled at something in the show or looked proudly on at his children's performance, she lost a little more of her heart to him.

It was an adorable show, she had to admit, filled with staged karate fights, bad guys, fancy costumes, a couple of handsome princes and plenty of singing and dancing.

Olive, beside her, watched the whole thing with wide, bright eyes and an enthralled expression. Rosie suspected Emma might have dozed off. Poor thing. She didn't think her daughter had been sleeping well, at least judging by the creak of floorboards upstairs above Rosie's own bedroom at all hours.

The show wasn't long, perhaps an hour. When the last notes of the final number had been sung, the audience erupted with uproarious applause.

The children in their royal clothing and belted karate uniforms looked delighted at the reaction and took several bows.

When the houselights came up, rather than going backstage, the children came out to look for their respective families.

Zara and Finn both found them quickly and rushed over. They went to their dad first, who hugged them both tightly, exclaiming over their performance. After they received the same treatment from their grandmother, Zara turned to Rosie, Olive and Emma.

"You came!" The girl looked delighted.

"And I'm so glad we did," Rosie answered. "What a great job you all did. I loved the whole thing. The part where the princesses all had to fight the bad guys in the forest had me on the edge of my seat."

"That's my favorite part, too," Zara confided. She looked bright and animated, obviously riding an adrenaline high from the performance.

"Guess what, Dad?" Finn said. "They have refreshments. Cookies and juice out where you pay for the tickets. Can we go have a cookie? I'm starving!"

"Could I have a cookie?" Olive asked.

"Yeah. They're for everyone," Finn said.

Together, they made their way out to the foyer, where parents and children alike were chatting in small groups.

Rosie stopped to talk with several people she knew, but eventually she and Andrew found their way back together at the refreshment table, where she grabbed a glass of lime-infused water and he picked out a lemon sugar cookie.

Rosie wasn't sure how it happened, but they moved together to the edge of the crowd, to a corner where he leaned down, his gaze intense.

"I miss you, Rosie," Andrew said softly, his eyes searching her face.

She blinked, a bit taken aback. "How can you miss me? You only saw me a few days ago."

He took a step closer, lowering his voice so only she could hear. "I haven't been able to stop thinking about you. I think we need to revisit our terms. I don't want to wait until Stormhaven is done and I turn in my book to see you again."

"You're seeing me now," she countered, feeling her cheeks warm, hoping everyone else was too busy with snacks to notice their conversation.

He smiled, but there was a hint of longing behind it. "And it only makes me want more."

Rosie looked away, struggling to control her racing heartbeat. "Nothing has changed. If anything, my life has gotten even more complicated since Pam left."

Andrew's brow furrowed, disappointment flickering in his eyes. "I get it. Doesn't mean I have to like it."

She hesitated for a brief second, then went on before she could think better of it. "I will have Olive tomorrow. If you and the kids don't have anything else planned, we could all go down to the beach. The kids could run around, and we can talk. No stress, no expectations."

Andrew's face brightened. "That sounds perfect. Just us, the ocean and fresh air. I'd like that."

Rosie nodded, feeling a hesitant warmth blossom in her chest despite the chaos around her.

His kids came over to introduce their father to some of the friends they had made preparing for the production. Rosie made her way toward Emma and Olive, who were chatting with Emma's friend Josie, there with her two children.

"Mom," Emma said in an undertone when Josie was showing Olive and her children a large carved statue of a ballerina in a nook of the foyer. "Is something going on with you and Andrew Morgan?"

Rosie flushed. "Why would you say that?"

Emma arched a brow. "Maybe because the two of you are generating enough electricity to power the Wood Briar downtown district for a year."

"Don't be silly. I'm a grandmother."

"And he's a father. That doesn't mean either of you is dead." Emma studied her carefully. "Do you like him?"

Rosie thought of her conflicted feelings for Andrew. She very much suspected *like* was a mild word for her growing feelings. She was in grave danger of falling for the man. "I do," she admitted.

"And he obviously likes you. I say go for it. You're not exactly ancient. You have years worth of life left. Might as well enjoy them while you can."

"You don't think it would be strange if I started dating again?"

"I think it would be amazing, especially if you start dating a great guy like Andrew. In case you forgot, he does happen to be my favorite author. Plus, he seems like a very nice person."

He was. Rosie sighed. "Are you ready to go?"

Emma gave her a look as if she knew perfectly well her mother was avoiding the conversation by changing the subject but she simply nodded. "Yes. It's past Olive's bedtime. I'll grab her."

Before they could go outside, sirens suddenly split through

the night as emergency vehicles raced past the community center, lights flashing.

A fire truck passed first, followed by a second ladder truck, along with an ambulance and paramedic vehicle.

"What's going on?" Rosie asked, going to the window. "Looks like a bad accident."

"It wasn't." Susan Ramsay—the wife of Rosie's favorite plumbing subcontractor, who was also a volunteer firefighter—spoke up.

"Jeff got a call two minutes ago. He already took off. Good thing we drove separately or I would be stuck here. This is the real thing. Apparently there's a fire downtown. They've called in everybody."

"Whoa," Emma said, looking shocked. "Did Jeff say where it was?"

Susan shook her head just as Rosie and Emma received simultaneous texts. Hers was from Sylvia and she assumed Emma's was as well.

Heard on the scanner. The bookstore is on fire. One person injured. They've called out the EMTs.

"Oh no," Emma exclaimed. "Mom, did Grandma text you, too?"

Rosie nodded, feeling sick. This couldn't be happening. Not the bookstore, especially after Emma had poured so much energy into renovating the place.

Her daughter had turned pale, reaching out to a nearby pillar for support. "Bryce is working there tonight after hours! He was installing more shelving."

"What's wrong, Mommy?" Olive asked, picking up on her mother's distress but not the cause of it.

Emma looked helplessly at her child until Nancy Morgan stepped up. “If it’s the bookstore on fire, you two need to be at the scene. Why don’t you go take care of what you need to do? We’ll drop Olive back at Sylvia’s place on our way home.”

“Thank you,” Rosie said, filled with a vast relief.

Emma gave her daughter a hug and told her she would be home soon, then Nancy reached for the little girl’s hand as Emma and Rosie rushed out of the community center.

Only after they were in Rosie’s Volvo and hurrying downtown did Emma speak.

“Mom. What if he’s hurt? Or worse?”

Rosie couldn’t bear thinking about all the grim possibilities. She reached across and squeezed her daughter’s hand. “He’s strong. He’ll be okay. I’m sure of it.”

She gripped the steering wheel tightly as she navigated the familiar streets of their town, now eerily transformed by the flashing lights of the emergency vehicles that cast long shadows.

She struggled to keep her breathing steady. She needed to be strong for Emma, but fear for Bryce clawed at her insides.

CHAPTER THIRTY-EIGHT

—

Emma

THE COMMUNITY CENTER WAS ONLY A MILE AWAY FROM THE bookstore, but by the time they reached downtown, Emma felt as if they had crossed the Sahara by foot.

Bryce couldn't be hurt. He couldn't be.

She replayed her last conversation with him, his earnestness and the sincerity with which he told her he had feelings for her.

Why had she been so stupidly stubborn? Why had she not taken the glowing opportunity he'd offered her?

She knew why.

At heart, she didn't feel like she deserved to be happy. She carried the choices she had made in her life like an iron anchor around her neck and couldn't figure out how to break free.

She couldn't bear the idea that he might be hurt in any way.

Hurry.

She didn't say the word, but she thought it. Her mom was driving fast, but it didn't feel fast enough.

Finally, *finally*, Rosie pulled into a parking place as close as she could get. The acrid smell of smoke hit them as soon as they opened their doors. Even from here, Emma could see the unearthly glow of flames licking at the windows.

Her legs felt weak as she hurried toward the bookstore alongside her mother.

"At least the store was closed," Rosie said. "I would have hated if any customers were injured."

"I don't want *anyone* injured. If Bryce is hurt, I don't know what I'll do." Regret and fear battled inside her. Why had she pushed him away?

Her mother gave her a careful look, and Emma knew she had revealed far too much about her feelings for the man. What did it matter, especially if something had happened to him?

She picked up her pace. She had to know that he was all right.

She was in love with him.

As she raced toward the scene, the truth of it seemed to flash through her head with every strobe of the rescue vehicle lights.

She was in love with Bryce Kendall.

With his humor, with his strength, with his goodness. She was in love with the kindness with which he treated her daughter, with the energy and attention to detail he brought to the renovation as he worked so hard to bring life back to the bookstore and especially with the dignity and tenderness he always offered her.

Bryce knew her past yet he still treated her like someone deserving of honor and respect. And love.

She wasn't sure how it happened, especially when she had fought so hard against it, but she could no longer dispute the solid truth. She was in love with him. And if he was safe, she planned to tell him.

She ran unerringly toward the ambulance, where paramedics were working on a person sitting on the back bumper. It was Bryce, she saw, as vast relief flooded her like those fire hoses attacking the flames.

He was sitting upright, speaking with the paramedics. His features were serious, unsmiling and covered in soot, but he was alive.

"Bryce!"

She rushed toward him. Without thinking, she threw her arms around him.

He was here.

He was here and alive and alert, talking to the paramedics.

A vast sense of relief surged through her. Only then did she realize how very terrified she had been that he had been seriously injured.

He hugged her, and she listened to his heartbeat, feeling each beat against her ear. He smelled of smoke and burned paper, with perhaps a hint of singed hair, but she didn't care.

"I was so scared. We saw the fire trucks coming this way and then the ambulance. Grandma said she heard on the scanner that one person had been injured. I knew it had to be you. Are you all right?"

Bryce looked stunned at Emma's reaction and her obvious concern for him. He blinked, seemingly at a loss for words before responding.

"I'm okay. Smoke inhalation." His voice sounded raspy, gruff. "I stayed too long trying to put it out with the fire extinguisher after I called in the fire. I'm so sorry about the bookstore, Emma. I don't know exactly what happened. I was working on the shelving units when I thought I smelled smoke coming from behind the wall in the office. I was trying to locate it when there was a small explosion and smoke started filling the room. I tried to contain it, but it spread too quickly. They're thinking it was electrical."

He coughed, still looking shaken by the experience.

"You're burned." She took in the white bandage on his hand and felt her knees buckle.

"I'm okay. I got too close to the flames when I was trying to put it out. I'll be all right. I'm afraid the bookstore will not."

"That doesn't matter," Emma said.

"The only thing that matters is that no one was hurt," her mother said as she joined them. "All that work you did to renovate, though. Do you think they can save any of it?"

"I hope so," Bryce answered. "The sprinklers came on like they're supposed to but I'm pretty sure the water probably ruined most of the books. Whatever the sprinklers didn't ruin, the fire hoses probably did. I'm so sorry. You've worked so hard the past month to turn things around. I wanted you to succeed here, Emma. I wanted everything to be perfect for you."

Her heart ached with love for him. "We'll rebuild," she said. "We can do it together."

Her mother looked doubtful. "Maybe at this point, we think about cutting our losses and walking away. Since the day I bought it, The Rainy Day Bookshop has been a struggling bookstore and has barely turned a profit. Maybe we should stop throwing good money after bad. We could sell the building once and for all."

"No way," Emma said. "You love this place."

Her mother's features softened. "I do. I always have. But maybe this is a sign that I can't do everything."

"Or maybe," Emma said, "this is a sign that you should return to running The Rainy Day Bookshop yourself. Let Bryce step up to handle things at Lucas Construction. He's more than capable. You know he is."

"Of course he is."

"You can take over rebuilding the bookstore. Make it exactly what you've always dreamed it could become, Mom."

Her mother and Bryce both looked stunned at the suggestion. This wasn't the time to make any big decisions, especially when they still didn't know how extensive the damage would be, but perhaps it would give her mother something to think about.

"You need to keep that oxygen mask on, Kendall." The EMT had gone to school with her and Bryce, Emma realized. Kelly Miller didn't look happy at any of them as she bustled around her patient.

Emma knew she should probably get out of the way but she wasn't willing to relinquish her hold on him.

She didn't want to let go right now . . . or ever.

CHAPTER THIRTY-NINE

—

Bryce

EVERY BREATH FELT LIKE RAZOR BLADES SLICING AT HIS LUNGS but Bryce didn't care. The only thing that mattered was Emma. He would never forget the way she had run to him, her face distressed, her eyes wild with fear.

She had rushed to him and wrapped her arms around him as if she couldn't bear to let him go.

He couldn't keep up with her quicksilver moods. The last time they spoke, she had pushed him away, making it clear she wasn't interested in anything but friendship between them. Yet she had cried his name with so much emotion in it, he felt like his head was spinning from far more than the smoke.

As soon as he smelled something wrong in the bookstore, all he could think about was protecting Emma's dream.

He couldn't let her fail. He didn't want her to leave town again, even if they could never be together. Yeah, that would mean he once more would be stuck at the edges of her life, but none of that mattered.

But now she was here, and she hadn't left his side since she had rushed up to him. That had to mean something, didn't it?

"What's the verdict?" he asked Kelly Miller.

"We need to transport you to the ER so the docs can check you out. Sorry, man. Protocol."

"I'm fine. A little burn on my hand, but it's nothing. I've had worse cooking chili in my kitchen."

"I don't make the rules," Kelly informed him. "You were

injured in a fire so you need to be checked out. I don't expect they'll keep you, but we have to do our job."

Bryce sighed in resignation, aware he didn't have a choice in the matter unless he jumped off the ambulance and made his way home through the darkness.

"You can ride along with him if you want," Kelly said to Emma as she took in their still-entwined fingers.

She looked startled but nodded. "Yes. I'll go with you."

"What about Olive?" he had to ask.

"She's with my grandma. I'm sure she'll be okay. She can sleep there tonight and I'll get her in the morning," she replied. "Right now making sure you're okay is the priority."

He wasn't about to argue. Bryce couldn't remember the last time someone had wanted to take care of him. It left him feeling uneasy but also more touched than he had been in a long time.

In the end, they agreed she should drive his truck to the hospital so he would have a way home, since Wood Briar wasn't exactly overflowing with taxis or rideshare services.

He didn't want to let go of her but comforted himself to know it would only be for a short time.

The next few hours were a blur of tests. Blood work, X-rays, consultations with a pulmonologist and burn specialist. While Bryce wasn't a fan of hospitals, this time he didn't mind, with Emma by his side.

He did feel vulnerable and more than a little embarrassed to be stretched out on an emergency room gurney wearing the stupid hospital gown they put on him. But having Emma nearby, solicitous and concerned, made all of that awkwardness fade into the background.

Fortunately, the doctors eventually cleared him to go home. To his further embarrassment, though, the medical staff insisted on wheeling him out to his pickup truck for her to drive him home.

"Now, you're going to want to make sure someone stays with him tonight," the male nurse said. "The pain meds might make him a little woozy."

Emma nodded. "I'll make sure someone is there," she said.

He was so damn tired, Bryce wanted to lean his head against the seat and go to sleep. Maybe that's what they meant about the pain meds making him woozy. He hadn't wanted to take them at all but apparently the burns on his hand and arm were more serious than initially thought.

"I'll stay with you," Emma said as she drove with deliberation and caution toward his house. "I need to make sure my mom and grandma are okay with taking care of Olive. I'm sure it will be no problem. I checked in with my mom after we arrived at the hospital and she already had Olive tucked into bed. She was planning on having her tomorrow anyway."

"You don't have to stay with me," he said.

"I told the nurse I would."

"I'll be fine. I've got Pearl."

He was glad again that he hadn't taken his dog with him to the bookstore that evening. He had thought about it but she had been with him at another jobsite all day and seemed happy to be home, stretched out on her dog bed.

"Unfortunately for you," Emma said, "Pearl lacks opposable thumbs to call for help if the need arises. It's fine. I'm happy to stay. Either that or you can come to my mom's place. Which do you prefer?"

"My house," he said.

"Smart move, unless you want a little girl jumping all over you, a rooster crowing to wake you up at the crack of dawn and a yippy dog making a nuisance of herself."

He wanted to tell her he would be fine on his own, but fatigue weighed on him, sucking him under like an anchor around his ankles. He must have drifted off, much to his dismay. When he awoke, she was pulling into his driveway.

"Here you are. Safe and sound," she said, then bustled out to open the door for him.

"Thank you for being my chauffeur."

"You injured yourself trying to save my bookstore, Bryce. I'm not going to leave you to fend for yourself."

He pulled out his house keys from his pocket, grateful they weren't on the same side as his injured hand. When he unlocked the door, Pearl padded toward him, tail wagging.

He petted her with his uninjured hand and led the way into his house. He had made a few changes since his mother first went into a care center. New paint, new wood floors, new windows. It was clean and functional but had never felt particularly homey.

"That looks like a perfect place for me to sleep," Emma said, pointing to the sofa in the family room. He could attest that it was comfortable enough, since he often fell asleep there himself while stretched out watching a ball game on TV.

"You really don't have to stay, Emma. I'll be fine."

He was completely unused to having someone watch over him and didn't quite know how to handle the situation.

"I'm staying," she said firmly. "I only need a pillow and a blanket."

"I'm not going to sleep well, knowing you're out here on the couch. Why don't you take the bed and I'll take the couch?"

Or we could both take the bed.

The words remained unspoken between them. She had pushed him away, he reminded himself. She had told him clearly that she wasn't interested in more than friendship with him.

"I'm not the one with a deep second-degree burn," she countered. "Please don't be difficult, Bryce."

He sighed, realizing arguing was pointless. "Fine. Thank you, Emma. I hate to ask, but I need a shower desperately. I smell like, well, a burning building."

"Are you okay to shower?"

"They said I can if I use one of the plastic sleeves they gave me. I'm not sure I can put it on by myself," he admitted.

"Of course," she said, though she seemed to have gone a little pink.

He led the way to his bedroom, with its en suite bathroom. She brought along the package of supplies from the hospital.

"You should, um, probably take off your shirt first."

He would be throwing away this smoky shirt as soon as possible. Bryce tried to work his way out of the T-shirt, doing his best to hide a wince when he moved his arm wrong.

"Let me help you," she said. She moved close to him and he could smell her, clean and fresh and lovely, like a spring rain shower on a flower garden.

He closed his eyes, wanting to brand her touch, her scent, into his memory.

When he opened them, he saw her eyes were glistening. "Hey. What's wrong?"

"Your poor arm," she whispered.

"It will be fine. I've had much worse."

She didn't seem to take any comfort from his words. A tear trickled down her cheek.

"I was so scared," she whispered. "When I heard about the fire, I thought . . ." Her voice broke.

Bryce reached for her, pulling her against his now bare chest. "Hey, I'm okay. I'm right here."

Emma's composure crumbled. She leaned forward, burying her face in his shoulder as she began to sob.

"I'm sorry," she murmured against his chest. "You're the one injured. I should be comforting you."

"This is the best I've felt since you pushed me away the other day," he told her solemnly, meaning every word.

Her gaze met his, murky green with emotion. "Me, too," she admitted.

He gazed down at her, then finally surrendered to what he had been wanting to do all evening. Hell, it felt like what he had been wanting to do all of his life. He lowered his mouth to hers and kissed her with all the pent-up tenderness and longing inside him.

When he lifted his mouth from hers, she rested her cheek against his chest, listening to what he was certain must be a rapid heartbeat.

"Oh, Bryce. I've been such a fool."

He tilted her chin up so he could meet her gaze. "About what?"

"Pushing you away. Giving in to my fear." She swallowed. "Tonight when I thought you were in danger, all I could think about was how I wish I had told you how much I . . . that I . . ." Her voice trailed off.

She took a deep breath. "How much I'm coming to care about you. I . . . I'm falling in love with you."

Joy surged through him, white-hot and fiery and he gave a rough laugh before he kissed her again. He wanted to pull her onto his bed beside them, injured arm be damned. "Are you sure about this, Emma? About me?"

She nodded, then bit her lip. "You are . . . everything I've always dreamed of. Caring, kind, decent. I knew it from the moment I came back to town. I also knew you were far too good for someone like me. That's why I pushed you away."

"That's the dumbest thing I've ever heard you say."

"It's true, though. I'm an addict. I've been clean for more than four years but I will always be an addict. You deserve someone who can come to you without all the baggage I carry around."

Bryce cupped her face with his uninjured hand. "Emma, I don't want anyone else. I want you. I've wanted you since we were kids. Your past, your struggles—they're part of what makes you who you are. And I love who you are."

Tears spilled down Emma's cheeks. She looked afraid to believe this could be real. "That's the pain meds talking."

"No. That's my heart talking. The heart that has been yours for most of our lives."

He pulled her close, capturing her lips in a tender kiss. As they parted, both breathless, Emma rested her forehead against his.

"Stay with me tonight?" Bryce whispered. "Here, in my bed. I won't be good for anything but holding you, I'm afraid. Tonight, anyway. On the other hand, I tend to heal pretty fast. Who knows about tomorrow?"

"That sounds absolutely perfect," she said, her smile radiant and her eyes bright with an emotion that stole his breath.

Bryce gazed at Emma, his heart swelling with joy and contentment. After years of longing and missed opportunities, he finally had everything he had ever dreamed of. The woman he loved by his side.

As he held her close, Bryce suddenly knew without question that this moment, forged in fire and loss and pain, marked a beautiful beginning to the life they would share together.

CHAPTER FORTY

—

Andrew

THE DAY AFTER THE FIRE AT THE RAINY DAY BOOKSHOP, ANdrew sat in a beach chair next to Rosie on Crescent Beach, watching the three children giggle as they raced back and forth trying to avoid the waves licking at the sand.

It was a beautiful summer afternoon on the Oregon coast, pleasant and sunny, with high clouds that rolled across the sky.

He leaned back in the chair, breathing in the scent of sea and sand. "I'm glad you decided to stick with our plan to come to the beach, Rosie. I thought for sure you would want to cancel, with everything you have going on," he said.

"I needed this," she said, lifting her face to the sun. "My brain has been caught in an endless loop of worry and stress. A distraction is exactly the thing to take my mind off it all. Olive needed it, too. She was so upset to find out about the bookstore. She loved that place. We called it our magical land of books."

"That describes every bookstore, doesn't it?" Andrew commented.

Rosie smiled, though her eyes remained sad. Andrew wanted to take all the pain away from this woman—this strong, courageous woman who had endured so very much in her life.

"Have you figured out what you're going to do yet? Is the bookstore beyond rebuilding?"

"No, actually. Surprisingly, for all the flames and fuss last night, it sustained little actual structural damage. Most of the brick is still intact and the actual fire was mostly contained to the office and the new section Bryce was renovating."

"That's a relief, I imagine."

"Because of the smoke and water damage, the books are all a loss, unfortunately. If we do rebuild, we're going to have to start over with all new inventory."

"That's too bad."

"That's the part I hate the most. It feels like a tragedy. I know it's not. They're only books, not people, but it still hurts."

"Books are priceless to those who love them. I get it, maybe more than most people would. I lost years' worth of books in the wildfire. Research books, my own early backlist titles, some signed first editions from friends and fellow writers. It's an incalculable loss that all the insurance in the world could never cover."

"I feel silly being so depressed about a business loss when you and your children lost your home and your memories."

"We still have the memories. Just not the tangible ones. And you're not silly. The bookshop was beloved, not only by you but by the whole community. I'm sure everyone in Wood Briar is hoping you decide to rebuild."

She sighed. "It won't be that hard to rebuild. I just don't know if it's worth the effort."

"What is your gut telling you?"

She gave a rueful smile, looking soft and lovely in the afternoon sunshine. "The same thing my gut told me when I wanted to buy the bookstore a decade ago, despite it never really making a profit. Towns like Wood Briar need a bookstore. It's more than pages and shelves. It's a sanctuary, a bridge to other worlds, a beacon of knowledge that lights up the whole town."

"There's your answer."

She released a breath, smiling as she watched her granddaughter kneel in the sand to point out something to Finn and Zara.

"Emma suggested last night that I should step away from the construction company and handle the renovation of the bookstore myself. She said that way I can truly fulfill my vision for what I wanted it to become when I bought it."

"What do you think about that?"

Her laugh sounded ragged around the edges. "It sounds wonderful. That's one of the things chasing around and around in my thoughts. When Lucas Construction began to falter a few years after Gary died, I buried my dreams for the bookshop. I didn't feel like I had any other choice. I felt I had an obligation to our employees as well as our community. We had signed contracts we weren't going to be able to fulfill if I didn't step up."

"Makes sense."

"And at the time, I was so lost in my grief and so busy worrying about Emma, it didn't really matter what I did. The construction company or the bookstore. I didn't really care about any of it."

"What about now?"

She gave a rough laugh. "I think I would like to run the bookstore. Is that crazy?"

"Not at all. If it was always your dream, you should go for it. What about the construction company?"

"That's the funny thing. Emma pointed out last night that Bryce would be more than capable of running it. She's absolutely right. He's young but he's sharp, honest, hardworking. And older than Gary and I were when we started the company."

"Didn't you say Emma wanted in at the construction company, too?"

"Yes. Who would have ever thought she would be interested? But she said it's been her dream since she was a girl, when her dad used to take her to jobsites. I don't expect I will step away completely but I would love to hand over the day-to-day operations to her and Bryce. Their hearts are in it. Mine has never really been."

"Your heart has always wanted to run a bookstore."

She laughed. "Yes. I guess that's it."

"Well, when the bookstore is done, I know a local author you might be able to talk into doing a few events there."

Her face lit up. "Would you, even though you hate book signings?"

"I don't hate book signings. Even if I did, though, I would still do them at The Rainy Day Bookshop for you."

Of course, he might require a few concessions from the bookstore owner in his rider, like more of her intoxicating kisses, but he decided this might not be the best time to let her know his conditions.

"That would be fantastic," she exclaimed. "I'm going to hold you to it."

They watched the sunlight on the water and Andrew found himself more at peace than he could remember being in a long time. When he had packed up his children and his life and moved here to Wood Briar, he wanted to leave behind the sadness and pain of losing Tracy, losing their house.

He had found so much more than he ever would have imagined.

"Speaking of Emma and Bryce, I haven't had a chance to tell you the biggest news of the day," she said.

"Bigger than your bookstore catching on fire?"

"A million times bigger! Emma stayed overnight at his place after the fire. This morning Olive and I went to pick her up and guess what? They were kissing on the porch to say goodbye."

"Does that mean Emma is more likely to stay in town?"

"I think so. It's better than I ever dreamed. I always thought they would be perfect together, but I never thought they would see that, too. She was glowing this morning. I wish you could have seen her."

Andrew found her enthusiasm for her daughter's happiness utterly charming. It was one more thing that drew him to Rosie—her capacity for joy, even in the face of adversity.

"That's wonderful news," he said. "I'm happy for Emma and Bryce. And for you, too. I can see how much it means to you."

Rosie's eyes sparkled. "It does. After everything that's happened, seeing Emma so happy? It's like a rainbow after a storm."

She was a remarkable woman. Despite losing her husband and putting her own dreams on hold for years, Rosie still found so much joy in the happiness of others. It was one of the things he admired most about her.

"Dad, can we fly the kite now?" Finn called out.

He looked over to see the three children struggling with the colorful kite shaped like a jellyfish that he had picked up before they came down to the beach.

"You got it, kiddo," Andrew replied, standing up. He turned to Rosie. "Care to join us? I have to admit, I'm not much of an expert at kite flying."

Rosie laughed, her green eyes dancing. "Well, you're in luck. I happen to be a kite-flying champion. Come on. I'll show you all my tricks."

"Not all of them, I hope. Save a few for later, when the kids aren't with us," he murmured.

She laughed outright at that, exactly as he hoped. "You are incorrigible, Andrew Morgan."

No one had ever called him that before. He decided he liked it.

They walked over to the children and Rosie took charge, showing them all how to hold the kite and when to release it, letting out more string from the spool. Andrew watched in admiration as she patiently guided them, her natural warmth and kindness shining through.

When it was Andrew's turn, Rosie stood close beside him, her hand gently guiding his on the kite string. "Like this," she said softly, and together they sent the kite soaring into the sky.

As they stood side by side, watching the kite dance on the wind, Andrew couldn't help thinking what a good team they made.

The sun was beginning to set, painting the sky in brilliant oranges and pinks. The children cheered as the kite swooped and soared above them, their laughter carried on the sea breeze.

Andrew glanced at Rosie, her face aglow in the fading sunlight, and felt a surge of hope for the future. He didn't know exactly where this journey with Rosie would lead, but he knew that whatever challenges lay ahead, he wanted to face them with her.

As if sensing his gaze, Rosie turned to him with a soft smile. "Thank you for today, Andrew. For everything."

He reached out and squeezed her hand gently. "Anytime," he replied, his voice filled with warmth and promise.

They stood hand in hand, watching the kite and the children, basking in the simple joy. And as the sun dipped below the horizon, Andrew was certain this was the beginning of something beautiful.

EPILOGUE

—

Rosie

One year later

"Look at her. Our girl is gorgeous, isn't she?" Sylvia crowed, taking in Emma in the stunning wedding dress the three of them had picked out in Portland months ago. Rosie's heart swelled with joy as she adjusted Emma's veil.

"Oh, sweetheart. You look absolutely beautiful," Rosie whispered, her voice thick with emotion.

Emma turned to face her mother and grandmother, her own eyes shining. "I can't believe this day is finally here."

Rosie cupped her daughter's face gently. "Your dad would be so happy to see you marrying a good man like Bryce. He would be so proud of the woman you've become."

A moment of understanding passed between them, healing old wounds and forgiving past mistakes. They embraced, careful not to wrinkle Emma's gown.

Sylvia, not to be left out, wrapped her arms around both of them, making Emma laugh and hug her grandmother.

When Rosie pulled away, she looked out the window of her house toward the flower-covered arbor where Emma and Bryce would shortly exchange vows overlooking the Pacific.

She spotted Olive in her flower girl dress sitting by Zara and Finn, the three of them with their heads together, probably concocting some mischief or other.

Her heart warmed at the sight of her granddaughter laughing with Andrew's children. Then she saw him, tall, handsome and hers, saying something to the children, who laughed in response.

After chatting for a while, he ushered Olive back inside, most likely for her to get ready for the bridal procession. As they walked inside, the little girl let go of Andrew's hand and immediately rushed to her mother. "You look like a princess, Mama."

Emma hugged her daughter, who couldn't be happier to be gaining a new stepfather in Bryce.

Rosie went to Andrew's side, seeking his steadying presence.

"Everything okay with the bride?"

"She's nervous. I'm nervous. We're all nervous, except maybe Olive."

Andrew's eyes softened as he took in the sight of her. "No matter how lovely a bride Emma will be," he murmured, "she doesn't hold a candle to her mother."

He leaned in and kissed her softly, making Rosie's heart swell with love.

The past year had been a time of healing and growth for both of them. Andrew's latest book had stayed on bestseller lists for months, and the second movie made from The Starbound Chronicles books had been an even bigger hit than the first.

He and the children had already made Stormhaven a home. The house was elegant and graceful but it was no showplace. It was filled with school calendars and toy clutter and a media room that was the envy of all their friends.

The bookstore renovation was done as well. Rosie had overseen the work herself, with input from Emma, Bryce and Sylvia. Newly reopened, The Rainy Day Bookshop was now bright and spacious, a haven for everyone in town.

She loved running it—and loved more seeing Bryce and Emma thrive under the challenge of taking over most of the operations of Lucas Construction.

Everything was perfect.

Well, almost perfect.

Rosie's mind drifted to the burning question Andrew had posed to her a month ago, the one she had asked him to put on hold until after Emma and Bryce were married.

Now, with her daughter about to walk down the aisle, the time felt right.

"Do you remember that question you asked me on the beach last month?" she began.

Andrew froze, then his eyes gleamed with mischief. "Hmm. I think so. Didn't I ask whether you wanted to go out for Chinese or Indian food?"

Rosie made a face at his teasing. "Ha ha, no. The other one. I told you I wanted to wait until after Emma and Bryce were married before I gave you my answer. They're not quite married yet, but they will be within the hour. I want to give you my answer now."

Andrew's expression shifted into one of anticipation. "Okay, what will it be? Chinese or Indian, then?" he joked, but his voice held a hint of nervous exhilaration.

"You know what I mean," Rosie said, her heart racing. "My answer is yes. How could it ever be anything else? I love you with all my heart. I want to marry you. I want to help you raise Zara and Finn. I want to live in Stormhaven with you. I want to build a future together."

His features lit up with delight. With a radiant smile, he pulled Rosie close, kissing her with a tenderness that stole her breath.

As he drew his head away, Sylvia cleared her throat. "Um, guys? Isn't this supposed to be Emma's big day?"

Rosie felt her face heat. "Yes. It is. You're right. This is her day, and it's going to be perfect."

The rest of the day was a whirlwind of emotion and celebration. As Rosie watched Emma and Bryce exchange vows, her hand firmly clasped in Andrew's, she didn't cry. She was too happy for that, filled with a sense of incomparable peace.

While the newlyweds shared their first dance, Rosie leaned into Andrew's embrace, her heart full to bursting. She knew that whatever the future held, they would face it together, surrounded by books, laughter and an abundance of love.